Enid Blyton's

MALORY TOWERS

Enid Blyton's

MALORY TOWERS

containing
First Term at Malory Towers
Second Form at Malory Towers
Third Year at Malory Towers

complete and unabridged

Illustrated by Jenny Chapple

DEAN
in association with
Methuen Children's Books

The Enid Blyton Newsletter

Would you like to receive The Enid Blyton Newsletter?
It has lots of news about Enid Blyton books, videos, plays, etc.
There are also puzzles and a page for your letters.
It is published three times a year and is free for children
who live in the United Kingdom and Ireland.

If you would like to receive it for a year, please write to:
The Enid Blyton Newlsetter, PO Box 357, London WC2N 6QB,
sending your name and address. (UK and Ireland only.)

First Term at Malory Towers first published 1946
Second Form at Malory Towers first published 1947
Third Year at Malory Towers first published 1948
This edition published in 1991 by Dean,
in association with Methuen Children's Books
Michelin House, 81 Fulham Road, London SW3 6RB
Reprinted 1991 and 1992
Copyright © Darrell Waters Limited
1946, 1947 and 1948

ISBN 0 603 55001 0

Enid Blyton is a registered trademark of
Darrell Waters Limited

A CIP catalogue record for this book
is available from the British Library

Printed in Great Britain by The Bath Press

FIRST TERM AT
MALORY TOWERS

CONTENTS

1   OFF TO BOARDING SCHOOL

DARRELL RIVERS looked at herself in the glass. It was almost time to start for the train, but there was just a minute to see how she looked in her new school uniform.

'It's jolly nice,' said Darrell, turning herself about. 'Brown coat, brown hat, orange ribbon, and a brown tunic underneath with an orange belt. I like it.'

Her mother looked into Darrell's room, and smiled. 'Admiring yourself?' she said. 'Well, I like it all too. I must say Malory Towers has a lovely school uniform. Come along, Darrell. We don't want to miss the train your very first term!'

Darrell felt excited. She was going to boarding school for the first time. Malory Towers did not take children younger than twelve, so Darrell would be one of the youngest there. She looked forward to many terms of fun and friendship, work and play.

'What will it be like?' she kept wondering. 'I've read lots of school stories, but I expect it won't be quite the same at Malory Towers. Every school is different. I do hope I make some friends there.'

Darrell was sad at leaving her own friends behind her. None of them was going to Malory Towers. She had been to a day-school with them, and most of them were either staying on there or going to different boarding schools.

Her trunk was packed full. On the side was painted in big black letters DARRELL RIVERS. On the labels were the letters M.T. for Malory Towers. Darrell had only to carry her tennis racket in its press, and her small bag in which her mother had packed her things for the first night.

'Your trunks won't be unpacked the first evening,' she said. 'So each girl has to take a small hand-bag with her nighty and tooth-brush and things like that. Here is your ten-shilling note. You must make that last a whole term, because no girl in your form is allowed to have more pocket-money than that.'

'I shall make it do!' said Darrell, putting it into her purse. 'There won't be much I have to buy at school! There's the taxi waiting, Mother. Let's go!'

She had already said good-bye to her father, who had driven off to his work that morning. He had squeezed her hard and said,' Good-bye and good luck, Darrell. You'll get a lot out of Malory Towers, because it's a fine school. Be sure you give them a lot back!'

Now they were off at last, the trunk in the taxi too, beside the driver. Darrell put her head out to take a last look at her home. 'I'll be back soon!' she called, to the big black cat who sat on the wall, washing himself. 'I'll miss you all at first but I'll soon settle down. Shan't I, Mother?'

'Of course,' said her mother. 'You'll have a lovely time! You won't want to come home for the summer holidays!'

They had to go up to London to catch the train for Cornwall, where Malory Towers was. 'There's a special train always, for Malory Towers,' said Mrs. Rivers. 'Look, there's a notice up. Malory Towers. Platform 7. Come along. We're in nice time. I'll stay with you a few minutes and see you safely with your house-mistress, and her girls, then I'll go.'

They went on to the platform. A long train was drawn up there, labelled Malory Towers. All the carriages were reserved for the girls of that school. The train had different labels stuck in the windows. The first lot said ' North Tower.' The second lot said ' South Tower.' Then came compartments labelled 'West Tower' and others labelled 'East Tower'.

'You're North Tower,' said her mother. 'Malory Towers has four different boarding houses for its girls, all topped by a tower. You'll be in North Tower, the Head Mistress said, and your house-mistress is Miss Potts. We must find her.'

Darrell stared about her at the girls on the crowded platform. They all seemed to be Malory girls, for she saw the brown coats and hats, with the orange ribbons, everywhere. They all seemed to know one another, and laughed and chattered at the tops of their voices. Darrell felt suddenly shy.

'I shall never never know all these girls!' she thought, as she stared round. 'Gracious, what big ones some of them are! They look quite grown-up. I shall be terrified of them.'

Certainly the girls in the top forms seemed very grown-up to Darrell. They took no notice at all of the little ones. The younger girls made way for them, and they climbed into their carriages in a rather lordly manner.

'Hallo, Lottie! Hallo, Mary! I say, there's Penelope! Hi , Penny, come over here. Hilda, you never wrote to me in the hols., you mean pig! Jean, come into our carriage!'

The gay voices sounded all up and down the platform. Darrell looked for her mother. Ah, there she was, talking to a keen-faced mistress. That must be Miss Potts. Darrell stared at her. Yés, she liked her—she liked the way her eyes twinkled—but there was something very determined about her mouth. It wouldn't do to get into her bad books.

Miss Potts came over and smiled down at Darrell. 'Well, new girl!' she said. 'You'll be in my carriage going down—look, that one over there. The new girls always go with me.'

'Oh, are there new girls besides me—in my form, I mean ? ' asked Darrell.

'Oh, yes. Two more. They haven't arrived yet. Mrs Rivers, here is a girl in Darrell's form—Alicia Johns. She will look after Darrell for you, when you've said good-bye.'

'Hallo,' said Alicia, and two bright eyes twinkled at Darrell. 'I'm in your form. Do you want to get a corner-seat ? If so, you'd better come now.'

'Then I'll say good-bye, dear,' said Mrs. Rivers, cheerfully, and she kissed Darrell and gave her a hug. 'I'll write as soon as I get your letter. Have a lovely time ! '

'Yes, I will,' said Darrell, and watched her mother go down the platform. She didn't have time to feel lonely because Alicia took complete charge of her at once, pushed her to Miss Potts's carriage, and shoved her up the step. 'Put your bag in one corner and I'll put mine opposite,' said Alicia. 'Then we can stand at the door and see what's happening. I say—look over there. Picture of How Not to Say Good-bye to your Darling Daughter ! '

Darrell looked to where Alicia nodded. She saw a girl about her own age, dressed in the same school uniform, but with her hair long and loose down her back. She was clinging to her mother and wailing.

'Now what that mother should do would be to grin, shove some chocolate at her and go ! ' said Alicia. 'If you've got a kid like that, it's hopeless to do anything else. Poor little mother's darling ! '

The mother was almost as bad as the girl. Tears were running down her face too. Miss Potts walked firmly up to them.

'Now you watch Potty,' said Alicia. Darrell felt rather shocked. Potty ! What a name to give your house-mistress. Anyway, Miss Potts didn't look in the least potty. She looked thoroughly all-there.

'I'll take Gwendoline,' she said to the girl's mother.

'It's time she went to her carriage. She'll soon settle down there, Mrs. Lacey.'

Gwendoline appeared ready to go, but her mother clung to her still. Alicia snorted. ' See what's made Gwendoline such an idiot ? ' she said. ' Her mother ! Well, I'm glad mine is sensible. Yours looked jolly nice too—cheerful and jolly.'

Darrell was pleased at this praise of her mother. She watched Miss Potts firmly disentangle Gwendoline from her mother and lead her towards them.

' Alicia ! Here's another one,' she said, and Alicia pulled Gwendoline up into the carriage.

Gwendoline's mother came to the carriage too and looked in. ' Take a corner-seat, darling,' she said. ' And don't sit with your back to the engine. You know how sick it makes you. And . . .'

Another girl came up to the carriage, a small, sturdy girl, with a plain face and hair tightly plaited back. ' Is this Miss Potts's carriage ? ' she asked.

' Yes,' said Alicia. ' Are you the third new girl ? North Tower ? '

' Yes. I'm Sally Hope,' said the girl.

' Where's your mother ? ' asked Alicia. ' She ought to go and deliver you to Miss Potts first, so that you can be crossed off her list.'

' Oh, Mother didn't bother to come up with me,' said Sally. ' I came by myself.'

' Gracious ! ' said Alicia. ' Well, mothers are all different. Some come along and smile and say good-bye, and some come along and weep and wail—and some just don't come at all.'

' Alicia—don't talk so much,' came Miss Potts's voice. She knew Alicia's wild tongue. Mrs. Lacey suddenly looked annoyed, and forgot to give any more instructions to Gwendoline. She stared at Alicia angrily. Fortunately the guard blew his whistle just then and there was a wild scramble for seats.

Miss Potts jumped in with two or three more girls. The door slammed. Gwendoline's mother peered in, but alas, Gwendoline was on the floor, hunting for something she had dropped.

'Where's Gwendoline!' came Mrs. Lacey's voice. 'I must say good-bye. Where's . . .'

But the train was now puffing out. Gwendoline sat up and howled.

'I didn't say good-bye!' she wailed.

'Well, how many times did you want to?' demanded Alicia. 'You'd already said it about twenty times.'

Miss Potts looked at Gwendoline. She had already sized her up and knew her to be a spoilt, only child, selfish, and difficult to handle at first.

She looked at quiet little Sally Hope. Funny little girl, with her tight plaits and prim, closed-up face. No mother had come to see her off. Did Sally care? Miss Potts couldn't tell.

Then she looked at Darrell. It was quite easy to read Darrell. She never hid anything, and she said what she thought, though not so bluntly as Alicia did.

'A nice, straightforward, trustable girl,' thought Miss Potts. 'Can be a bit of a monkey, I should think. She looks as if she has good brains. I'll see that she uses them! I can do with a girl like Darrell in North Tower!'

The girls began to talk. 'What's Malory Towers like?' asked Darrell. 'I've seen a photograph of it, of course. It looked awfully big.'

'It is. It's got the most gorgeous view over the sea, too,' said Alicia. 'It's built on the cliff, you know. It's lucky you're in North Tower—that's got the best view of all!'

'Does each Tower have its own schoolrooms?' asked Darrell. Alicia shook her head.

' Oh, no ! All the girls from each of the four Tower houses go to the same classrooms. There are about sixty girls in each house. Pamela is head of ours. There she is over there ! '

Pamela was a tall, quiet girl, who had got into the carriage with another girl about her own age. They seemed very friendly with Miss Potts, and were eagerly discussing with her the happenings planned for the term.

Alicia, another girl called Tessie, Sally and Darrell chattered too. Gwendoline sat in her corner and looked gloomy. Nobody paid her any attention at all, and she wasn't used to that !

She gave a little sob, and looked at the others out of the corner of her eye. Sharp Alicia saw the look and grinned. ' Just putting it on ! ' she whispered to Darrell. ' People who really do feel miserable always turn away and hide it somehow. Don't take any notice of our darling Gwendoline.'

Poor Gwendoline ! If she had only known it, Alicia's lack of sympathy was the best thing for her. She had always had far too much of it, and life at Malory Towers was not going to be easy for her.

' Cheer up, Gwendoline,' said Miss Potts, in a cheerful tone, and immediately turned to talk to the big girls again.

' I feel sick,' announced Gwendoline at last, quite determined to be in the limelight and get sympathy somehow.

' You don't look it,' said the downright Alicia. ' Does she, Miss Potts ? I always go green when I feel sick.'

Gwendoline wished she could really be sick ! That would serve this sharp-tongued girl right. She leaned back against the back of the seat, and murmured faintly. ' I really do feel sick ! Oh, dear, what shall I do ? '

' Here, wait a bit—I've got a paper bag,' said Alicia, and fished a big one out of her bag. ' I've got a brother who's always sick in a car, so Mother takes paper bags with her wherever she goes, for Sam. I always think it's funny to see him stick his nose in it, poor Sam—like a horse with a nose-bag ! '

Nobody could help laughing at Alicia's story. Gwendoline didn't, of course, but looked angry. That horrid girl, poking fun at her again. She wasn't going to like her at all.

After that Gwendoline sat quiet, and made no further attempt to get the attention of the others. She was afraid of what Alicia might say next.

But Darrell looked at Alicia with amusement and liking. How she would like her for a friend ! What fun they could have together !

2   MALORY TOWERS

IT was a long journey to Malory Towers, but as there was a dining-car on the train, and the girls took it in turns to go and have their midday meal, that made a good break. They had tea on the train too. At first all the girls were gay and chattery, but as the day wore on they fell silent. Some of them slept. It was such a long journey !

It was exciting to reach the station for Malory Towers. The school lay a mile or two away, and there were big motor coaches standing outside the station to take the girls to the school.

' Come on,' said Alicia, clutching hold of Darrell's arm. ' If we're quick we can get one of the front seats in a coach, beside the driver. Hurry ! Got your bag ? '

' I'll come too,' said Gwendoline. But the others were gone long before she had collected her belongings. They climbed up into front seats. The other girls came out in twos and threes, and the station's one and only porter helped the drivers to load the many trunks on to the coaches.

' Can we see Malory Towers from here ? ' asked Darrell, looking all round.

' No. I'll tell you when we can. There's a corner where we suddenly get a glimpse of it,' said Alicia.

' Yes. It's lovely to get that sudden view of it,' said Pamela, the quiet head-girl of North Tower, who had got into the coach just behind Alicia and Darrell. Her eyes shone as she spoke. ' I think Malory Towers shows at its best when we come to that corner, especially if the sun is behind it.'

Darrell could feel the warmth in Pamela's voice as she spoke of the school she loved. She looked at her and liked her.

Pamela saw her look and laughed. ' You're lucky, Darrell,' she said. ' You're just beginning at Malory Towers ! You've got terms and terms before you. I'm just ending. Another term or two, and I shan't be coming to Malory Towers any more—except as an old girl. You make the most of it while you can.'

' I shall,' said Darrell, and stared ahead, waiting for her first glimpse of the school she was to go to for at least six years.

They rounded a corner. Alicia nudged her arm. ' There you are, look ! Over there, on that hill ! The sea is behind, far down the cliff, but you can't see that, of course.'

Darrell looked. She saw a big, square-looking building of soft grey stone standing high up on a hill. The hill was really a cliff, that fell steeply down to the sea. At each end of the gracious building stood rounded towers. Darrell could glimpse two other towers behind as well, making four in all. North Tower, South, East and West.

The windows shone. The green creeper that covered parts of the wall climbed almost to the roof in places. It looked like an old-time castle.

' My school ! ' thought Darrell, and a little warm feeling
came into her heart. ' It's fine. How lucky I am to be
having Malory Towers as my school-home for so many
years. I shall love it.'

' Do you like it ? ' asked Alicia, impatiently.

' Yes. Very much,' said Darrell. ' But I shall never
never know my way about it ! It's so big.'

' Oh, I'll soon show you,' said Alicia. ' It's surprising
how quickly you get to know your way round.'

The coach turned another corner and Malory Towers
was lost to sight. It came into view again, nearer still,
round the next corner, and it wasn't very long before all the
coaches roared up to the flight of steps that led to the great
front door.

' It's just like a castle entrance ! ' said Darrell.

' Yes,' said Gwendoline, unexpectedly, from behind them.
' I shall feel like a fairy princess, going up those steps ! '
She tossed her loose golden hair back over her shoulders.

' You would ! ' said Alicia, scornfully. ' But you'll
soon get ideas like that out of your head when Potty gets
going on you.'

Darrell got down and was immediately lost in a crowd of
girls, all swarming up the steps. She looked round for
Alicia, but she seemed to have disappeared. So up the
steps went Darrell, clutching her small bag and racket,
feeling rather lost and lonely in the chattering crowd of
girls. She felt in quite a panic without the friendly Alicia !

After that things were rather a blur. Darrell didn't
know where to go and she didn't know what to do. She
looked vainly for Alicia, or Pamela, the head-girl. Was
she supposed to go straight to North Tower ? Everyone
seemed to know exactly what to do and where to go, except
poor Darrell !

Then she saw Miss Potts, and felt a wave of relief. She
went up to her, and Miss Potts looked down, smiling.

'Hallo! Feeling lost? Where's that rascal of an Alicia? She ought to look after you. All North Tower girls are to go there and unpack their night-bags. Matron is waiting for you all.'

Darrell had no idea which way to go for North Tower, so she stood by Miss Potts, waiting. Alicia soon re-appeared again, accompanied by a crowd of girls.

'Hallo!' she said to Darrell. 'I lost you. These are all girls in our form, but I won't tell you their names just now. You'll only get muddled. Some are North Tower girls, but some belong to the other houses. Come on, let's go to North Tower and see Matron. Where's darling Gwendoline?'

'Alicia,' said Miss Potts, her voice stern, but her eyes twinkling. 'Give Gwendoline a chance!'

'And Sally Hope? Where's she?' said Alicia. 'Come on, Sally. All right, Miss Potts, I'll take them along to North Tower, and nurse them a bit!'

Sally, Gwendoline and Darrell followed Alicia. They were in a big hall, that had doors leading off on either side, and a wide staircase curving upwards.

'The assembly hall, the gyms., the lab., the art-rooms, and the needlework room are all on this side,' said Alicia. 'Come on, we'll cross the Court to get to our tower.'

Darrell wondered what the Court was. She soon found out. Malory Towers was built round a large oblong space, called the Court. Alicia took her and the others out of a door opposite the entrance they had come in by, and there lay the Court surrounded on all sides by the buildings.

'What a lovely place!' said Darrell. 'What's that sunk piece in the middle?'

She pointed to a great circle of green grass sunk a good way below the level of the Court. Round the sloping sides of the circle were stone seats. It looked like an open-air circus ring, the ring sunk low, and the stone seats rising upwards around it, Darrell thought.

' That's where we act plays in the summer,' said Alicia.
' The players perform in the ring, and the audience sit
round on those stone seats. We have good fun.'

Round the sunk circle, on the level, was a beautifully
set out garden, with roses and all kinds of flowers planted
there. Green lawns, not yet cut by the gardeners, were
set between the beds.

' It's warm and sheltered in the Court,' said Darrell.

' It's too hot in the summer,' said Alicia, steering them
all across the Court to the opposite side. ' But you should
see it in the Easter term ! When we come back, in January,
leaving our own homes in frost and maybe snow, we find
snowdrops and aconites and primroses blooming in all the
beds here, in the sheltered Court. It's gorgeous. Well,
look at the tulips coming out here already, and it's only
April ! '

At each end of the hollow oblong of buildings was a
tower. Alicia was making for North Tower. It was
exactly like the other three. Darrell looked at it. It was
four storeys high. Alicia stopped short just outside.

' On the ground floor there's our dining-hall, our common
rooms, where we go when we're not in class, and the kitchens.
On the second floor are the dormies, where we sleep—
dormitories, you know. On the third floor are more dormies. On the top floor are the bedrooms of the staff, and
the box rooms for our luggage.'

' And each house is the same, I suppose ? ' said Darrell,
and she looked up at her tower. ' I wish I slept right at
the top there, in the tower itself. What a lovely view I'd
have ! '

Girls were going in and out of the open door at the
bottom of North Tower. ' Buck up ! ' they called to
Alicia. ' Supper's in a few minutes' time—something good
by the smell of it ! '

' We always get a jolly good supper the day we arrive,'

said Alicia. 'After that—not so good ! Cocoa and biscuits, something like that. Come on, let's find Matron.'

Each of the Tower houses had its own matron, responsible
for the girls' health and well-being. The matron of North
Tower was a plump, bustling woman, dressed in starched
apron and print frock, very neat and spotless.

Alicia took the new girls to her. 'Three more for you
to dose and scold and run after ! ' said Alicia, with a grin.

Darrell looked at Matron, frowning over the long lists
in her hand. Her hair was neatly tucked under a pretty
cap, tied in a bow under her chin. She looked so spotless
that Darrell began to feel very dirty and untidy. She
felt a little scared of Matron, and hoped she wouldn't
make her take nasty medicine too often.

Then Matron looked up and smiled, and at once Darrell's
fears fell away. She couldn't be afraid of a person who
smiled like that, with her eyes and her mouth and even her
nose too !

'Now let me see—you're Darrell Rivers,' said Matron,
ticking off her name on a list. 'Got your health certificate
with you ? Give it to me, please. And you're Sally Hope.'

'No, I'm Gwendoline Mary Lacey,' said Gwendoline.

'And don't forget the Mary,' said Alicia, pertly. 'Dear
Gwendoline Mary.'

'That's enough, Alicia,' said Matron, ticking away down
her list. 'You're as bad as your mother used to be. No,
worse, I think.'

Alicia grinned. 'Mother came to Malory Towers when
she was a girl,' she told the others. 'She was in North
Tower too, and Matron had her for years. She sent you
her best love, Matron. She says she wishes she could
send all my brothers to you too. She's sure you're the
only person who can manage them.'

'If they're anything like you, I'm very glad they're not
here,' said Matron. 'One of the Johns family at a time

is quite enough for me. Your mother put some grey hairs into my head, and you've certainly done your bit in adding a few more.'

She smiled again. She had a wise, kindly face, and any girl who fell ill felt safe in Matron's care. But woe betide any pretender, or any lazy girl or careless one! Then Matron's smile snapped off, her face closed up, and her eyes glinted dangerously!

A big gong boomed through North Tower. 'Supper,' said Matron. 'Unpack your things afterwards, Alicia. Your train was late and you must all be very tired. All first-formers are to go to bed immediately after supper tonight.'

'Oh, *Ma*tron!' began Alicia, groaning. 'Can't we just have ten minutes after . . .'

'I said im*mediate*ly, Alicia,' said Matron. 'Go along now. Wash your hands quickly and go down. Hurry!'

And in five minutes time Alicia and the others were sitting down, enjoying a good supper. They were hungry. Darrell looked round at the tables. She was sure she would never know all the girls in her house! And she was sure she would never dare to join in their laugh and chatter either.

But she would, of course—and very soon too!

3   FIRST NIGHT AND MORNING

AFTER supper, obeying Matron's command, all the first-formers went up to their dormitory. Darrell was delighted with the room. It was long, and had windows all down the length of it, which, to Darrell's joy, overlooked the sea. She stood there, hearing the faraway sound of waves on the beach, watching the slowly moving blue sea. What a lovely place this was!

'Buck up, Dreamy!' said Alicia's voice. 'Matron will be along in two ticks.'

Darrell turned. She looked at the room. It had ten beds in it, each divided from the next by a white curtain which could be drawn or pulled back as the girls wished.

Each girl had a white bed with a coloured eiderdown. The eiderdowns were different colours and made a pretty show as Darrell looked down the row of beds. In each cubicle there was a cupboard to hang things, and a chest of drawers with a mirror on top. There were wash-basins with hot and cold water at each end of the room.

The girls were busy unpacking their small bags. Darrell opened hers. She shook out her night-dress. She took her face-flannel, her tooth-brush and paste. A clean towel hung ready for her on a rail at the side of her chest of drawers.

'It will be fun to sleep here, with all the others,' thought Darrell. 'What fun we shall have talking at night. We could have dormy games too, I should think.'

All the first-formers were in the same dormy. Alicia was there, Darrell, Sally and Gwendoline. There were six other girls besides. They stared at the three new girls as they ran to and from the wash-basins, washing, and cleaning their teeth.

One of the girls looked at her watch. 'Get into bed, everyone!' she ordered. She was a tall, dark girl, quiet in her manner. Everyone but Gwendoline scrambled into bed. Gwendoline was still brushing out her fine golden hair. She was counting as she brushed it.

'Fifty-four, fifty-five, fifty-six . . .'

'Hey, you new girl—what's your name—get into bed!' ordered the tall dark girl again.

'I've got to brush my hair a hundred times each night,' protested Gwendoline. 'Now I've forgotten what number I got to!'

'Shut up and get into bed, Gwendoline Mary,' said Alicia, who was next to Gwendoline. ' Katherine is the head of our dormy. You've got to do what she says.'

'But I promised M-M-Mo . . .' began Gwendoline, tears welling up. 'I promised Mother to b-b-b-brush my hair a hundred times each night!'

'You can add the number of brushings you leave out tonight on to tomorrow night,' came the head-girl's cool voice. 'Get into bed, please.'

'Oh, just let me finish!' said Gwendoline and began frantically brushing again. 'Fifty-seven, fifty . . .'

'Shall I spank her with my brush, Katherine?' said Alicia, sitting up. Gwendoline gave a squeal and leapt into bed. The girls laughed. They all knew that Alicia had no intention of spanking Gwendoline.

Gwendoline lay down, angry. She determined to make herself miserable and cry. She thought of her mother, and her faraway home, and she began to sniff.

'Do blow your nose, Gwendoline,' said Alicia, sleepily.

'Stop talking,' said Katherine. There was silence in the room. Sally Hope gave a little sigh. Darrell wondered if she was asleep. The curtains between her bed and Sally's were pulled back. No, Sally was not asleep. She lay with her eyes wide open. There were no tears in them, but her face looked sad.

'Perhaps she's homesick,' thought Darrell, and thought of her home too. But she was too sensible to be silly about it, and too excited to be at Malory Towers to miss her home. After all, she had badly wanted to come, and here she was— and she meant to be very happy and have a lot of fun.

Matron arrived. She took a look down the beds. One or two of the girls were already fast asleep, tired out. Matron walked down the long room, twitched an eiderdown into place, turned off a dripping tap, and pulled the curtains across the windows, for it was still very light outside.

'Good night,' she said, in a low voice. 'And no talking, please!'

'Good night, Matron,' murmured those girls who were not yet asleep. Darrell peeped to see if Matron's nice smile was on her face. She caught sight of Darrell's peeping eyes and nodded, smiling. 'Sleep well!' she said, and went out quietly.

Gwendoline was the only one who tried to keep awake. What had Mother said to her? 'You'll feel dreadful tonight, I know, darling, but be brave, won't you?'

So Gwendoline was determined to lie awake and feel dreadful. But her eyes wouldn't keep open! They shut and soon Gwendoline was as fast asleep as the others. And at home her mother was dabbing her eyes, and saying, 'Poor little Gwen! I shouldn't have sent her away from me! I feel she's awake and crying her heart out!'

But Gwendoline was giving little contented snores, dreaming happily of how she would queen it over the girls here, be top of her form, and best at all games.

A loud bell awoke all the girls the next morning. At first Darrell couldn't imagine where she was. Then she heard Alicia's voice. 'Get up, lazy-bones! You've got to make your bed before breakfast!'

Darrell leapt out of bed. The sun poured into the room, for Katherine had drawn the curtains back. A loud chattering began. Girls hopped across the room to the wash-basins. Darrell dressed quickly, proud to put on her brown tunic with its brown-orange belt, just like all the other girls wore. She brushed her hair back and put in two slides to keep it tidy. Gwendoline left her hair loose over her shoulders.

'You can't have it like that,' said Alicia. 'Not in *school*, Gwendoline!'

'I've always had it like this,' said Gwendoline, an obstinate look coming over her pretty, silly little face.

'Well, it looks awful,' said Alicia.

'It does not!' said Gwendoline. 'You only say that because your hair is short and coarse.'

Alicia winked at Katherine, who was coming up. 'Better let dear Gwendoline show off her long, fine-as-silk hair, don't you think so?' she said, in a bland voice. 'Miss Potts might be delighted to see it like that.'

'My governess, Miss Winter, always liked it like this,' said Gwendoline, looking pleased.

'Oh—haven't you been to a school before? Have you just had a governess?' asked Alicia. 'That explains a lot.'

'What does it explain?' asked Gwendoline, haughtily.

'Never mind. You'll find out,' said Alicia. 'Ready, Darrell? That's the breakfast gong. Tuck your sheet in well. That's right. Gwendoline, fold up your nighty. Look at Sally—there's a new girl for you! Everything done to time, nobody's got to chivvy her round!'

Sally gave a little smile. She hardly said a word. She did not seem in the least shy, but she was so quiet and self-possessed that Darrell could hardly believe she was a new girl. She always seemed to know exactly what to do.

They all went down to the dining-hall. The long tables were ready, and girls were already seating themselves, greeting their house-mistress politely. Matron was there too, and a third grown-up, whom Darrell had not seen before.

'That's Mam'zelle Dupont,' whispered Alicia. 'We've got two French mistresses at Malory Towers. One's fat and jolly and the other's thin and sour. We've got the fat and jolly one this term. They've both got simply awful tempers, so I hope you're pretty good at French.'

'Well, no, I'm not really,' said Darrell, wishing she was.

'Mam'zelle Dupont hates Mam'zelle Rougier and Mam'zelle Rougier hates Mam'zelle Dupont,' went on Alicia. 'You should see the fur fly sometimes. Matron

has to be sent for to calm them down when they get too
bad ! '

Darrell's eyes opened wide.   Katherine, across the table,
laughed. ' Don't believe all that Alicia says,' she said.
' Her tongue runs away with her sometimes.   Nobody has
ever seen our two Mam'zelles fly at each other's throats yet.'

' Ah, but they will one day—and I hope I'll be there to
see it,' said Alicia.

Mam'zelle Dupont was short, fat and round.   She wore
her hair in a little bun on top.   Her eyes, black and beady,
were never still.   She wore a black frock that fitted her
perfectly, and well-fitting black shoes on her tiny feet.

She was short-sighted but she would not wear glasses.
She had instead a pair of long-handled glasses, called
lorgnettes, which she wore dangling on a long black ribbon.
These she used when she wanted to see anything at close
quarters, holding them to her eyes with her hand.

Alicia, who was a good mimic, could keep her class in
fits of laughter, blinking like poor Mam'zelle, and holding
imaginary glasses up to her nose.   But she was just as
much in awe of Mam'zelle Dupont as anyone else, and
did not rouse her hot temper if she could help it.

' New girls must go to see the Head Mistress after breakfast,' announced Miss Potts.   ' There are three in the first
form, two in the second form, and one in the fourth.   You
can all go together.   Join us in the assembly room for
Prayers later.   Pamela, will you take the new girls to the
Head, please ? '

Pamela, head-girl of North Tower House, rose.   The
new girls stood up, Darrell among them.   They followed
Pamela.   She took them out of the door that let into the
Court, and then in through another door set in the building
that ran between East and North Tower.   The Head
Mistress's rooms were there, and so was the San. or sana-
torium, where any sick girl went.

They came to a door painted a deep cream colour. Pamela knocked. A low voice said ' Come in ! '

Pamela opened the door. ' I've brought the new girls to you, Miss Grayling,' she said.

' Thank you, Pamela,' said the low voice again, and Darrell saw a grey-haired woman sitting at a desk, writing. She had a calm, unwrinkled face, eyes that were startlingly blue, and a very firm mouth. Darrell felt frightened of this calm, low-voiced Head Mistress, and hoped she would never have to be sent to her for misbehaviour !

The new girls stood in a row before the Head, and Miss Grayling looked at them all closely. Darrell felt herself going red, she couldn't imagine why. Her knees felt a bit wobbly too. She hoped Miss Grayling wouldn't ask her any questions, for she was sure she wouldn't be able to say a word !

Miss Grayling asked them their names, and spoke a few words to each girl. Then she addressed them all solemnly.

' One day you will leave school and go out into the world as young women. You should take with you eager minds, kind hearts, and a will to help. You should take with you a good understanding of many things, and a willingness to accept responsibility and show yourselves as women to be loved and trusted. All these things you will be able to learn at Malory Towers—if you *will*. I do not count as our successes those who have won scholarships and passed exams., though these are good things to do. I count as our successes those who learn to be good-hearted and kind, sensible and trustable, good, sound women the world can lean on. Our failures are those who do not learn these things in the years they are here.'

These words were spoken so gravely and solemnly that Darrell hardly breathed. She immediately longed to be one of Malory Towers' successes.

'It is easy for some of you to learn these things, and hard for others. But easy or hard, they must be learnt if you are to be happy, after you leave here, and if you are to bring happiness to others.'

There was a pause. Then Miss Grayling spoke again, in a lighter tone. 'You will all get a tremendous lot out of your time at Malory Towers. See that you give a lot back!'

'Oh!' said Darrell, surprised and pleased, quite forgetting that she had thought she wouldn't be able to speak a word, 'that's *exactly* what my father said to me when he said good-bye, Miss Grayling!'

'Did he?' said Miss Grayling, looking with smiling eyes at the eager little girl. 'Well, as you have parents who think in that way, I imagine you will be one of the lucky ones, and will find that the things I have been speaking of will be easy to learn. Perhaps one day Malory Towers will be proud of you.'

A few more words and the girls were told to go. Very much impressed they walked out of the room. Not even Gwendoline said a word. Whatever they might do, in the years to come at Malory Towers, each girl wanted, at that moment, to do her best. Whether or not that wish would last, depended on the girl.

Then they went to the Assembly Hall for Prayers, found their places, and waited for Miss Grayling to come to the platform.

Soon the words of a hymn sounded in the big hall. The first day of term had begun. Darrell sang with all her might, happy and excited. What a lot she would have to tell her mother when she wrote!

ALL the school met each morning for prayers. The girls stood together in their classes—first-formers of North Tower, South, East, and West Tower, all together, and so on.

Darrell took a nervous look at her class. What a big one it seemed! About twenty-five or thirty girls, surely. Miss Potts, her house-mistress, was also the first-form mistress. There was Mam'zelle Dupont, singing lustily, and the teacher beside her must be the other French mistress. But how different! She was skinny, tall and bony. Her hair too was done up in a little bun, but at the back instead of on top. Darrell thought she looked bad-tempered.

Alicia told her which the other mistresses were. 'That's the history mistress, Miss Carton over there—see her—the one with the high collar and pince-nez glasses on her nose. She's frightfully clever, and awfully sarcastic if you don't like history. And that's the art mistress, Miss Linnie—she's awfully nice. Very easy-going.'

Darrell hoped she would have a lot to do with Miss Linnie, if she was easy-going. She looked nice. She was young and had red hair done in little curls.

'That's the music-master—Mr. Young—see him? He's always either in a very good temper or a very bad one. We always try and find out which, when he takes us for music or singing.'

The matrons of the four houses were at Prayers too. Darrell saw her own Matron, looking a little stern, as she always did when she was thinking hard of what she was doing. Alicia began whispering again.

'And that's . . .'

Miss Potts's eye swung round to her, and Alicia immediately stopped whispering and studied her hymn-book. Miss

Potts did not look kindly on people who whispered **at any** time, least of all in Prayers.

Prayers over, the girls filed off to their various classrooms. These ran all along the west side of Malory Towers, and soon that building was filled with the sound of hurrying feet, laughter and chattering. There was no rule about silence in the corridors in the part of the building where the classrooms were.

The first-formers filed into their own classroom, a room with a lovely view over the sea. It was a big room, with the mistress's desk at one end, and cupboards at the other. Desks and chairs were arranged in orderly rows.

'Bags I one by the window!' said a fat girl and plumped herself down there.

'Bags I one too,' said Gwendoline. But the fat girl stared in surprise.

'You're new aren't you? Well, you can't choose your own seat, then. New girls have to take the desks left over when the old girls have chosen the ones they want.'

Gwendoline went red. She tossed her golden hair back over her shoulders and looked sulky.

She stood close by the desk she had chosen, not quite daring to take it, but too obstinate to leave it. A small wiry girl pushed her away.

'Bags I this desk! Hallo, Rita! Did you have nice hols.? Awful to be back with old Potty, isn't it?'

Darrell stood and waited till she saw that all the girls except herself, Sally and Gwendoline and one or two others, had desks. Then she slipped into one beside Alicia, glad of her good luck. Alicia was exchanging news with a girl on the other side of her. She seemed to be very friendly indeed with her.

She turned to Darrell. 'Darrell, this is my friend, Betty Hill. We always sit next to each other. But Betty is in West House, worse luck.'

Darrell smiled at Betty, who was a lively-looking girl, with wicked brown eyes and hair that fell over her forehead. She liked Betty but she was sorry to hear that Alicia had a friend already. She had rather hoped that Alicia would be *her* friend. She didn't particularly want either Sally or Gwendoline.

'Sh!' said the girl at the door. 'Here comes Potty!'

There was silence at once. The girls stood up, and looked straight before them as they heard the quick, light steps of their form-mistress coming down the corridor outside. She swept into the room, nodded to the girls and said, 'You can sit!'

They sat down and waited in silence. Miss Potts took out her list of names and checked them all, tracking down a few more new girls in the other houses. Then she turned to the expectant faces before her.

'Well!' she said, 'the summer term is always the best of the lot, with swimming and tennis, picnics and rambles. But please don't make the mistake of thinking that the summer term is nothing *but* a picnic. It isn't. It's good hard work too. Some of you are taking exams. next term. Well, work hard this term, and you'll find the exams. easy next term. But slack this term, and I promise you I shall hear some groans and grumbles *next* term!'

She paused. Then she looked hard at two or three girls. 'Last term there were one or two girls who seemed to like to be bottom every week,' she said. 'Leave that place to the new girls, please, and go up a few places! I never expect much of new girls their first term—but I *shall* expect quite a lot of you.'

A few girls went red. Miss Potts went on talking. 'I don't really think I've any brainless girls this term,' she said, 'though I don't know much about the new girls, of course. If you are brainless and near the bottom, we shan't blame you, of course—but if you've got good brains

and are down at the bottom, I shall have a lot to say.   And
you know what *that* means, don't you ? '

'Yes,' answered most of the girls, fervently.   Miss Potts
smiled, and her keen face lit up for a moment. 'Well,
now, after all those threats, let's get on.   Here's a list of
things each girl must have.   If anyone lacks any of them,
she must go to Katherine, head-girl of the form, and get
them from her at the end of the lesson.   I will give ten
minutes for that.'

Soon a lesson was in full swing.   It was maths., and Miss
Potts was giving a quick test-paper to see what standard
the new girls were up to, and whether the whole form could
work together or not.   Darrell found the paper quite easy,
but Gwendoline groaned and grunted terribly, her golden
hair all over the desk.

'What's the matter, Gwendoline ? ' enquired Miss Potts,
unsympathetically.

'Well, my governess, Miss Winter, never showed me
how to do sums like this,' wailed Gwendoline. 'She put
them down quite differently.'

'You'll have to learn *my* way now,' said Miss Potts.
And Gwendoline—why haven't you done your hair this
morning ? '

'I *did*,' said Gwendoline, raising her big pale blue eyes.
'I brushed it well.   I gave it forty . . .'

'All right, I don't want details,' said Miss Potts.   'You
can't come to class with it like that.   Plait it after Break.'

'*Plait* it ! ' mourned poor Gwendoline, whilst the rest
of the class began to giggle.   'But I've never . . .'

'That's enough,' said Miss Potts.   'If you can't plait
it and keep it tidy, perhaps your mother could have it cut
short next holidays.'

Gwendoline looked so horrified that it was all Darrell
could do to keep from laughing out loud.

'I told you so ! ' whispered Alicia, as soon as Miss Potts

turned to write something on the blackboard. Gwendoline glared angrily at her and made a face. As if Mother would *dream* of cutting off her beautiful fine sheet of hair. And now to think she'd got to plait it. Why, she didn't even know *how* to plait! Gwendoline was so lost in sulky thought that she hardly answered any of the maths. questions.

The morning went on. Break came and the girls rushed out to play where they liked. Some went for a quick game on one of the many tennis-courts. Some went for a ramble in the grounds. Others lay about in the Court, talking. Darrell would have liked to go with Alicia, but she was with Betty, and Darrell felt sure they wouldn't want a third person. She looked at the other new girls. Two of them, whom she didn't know, had made friends already. Another girl, who had a cousin in the same form, went off with her. Gwendoline was not to be seen. Perhaps she had gone to plait her hair!

Sally Hope was sitting on the grass alone, no expression at all on her closed-up face. Darrell went over to her. 'What do you think of Malory Towers?' she said. 'I think it's fine.'

Sally looked up primly. 'It's not bad,' she said.

'Were you sorry to leave your other school?' asked Darrell. 'I wanted to come to Malory, of course, but I hated leaving all my friends. Didn't you hate leaving all your friends too?'

'I don't think I had any, really,' said Sally, considering. Darrell thought that was queer. It was hard to get anything out of Sally. She was polite and answered questions, but she didn't ask any in return.

'Well, I hope I don't have to make *her* my friend!' thought Darrell, at last. 'Gracious, here's Gwendoline! *Does* she think she's plaited her hair? It's all undone already!'

'Is my hair all right?' said Gwendoline, in a plaintive

Sally was sitting on the grass alone

voice. ' I've tried and tried to plait it. It was beastly of
Miss Potts not to let me wear it as I've always worn it. I
don't like her.'

' Let *me* plait it for you,' said Darrell, jumping up. ' It
doesn't look to me as if you know *how* to plait, Gwendoline ! '

She plaited the golden hair deftly and quickly into
long braids and tied the ends with bits of narrow ribbon.

' There ! ' she said, swinging Gwendoline round to look
at her. ' You look *much* nicer ! '

Gwendoline scowled, and forgot to thank Darrell for her
help. Actually, she did look much nicer now. ' How
spoilt she is ! ' thought Darrell. ' Well, little as I want
Sally for a friend, I want Gwendoline even less. I should
want to slap her for all her silly airs and graces ! '

The bell went, and scores of girls raced in to their classrooms. Darrell raced too. She knew where her classroom
was. She knew the names of a lot of her form. She would
soon be quite at home at Malory Towers !

5   THE FIRST WEEK GOES BY

DARRELL soon began to settle down. She learnt the
names not only of the girls in her form at North Tower,
but of every girl there, from the head-girl Pamela, down
to Mary-Lou, the youngest but one in the first form.
Darrell herself was the youngest girl in North Tower, she
found, but she felt that Mary-Lou was very much younger.

Mary-Lou was a scared mouse of a girl. She was frightened of mice, beetles, thunderstorms, noises at night, the
dark, and a hundred other things. Poor Mary-Lou, no
wonder she had big scared eyes. Darrell, not easily scared
of anything, laughed when she saw poor Mary-Lou rush

to the other side of the dormy because she saw an earwig on the floor.

There were ten girls in the first-form dormy at North Tower. Katherine, the quiet head-girl. Alicia, the talk-ative, unruly-tongued monkey. The three new girls, Darrell, Gwendoline, and Sally. Mary-Lou, with her big scared eyes, always ready to shy back like a nervous horse, at anything unexpected.

Then there was clever Irene, a marvel at maths. and music, usually top of the form—but oh, how stupid in the ordinary things of life. If anyone lost her book it was Irene. If anyone went to the wrong classroom at the wrong time it was Irene. It was said that once she had gone to the art-room, thinking that a painting lesson was to be taken there, and had actually sat there for half-an-hour, apparently waiting for Miss Linnie to come. What she thought had happened to the rest of the class, no one knew.

'But *how* could you sit there all that time and not even *wonder* why nobody came!' said Katherine, in amazement. 'What were you thinking of, Irene?'

'I was just thinking of a maths. problem that Potty set us, that's all,' said Irene, her eyes shining through her big glasses. 'It was rather an interesting one, and there were two or three ways of getting it right. You see . . .'

'Oh, spare us maths. out of school!' groaned Alicia. 'Irene, I think you're bats!'

But Irene wasn't. She was a most intelligent girl, who, because her mind was always so deeply at work at something, seemed to forget the smaller, everyday things of life. She had a sense of fun too, and when she was really tickled she came out with a tremendous explosive giggle that startled the class and made Miss Potts jump. It was Alicia's delight to provoke this explosion sometimes, and upset the class.

The other three girls in the form were Jean, a jolly, shrewd girl from Scotland, very able at handling money for various school societies and charities; Emily, a quiet studious girl, clever with her needle, and one of Mam'zelle's favourites because of this; and Violet, a shy, colourless child, very much left out of things because she never seemed to take any interest in them. Half the form never even noticed whether Violet was with them or not.

That made up the ten girls. Darrell felt that she had known them for years after she had lived with them only a few days. She knew the way Irene's stockings always fell down in wrinkles. She knew the way Jean spoke, clipped and sharp, in her Scots accent. She knew that Mam'zelle disliked Jean because Jean was scornful of Mam'zelle's enthusiasms and emotions. Jean herself never went into ecstasies about anything.

Darrell knew Gwendoline's sighs and moans over everything, and Mary-Lou's scared exclamations of fear at any insect or reptile. She liked Katherine's low, firm voice, and air of being able to cope with anything. She knew a great deal about Alicia, but then, so did everyone, for Alicia poured out everything that came into her head, she chattered about her brothers, her mother and father, her dogs, her work, her play, her knitting, her opinion of everything and everybody under the sun.

Alicia had no time at all for airs and graces, pretences, sighs, moans or affectations. She was as downright as Darrell, but not so kind. She was scornful and biting when it pleased her, so that girls like Gwendoline hated her, and those like scared Mary-Lou feared her. Darrell liked her immensely.

'She's so lively,' she thought to herself. 'Nobody could be dull with Alicia. I wish I was as interesting as she is. Everyone listens when Alicia speaks, even when she says something unkind. But nobody pays much attention when I want to say something. I do really like Alicia, and I wish she hadn't got Betty for a friend. She's just the one I would have chosen.'

It took Darrell longer to know the first-formers who came from the other Towers. She saw them in class, but not in the common room or dormies, for the first-formers of the other Towers had their own rooms, of course, in their own Towers. Still, it was enough to know her own Tower girls for a start, Darrell thought.

She didn't know very much about the older girls in her Tower, for she didn't even meet them in the classroom. She saw them at Prayers in the morning, sometimes during the singing-lesson, when Mr. Young took more than one class at a time, and sometimes on the tennis-courts and in the swimming-pool.

She heard a few things about some of them, of course. Marilyn, sixth-former, was captain of the games, and most of the girls liked her immensely. ' She's fair and really takes a lot of trouble to coach even the first-formers,' said Alicia. ' She's as good as old Remmington, the games-mistress, any day. *She* won't bother with the duds, but Marilyn *does*.'

Everyone appeared to look up to Pamela, the head-girl, too. She was clever, and rather literary. It was said that she was already writing a book. This impressed the first-formers very much. It was hard enough to write a decent composition, let alone a book.

No one seemed to like two girls called Doris and Fanny. ' Too spiteful for words,' said Alicia, who, of course, could always give an opinion immediately about anyone or anything, from Winston Churchill down to the little boy belonging to the Tower House cook. ' They're frightfully pi.'

' What do you mean—pi ? ' said Gwendoline, who hadn't apparently heard that word before.

' Golly—what an ignoramus you are ! ' said Alicia. ' Pi

means pious. Religious in the wrong way. Thinking they're wonderful and nobody else is. Trying to stop people's pleasure. They're a sickening pair. Always on the prowl and on the snoop. Once, when I slipped across the Court in the middle of the night to join Betty Hill, in West Tower for a midnight feast, Doris saw me out of the window, and lay in wait for me to come back. Beast.'

' Did she catch you ? ' asked Mary-Lou, her eyes wide with alarm.

' 'Course she didn't ! You don't think I'd let myself be caught by the Pi Sisters, do you ? ' said Alicia, scornfully. ' I spotted her when I came back, and shut her in the boot-cupboard.'

Irene gave one of her loud explosive giggles and made them all jump. ' I'd never think of the things *you* think of, Alicia ! ' she said. ' No wonder the Pi Sisters glare at you in Prayers each morning. I bet they'll watch out for you to do something you shouldn't, and tell on you.'

' And I bet I'll get the better of them ! ' said Alicia, grimly. ' If they try any tricks on me, I'll try a few on them ! '

' Oh, do, do,' begged Darrell, who had a great weakness for jokes and tricks. She didn't always dare to do them herself, but she was always ready to back up any one else who did.

Darrell soon got to know all the different classrooms too. She knew the art-room, with its clear north light. She hadn't yet had a lesson in the lab. or laboratory, which looked a bit frightening. She loved the great gym. with all its apparatus of swings, ropes, vaulting-horses and mattresses. She was good at gym. So was Alicia, who could climb like a monkey, and was as strong as a horse. Mary-Lou, of course, was too scared to do anything unless she was made to.

It was fun, the way all the girls slept in the Towers, and had their lessons in the other parts of the great building.

Darrell knew where the teachers lived now in the building facing south, except those who, like Miss Potts, and Mam'zelle, lived in with the girls, to keep an eye on them. She began to wonder how she could have felt so lost and over-awed when she first arrived. She didn't feel a bit like a new girl now.

One of the things that Darrell liked best of all was the big swimming-pool down by the sea. This had been hollowed out of a stretch of rocks, so that it had a nice rocky, uneven bottom. Seaweed grew at the sides, and sometimes the rocky bed of the pool felt a little slimy. But the sea swept into the big natural pool each day, filled it, and made lovely waves all across it. It was a sheer delight to bathe there.

The coast itself was too dangerous for bathing. The tides were so strong, and no girl was allowed to swim in the open sea. But anyone was safe in the pool. One end was quite deep, and here there were diving-boards and a chute, and a fine spring-board for running dives. Mary-Lou and Gwendoline were terrified of the pool, Mary-Lou because she was afraid of water, anyhow, and Gwendoline because she hated the first cold plunge. Alicia's eyes always gleamed when she spied the shivering Gwendoline, and the poor girl so often had an unexpected push into the water that she soon began to step in hurriedly whenever she saw Alicia or Betty coming near.

The first week went very slowly. There was a lot to learn and know, things were so new and exciting. Darrell loved every minute, and soon got into the way of things. She was naturally quick and responsive, and the girls soon accepted her and liked her.

But they neither accepted nor liked poor Gwendoline, and as for Sally Hope, after trying in vain to draw her out a little, and get her to talk of her family and home, the girls let her live in her shell, and not come out of it at all.

' First week gone ! ' announced Alicia, some days later.
' The first week always crawls. After that the days fly,
and it's half-term in no time, and when that's gone we're
looking forward to the hols. You've soon settled in,
haven't you, Darrell ? '

' Oh, *yes*,' said Darrell. ' I love it. If every term is as
nice as this, I shall be thrilled ! '

' Ah, you wait,' said Alicia. ' Everything's always all
right at first—but when you've had a wigging or two from
Mam'zelle, and been dosed by Matron, and kept in by
Potty, and slated by Miss Remmington, and ticked off by
one of the older girls, and . . . ! '

' Oh, stop ! ' cried Darrell. ' Nothing like that will
happen, Alicia. Don't try and frighten me ! '

But Alicia was right, of course. Things were not going
to be quite so smooth and easy as Darrell thought !

6   ALICIA'S LITTLE JOKE

DARRELL had good brains and she had been taught how
to use them. She soon found that she could easily do the
work of her class, and in such things as composition was
ahead of most of the others. She felt pleased.

' I thought I'd have to work much much harder than at
my old school,' she thought to herself. ' But I shan't !
It's only maths. I'm not so good at. I wish I was as good
as Irene at maths. She does things in her head that I
can't even do on paper.'

So, after the first week or two, Darrell relaxed a little, and
did not worry herself too much about her work. She began
to enjoy amusing the class a little, just as Alicia did. Alicia
was thrilled to have someone to help her in her mischief.

Betty Hill went much further than Alicia. Darrell sometimes wondered if there was anything she would stop at. There were two mistresses that Betty and Alicia played up to. One was Mam'zelle Dupont, the other was a quiet, gentle mistress who took needlework, and sometimes took prep. time at night. Miss Davies never seemed to realize that Alicia and Betty could play tricks on her. Mam'zelle did realize it, but was taken in all the same.

'Did you ever hear how Betty put a white mouse into Mam'zelle's desk one day ? ' said Alicia. 'Poor little thing, it couldn't get out, and suddenly, in despair, it pushed up the little ink-pot, and stuck its nose out of the ink-pot hole. Mam'zelle nearly had a fit.'

'What did she do ? ' asked Darrell, with great interest.

'Flew out of the room as if a hundred dogs were after her ! ' said Alicia. 'When she was gone we took the mouse out quickly, and Betty hid it down her neck. So, when Mam'zelle ventured back, and ordered one of us to turn her desk out and get the mouse, there was none to be found. Mam'zelle thought her eyes had gone wrong ! '

'Oh, I *do* wish I'd been there ! ' sighed Darrell. 'Alicia, *do* do something funny like that. Do something in maths., can't you ? I know Miss Potts is going to go for me over my maths. prep., and something like that would take her mind away from me ! '

'What ! Play a trick like that in Potty's class ! ' said Alicia, scornfully. 'Don't be silly. Potty's up to everything. You can't fool *her* ! '

'Well—in Mam'zelle's class, then,' begged Darrell. 'I like Mam'zelle, but I haven't seen her in a temper yet and I'd like to. *Do*, do play a trick in her class.'

Alicia felt that she would have a most admiring spectator in Darrell, if only she could think of something. She screwed her forehead into wrinkles and thought hard.

Betty prompted her. 'Can't you think of something

Sam or Roger or Dick did last term ? ' she asked. She turned to Darrell. ' Alicia's three brothers all go to the same school,' she said. ' And there's a master there called Toggles—at least that's what the boys call him—and he's such a dud the boys can play any trick they like on him and get away with it.'

Darrell thought Roger, Sam, and Dick sounded fine brothers to have. She wished she had a brother too. But she had only a younger sister.

' There's one thing Roger did last term that was quite funny,' said Alicia, suddenly. ' I believe we could do it. But you and Betty will have to help, Darrell.'

' Oh, I'd *love* to,' said Darrell. ' What is it ? '

' Well, Roger pretended to be deaf,' said Alicia. ' And everything old Toggles asked him he pretended to hear wrong. When Toggles said " Johns, sit still in your chair ! " Roger said " Give you a cheer, sir ? Certainly ! Hip, hip, hip, hurrah ! "

Darrell laughed. ' Oh, Alicia ! That would be fun ! Do, do pretend to be deaf, please do. We'll play up to you like anything. We will really. Do it in Mam'zelle's class.'

The first form soon heard that Alicia was going to pull Mam'zelle's leg, and were thrilled. The first excitement of coming back to school had worn off. The girls were restless and ready for a bit of excitement.

' Now,' said Alicia, ' I'll pretend to misunderstand what Mam'zelle says—and then you can repeat it very loudly, Darrell, and then you, Betty, and then the rest of the class. See ? We'll have some sport.'

Mam'zelle, all unsuspicious of this deep-laid plot, entered the first-form classroom smiling brightly the next morning. It was a beautiful summer day. She had had two letters from home, giving her the news that she had a new little nephew. She had on a new brooch, and had washed her hair the night before. She was feeling in a very good temper.

She beamed round at the class. 'Ah, my dear girls!'
she said. 'We are going to do some very very good
French today, *n'est ce pas*? We are going to be better
than the second form! Even Gwendoline will be
able to say her verbs to me without one, single, mistake!'

Gwendoline looked doubtful. Since she had been at
Malory Towers her opinion of her governess at home had
gone down. Miss Winter didn't seem to have taught her half
the things she ought to have known! On the other hand,
thought Gwendoline, she had raved over her hair and blue
eyes, she had praised the sweetness of Gwendoline's temper,
and said how graceful she was in all she did. That kind
of thing was most enjoyable to a person like Gwendoline.
But a little more learning would have been very useful to
her at Malory Towers.

She wished she had learnt a lot more French. Mam'zelle
had exclaimed at the little she knew, and had even suggested
extra French lessons in order to get her up to the average
standard of the form. But so far Gwendoline had been
able to avoid extra lessons, and she was quite determined to
go *on* avoiding them! French five times a week was bad
enough without extra time tagged on.

She smiled back rather doubtfully at Mam'zelle, hoping
that Alicia would soon begin her performance, so that
Mam'zelle's attention would not be directed at her.
Mam'zelle beamed round again. She thought the girls
looked eager and responsive this morning. The dear girls!
She would tell them about her new little nephew. That
would please them, no doubt!

Mam'zelle could never stop herself from talking about
her beloved family in France, if she had had news of them.
Usually the girls encouraged her, because the more they
heard about *la chère* Josephine, and *la mignonne* Yvonne,
and *la méchante* Louise, the less they heard about verbs and

genders. So they were delighted when Mam'zelle informed them of her new nephew.

' *Il est appelé, Jean*—he is called John. *Il est tout petit,
oh, tout petit!* ' Mam'zelle held up her two hands and
measured a small distance between them to show how little
her new nephew John was. ' Now, what does that mean ?
Il—est—tout—petit. Who will tell me ? '

Alicia was sitting in an attitude of strained attention,
leaning forward as far as possible over her desk, one of her
hands behind her ear. Mam'zelle noticed her.

' Ah, Alicia, you did not hear me very well ? I will repeat. *Il—est—tout—petit.* Repeat to me, please.'

' Pardon ? ' said Alicia, politely, and put both hands
behind her ears.

Darrell wanted to giggle already. She tried to keep her
face straight.

' Alicia ! What is wrong with you ? ' cried Mam'zelle.
' Can you not hear ? '

' What do I fear ? Why, nothing, Mam'zelle,' said Alicia,
looking slightly surprised. Somebody giggled and then
smothered it quickly.

' Mam'zelle said " Can you not *hear* ? " ' repeated Betty
in a loud voice to Alicia.

' Beer ? ' said Alicia, more astonished, apparently, than
ever.

' CAN YOU NOT HEAR ? ' shouted Darrell, joining in the
game. And the class joined in too. ' CAN YOU NOT HEAR ? '

Mam'zelle banged on her desk. ' Girls ! You forget
yourselves. What a noise to make in class.'

' Mam'zelle, perhaps Alicia is DEAF,' said Darrell, speaking
as if Mam'zelle herself were deaf. ' Maybe she has ear-ache.'

' Ah, *la pauvre petite!* ' cried Mam'zelle, who suffered
from ear-ache herself at times, and was always very sympathetic towards anyone else who did. She bellowed at
Alicia.

'Have you ear-ache?'

'A rake? I don't want a rake, thank you, Mam'zelle,' replied Alicia. 'I'm not gardening today.'

This was too much for Irene, who let out one of her explosive laughs, making the girls in front of her jump.

'*Tiens!*' cried Mam'zelle, jumping too, 'what was that? Ah, you Irene—why do you make that extra-ordinary noise? I will not have it.'

'Can't help sneezing sometimes, Mam'zelle,' stuttered Irene, burying her nose in her handkerchief as if she was about to sneeze again. Curious noises came from her as she tried to choke back her giggles.

'Alicia,' said Mam'zelle, turning back to the mischief-maker, who at once put both hands behind her ears, and frowned as if trying her best to hear. 'Alicia, do not talk to me of rakes. Tell me, have you a cold?'

'No, I've no gold, only a ten-shilling note,' answered Alicia, much to Mam'zelle's mystification.

'Mam'zelle said COLD not GOLD,' explained Darrell at the top of her voice.

'You know—COLD, the opposite of HOT,' went on Betty, helpfully. 'Have you a COLD?'

'HAVE YOU A COLD?' roared the class, coming in like a well-trained chorus.

'Oh, *cold!* Why don't you speak clearly, then I should hear you,' said Alicia. 'Yes—I've had a cold, of course.'

'Ah—then it has affected your poor ears,' said Mam'zelle. 'How long ago was this cold, Alicia?'

Darrell repeated this question at the top of her voice, followed by Betty.

'Oh—when did I have it? About two years ago,' said Alicia. Irene buried her nose in her hanky again. Mam'zelle looked a little blank.

'It is of no use the poor child trying to follow the French lesson,' said Mam'zelle. 'Alicia, sit by the window in the sun and read your French book to yourself. You cannot hear a word we say.'

Alicia looked enquiringly at Darrell, as if she hadn't heard. Darrell obligingly repeated it all at the top of her voice. Betty unfortunately was too overcome by a desire to laugh to be able to repeat it too. But the rest of the class obliged with a will.

'YOU CANNOT HEAR A WORD WE SAY!' they chorused.

The door opened suddenly and a most irate Miss Potts looked in. She had been taking Form 2 next door, and could not imagine what the shouting was in Form 1.

'Mam'zelle, excuse my interrupting you, but is it necessary for the girls to repeat their French lesson so very loudly?' she asked.

'Ah, Miss Potts, I am so sorry. But it is not for me the girls repeat words so loudly, it is for the poor Alicia,' explained Mam'zelle.

Miss Potts looked most surprised. She looked at Alicia. Alicia felt uncomfortable. She also looked as innocent as she could. But Miss Potts was always on the alert when Betty or Alicia looked innocent.

'What do you mean, Mam'zelle?' she snapped. 'Has Alicia suddenly gone deaf? She was all right this morning.'

'She is quite, quite deaf now,' Mam'zelle assured her. Miss Potts looked sharply at Alicia.

'Come to me at Break, Alicia,' she said. 'I would like a few words with you.'

Nobody dared repeat these words to Alicia, but Mam'zelle herself obliged. She shouted across to Alicia.

'Miss Potts says, will you . . .'

'Don't bother to repeat what I said, Mam'zelle,' said Miss Potts. 'Alicia will come all right. I shall expect you at eleven, Alicia. And please stand up when I speak to you.'

Alicia stood up, her face a flaming red. Miss Potts

went out of the room, and she did not shut the door very quietly. Mam'zelle disliked people who banged doors.

'Ah, this door, it goes through my poor head!' she said. 'Miss Potts, she is very good and clever, but she does not have the head-ache, as I do . . .'

'Nor the ear-ache,' put in Darrell, but no one raised a giggle. Miss Potts's entry and fierceness had damped the cheerfulness of the class considerably.

Alicia said no more about her ear-ache. She took a book and sat down by the window in the sunshine, feeling sure that Miss Potts would not appear again. She thought she might as well get something out of her performance! Mam'zelle took no further notice of her, and devoted herself to a whole-hearted search for someone in Form 1 who could and would conjugate a whole French verb properly. Not finding anyone really good, she lost the good temper she had entered with that morning, and gave the class a bad time.

She stalked out when the bell for Break went. The girls crowded round Alicia. 'Oh, Alicia! I nearly died when you said " beer ".'—'Wasn't it a shame Potty coming in like that?'—'Will you get into a fearful row, Alicia?'

'Darrell nearly yelled the roof off!' said Irene. 'I almost burst with trying not to laugh.'

'I must go and hear what Potty has to say,' said Alicia. 'Pity I forgot she was taking Form 2 next door! So long, girls!'

7   DARRELL LOSES HER TEMPER

ALICIA got a good scolding, and extra prep. She came out from Miss Potts's room, and ran straight into Mam'zelle. 'Have you been to see Miss Potts, Alicia?' asked Mam'zelle, thinking that perhaps Alicia hadn't heard what Miss Potts had said.

' Oh, yes, thank you, Mam'zelle,' said Alicia, and walked off. Mam'zelle stared after her. How queer ! Alicia had heard perfectly what she had said. Could ears get better so quickly then ? Mam'zelle stood still and frowned. Miss Potts came out of her room and saw her.

' If Alicia shows any further signs of deafness, send her to me,' said Miss Potts, coldly. ' I can always cure it at once.'

She walked off. Mam'zelle began to breathe quickly. ' 'The bad girl, Alicia !—She has pulled my foot,' said Mam'-zelle, who sometimes got a little mixed ! ' She has hoodle-winked me ! Never again will I believe her, the bad girl.'

Darrell had thoroughly enjoyed the absurd affair. How cleverly Alicia had pulled it off ! She looked at her admir-ingly, and Alicia liked the admiration. It always egged her on to further misbehaviour. Mary-Lou stared at her too, as if she was somebody most remarkable. Alicia went up and took Darrell's arm.

' We'll think of something else soon,' she said. ' You and I and Betty. We'll be the Bold Bad Three, or something like that ! '

' Oh, *yes* ! ' said Darrell, thrilled at the idea of being one of a gang with Betty and Alicia. ' Do let's ! Maybe I could think of something, too.'

It was decided, however, that it would be best not to try anything further until a little time had gone by. Perhaps something could be tried on Miss Linnie next.

Gwendoline was jealous of the way Alicia and Betty, recognized leaders in the first form, had made friends with Darrell. After all, Darrell was as new as she herself was. And she, Gwendoline, was much prettier, and had, she was sure, much more charm of manner.

She took Sally Hope into her confidence. ' I don't like the way Darrell Rivers pushes herself forward all the time,

do you ? ' she said to Sally. ' Thinking she's so marvellous !
Chumming up with Alicia and Betty. Not that I would if
they asked me.'

Sally didn't look very interested, but Gwendoline didn't
mind. She went on grumbling about Darrell. ' She
thinks she's got such good brains, she thinks she plays such
a marvellous game of tennis, she thinks she's so good at
swimming ! I've a good mind to show her that I'm *twice*
as good as she is ! '

' Well, why don't you ? ' said Sally, bored. ' Instead of
showing everyone you're twice as bad ! '

Gwendoline was annoyed. To think that the quiet little
Sally Hope should say such a thing to her ! She looked
at Sally as if she would like to wither her up.

' All right,' said Gwendoline, grandly. ' I *will* just show
you, Sally. I haven't really tried before, because it didn't
seem worth it. *I* didn't want to come to Malory Towers,
and Mother didn't want me to either. It was Daddy that
made me come. I did marvellously with my governess,
Miss Winter, and I could do marvellously now, if only I
thought it was worth while ! '

Alicia came up and heard this curious speech. She
laughed loudly.

' You can't play tennis, you can't swim, you squeal when
your toe touches the cold water, you don't even know all
your twelve times table, baby ! And then you talk of it not
being worth while to show what you can do ! You can't
do a thing and never will, whilst you have such a wonderful
opinion of yourself ! '

Sally laughed too, and that made Gwendoline angry.
How she would like to slap them both ! But Miss Winter
had always said that a little lady kept her hands to herself.
Anyway, it would be decidedly dangerous to slap Alicia.

Gwendoline walked off, her nose in the air. ' Dear
Gwendoline Mary,' remarked Alicia, in a loud voice.

'Mummy's pet, Daddy's darling, Miss Winter's prize pupil. And can't do fractions properly yet!'

That evening the girls were in the swimming-pool, having a lovely time. Alicia swam under water the whole width of the pool, and then back again. Everyone applauded her.

'How *can* you hold your breath all that time?' cried Darrell. 'I wish I could! Do it again, Alicia, when you've got your breath.'

'The water's got properly into my ears this time!' said Alicia, shaking her head violently. 'They feel all bunged up. I'll wait till they're clear. I'll do a spot of diving.'

She was just as good a diver as a swimmer. Gwendoline, paddling about in the shallow end, envied her. She was certain *she* could swim and dive better than Alicia—if only she could get over the unpleasant beginnings. She did hate the first cold plunge. She couldn't bear going under the water. She spluttered and gasped if she got water up her nose, and felt as if she was drowning.

There was only one person worse than she was, and that was poor Mary-Lou. No one teased Mary-Lou too much. It was too like teasing a small, bewildered kitten. Gwendoline saw her floundering about near her, and, because she knew Mary-Lou was even more afraid of the pool than she was, she felt a sense of power.

She waded over to Mary-Lou, jumped on her suddenly and got her under the water. Mary-Lou had no time to scream. She opened her mouth and the water poured in. She began to struggle desperately. Gwendoline, feeling the struggles, spitefully held her under longer than she had intended to. She only let her go when she felt a sharp slap on her bare shoulder.

She turned. It was Darrell, trembling with rage, looking as if she was shivering, so great was her anger. 'You beast!' shouted Darrell. '*I* saw you duck poor Mary-Lou—and you know how scared she is. You nearly drowned her!'

She pulled Mary-Lou to the surface, and held her there, gasping and choking, blue in the face, almost sick with the amount of salt water she had swallowed.

Girls began to swim across to the scene of excitement. Darrell, her voice shaking with rage, addressed Gwendoline again. 'You just wait a minute! I'll duck *you* under, Gwendoline, and see how *you* like it!'

Mary-Lou was clinging with all her might to Darrell. Gwendoline, rather scared by the anger in Darrell's voice, thought it would be just as well if she got out of the pool before Darrell or somebody else carried out the threat. She began to wade towards the steps that led down into the pool.

Just as she was climbing up them, Darrell, who had given the weeping Mary-Lou to Alicia, caught her up.

'I'm not going to duck you, you little coward!' she cried. 'But I *am* going to show you what happens to people like you!'

There came the sound of four stinging slaps and Gwendoline squealed with pain. Darrell's hand was strong and hard, and she had slapped with all her might, anywhere she could reach as Gwendoline hastily tried to drag herself out of the water. The slaps sounded like pistol-shots.

'Hey, Darrell!' came the voice of the head-girl of her dormy, Katherine. 'Stop that! What are you thinking of? Leave Gwendoline alone!'

Still blazing, Darrell rounded on Katherine. 'Somebody's got to teach that cowardly Gwendoline, haven't they?'

'Yes. But not *you*,' said Katherine, coolly. 'You put yourself in the wrong, slapping about like that. I'm ashamed of you!'

'And *I'm* ashamed of *you*!' burst out Darrell, much to everyone's amazement. 'If *I* were head-girl of the first form I'd jolly well see that girls like Gwendoline learnt to swim and dive and everything, and left people like Mary-Lou alone. See?'

No one had ever seen Darrell in a temper before. They stared. ' Get out of the pool,' ordered Katherine. ' Go on, get out. It's a good thing no mistress saw you doing that.'

Darrell got out, still trembling. She went to where she had flung down her towel-cloak and put it round her. She climbed up the cliff slowly, her heart pounding.

Hateful Gwendoline! Horrid Katherine! Beastly Malory Towers!

But before she reached the top of the cliff and came to the little gate that led into the grounds of Malory Towers, Darrell's anger had all gone. She was dismayed. How *could* she have acted like that ? And she had absolutely *meant* always to keep her temper now, and never let that white-hot flame of rage flare up as it used to do when she was smaller.

Very much subdued, Darrell went back to the school, dried herself and changed. She had been publicly scolded by Katherine. Nobody had backed her up at all, not even Alicia. She had shouted at the head-girl of her form. She had behaved just as badly to Gwendoline as Gwendoline had behaved to Mary-Lou—except that it must have been sheer cruelty that made Gwendoline almost drown Mary-Lou, and it was anger, not cruelty, that made her slap Gwendoline so hard. Still—anger was cruel, so maybe she *was* just as bad as Gwendoline.

She felt sorry she had slapped Gwendoline now. That was the worst of having such a hot temper. You did things all in a hurry, without thinking, and then, when your temper had gone, you were terribly ashamed, and couldn't manage to feel better until you had gone to say you were sorry to the person you had hurt, and whom you still disliked heartily.

Darrell heard somebody sniffling in the changing-room. She looked to see who it was. It was Gwendoline, dolefully examining the brilliant red streaks down her thighs. That was where Darrell had slapped her. Gwendoline sniffed loudly.

'I shall write and tell Mother,' she thought. 'If only she could see those red streaks—why, you can see all Darrell's fingers in this one!'

Darrell came up behind her and made her jump. 'Gwendoline! I'm sorry I did that. I really am. I was just so awfully angry I couldn't stop myself.'

Gwendoline was neither generous nor gracious enough to accept such a natural apology. She drew herself up and looked at Darrell as if she smelt nasty.

'I should hope you *are* sorry!' she said contemptuously. 'I shall write and tell my mother. If she thought girls at Malory Towers would behave like you do, she'd never have sent me here!'

8   DARRELL—AND GWENDOLINE

THE girls left in the pool discussed the sudden happenings with interest and much surprise.

'Who would have *thought* quiet old Darrell would have lashed out like that!'

'She can't be allowed to cheek Katherine. That was jolly rude of her.'

'Katherine, are you going to do anything about it?'

Katherine was now out of the pool, her usually calm face red and disturbed. She had liked Darrell so much—and now in one minute she had quite a different idea of her! Alicia was puzzled too. She shook her head from side to side, trying to get the water out of her ears. Who would have thought Darrell had such a temper?

'Come into the common room, North Tower girls, as soon as you are dressed,' said Katherine at last, in her usual cool voice. The girls looked at one another. A first-form meeting! About Gwendoline and Darrell, they supposed. They tore off up the cliff, and poured into the changing-room, chattering loudly. Neither Gwendoline nor Darrell was there.

Gwendoline had gone up to her dormy, to get some cold cream for her red-streaked legs. They didn't need cold cream, of course—but she meant to make as much fuss as she could! She had always been jealous of Darrell, and she was jolly glad she had got something against her. Coming up and apologizing like that—she didn't mean a word of it, Gwendoline was sure!

The rest of the first-form North Tower girls, eight of them, met in the common room. Katherine sat herself on a desk and looked round.

'I am sure you are all agreed that, much as we like Dar-rell, we can't pass behaviour of that sort,' she began.

'Oh, Katherine—don't row her!' begged Mary-Lou's small voice. 'She saved me from drowning, she really did.'

'She didn't,' said Katherine. 'Gwendoline isn't such an idiot as to drown anyone. I suppose she just suddenly felt spiteful after being teased by the others for not trying to swim properly.'

Mary-Lou was firmly convinced that Darrell was a heroine. She had suffered such agonies under the water, and had really and truly thought she was drowning—and then along had come strong, angry Darrell. How could Kath-erine judge her anyhow but kindly? Mary-Lou didn't dare to say any more, but she sat with a worried, anxious look on her face, wishing she could speak up for Darrell bravely and fearlessly. But she couldn't.

'I think,' said Irene, 'that Darrell should certainly

apologize to Katherine for being cheeky to her. And if she won't, we'll send her to Coventry. We won't speak to her for a week. I must say I'm surprised at Darrell.'

'Well, *I* think she must apologize to Gwendoline too,' said Katherine. ' I heard those slaps right at the other end of the pool ! That's much more important than apologizing to me.'

' But how *much* more unpleasant ! ' murmured Alicia. ' How I should hate to have to say I was sorry for anything to darling Gwendoline Mary ! '

' Aren't you going to address a few words to Gwendoline too ? ' asked Jean.

'Yes,' said Katherine. 'Of course. Now, I wonder where Darrell is. Oh, dear, I do hope she won't kick up a fuss about apologizing to Gwendoline. If she's still in a flaming temper she won't be easy to deal with. I don't *want* to report her, or to send her to Coventry. I never imagined she could be such a little spitfire.'

Just as she finished this speech, the door opened and Darrell herself walked in. She looked surprised to see the girls sitting about, silent and serious. Katherine opened her mouth to speak to her, astonished to see Darrell looking so calm.

But before she could say a word, Darrell walked right up to her. ' Katherine, I'm most awfully sorry I spoke to you like that. I can't think how I could. I was in such a temper, I suppose.'

The wind was completely taken out of Katherine's sails. Instead of glaring at Darrell, she smiled. ' That's all right,' she said, rather awkwardly. ' I saw you were in a rage. But, Darrell . . .'

' That's an awful fault of mine,' said Darrell, rubbing her nose as she always did when she felt ashamed of herself. ' My temper, I mean. I've always had it. I get it from Daddy, but he keeps his temper for something worth while

—I mean he only loses it when there's some really big reason. I don't. I go and lose it for silly little things. I'm awful, Katherine! But honestly I had made up my mind when I came to Malory Towers that I wouldn't lose it any more.'

The girls, who had looked coldly at Darrell when she had marched into the room, now regarded her with warm liking. Here was a person who had a fault, and who said so, and was sorry about it, and didn't attempt to excuse herself. Who could help warming to a person like that?

'Well,' said Katherine, 'you managed to lose it all right this evening! I think Gwendoline deserved all she got, Darrell—but you shouldn't have been the one to give it to her. I'm the one to tick her off, or Pamela, or even Miss Potts. Not you. Just imagine what the school would be like if we could all lose our tempers and go about slapping people when we felt like it!'

'I know,' said Darrell. 'I've thought all that out myself. I'm much more ashamed of myself, Katherine, than you are of me. I wish you'd believe me.'

'I do,' said Katherine. 'But I'm afraid, Darrell, you'll have to do something unpleasant, that you'll hate doing, before we can regard this matter as finished.'

'Oh—what's that?' asked Darrell, looking really alarmed.

'Well, you'll have to apologize to Gwendoline,' said Katherine, expecting an outburst from Darrell at once.

'Apologize to Gwendoline? Oh, I've done *that*,' said Darrell, with relief. 'I thought you meant I had to do something really awful. I'm always sorry very soon after I've lost my temper. I told you that. And that means I have to go and *say* I'm sorry!'

The girls stared at Darrell, who shook back her black curls and gazed with clear eyes at Katherine. Why, they hadn't needed to have a meeting at all! They hadn't needed to judge Darrell and set her to make amends. She had judged herself and made amends herself. The girls looked at her with admiration and Mary-Lou could hardly keep still. What a wonderful person Darrell was, she thought!

'Of course,' went on Darrell, ' I still think that Gwendoline did a beastly thing to Mary-Lou—and I think it's a pity too that Mary-Lou doesn't pull herself together so that spiteful people like Gwendoline can't tease her.'

Mary-Lou crumpled up. Oh! Darrell thought her feeble and weak and frightened. And she was too. She knew she was. She knew that a strong person like Darrell could never really like a stupid person like Mary-Lou. But how she wished she would!

Gwendoline opened the door and came in, looking like a martyr. She had undone her hair so that it lay in a golden sheet over her shoulders again. She evidently fancied herself as an ill-used angel or something of the kind.

She heard the last few words that Darrell spoke, and flushed red. ' Spiteful people like Gwendoline can't tease her!' That was what she heard.

'Oh—Gwendoline. The next time you want to give anyone a nasty fright, choose someone able to stand up to you,' said Katherine, her voice sounding rather hard. ' And please tell Mary-Lou you're sorry you were such a beast. You gave her an awful fright. Darrell has apologized to you, and you can jolly well do *your* bit, now!'

'Oh—so Darrell said she apologized to me, did she?' said Gwendoline. ' Well, *I* don't call it an apology!'

'You fibber!' said Darrell, in amazement. She swung round to the girls. ' I *did*!' she said. ' You can believe which you like, me or Gwendoline. But I *did* apologize—straightaway too.'

Katherine glanced from Darrell's hot face to Gwendoline's sneering one. ' We believe *you*,' she said, quietly. Her voice hardened again. ' And now, Gwendoline, in front of

us all, please, so that we can hear—what have you got to say
to Mary-Lou ? '

Gwendoline was forced to say she was sorry. She
stammered and stuttered, so little did she want to say the
words, but, with everyone's eyes on her, she had to. She
had never said she was sorry for anything before in her life,
and she didn't like it. She hated Darrell at that moment—
yes, and she hated that silly Mary-Lou too·!

She went out of the room almost in tears. There was a
sigh of relief as she left. 'Well, it's a good thing *that*'s over ! '
said Irene, who hated scenes. ' I'm off to one of the practice
rooms. I feel a little music will be good after this upset ! '

She went off to play the piano to herself in one of the
many practice rooms. She would soon forget about everything but the melody she was playing. But the others
didn't forget so easily. It hadn't been nice to see Darrell
lose control of herself, but everyone agreed that it served
Gwendoline right to get a slapping.

The girls compared the natural, generous way in which
Darrell had said she was sorry with the grudging, stammering
words that Gwendoline had spoken to the embarrassed
Mary-Lou. Gwendoline certainly hadn't come out of the
affair at all well. And she knew it too. She felt humiliated.
What a fuss to make over a joke ! Why, the girls often
ducked one another ! Anyway, she *would* write to her
mother about being slapped by that beast of a Darrell !
That would make all the girls sit up.

She went back to the common room, and opened her
locker. Her writing-paper was in there. She took out a
pad and sat down. She did not usually enjoy writing to
her mother. She thought it a bore ! She had not written
to Miss Winter at all since she had come to Malory Towers,
though the governess had written to her three times a week.
Gwendoline rather despised the people who liked her, and
was spiteful towards those that didn't.

'I'm writing to my mother,' she announced to the girls around. Some were sewing, some were reading. It was a free hour for them before supper-time. Nobody took any notice of Gwendoline's remark except Jean.

'Not the day for writing home, is it now?' she said. 'What's come over you, Gwendoline, to be sending home in the middle of the week, when you sigh and groan over your Sunday letter fit to make us all hold our hands over our ears!'

'I'm writing to tell Mother how Darrell slapped me,' said Gwendoline, clearly, so that everyone could hear. 'I'm not going to stand that sort of thing. Mother won't, either.'

Katherine got up. 'I'm glad you told me what you were going to do,' she said. 'I'll go and get *my* writing-pad too. I am sure you won't tell your mother what led up to your slapping! But *I* will!'

Gwendoline flung down her pen in a fury. She tore the sheet she had begun, right off the pad and crumpled it up. 'All right,' she said. 'I won't write. I'm not going to have you telling tales of me to my people. What a beastly school this is! No wonder Mother didn't want to send me away from home.'

'Poor darling Gwendoline,' said Alicia, as the angry girl flung out of the room. 'She just can't do *any*thing she wants! I must say I think Malory Towers is going to be jolly good for her!' She shook her head violently again, and Darrell looked at her in surprise.

'Why do you keep doing that?' she asked.

'I told you. I can't seem to get the water out of my ears,' said Alicia. 'They feel blocked. I *say*—I do hope I shan't be deaf tomorrow! I did go deaf once before when I swam under water for ages!'

'Oh, Alicia! How funny it would be if you really did go deaf tomorrow in Mam'zelle's class!' said Darrell, heartlessly. 'Oh, dear. I can't imagine what would happen!'

'Well, *I* can!' said Alicia. 'Let's hope my ears get right before the morning!'

9   ALICIA IN TROUBLE

THE affair at the Pool had a good many results. First, it made Mary-Lou follow Darrell about like a dog that has found its master and doesn't mean to leave it! She was always there to fetch and carry for Darrell. She tidied her desk for her. She even tidied the drawers in her dressing-table, and offered to make her bed each day.

But Darrell didn't like that sort of thing. 'Don't,' she said to Mary-Lou. 'I can do things for myself. Why should you make my bed? You know we're all supposed to make our own, Mary-Lou. Don't be daft.'

'I'm not,' said Mary-Lou gazing at Darrell out of her big, wide eyes. 'I'm only just trying to make a—a little return to you, Darrell—for—for saving me from drowning.'

'Don't be silly,' said Darrell. 'You wouldn't have drowned, really. I know that now. And anyway I only slapped Gwendoline hard! That was nothing.'

But it didn't in the least matter what Darrell said, Mary-Lou persisted in adoring her, and being on the watch for anything she could do. Darrell found chocolates put inside her desk. She found a little vase of flowers always on her dressing-table. But it irritated her and made her cross. She could not see Mary-Lou's timid reaching-out for a friendship that might help her. Mary-Lou was so weak. She needed someone strong, and to her Darrell was the finest girl she had ever met.

The others teased Darrell about Mary-Lou's attentions.
' Has the little dog wagged its tail for you today ? ' asked
Alicia.

' I wish *I* had some one to put bee-yoo-tiful flowers on
my dressing-table ! ' said Irene.

' Just like Darrell to encourage silly nonsense like that ! '
said Gwendoline, who was jealous of all Mary-Lou's friendly
little attentions to Darrell.

' She doesn't encourage it,' said Katherine.   ' You can
see she doesn't.'

Another result of the Pool affair was that Gwendoline
really did feel bitter towards Darrell now. She had never
in her life been slapped by anyone, and she couldn't forget
it. Not even her mother had slapped her ! It would have
been very much better for spoilt, selfish Gwendoline if a
few smacks had come her way when she was small. But
they hadn't, and now the four or five slaps she had received
from Darrell seemed to her, not a sudden flash of temper,
soon to be forgotten, but a great insult somehow to be
avenged.

' And one day I'll pay her back, see if I don't ! ' thought
Gwendoline to herself.   ' I don't care how long I wait.'

The third result of the Pool affair was that Alicia really
did go deaf through swimming under water so long. It
was not a deafness that would last very long, Alicia knew.
Suddenly her ears would go ' pop ' inside, and she would be
able to hear as well as ever.   But in the meantime it was
really very annoying to think that just after she had *pretended*
to be deaf, she really had become deaf.   Whatever would
Mam'zelle say this time ?

It was unfortunate for Alicia that she sat at the back of
the room, in the last row but one.   Anyone with normal
hearing could hear perfectly well, even in the back row, but
Alicia with both ears ' blocked,' as she called it, found it
extremely difficult to catch every word that was said.

To make matters worse, it was not Mam'zelle Dupont who took French that day, but Mam'zelle Rougier, thin, tall and bony. She was rarely in a good humour, as her thin lips, always tightly pressed together, showed. It was funny, Alicia thought, how bad-tempered people nearly always had thin lips.

Mam'zelle Rougier had a soft voice, which, however could become extremely loud when she was angry. Then it became raucous, like a rook's, and the girls hated it.

Today she was taking the beginnings of a French play with the girls. They nearly always had to learn one each term, taking different parts. Sometimes they performed it at school concerts, but often they didn't perform it at all, merely taking it in class.

' Now,' said Mam'zelle Rougier, ' today we will discuss the play, and perhaps give out the parts. Maybe one or two of the new girls are good at French, and can take the leading parts. That would be so nice ! I cannot think any of the old girls would mind that ! '

They wouldn't ! The less learning they had to do, the better ! The new girls smiled in a sickly fashion. They thought Mam'zelle Rougier's little jokes were feeble.

' Now, first we will see who took the chief parts in last term's play,' said Mam'zelle. ' You, Alicia, what part did you play ? '

Alicia didn't hear, so she didn't answer. Betty nudged her. ' What part did you take in last term's play ? ' she said, loudly.

' Oh ! Sorry, Mam'zelle, I didn't catch what you said,' said Alicia. ' I took the part of the shepherd.'

' I thought that was in the term before,' said Mam'zelle. Alicia again couldn't catch what she said. Betty repeated it loudly. ' MAM'ZELLE SAID SHE THOUGHT THAT WAS IN THE TERM BEFORE,' said Betty.

Mam'zelle was astonished. Why should Betty repeat

everything she said like that ? Then suddenly she remembered something Mam'zelle Dupont had told her about Alicia—ah, yes, the bad naughty girl ! She had pretended to be deaf, hadn't she—and here she was again, playing the same trick on Mam'zelle Rougier.

' Ah non, non ! ' said Mam'zelle Rougier to herself angrily. ' It is too much ! I will not have it.'

' Alicia,' she said, patting the little bun at the back of her head, ' you are a funny girl and you do funny things, *n'est ce pas* ? But I also, I am funny and I do funny things. I would like you to write out for me in French, fifty times in your best handwriting, " I must not be deaf in Mam'zelle Rougier's class." '

' What did you say, Mam'zelle ? ' asked Alicia, having caught her own name at the beginning, but very little else. ' I couldn't quite hear.'

' Ah, *cette méchante fille !* ' cried Mam'zelle, losing her temper as suddenly as she always did. ' Alicia, *écoutez bien !* Listen well ! You shall write me out " I must not be deaf in Mam'zelle Rougier's class " ONE HUNDRED TIMES ! '

' But you said fifty just now,' said Betty, indignantly.

' And you too, you shall write out " I must not interrupt," one hundred times ! ' stormed Mam'zelle. The class was silent. They knew Mam'zelle Rougier in this mood. She would be handing out a thousand lines soon to somebody. She was the most irritable teacher in the whole school.

Betty whispered to Alicia as soon as Mam'zelle was writing something on the board, but, seeing that poor Alicia couldn't hear her whisper, she scribbled a message on a bit of paper.

' You've got to write out a hundred lines for M. For goodness' sake don't say you can't hear anything else, or vou'll get a thousand ! She's in a real paddy ! '

Alicia nodded. And whenever Mam'zelle asked her if she had heard what was said, she answered politely, ' Yes, thank you, Mam'zelle,' hoping she would be forgiven for the story !

Miss Potts came for the next lesson. Mam'zelle stopped and spoke to her, with a gleam in her eye. ' Alas, Miss Potts, one of your girls, Alicia, has again got a deafness in her ear. It is sad, is it not ? Such a young and healthy girl ! '

With this parting shot Mam'zelle Rougier disappeared. Miss Potts looked at Alicia coldly.

' I shouldn't have thought that even *you* were foolish enough to try the same trick twice, Alicia,' she said. Poor Alicia ! She didn't hear what Miss Potts said, but gazed at her enquiringly.

' You can leave your desk and come to one of the front ones,' said Miss Potts. ' Jean, change places with Alicia, please. You can change over the contents of your desk later.'

Jean stood up, very pleased to think that she could leave the front row, which was always under Miss Potts's eye, and go to one of the much-sought-after back rows. It was easy to whisper in the back row, and easy to play tricks or pass notes there. Alicia didn't move because she really hadn't heard. There was suddenly a curious buzzing noise in her ears.

' You've got to move, idiot ! ' said Betty in a loud whisper. ' Go on—go to Jean's place.'

Alicia realised what was happening. She was full of dismay ! What, leave the back seat she liked so much, leave her seat beside Betty—and go to the front row, under every teacher's eagle eye. Everyone knew that the front row had no fun at all !

' Oh, Miss Potts,' she began, in dismay. ' Honestly..I *am* deaf ! It's all that under-water swimming ! '

' You thought—or pretended you were deaf the other day,' said Miss Potts, unfeelingly. ' How in the world am I supposed to know when you are and when you aren't, Alicia ? '

' Well, I really *am* this time,' said Alicia, wishing her ears wouldn't buzz so. ' Please, Miss Potts, let me stay here ! '

'Now, Alicia,' said Miss Potts, speaking in loud, clear tones so that, deaf or not, Alicia would be sure to hear, 'listen to me, and tell me if you agree with me or not. If you are *not* deaf, but playing a trick, it would be best to have you out here under my eye. If you *are* deaf and can't hear in the back row, then it is only common sense that you should be placed out here where you can. What do you think about it?'

Alicia, of course, could not do anything but agree. She sat rather sulkily down in Jean's place. She could, of course, hear much better there. Then a funny thing happened. First one of her ears went 'pop' and then the other. She shook her head. Goody, goody! Her ears had gone pop and were all right again. She could hear as well as ever.

She was so pleased that she whispered to Mary-Lou, next to her. 'My ears have gone pop. I can hear!'

Miss Potts had extremely sharp hearing. She caught the whisper and turned round from the board. 'Will you kindly repeat what you said, Alicia?' she said.

'I said "My ears have gone pop. I can hear!"' said Alicia.

'Good,' said Miss Potts. 'I thought you would probably find you could hear all right in the front there.'

'But Miss Potts, I . . .' began Alicia.

'That's enough,' said Miss Potts. 'Let us begin this lesson please without wasting any more time on your ears, deaf or not.'

Alicia was cross because Jean and she had to change over the contents of their desks in Break. She hated being out in the front. Jean was very cheerful about the change.

'I wished hard enough I could be at the back,' she said. 'And now I am.'

'It's not fair,' grumbled Alicia. 'I really *was* deaf this morning—and then my ears suddenly got right. Miss Potts ought to have believed me.'

Darrell, who was helping, couldn't help laughing. Alicia was not in a mood to be teased, and she scowled.

'Oh, Alicia, I know it's unkind of me to laugh,' said Darrell, 'but honestly it's funny! First you pretend to be deaf, and pull Mam'zelle's leg well. Then you really *do* get deaf, and nobody believes it! It's just like that fable of the shepherd boy who called "wolf wolf!" when there wasn't a wolf, and then, when there really was, and he called for help, nobody came because nobody believed him!'

'I thought you were my friend,' said Alicia, stiffly. 'I don't like being preached at.'

'Oh, I'm not preaching, really I'm not!' said Darrell. 'Listen, Alicia, I'll write out half your lines for you, I will really! It would take you ages to write out a hundred, and I know you hate writing. I love it.'

'All right. Thanks very much,' said Alicia, cheering up. So Mam'zelle Rougier was presented with one hundred lines that evening, half of them rather badly written and the other half quite nicely written. 'Strange that a child should write so badly on one side of the paper and so well on the other!' said Mam'zelle wonderingly. But fortunately for Alicia Mam'zelle got no further than wondering about it!

10   A QUEER FRIENDSHIP

IT was very hot. The girls simply lived for their time in the swimming-pool. They groaned when the tide was out and they couldn't bathe. Fortunately the pool was an enormous one, and would take practically the whole school when the tide was in.

Darrell loved to have a game of tennis and then sprint down to the pool to bathe. Oh, the delicious coolness of the water then ! She couldn't understand how Gwendoline or Mary-Lou could possibly shrink from getting in. But they insisted that the hotter the day, the colder the water felt, and they didn't like it.

' But that's what's so *lovely* about the water,' said Darrell. ' Feeling so cold on such a blazing hot day as this ! If you could only make up your minds to plunge in instead of going in inch by inch, you'd love it. You're awful cowards, both of you.'

Neither Mary-Lou nor Gwendoline liked being called cowards. Mary-Lou always felt very hurt when Darrell so carelessly lined her up with Gwendoline, and scorned her, too, for her timidity. She tried her hardest to make Darrell pleased with her by running after her more than ever, even to tidying her locker in the common room, which exasperated Darrell because Mary-Lou always altered her arrangement of things.

' *What's* happened to my sweets ? I *know* I put them in the front here. And where's my writing-pad ? Blow, and I'm in such a hurry, too ! '

And out would come every single thing in the locker, higgledy-piggledy on the floor ! Mary-Lou would look on mournfully.

' Oh—I tidied them all so nicely for you,' she would say.

' Well, *don't* ! ' Darrell would order. ' Why don't you go and bother with somebody else's things ? You always seem to make a bee-line for mine. You seem to have got a craze for tidying things and putting them away. You go and do Alicia's—they're much untidier than mine ! Just leave mine alone ! '

' I only do it to help you,' Mary-Lou would murmur. It was awful to have such an admiration for somebody and for them to find it a nuisance. Perhaps Darrell *would* like her to tidy Alicia's things. She knew Darrell liked Alicia very much. Very well, then, she would help Alicia too.

But Alicia could not bear it any more than Darrell, and when poor Mary-Lou succeeded in breaking the glass of her mother's photograph, Alicia forbade her ever to touch any of her things again.

' Can't you *see* when you're a nuisance ? ' she said. ' Can't you see we don't want a little ninny like you always flapping round us ? Look at that photograph ! Smashed to bits just because you started messing around.'

Mary-Lou wept. She was always scared when anyone ticked her off. She went out of the room and bumped into Gwendoline in the passage.

' Hallo ! Crying again ! Whatever's up now ? ' asked Gwendoline, who was always interested in other people's rows, though never sympathetic.

' Nothing. It's only that Alicia and Darrell are always so hard on me when I want to help them,' wept poor Mary-Lou, feeling very sorry for herself.

' Oh, what do you expect from people like Alicia and Darrell—yes and Betty too ? ' asked Gwendoline, delighted to get in a few hard words about her enemies. ' Always so cocksure of themselves, and so ready with their tongues. I can't imagine why you want to make friends with them.'

' I've just broken the photograph of Alicia's mother,' said Mary-Lou, wiping her eyes. ' That's what the trouble was really about.'

' Well, you may be sure Alicia won't forgive you for *that*,' said Gwendoline. ' She'll have her knife into you now. She just adores her mother, and nobody is ever allowed to handle that photograph. You've done it now, Mary-Lou ! '

As she spoke, a perfectly wonderful idea came into Gwendoline's head. She stopped and thought a moment, her eyes shining. In one moment she saw how she could get even with Alicia and Darrell, yes, and give that stupid

little Mary-Lou a few bad moments too. Mary-Lou looked
at her curiously.

'What's the matter, Gwendoline?' she asked.

'Nothing. Just an idea,' said Gwendoline. To Mary-
Lou's intense surprise she suddenly slipped her arm through
the younger girl's.

'You be friends with *me*,' she said, in a honeyed voice.
'*I* shan't treat you like Darrell does, and Alicia. I haven't
a wicked tongue like Alicia, or scornful eyes like Darrell.
Why don't you make friends with me? *I* shouldn't jeer at
you for any little kindnesses, I can tell you.'

Mary-Lou looked at Gwendoline doubtfully. She really
didn't like her, but Gwendoline smiled at her so sweetly
that she felt grateful. And Alicia and Darrell really *had*
been horrid to her when she had tried to do things for them.
Then she remembered how Gwendoline had held her under
the water.

She took her arm away from Gwendoline's. 'No,' she
said, 'I can't be friends with you, Gwendoline. You were
very cruel to me that day in the pool. I've had dreams
about it ever since.'

Gwendoline was angry to think that the stupid, feeble
little Mary-Lou should refuse to be friends with her. But
she still went on smiling sweetly. She took Mary-Lou's
arm again.

'You know I didn't mean anything that time in the pool,'
she said. 'It was just a joke. You've often seen the others
being ducked. I'm sorry I ducked you so hard. I didn't
realize you were so frightened.'

There was something very determined about Gwendoline,
when she had made up her mind about anything. Mary-
Lou didn't know how to get away. So, as usual, she
surrendered.

'Well,' she said, hesitatingly, 'well—if you *really* didn't
mean to hurt me, that time in the pool, Gwendoline, I'll

be friends. But I'm not going to talk against Darrell or Alicia.'

Gwendoline gave her arm a squeeze, bestowed another honeyed smile on the perplexed Mary-Lou and walked off to think out her suddenly conceived plan in peace.

' It's marvellous ! ' she thought. ' Everyone knows how fed-up Darrell is with Mary-Lou, because she's always tagging after her, and soon everyone will know how cross Alicia is because she has broken her mother's photograph. So, if *I* start playing a few tricks on Mary-Lou, everyone will think it is Darrell or Alicia getting back at her ! And oh, goody, goody, Alicia has to sit by Mary-Lou now ! That makes it easier still.'

She sat down in the Court and thought out her plan. She meant to revenge herself on the three people she disliked. She would scare Mary-Lou to death—but she would make everyone think it was Alicia and Darrell ! Then they would be blamed, and punished.

' And if I make close friends with Mary-Lou nobody would ever *think* I had anything to do with things,' thought Gwendoline, in delight. ' Really, I'm very clever. I bet no one else in the whole of the first form could think of a plan like this.'

She was right. They couldn't—but not because they weren't clever enough—but just because they weren't mean enough. Gwendoline couldn't see that. She couldn't even see that she was doing a mean thing. She called it ' giving them all a lesson ! '

She laid her plans very carefully. She would wait her time, till Alicia or Darrell were carrying out the duty of tidying the classroom and filling the vases with water. Then everyone would know they and they only had been in the classroom and so had the opportunity of slipping anything into anyone's desk, or taking something out.

She would pop a blackbeetle into Mary-Lou's desk—or

a few worms—or even a mouse if she could get hold of it. But no—Gwendoline quickly ruled out mice because she was so scared of them herself. She didn't much like black-beetles or worms either, but she could manage to scoop those up into a match-box or something.

She could do that. And she could remove Mary-Lou's favourite pencils and hide them in Alicia's locker. That would be a cunning thing to do! She might put one or two of Mary-Lou's books in Darrell's locker too. And how sympathetic she would be with Mary-Lou when she found out these tricks!

Gwendoline began poking round the garden to see what insects she could find. Jean, who was a good gardener, and liked to give a hand with the school garden at times, was most amazed to see Gwendoline poking about in the beds with a trowel.

'What *are* you doing?' she asked. 'Looking for a bone you've buried?'

'Don't be silly,' said Gwendoline, angry that Jean should have come across her. 'Can't I do a little gardening? Are you to be the only one?'

'Well, what gardening are you doing?' demanded Jean, who always liked to know the ins and outs of everything that aroused her curiosity.

'Just digging,' said Gwendoline. 'Making the earth a bit loose. It's so dry.'

Jean gave a snort. She had a wonderful variety of snorts, which she kept mainly for Gwendoline, Sally and Mary-Lou. Gwendoline dug viciously with her trowel, wishing she could put a worm down Jean's neck. But probably Jean wouldn't mind, anyway.

Gwendoline didn't like to look for worms after that. She decided to look for spiders. But when she saw a large one in the wood-shed she almost ran out helter-skelter herself! Still, it was *such* a large one, it would be just the thing for Mary-Lou's desk. It would come running out marvellously!

Somehow Gwendoline caught it, though she shivered as she clapped a flower-pot over it. She managed to get it into a little cardboard box. Then, feeling very clever, she slipped away to the common room, meaning to hide the spider in its box away in her locker until the right moment came.

She led the conversation round to spiders that evening. 'I got my head caught in a web in the shed today,' she said. 'Oooh, it did feel horrid. I don't like spiders.'

'My brother Sam once had a tame spider,' began Alicia, who could always be relied on to produce a bit of family history at any moment. 'It lived under a fern in our greenhouse, and it came out every evening for a drink of water, when Mother watered the ferns.'

'Oooh! I should have hated to see it!' said Mary-Lou, with a shudder. 'I'm terrified of spiders.'

'You're an idiot,' said Alicia, still cross over the broken photograph. 'Terrified of this, scared of that—what a life you lead, Mary-Lou. I've a good mind to catch a large spider and put it down your neck!'

Mary-Lou turned pale. The very thought made her heart jump in fright. 'I should die if you did that!' she said, in a low voice.

'Cowardy custard,' said Alicia, lazily. 'Well—wait till I get a spider!'

Gwendoline said nothing—but how she rejoiced! Could anything be better! Alicia had said more than she could possibly have hoped she would say—and what was more, every North Tower first-former had heard it. It was marvellous!

'I'll wait till Monday, when Alicia and Darrell are on duty in the classroom,' she thought. 'Then I'll do the trick. It will teach them all a lesson!'

So, when Monday came, Gwendoline watched for her moment. She and Mary-Lou went about everywhere together now, much to the surprise and amazement of Darrell and Alicia and Betty. How could Mary-Lou chum up with that awful Gwendoline, especially after that cruel ducking? And why was Gwendoline sucking up to Mary-Lou? It seemed very queer to the first-formers.

Gwendoline's chance came, and she took it. She was told to go and fetch something from her common room, ten minutes before afternoon school. She tore there to get it, then raced to the first-form classroom with the cardboard box. She opened it and let the great, long-legged spider run into the desk. It ran to a dark corner and crouched there, quite still.

Gwendoline hurried away, certain that no one had seen her. Two minutes later Darrell and Alicia strolled in to fill the flower-vases with water. Ah, luck was with Gwendoline just then!

11   THE SPIDER AFFAIR

THE first lesson that afternoon was mental arithmetic. The girls groaned over this, except the quick ones, like Irene, who delighted in it. But it meant that there was no need for anyone to open a desk, because it was all oral work.

Miss Potts was lenient with the girls, for it was a very hot afternoon. Darrell was glad that Miss Potts was not as exacting as usual, for arithmetic was not her strong point, especially mental arithmetic.

The next lesson was to be taken by Mam'zelle Dupont. It was to be a French conversation lesson, in which the girls would endeavour to answer all Mam'zelle's simple questions in French. Miss Potts left, and Mam'zelle arrived, not quite so beaming as usual, because of the heat. She was too plump to enjoy the hot weather, and little beads of perspiration shone on her forehead as she sat down at the big desk, opposite the rows of girls.

' *Asseyez-vous*,' she said, and the girls sat down thankfully, feeling that the only lesson they would really enjoy that weather would be a swimming lesson.

The lesson proceeded slowly and haltingly. The flow of French conversation was not at all brisk on the girls' part, and the constant pauses began to irritate Mam'zelle.

' Ah ! ' she cried at last, ' it is too hot to make conversation with such stupid ones as you are this afternoon ! Get out your grammar books and I will explain a few things to you that will help your conversation if you can get them into your so-stupid heads ! '

The girls opened their desks to get out their grammar books. Gwendoline watched eagerly to see what would happen when Mary-Lou opened hers. But nothing did happen. Mary-Lou had neither seen the spider nor disturbed it. She shut her desk.

All the girls opened their grammar books at the page Mam'zelle commanded. Then Mary-Lou found that she had her English grammar instead of her French one. So she re-opened her desk to get the right book.

' *Que faites vous*, Mary-Lou ? ' demanded Mam'zelle, who hated desks being opened and shut too often. ' What are you doing ? '

Mary-Lou stuffed her English grammar into the back of her desk and pulled out the French one. The spider, feeling itself dislodged by the book, ran out in a fright. It ran almost up to Mary-Lou before she saw it. She let the desk-lid drop with a terrific bang and gave a heart-rending scream.

Everyone jumped in alarm. Mam'zelle leapt to her

feet, sending a pile of books clattering from her desk to the floor. She glared at Mary-Lou.

' *Tiens !* What is this noise ! Mary-Lou, have you gone mad ? '

Mary-Lou couldn't speak. The sight of the enormous spider apparently running straight at her had completely undone her. She scraped her chair away from her desk, and stared at it as if she expected the spider to jump through the lid.

' Mary-Lou ! ' thundered Mam'zelle. ' Tell me what is the matter with you ? I demand it ! '

' Oh, Mam'zelle—there's a—there's a simply enormous —giant—spider in my desk ! ' stammered Mary-Lou, quite pale.

' A spider ? ' said Mam'zelle. ' And you make this fuss, and call out so loudly that we all jump in fear ! Mary-Lou, be ashamed of yourself ! I am angry with you. Sit down.'

' Oh—I—I daren't,' said Mary-Lou, trembling. ' It might come out. Mam'zelle, it's enormous.'

Mam'zelle wasn't quite sure whether she really believed in this spider or not. What with Alicia's deafness last week and one thing and another. . . .

Irene giggled. Mam'zelle fixed her with a glare. ' We will see if this spider exists or not,' she said, firmly. ' And I warn you, Mary-Lou, if this is again a trick, and there is no spider, you will go to Miss Potts for punishment. I wash my hands of you.'

She advanced to the desk. She threw open the lid dramatically. Mary-Lou drew in her breath and got away as far as she could, looking at the inside of the desk with scared eyes.

There was no spider to be seen. It had, of course, retreated to the darkest corner it could find again. Mam'zelle swept the desk with a searching glance and then turned on poor Mary-Lou.

'Bad girl,' she said, and stamped her foot. 'You, so quiet and good, you too deceive me, the poor Mam'zelle! I will not have it.'

'Mam'zelle, *do* believe me,' begged Mary-Lou, in despair, for she could not bear to be scolded like that. 'It *was* there—an enormous one.'

Mam'zelle rummaged violently among the books in the desk. 'No spider! Not one!' she said. 'Tell me, where has it gone, if it is still in there?'

The spider was alarmed by the violent rummaging. It suddenly hurried out from its hiding-place, and ran on to Mam'zelle's hand and up her arm.

Mam'zelle stared at the enormous thing as if she really could not believe her eyes. She gave a shriek even louder than Mary-Lou had given! She too was scared of spiders, and here was a giant specimen running over her person!

Irene exploded. That was the signal for the class to enter into the fun, and one and all scrambled over to Mam'zelle.

'Ah, where is it, the monster? Girls, girls, can you see it?' wailed Mam'zelle.

'It's here,' said wicked Alicia and ran a light finger down Mam'zelle's spine. She gave a scream, thinking that it was the spider running there. 'Take it off! I beg you, Alicia, remove it from me!'

'I think it must have gone down your neck, Mam'zelle,' said Betty, which nearly made Mam'zelle have a fit. She immediately felt sure that it was all over her, and began to shiver and tremble.

Alicia tickled the back of her neck and she leapt in the air. 'Oh, la la! Oh, la la! What a miserable woman I am! Where is this monster? Girls, girls, tell me it is gone!'

There was now a complete uproar in the first-form room. Miss Potts, again in the second-form room, was amazed and exasperated. What *could* her form be doing now ? Had Mam'zelle left them alone, and had they all gone mad ?

'Go on with your maps for a minute,' she said to the second form, who were glancing at one another in astonishment, as they heard the noise from the first-form room. She left the room and went rapidly to the door of the first form.

She opened it and the noise hit her like something solid. Worse than Break, she thought grimly. At first she could not see any mistress there at all, and thought that the girls were alone. Then she caught sight of Mam'zelle's head in the middle of a crowd of girls. What *was* happening !

'Girls ! ' she said, but her voice went unheard. 'GIRLS ! '

Irene suddenly saw her and started to nudge everyone. 'Look out—here's Potty,' she hissed.

The girls flowed back from Mam'zelle as if they were water ! In a trice every one was by her desk. Mam'zelle stood alone, trembling, wondering what was happening. Where had that monster of a spider gone ?

'Mam'zelle, really ! ' said Miss Potts, almost forgetting the rule the staff had of never finding fault with one another before the girls. 'I simply cannot think what happens to this class when you take it ! '

Mam'zelle blinked at Miss Potts. 'It was a spider,' she explained, looking up and down herself. 'Ah, Miss Potts, but a MONSTER of a spider. It ran up my arm and disappeared. Ah-h-h-h-h ! I seem to feel it everywhere.'

'A spider won't hurt you,' said Miss Potts, coldly and unfeelingly. 'Would you like to go and recover yourself, Mam'zelle, and let me deal with the first form ? '

'Ah non ! ' said Mam'zelle, indignantly. 'The class, it is good—the girls, they came to help me to get this monster of a spider. So big it was, Miss Potts ! '

Miss Potts looked so disbelieving that Mam'zelle exaggerated the size of the spider, and held out her hands to show Miss Potts that it was at least as big as a fair-sized frog.

The girls had enjoyed everything immensely. What a French lesson! Gwendoline had enjoyed it too, especially as she was the cause of it, though nobody knew that, of course. She sat demurely in her desk, watching the two mistresses closely.

And then suddenly she felt something running up her leg! She looked down. It was the spider! It had left Mam'zelle a long time ago, and had secreted itself under a desk, afraid of all the trampling feet around. Now, when peace seemed restored, the spider wanted to seek a better hiding-place. It ran over Gwendoline's shoe, up her stocking and above her knee. She gave a piercing scream. Everyone jumped again. Miss Potts turned fiercely.

'Gwendoline! Go out of the room! How dare you squeal like that! No, don't tell me you've seen the spider. I'm tired of the spider. I'm ashamed of you all!'

Gwendoline shook herself violently, not daring to scream again, but filled with the utmost horror at the thought of the spider creeping over her.

'It *was* the spider!' she began. 'It . . .'

'GWENDOLINE! What did I tell you! I will NOT hear another word of the wretched spider!' said Miss Potts, raising her voice angrily. 'Go out of the room. The whole class can go to bed one hour earlier tonight as a punishment for this shameful behaviour, and you, Gwendoline, can go two hours earlier!'

Weeping, Gwendoline ran from the room. As soon as she got outside she examined herself carefully and tremblingly to see if the spider was still anywhere about her. To her enormous relief she suddenly saw it running down the passage.

She leant against the wall. How tiresome of that spider to come to her, when it might have gone to anyone else! Now she had got to have double punishment. Still, she would soon put it about that Alicia and Darrell had planted

A spider was running up her leg!

the spider in Mary-Lou's desk! How sickening of Miss Potts to pounce on her like that. *She* couldn't help it if the spider came to her.

But perhaps after all it was a good thing that Miss Potts had come into the room and heard it all. Perhaps Gwendoline might even drop a hint to Miss Potts about Alicia and Darrell putting the spider in the desk.

Miss Potts came out of the room at this moment. She eyed Gwendoline with dislike.

' Miss Potts, the spider ran away down there,' said Gwendoline, pointing, anxious to get back into Miss Potts's good books.

Miss Potts took not the slightest notice but swept into the second-form classroom, and the door shut. Gwendoline felt very small. Now what was she to do ? Stay out here—or go back into the classroom ? She didn't want to be found out there if by any chance Miss Grayling, the Head, came by. She decided to risk going back. She opened the door and sidled in.

'Ha! You are back again! And who told you to come ?' demanded Mam'zelle, now ashamed of her part in the affair, and ready to vent her humiliated feelings on anyone she could. ' You screamed and made Miss Potts white and angry ! '

'Well, Mam'zelle, you screamed too,' protested Gwendoline, in an injured tone. ' Louder than I did, I should think.'

Mam'zelle rose in her seat, and for all her smallness she seemed enormous to Gwendoline just then. Her beady black eyes flashed.

' You would be rude to *me*, Mam'zelle Dupont! You would argue with *me*, who have taught here for twenty years ! You—you . . .'

Gwendoline turned and fled. She would rather stand outside the door all day long than face Mam'zelle when she looked like that !

12   SHARP WORDS

THE Spider Affair, as it was called, went all over the school before the day was out. It caused a great deal of laughter. When Mam'zelle Rougier heard of it she sneered.

'To think that a Frenchwoman should be so foolish!' she said. 'Now *I* do not mind spiders or earwigs or moths or even snakes! Mam'zelle Dupont should be ashamed to make such an exhibition of herself!'

The first form talked about it more than anyone else, of course. They squealed with laughter whenever they thought of poor Mary-Lou, Mam'zelle, and Gwendoline all falling victims to the same spider.

'Jolly clever spider! said Irene. 'It knew the only three people in the form that would be scared of it. I take my hat off to that spider.'

'I can't think why it chose *my* desk,' said Mary-Lou.

'No. That was a shame,' said Gwendoline. 'Poor Mary-Lou! It must have been an awful shock for you when you saw it. I wonder who put it there?'

There was a silence. For the first time it occurred to the first form that the spider might have been put there on purpose. They looked at one another.

'It was a dirty trick to put it into poor Mary-Lou's desk,' said Jean. 'She can't *help* being scared of things, I suppose, and she almost jumped out of her skin when she saw it. I should have thought any joker in our form would have been decent enough to have popped it into, say, Alicia's desk!'

'Not if it happened to be *Alicia* who popped it in!' said a sly voice. 'You do so love playing tricks, don't you, Alicia? You and Darrell were in the first-form room before afternoon school. And I'm sure we all remember you saying you'd like to put a spider down Mary-Lou's neck ! '

It was Gwendoline speaking. Alicia glanced at her. ' Well, I didn't do it,' she said. ' Nor did Darrell. Sorry to disappoint you, darling Gwendoline Mary, but we just didn't. If it was anyone, I should think it was you ! '

' Mary-Lou is my friend,' said Gwendoline. ' I wouldn't do that to her.'

' Well, if you'd almost drown her one week, I should think you could quite well bring yourself to put a spider in her desk the next week,' said Darrell.

' It's pretty funny that you and Alicia were the only ones in the classroom before afternoon school,' persisted Gwendoline, angry that no one seemed to have agreed with her suggestion.

' Shut up,' said Katherine, shortly. ' We *know* it wasn't either Darrell or Alicia, because they *say* so ! The spider must have got in there by accident, and that's that.'

' Well, *I* think . . .' began Gwendoline, but the class took up a chant at once.

' Shut up, Gwendoline ; Gwendoline, shut up ! Shut *up*, Gwendoline ; Gwendoline, shut *up* ! '

There was nothing to do but shut up. Gwendoline was sulky and exasperated. It had been such a good idea, and all that had resulted from it was a double punishment for her, and a complete failure to make anyone believe that Alicia or Darrell had played the trick. True, the first formers had had to go to bed an hour earlier, but they had all voted it was worth it.

Gwendoline felt vicious about the whole affair. She determined not to be put off by her first failure but to go on doing things to Mary-Lou, so that in the end the class would have to put them down to tricks by Alicia and Darrell. She thought too she would also hint to Miss Potts that she thought Alicia and Darrell were at the bottom of things.

But she didn't get very far with this. She had to go and see Miss Potts about some returned homework, and stood very meekly beside her, in the little room that Miss Potts shared with Mam'zelle Dupont at North Tower.

'Miss Potts, I was awfully sorry about that spider affair the other day,' she began. 'Of course, Alicia and Darrell were in the classroom beforehand, and I'm sure they know something about it. I heard Alicia say . . .'

Miss Potts looked up. 'Are you trying to sneak?' she said. 'Or in more polite language, to tell tales? Because if so, don't try it on me. At the boarding school I went to, Gwendoline, we had a very good punishment for sneaks. All the girls in the sneak's dormy gave her one good spank with the back of a hair-brush. You may have a lot of interesting things to tell me but it's no use expecting me to listen. I wonder if the girls here have the same punishment for sneaks. I must ask them.'

Gwendoline went flaming red. A sneak! Fancy Miss Potts daring to call her, Gwendoline Mary Lacey, a sneak! All because she had just wanted to drop a kindly hint. Gwendoline didn't know what to say. She felt as if she would like to burst into tears, but Miss Potts always got very impatient with girls who did that. She went out of the room, longing to slam the door as she often did at home. But she didn't dare to here.

She felt very sorry for herself. If her mother knew what an awful school she had come to she would take her away at once. Miss Winter, too, would be horrified. But Gwendoline wasn't quite so sure about her father. He could say things at times very like the things Miss Potts said.

The week went by. It was a very pleasant week, hot with a cool breeze that made games and swimming even more pleasure than usual. Alicia and Betty were practising hard for the school sports. Both were excellent swimmers and divers. Darrell tried to imitate all they did.

She was good, too, but not quite so good as they were. But she was quite fearless, and dived off the highest diving-boards, and went down the chute in all kinds of peculiar positions.

The only unhappy person that week was Mary-Lou. She got into a lot of trouble over many little things. For instance, her clothes in the changing-room had been thrown down in a pool of water, and were soaking wet. She had to take them to Matron to be dried.

Matron was cross. 'Mary-Lou! Can't you hang your things up properly in that changing-room? You know there are always puddles on the floor from the girls coming in and out from the pool.'

'I did hang them up, Matron,' said Mary-Lou, mildly. 'I know I did.'

Then Mary-Lou's tennis racket suddenly showed three broken strings. They were not frayed, but looked as if they had been cut. Mary-Lou was upset.

'My new racket!' she said. 'Look, Gwendoline, who would think a new racket could go like that?'

'It couldn't,' said Gwendoline, pretending to examine it very closely. 'These strings have been cut, Mary-Lou. Someone's been playing a dirty trick on you. What a shame.'

Mary-Lou was miserable. She couldn't believe that she had any enemies. But when she found buttons cut off her Sunday dress she knew that someone was being unkind and mean. Gwendoline comforted her.

'Never mind. *I'll* sew them on for you! I hate sewing, but I'll do it for you, Mary-Lou.'

So, making a great show of it, Gwendoline sewed on the six blue buttons one night. The first-formers stared at her in surprise. They knew she never mended anything if she could help it.

'How did those buttons come off?' asked Jean.

'That's what *I'd* like to know,' said Gwendoline smugly.

'Six buttons, all ripped off! I'm putting them on for Mary-Lou, because I'm so sorry that anyone should play her such a dirty trick. And I'd like to know who cut the strings of her tennis racket, too.'

The first-formers looked at one another. It certainly was queer the way things had been happening to poor Mary-Lou lately. Even her prayer-book had disappeared. And some of her pencils had gone. True, they had been found in Alicia's desk—but everyone had thought that was just an accident. Now they began to wonder if some one had put them there. Not Alicia. Alicia wouldn't do a thing like that. But Somebody.

It was getting near half-term. Many of the girls were excited, because some of them were expecting visits from their parents. Any parent who lived not too far away would be sure to come. Darrell was thrilled because her father and mother were coming. They lived a long way away, but had decided to take a week's holiday in Cornwall, and come and see Darrell in the middle of it.

The girls began to talk about their families. 'I wish my three brothers could come,' said Alicia. 'We'd have some sport then.'

'I wish my little sister could come,' said Jean. 'I'd love to show her Malory Towers.'

'Is *your* mother coming, Sally?' asked Mary-Lou.

'No,' said Sally. 'She lives too far away.'

Darrell remembered something her mother had told her in a letter a week or two before. She had said that she had met Sally Hope's mother, and had liked her. She had said too that she had seen Mrs. Hope's baby, Sally's sister, a little girl of three months. Darrell had meant to tell Sally what her mother had said and had forgotten. Now she remembered it.

'Oh, Sally, I expect your mother won't come because of the baby,' she said.

Sally went stiff.   She stared at Darrell as if she couldn't believe her ears.   Her face went quite white, and when she spoke she sounded as if she were choking.

'You don't know what you're talking about,' she said. 'What baby?   We haven't a baby!   My mother won't be coming because it's so *far*, I tell you!'

Darrell was puzzled.   'But Sally—don't be silly—my mother said in a letter that she had *seen* your baby sister —she's three months old, she said.'

'I haven't *got* a baby sister!' said Sally, in a low, queer voice.   'I'm the only one.   Mother and I have been everything to each other, because Daddy has had to be away such a lot.   I haven't *got* a baby sister!'

The girls looked at Sally curiously.   Whatever could be the matter with her?   She sounded so queer.

'All right,' said Darrell, uneasily.   '*You* ought to know, I suppose.   Anyway, I expect you'd like a sister.   It's nice having one.'

'I should hate a sister,' said Sally.   'I wouldn't share my mother with anyone!'

She walked out of the room, her face as wooden as ever. The girls were really puzzled.   'She's a funny one,' said Irene.   'Hardly ever says anything—all closed up, some-how.   But sometimes those closed-up people burst open suddenly—and then, look out!'

'Well, I shall certainly write and tell Mother she's mis-taken,' said Darrell, and she did so, then and there.   She told Sally the next time she saw her.

'I'm sorry I made that mistake about your having a sister,' she said to Sally.   'I've written to tell Mother you said you hadn't one.   She must have mistaken what your mother said.'

Sally stood still and glared at Darrell as if she suddenly hated her.   'What do you want to go interfering for?' she burst out.   'Leave me and my family alone!   Little busybody, always sticking your nose into other people's affairs!'

Darrell's temper flared up. 'I don't,' she said. 'You guard your tongue, Sally. I never meant to interfere, and I can't think what all the fuss is about. Either you have a sister or you haven't. *I* don't care.'

'You tell your mother not to interfere either!' said Sally. 'Writing letters about my family!'

'Oh, don't be so *silly*!' flared back Darrell, really exasperated now. 'Anyone would think there was a deep, dark mystery, the way you go on! Anyway, I'll just see what my mother says when she next writes to me—-and I'll tell you.'

'I don't want to know. I won't know!' said Sally, and she put out her hands as if she was fending Darrell off. 'I hate you, Darrell Rivers—you with your mother who comes to see you off, and sends you things and writes you long letters and comes to see you! And you boast about that to me; you do it all on purpose. You're mean, mean, mean!'

Darrell was utterly taken about. What in the wide world did Sally mean? She watched the girl go out of the room, and sank down on to a form, completely bewildered.

13   HALF-TERM AT LAST!

THE girls became very excited at the beginning of half-term week. Many of them would see their parents on the Saturday—and Miss Remmington, the games-mistress, had suddenly decided to have a small edition of the Swimming Sports for the benefit of the parents. Everyone who visited Malory Towers was struck with the beautiful natural pool, and loved to see it.

' So it would be nice this half-term, as it's so hot, for your people to go down to the breezy pool, and see not only the beauties of the water, but the way their girls can swim and dive ! ' said Miss Remmington. ' We will have a pleasant time down there and then come back for a strawberry and cream tea, with ices ! '

What fun ! Darrell hugged herself with joy whenever she thought of it. She had got on so well with her swimming and diving, and she knew her parents would be pleased. And strawberries and ice-cream afterwards. How simply wizard !

But she was rather taken aback on Wednesday when the half-term places were read out. Instead of being in the first three or four, as she had hoped, she was tenth from the bottom. She could hardly believe her ears ! Katherine was top, Alicia was fifth, Betty was fourteenth, Gwendoline was bottom—Mary-Lou was sixth from the bottom, not very far below Darrell !

Darrell sat very quiet whilst the rest of the marks were read out. There were thirty or so girls in her form—and more than twenty of them had done better than she had. Surely, surely there must be some mistake ?

She went to Miss Potts about it, looking worried. ' Miss Potts,' she began, rather timidly, for the mistress was correcting papers and looked very busy, ' Miss Potts, excuse my interrupting you, but can I ask you something ? '

' What is it ? ' said Miss Potts, running her blue pencil across a line of writing.

' Well—it's about the form order,' said Darrell. ' Am I really so low down as that ? '

' Let me see—what were you ? Quite a long way down,' said Miss Potts, pulling the list to her and looking at it. ' Yes, that's right. I was surprised and disappointed, Darrell. You did so well in the first two weeks.'

' But Miss Potts,' said Darrell, and then stopped. She didn't know quite how to say what she wanted to say. She wanted to say that she had much better brains than at least half the form, so why was she so low? But somehow that sounded conceited.

However Miss Potts, who was very quick-minded, saw her difficulty. 'You have come to ask me how it is you are nearer the bottom than the top when you could so easily be among the top ones?' she said. 'Well, I'll tell you, Darrell. There are people like Alicia, who can play the fool in class and waste their time and everyone else's, and yet still come out well in their work. And there are people like you, who can also play the fool and waste their time—but unfortunately it affects their work and they slide down to the bottom. Do you understand?'

Darrell flushed very red and looked as if she could sink through the floor. She nodded.

'Yes, thank you,' she said, in a small voice. She looked at Miss Potts out of her clear brown eyes. 'I wouldn't have been so silly if I'd known it was going to affect my place in the form,' she said. 'I—I just thought as I had good brains and a good memory I'd be all right, anyhow. Daddy and Mother will be disappointed.'

'They probably will,' said Miss Potts, taking up her pencil again. 'I shouldn't copy Alicia and Betty too much if I were you, Darrell. You will be a finer character if you go along on your own, than if you copy other people. You see, what *you* do, you do whole-heartedly—so if you play the fool, naturally other things will suffer. Alicia is able to do two or three things quite well at one and the same time. That certainly has its points—but the best people in this world are the whole-hearted ones, if they can only make for the right things.'

'I see,' said Darrell. 'Like my father. He's whole-hearted. He's a surgeon and he just goes in for giving back people their health and happiness with all his heart—so he's marvellous.'

'Exactly,' said Miss Potts. ' But if he split himself up, so to speak, and dabbled in half a dozen things, he would probably not be nearly such a remarkable surgeon. And when you choose something worth while like doctoring— or teaching—or writing or painting, it is best to be whole-hearted about it. It doesn't so much matter for a second-rate or third-rate person. But if you happen to have the makings of a first-rate person and you mean to choose a first-rate job when you grow up, then you must learn to be whole-hearted when you are young.'

Darrell didn't like to ask Miss Potts if she thought she had the makings of a first-rate person in her, but she couldn't help hoping that she had. She went away rather subdued. What a pity she hadn't been whole-hearted over her work and got up to the top, instead of being whole-hearted over playing the fool with Alicia and Betty, and sliding down towards the bottom.

Gwendoline's mother and her old governess, Miss Winter, were coming on Saturday too. Gwendoline was very much looking forward to showing off in front of them. How small she would make Miss Winter feel, when she talked of her lessons and how wonderful she was at everything !

Mary-Lou's people were not coming and she was disappointed. Gwendoline spoke kindly to her. ' Never mind, Mary-Lou. You can keep with me and my mother and Miss Winter all day. I won't let you feel lonely.'

Mary-Lou didn't much want to keep with Gwendoline. She was tired of being pawed about by Gwendoline, and tired of the never-ending stories of her family, in all of which Gwendoline herself shone out brightly as someone really too marvellous for words.

But Gwendoline thoroughly enjoyed such a quiet listener as Mary-Lou, though she despised her for being weak enough to put up with so much.

When Darrell heard that Mary-Lou's people could not come on half-term Saturday she went to her. 'Would you like to come and be with my mother and father and me all day?' she said. 'They are taking me out to lunch in the car. We're having a gorgeous picnic.'

Mary-Lou's heart leapt. She gazed at Darrell in adoration and delight. To be asked by *Darrell* to share the half-term—could anything be nicer? Darrell had ticked her off so much lately, and found her such a nuisance—but now she had been decent enough to give her this invitation.

Then she remembered Gwendoline's invitation, and her face fell. 'Oh,' she said, 'Gwendoline's asked me to join *her*—and I said I would.'

'Well, go and tell her *I've* asked you, and that my father and mother would like to meet you,' said Darrell. 'I shouldn't think she'd mind.'

'Well—I don't know if I dare say that,' said timid Mary-Lou. 'She might be very angry—especially as she doesn't like you, Darrell.'

'I suppose that means you'd rather go with Gwendoline than with me,' said Darrell, unkindly. It always irritated her when Mary-Lou put on her 'scared' look. 'Well, go then.'

'*Darrell!* How can you say that?' cried Mary-Lou, almost in tears. 'Why—I'd—I'd—I'd give *anything* to come with you.'

'Well, go and tell Gwendoline then,' said Darrell. 'If you want a thing badly you can surely pluck up enough courage to get it. You're a terrible little coward.'

'Oh, I know,' said Mary-Lou, in despair. 'Don't keep on and on saying that! It only makes me worse! *You* tell Gwendoline, Darrell.'

'Certainly not,' said Darrell. '*I'm* not going to do your dirty work! Anyway, I'm not sure I want such a silly baby tagging on to me all half-term.'

She walked off, leaving Mary-Lou looking after her in despair. Jean, who was nearby and had overheard everything, felt a little sorry for Mary-Lou. She walked after Darrell.

'I think you're a bit hard on her,' she remarked, in her forthright Scots voice.

'Well, it's all for her good,' said Darrell. 'If I can *make* her have a little courage, she'll thank me for it. I said those things purposely, to shame her into going to Gwendoline and asking her.'

'You've shamed her all right, but not in the way that will make her pluck up her courage,' said Jean. 'You've given her the kind of shame that puts people into despair!'

Jean was right. Mary-Lou was quite in despair. The more she thought of going to Gwendoline and asking her if she minded her going with Darrell at half-term instead of with her, the more terrified she got. In the end she did go to find Gwendoline, but found that she didn't dare to ask her; which made it worse than ever! Poor Mary-Lou!

Gwendoline got to hear that Darrell had asked Mary-Lou for half-term, and she was pleased that Mary-Lou had not apparently wanted to go with her. She spoke to her about it.

'Fancy Darrell having the cheek to ask you, after *I'd* asked you!' she said. 'I'm glad you had the decency to refuse, Mary-Lou. You'd surely not want to go off with a girl like that, who thinks you're such a poor worm?'

'No,' said Mary-Lou, and couldn't say any more. If only she could have said yes, boldly, right out! But she couldn't.

The morning of half-term dawned bright and clear. It was going to be a super day. The sea glinted in the sunlight, as calm as a mirror. It would be high tide at two o'clock. The pool would be just right. What luck!

Girls took loads of camp-stools down to the pool and

set them up on the high rocky place above the pool, where the tide seldom reached. It was a fine place for watching. Darrell sang loudly as she went up and down, her heart leaping because she would see her parents that day. Mary-Lou did not sing. She looked sober and down-hearted. Sally Hope looked sober too—her face more 'closed-up' than ever, thought Darrell.

Alicia was in high spirits. Her mother and father were coming and one of her brothers. Betty's parents were not coming, so she was, of course, going to be with Alicia.

Darrell, catching sight of Sally trudging up the cliff, after taking down some camp-stools, was struck by the sad expression on her face. Impulsively she hailed her.

' Hi , Sally ! Sally Hope ! Your people aren't coming, are they ? Wouldn't you like to join me and my parents today ? I can ask anyone I like.'

' I'd rather not, thank you,' said Sally, in a stiff little voice, and went on up the cliff without another word.

' Well, she is a funny girl,' thought Darrell, feeling rather annoyed that the two girls she had so far asked hadn't either of them agreed to come with her. She went off to find someone else whose people were not coming. She really must get somebody, because her mother had said she would like to take another girl out too. ' Your own particular friend, if possible,' her mother had written.

But Darrell hadn't got a ' particular friend.' She would so much have liked Alicia, but Alicia was Betty's friend. She liked Irene, too, but Irene never seemed to feel the need of a friend. Her music made up to her for everything.

' Oh, well—what about asking Emily ? ' thought Darrell. She was not at all interested in the quiet, studious Emily, who always seemed to be sewing most industriously every evening. But Emily's people weren't coming, and no one had asked her to go out to lunch with them.

So she asked Emily, who blushed with pleasure and said

yes, she would be delighted to come. She seemed surprised that Darrell had asked her. Mary-Lou was almost
in tears when she saw the two of them going off to get
ready to meet Darrell's parents. She couldn't bear to
think that Emily was going to have the treat she would so
much have loved herself—but hadn't enough courage to get.

14   A REALLY LOVELY DAY

SOON the big drive in front of Malory Towers was crowded
with cars of all shapes and sizes. Parents climbed out of
them and looked for their girls. There were shrieks of
delighted welcome all over the place.

'Mummy! Daddy! I'm so glad you've come early!'

'Mother! I didn't expect you so soon! Oh, it's lovely
to see you again!'

Darrell was watching for her father and mother, too.
She soon saw her father's plain black car, which he drove
himself. And there was mother sitting beside him, looking
pretty in a new dress, and excited because she would so
soon see Darrell.

Darrell shot out of the doorway and down the drive like
an arrow, nearly knocking over Gwendoline, who was
waiting impatiently for her own mother. She flung herself
on her parents. 'Mother! I've been waiting and waiting! Oh, it's lovely to see you again! Hallo, Daddy—
did you drive all the way down?'

'Hallo, darling,' said her mother and looked at her in
pleasure. Darrell was brown and glowing with colour.
Her warm brown eyes were filled with delighted love. She
looked happy and 'on top of the world' as her father put
it to himself. Both her parents were pleased.

Darrell took them into the school, chattering at the top of her voice. 'You must see my dormy. You must see the very bed I sleep in—and I *must* show you the view out of our dormy window. It's super!'

In her intense excitement she had forgotten all about Emily, waiting patiently nearby. She suddenly saw her, and stopped.

'Oh—Emily! Mother, you said I could choose some one to come out with us—and here she is. This is Emily Lake, a girl in my form.'

Mrs. Rivers looked at Emily and was surprised. She had not expected a quiet sober little girl like this to be Darrell's chosen friend. She did not know that as yet Darrell had no definite friend. She shook hands with Emily, and said she was pleased she was coming out with them.

After that Emily tagged along behind them, listening to Darrell's excited chatter, and her parents' amused replies. She liked Darrell's parents. Her mother was pretty and amusing, and sensible too—and as for her father, well, any one would trust him at sight, thought Emily, gazing at his determined, good-looking face with its big dark eyes and intensely black eyebrows, just like Darrell's but bigger and shaggier.

Darrell was proud of her parents. She wanted to show them off. She saw Gwendoline with two women—one obviously her mother, with bright golden hair like Gwendoline's and a rather babyish, empty face. The other must be Miss Winter, the governess, thought Darrell. What an awful person!

Poor Miss Winter was not really awful. She was plain and poor and always eager to agree with everyone. She adored Gwendoline because she was pretty and graceful, and did not seem to see the selfishness and spoilt ways of the silly little girl.

Mary-Lou was with them, trying to smile, but really very unhappy. She didn't like either Mrs. Lacey or Miss Winter and she was beginning to feel horrified at some of the fibs that she had heard Gwendoline tell them.

'I'm almost the best at tennis in our form,' she heard Gwendoline say. 'I shouldn't be surprised if I'm put into a match-team, Mother!'

'Oh, darling—how clever you are!' said Mrs. Lacey, fondly. Mary-Lou stared at Gwendoline in surprise. Why, everyone knew Gwendoline was a real muff at all games!

'And Mam'zelle is very pleased with my French,' went on Gwendoline. 'I believe I might be top in that. She says I have a splendid accent.'

Miss Winter glowed. 'Oh, Gwen darling! Isn't that lovely now? I did my best with you, of course, but I was always afraid it was rather a *poor* best, because I've never been to France.'

Mary-Lou longed to say that Gwendoline was always bottom in the French class, but she did not dare to. How *could* Gwendoline stuff her people up with such a lot of lies? And how *could* they believe them?

'Are you going to go in for the swimming-match this afternoon?' asked Mrs. Lacey, looking fondly at Gwendoline, who today had her shining golden hair loose down her back, and looked, so her mother thought, like a real angel.

'No, I thought I wouldn't, Mother,' said Gwendoline. 'It's best to give the others a chance. After all, I've done well at so many things.'

'There's my sweet, unselfish girl!' said Mrs. Lacey, and squeezed Gwendoline's arm. Mary-Lou felt slightly sick.

Then Darrell spoilt it all! She passed by with her mother and father, and Mrs. Lacey was struck by her good looks and happy smile.

'*There's* a nice girl, dear!' she said to Gwendoline.
'Is she one of your friends? Let us speak to her.'

'Oh, no, she's not a friend of mine,' began Gwendoline,
but Mary-Lou, delighted at this praise of Darrell, was
calling to her. 'Darrell! Darrell! Mrs. Lacey wants to
speak to you.'

Darrell went over to Mrs. Lacey and was introduced
by a glowering Gwendoline. 'And are you going to go
in for the swimming-sports?' asked Mrs. Lacey, graciously.
'I hear dear Gwendoline is not, bless her.'

'Gwendoline! Oh, she can't swim a stroke!' said
Darrell. 'We always yell at her because she takes five
minutes putting one toe into the water. Don't we, Gwendoline?'

This was all said in good humour and fun—but Gwendoline could willingly have pushed Darrell over the cliff
at that moment! She went very red.

Mrs. Lacey really thought that Darrell was joking. She
laughed the tinkling laugh which she thought was so pretty.
'I suppose if Gwendoline entered she'd beat you all!' she
said. 'As she does at tennis—and lessons, I suppose.'

Darrell looked in astonishment at Gwendoline, who was
glaring at her, crimson in the face. 'Gwendoline's been
stuffing you up, I expect!' she said with a laugh, and went
off to join her own party.

'What a very outspoken, blunt sort of girl,' said Miss
Winter, puzzled and worried.

Gwendoline recovered herself. 'Oh, she's not a nice
girl,' she said. 'Nobody likes her. She hasn't got any
friend of her own at all—and you can see why. She's
always running other people down. Jealous, I suppose.
Don't you take any notice of her, Mother. Mary-Lou here
will tell you I'm first-rate at tennis and the rest!'

But that was beyond even timid Mary-Lou! She just
looked more scared than ever, and murmured something

about going to speak to Mam'zelle—and off she went, glad
to escape from the Lacey family for a few minutes.

On the way to the car, after Darrell had shown her
parents every single thing she could think of, from the
view up in North Tower, to the inside of her very well-
tidied desk, the Rivers family saw Sally Hope.

'Why, isn't that Sally Hope?' said Mrs. Rivers, stopping. 'I'm sure it is. There was a very good photograph
of her in her mother's drawing-room, when I went to tea
there the other day.'

'Yes. That's Sally,' said Darrell. 'Do you want to
speak to her, Mother?'

'Well, I have a message for her from her mother,' said
Mrs. Rivers. So Darrell raised her clear voice and called,
'Sally! Sally Hope! Come here a minute, will you?'

Sally must have heard Darrell, for everyone around
did. But if so, she took no notice at all. She plunged
down into a path that led through some bushes in the drive
and disappeared.

'Blow her!' said Darrell. 'I should have thought she
would have heard my yell. I asked her to come out with
us, Mother, but she wouldn't.'

'Come along,' said her father, opening the door of the
car. 'We'll go along the cliff and then take an exciting
road I've found that leads right down to a lonely little cove.
We'll have our lunch there.'

Darrell and Emily got in. Emily was enjoying herself.
Mrs. Rivers was so nice, and asked her so many questions
about herself. Usually people found Emily dull, and left
her alone. But Mrs. Rivers, thinking that Emily was
Darrell's chosen friend, was very anxious to know her
well.

She soon learnt that Emily was very fond of sewing.
Darrell listened to her chattering in astonishment. She
had never heard Emily talk so much before! Gracious,

A REALLY LOVELY DAY   103

hark at her describing the cushion-cover she was making
—the colours, the stitches and everything !

'It's always been a disappointment to me that Darrell
never took any interest in embroidery,' said Mrs. Rivers
to Emily. 'I'm very fond of it too. I've done the seats
of six of our chairs at home, in tapestry work.'

'Oh, *have* you ! ' exclaimed Emily. ' I've done some
too—but only two so far. I loved that work.'

'Perhaps you will be able to interest Darrell in sewing ! '
said Mrs. Rivers, laughing. ' It's as much as I can do at
home to get her to do a simple darn ! '

'Well, I'll teach Darrell to darn, if she likes,' said Emily,
eager to please this nice Mrs. Rivers.

Darrell was horrified. Gracious, she hadn't brought
Emily out to have her planning with her mother to teach
her darning ! She changed the subject at once, and told
them about Gwendoline and how she had been boasting
to her mother and governess.

Soon they were down on the beach, eating the most
gorgeous lunch Darrell had had that term. Cold chicken
and pickles—*pickles* ! There was never a pickle to be seen
at school. Little cardboard containers full of fresh salad
and mayonnaise sauce. Delicious ! Jam-tarts and slabs
of chocolate ice-cream. What a lunch !

'And ginger-beer to wash it down,' said Mrs. Rivers,
filling up the glasses. 'More chicken, Darrell ? There's
plenty.'

After lunch it was time to go back for the sports. Emily
was not in the swimming, so she said she would find Darrell's
parents good places to watch from. Darrell left them in
her care when she got back to Malory Towers to change.

It was such a happy day. Everyone seemed in a good
temper, and jokes flew about everywhere. Even the two
Mam'zelles went about arm-in-arm, a thing that they had
not done at all that term.

The swimming-sports were exciting. Mrs. Rivers was delighted with Darrell's strong swimming, graceful diving, and fearlessness. She was one of the best of the small girls. Some of the big girls were extremely clever in their diving, especially Marilyn, the sixth-form games-captain. Everyone cheered her as she did a graceful swallow-dive from the topmost board.

'And can you do all these things, darling?' Darrell heard Mrs. Lacey ask Gwendoline. Gwendoline, who was near Darrell and a few others, looked round warily, wishing her mother wouldn't ask such awkward questions in public.

'Well—not quite all,' she said, and Miss Winter patted her fondly on the shoulder.

'Always so modest,' she said, and Darrell could hardly stop herself laughing outright at the thought of Gwendoline being called modest. She looked scornfully at little Mary-Lou sitting near Gwendoline, wondering how she could possibly listen to all the bigger girl's boasting and yet say nothing.

At tea-time Darrell and Emily kept the plates of the grown-ups (and their own!) well supplied with strawberries and cream, and fetched ice-creams in plenty. What a lunch they had had—and now, what a tea! Besides the strawberries and ice-creams, there were little buns and cakes and biscuits of every kind. Malory Towers knew how to do things well!

'Mother! There's Sally Hope again!' said Darrell suddenly, catching sight of Sally's head in the distance. 'I'll get her in a minute. By the way, you never told me how that mistake about Sally's baby sister happened— the one you said she had got, and hasn't.'

'But Darrell dear—she *has* got a baby sister!' said her mother in surprise. 'I've seen her!'

'Well—whatever *does* Sally mean!' said Darrell. 'I really must get her and find out!'

15   A SUDDEN QUARREL

BUT Sally was not easy to find. She seemed to have completely disappeared again. It occurred to Darrell to wonder if Sally was avoiding her—but no, why should she ? There would be no reason for that.

She hunted everywhere for Sally. Nobody knew where she was. It was peculiar. Darrell went back to her parents, anxious not to lose any more of their company, for time was precious now.

'Well, *I* can't find Sally,' she said. 'She's completely vanished. Anyway, I'll give her her mother's message. What was it, Mother ? '

'Oh, her mother seemed a little worried about Sally, because it's her first term at boarding school, and Sally writes such funny wooden little letters,' said Mrs. Rivers. 'I showed Mrs. Hope some of *your* letters, darling. I knew you wouldn't mind ; and she said she did wish Sally would write more news to her, and send her letters like yours. She said she seemed to have lost touch with her completely. She was really very worried. She wanted me to speak to Sally and tell her she sent her fondest love, and was so sorry she couldn't come and see her this half-term. And she said her baby sister sent her hugs and kisses.'

'I'll tell her,' said Darrell, very puzzled. 'But Mother dear, Sally's awfully funny about things. She truly and honestly did tell me she hadn't got a sister, and she was furious with me for talking about her mother. She said I was interfering and all sorts of things.'

'Well—perhaps she was joking,' said Mrs. Rivers, also rather puzzled. 'Sally *does* know she's got a baby sister at home. For one thing, that was why she was sent to boarding school, so that the baby, who is rather delicate, could have all Mrs. Hope's care. It's a dear little thing.'

'Been losing your temper yet?' asked Darrell's father, with a twinkle in his eye. Darrell went red.

'Well—I did once,' she said. 'And after I'd made up my mind I wouldn't, too!'

'Oh, Darrell—you didn't lose it badly, I hope,' said her mother, anxiously.

Emily answered for Darrell. 'Oh, she just gave a most exasperating girl some jolly good slaps in the pool! You could almost hear them up at the Towers!'

'*Darrell!*' said her mother, shocked. Darrell grinned.

'I know. Awful of me, wasn't it. I shan't do it again. I've got my temper well in hand now.'

'We've all *wanted* to do a bit of slapping where that particular girl is concerned,' said Emily, 'so secretly we were rather pleased!'

They all laughed. Darrell felt so happy that she was sure she would never lose her temper again in her life! What a pity a day like this had to come to an end!

But it did come to an end. At about six o'clock the cars began to purr out of the big drive, and girls waved wildly. One by one their parents went, and the excited chattering died down. The girls went into their common rooms to talk over the events of the day.

After a while Darrell remembered the message she had for Sally Hope. She glanced round the common room. Sally wasn't there. Where was she? She seemed always to be disappearing!

'Where's Sally Hope?' asked Darrell.

'I believe she's in one of the music-rooms,' said Katherine. 'Goodness knows why she wants to practice today, when everyone is let off lessons!'

'I'll go and find her,' said Darrell, and walked off. She made her way to the music-rooms, where the girls did their

practising each day. They were tiny rooms, containing
only a piano, a stool, and a chair.

Music came from two of them. Darrell peeped into the
first one. Irene was there, playing softly to herself. She
didn't even see Darrell. Darrell smiled and shut the door.
Irene was certainly mad on music !

She came to the other practice room, from which music
was coming. It was not the entrancing melodies that Irene
had been playing, though, but plain five-finger exercises,
played over and over again, over and over again, in an
almost angry manner.

Darrell opened the door. Yes—Sally was there all right.
Good. Darrell went in and shut the door. Sally turned
round and scowled.

' I'm practising,' she said. ' Get out.'

' What's the matter with you ? ' said Darrell, feeling
annoyed immediately. ' You don't need to jump down
my throat like that. I've been trying to find you all day.
My mother wanted to speak to you.'

' Well, I didn't want to speak to her,' said Sally, and
began to thump out the irritating exercise again, up and
down, up and down.

' *Why* shouldn't you want to speak to my mother ? ' cried
Darrell, angrily. ' She had a message for you from *your*
mother.'

No answer. Up and down, up and down went Sally's
fingers on the notes, more loudly than ever. Darrell lost
her temper.

' Stop playing ! ' she shouted. ' Don't be so horribly
rude ! Whatever's the matter with you ! '

Sally put the loud pedal down and crashed the notes
more loudly than ever. Plainly she was not going to listen
to a word.

Darrell went near to her and put her mouth to her ear.

' Why did you say you haven't got a sister ? You *have*,

and that's why your mother couldn't come and see you !
But she sent you her love and said . . .'

Sally swung round from the piano, her face looking queer
and white. ' Shut up ! ' she said. ' Interfering little busybody ! Leave me alone. Just because you've been with
your mother all day long, and had her fussing round you, you
think you can come and taunt me like this ! I hate you ! '

' You're mad ! ' cried Darrell, and she struck her hand
on the piano, making a queer sound of clashing notes.
' You won't listen when I want to tell you things. But
you *shall* listen ! Your mother told mine that you only
write her funny wooden letters. . . . She said . . .'

' I *won't* listen ! ' said Sally, in a choking voice, and got
up from the stool. She pushed Darrell blindly away. But
Darrell could not bear to be touched when she was in a
temper, and she shoved back with all her might. She was
strong, and she sent Sally flying across the little room.
She fell across the chair, and lay there for a moment.

She put her hand on her stomach. ' Oh, it hurts,' she
said. ' Oh, you wicked girl, Darrell ! '

Darrell was still trembling with anger as Sally stumbled
out of the room. But almost immediately her rage went,
and she was overwhelmed with horror. How *could* she have
been so awful ? Sally was queer and silly and horrid, it
was true—but she, Darrell, had used her strength against
her to hurt her. She had lost her temper all over again,
after boasting to her parents only a little while ago that she
never would any more.

She ran to the door, eager to go after Sally and beg her
pardon. But Sally was nowhere to be seen. Darrell ran
back to the common room. No Sally there, either. She
sat down in a chair and rubbed her hot forehead. What a
scene ! How disgusting ! *Why* couldn't she manage her
temper ?

' What's up ? ' asked Alicia.

' Oh—nothing much. Sally was a bit difficult, that's all —and I lost my temper,' said Darrell.

' Idiot ! ' said Alicia. ' What did you do ? Slap her ? Give her some broth without any bread ? '

Darrell couldn't smile. She felt near tears. What a horrid ending to such a lovely day ! After all the excitement, and now this sudden row, she felt quite exhausted. She was not at all pleased when Emily came up with her sewing.

' I do think your people are nice,' began Emily, and started to chatter in a way she seldom did. How boring ! Darrell wanted to tell Emily to be quiet. If she had been Alicia she would—but as a rule she was kinder than the sharp-tongued Alicia, and did not like to hurt people's feelings. So she bore with Emily as patiently as she could.

Mary-Lou watched her from the other side of the room. She wanted to come over and join Emily and Darrell. But Gwendoline was pouring out reams of family history to her, and she had to listen. Also she was a little afraid that Darrell might snub her if she went across.

Darrell watched for Sally to appear in the common room. Perhaps she could slip over to her then and tell her she was sorry. She was ashamed of herself now, and she could only put it right by telling Sally. Oh, dear ! It was awful to have a temper that simply rose up out of the blue, before you even knew it was coming ! What *could* you do with a temper like that ?

Sally didn't come back to the common room. Soon the supper-bell went and the girls filed into the dining-room. Darrell looked about for Sally again. But still she wasn't there. This was really very queer.

Miss Potts noticed that there was an empty chair. ' Who's missing ? ' she said.

' Sally Hope,' said Darrell. ' I last saw her in one of the practice rooms—about an hour ago.'

'Well, go and fetch her said Miss Potts, impatiently.

'Oh, she left when I was there,' said Darrell. 'I don't know where she went to.'

'We'll get on without her then,' said Miss Potts. 'She must have heard the supper-bell.'

The girls chattered about the day they had had. Only Darrell was silent. Was Sally somewhere, very upset? What could be the matter with her? Why was she so queer about things? Was she unhappy about something?

Mary-Lou sniffed loudly. 'Where's your hanky?' asked Miss Potts. 'Haven't you got one? Oh, Mary-Lou, you know you must always have one. Go and get one at once. I can't bear that sniff of yours.'

Mary-Lou slipped out of the room, and ran up to the dormy. She didn't come back for a little while and Miss Potts became impatient.

'Really! It seems to take Mary-Lou all evening to find a hanky!'

There came the sound of running steps and the door of the dining-room was flung open. Mary-Lou came in, looking even more scared than usual.

'Miss Potts! Oh, Miss Potts! I've found Sally. She's lying on her bed in the dormy, and she's making an awful noise!'

'What sort of noise?' said Miss Potts, hurriedly getting up.

'A groaning sort of noise and she keeps holding herself and saying, "Oh, my tummy!"' said poor Mary-Lou, bursting into tears. 'Oh, Miss Potts, do go to her. She wouldn't even speak to me!'

'Girls, get on with your supper,' said Miss Potts, briskly. 'It sounds as if Sally has eaten too many strawberries and too much ice-cream. Katherine, go and tell Matron, please, and ask her to go up to your dormy.'

She swept out of the room. The girls began talking at

once, asking scared Mary-Lou all kinds of questions. Only Darrell still sat silent, a cold fear creeping round her heart.

She had flung Sally across the room, and Sally had fallen over that chair! She must have hurt herself in the stomach then. Darrell remembered how she had said, ' It hurts.' It wasn't too many strawberries and too much ice-cream. It was Darrell's temper that had caused the trouble !

Darrell couldn't eat any more supper. She slipped off to the common room to be by herself. Surely Sally wasn't *much* hurt ? Just bruised, perhaps. Surely Miss Potts would come in soon and say cheerfully, ' Well, well ! Nothing much wrong with Sally after all ! '

' Oh, I hope she does, I hope she does,' said poor Darrell, and waited impatiently and anxiously for the sound of Miss Potts's quick footsteps.

16   A BAD TIME FOR DARRELL

THE girls poured into the common room after their supper. They had half an hour before bedtime. They were tired after their exciting day, and some of them were sleepy already.

Alicia looked at Darrell in surprise. ' Why so gloomy ? ' she said.

' Well—I was just wondering about Sally,' said Darrell. ' Hoping she wasn't very ill.'

' Why ever should she be ? ' said Alicia. ' Lots of people can't eat strawberries without getting a pain or a rash. One of my brothers is like that.'

Alicia plunged into one of her bits of family history and Darrell listened gratefully. Alicia did not relate stories

that glorified herself, as Gwendoline always did—she
simply poured out amusing tales of the life she and her
brothers led in the holidays at home—and, if Alicia was
to be believed, the pranks they got up to were enough
to turn any mother's hair completely grey! However,
Alicia's mother had not seemed to Darrell to have any
grey hairs at all, when she had seen her that day.

The bed-time bell went for the first- and second-formers.
They put away their things at once. Matron did not show
much patience with laggards at bed-time. There were too
many girls to hustle into bed for that!

Miss Potts had not come back. Darrell felt her anxiety
creeping over her again. Perhaps Matron would know.
She would ask her about Sally as soon as she saw her
hovering around the bathrooms.

But Matron wasn't there. Mam'zelle was there instead,
beaming placidly at everyone, still in a good temper because
of the lovely day they had all had.

'Hallo, Mam'zelle! Where's Matron?' asked Alicia
in surprise.

'Looking after Sally Hope,' said Mam'zelle. 'Ah, the
poor child—she is in great pain.'

Darrell's heart sank. 'Is she—is she in the San. then?'
she asked. Girls who were ill were always put in the
San., which consisted of a good many nice rooms above
the Head Mistress's own suite of rooms. There was also
a special matron for the San. itself, a smiling, but strict
hospital nurse, who was extremely efficient not only at
dealing with any kind of school accident or illness, but
also at dealing with any kind of girl!

'Yes. Of course she is in the San. She is very ill,'
said Mam'zelle. Then, with her love of exaggerating, she
added a sentence or two that sent Darrell's heart down
into her boots. 'It is her poor tommy—no, tummy is
what you say, *n'est ce pas*. She has a big pain there.'

' Oh,' said Darrell. ' Do they—do they know what has caused the pain, Mam'zelle ? Has Sally hurt herself ? '

Mam'zelle didn't know. ' All I know is that it is not the strawberries and the ice-cream,' she said. ' Because Sally did not have any. She has told Matron that.'

That made it all the more certain, then, that it must have been Darrell's rough push and the fall that followed ! Poor Darrell ! She felt so miserable that Mam'zelle's sharp eyes noticed her downcast face and she began to wonder if here was another girl about to be ill !

' You feel all right, my little Darrell ? ' she said, in a sympathetic voice.

' Oh, yes, thank you,' said Darrell, startled. ' I'm just—well, just tired, I suppose.'

Darrell hardly slept at all that night. She was so horrified at what had happened. How could she have lost her temper so thoroughly, how could she have yelled at Sally like that and how *could* she have sent her flying across the room ? She, Darrell, was wicked ! It was true that Sally was queer and annoying, but that was no excuse for Darrell's behaviour.

Now Sally was ill and in pain. Had she said anything about Darrell losing her temper ? Darrell felt herself growing cold as she thought of what Miss Grayling might do if she heard.

' She would hear about my slapping Gwendoline too, and she would send for me and tell me I was a failure already,' thought Darrell. ' Oh, Sally, Sally, do get better by to-morrow ! Then I'll tell you I'm terribly sorry, and I'll try to make it up to you all I can.'

She fell asleep at last, and was very tired when the dressing-bell rang for them all to get up. Her first thought was Sally. She saw the girl's empty bed and shivered. How she hoped Sally would be back there that night !

She ran downstairs before any one else. She saw Miss Potts and went to her. ' Please,' she said, ' how is Sally ? '

Miss Potts thought what a kind child Darrell was. ' She's not at all well, I'm afraid,' she said. ' The doctor is still doubtful about what exactly is the matter. But she really seems rather ill, poor child. It was so sudden, too—she seemed all right yesterday.'

Darrell turned away, miserable. Yes, Sally had been all right till she had fallen across that chair. *She* knew what was the matter—but nobody else did ! It was plain that Sally hadn't told anyone of the quarrel.

It was Sunday. Darrell prayed hard for Sally all the time she was in church. She felt very guilty and ashamed. She also felt very much afraid. She felt that she ought to tell Miss Potts or Matron about the quarrel and how she had flung poor Sally across the room—but she was too frightened to tell !

Too frightened ! Darrell was so fearless in the usual way that it was something strange and queer to her to feel afraid. But she *was* afraid. Supposing Sally was very *very* ill ! Supposing—just supposing she didn't get better ! Supposing Darrell's temper caused all that !

She couldn't, couldn't tell anyone, because they would think her so wicked, and she would disgrace her mother and father. People would say " That's the girl whose temper caused her to be expelled from Malory Towers ! You know she made another girl terribly ill ! "

It would be awful to be sent away from Malory Towers in disgrace. She would never get over it. But she was sure Miss Grayling wouldn't keep her another day if she knew that she had caused Sally's illness and pain.

' I can't tell anyone, I can't ! ' thought poor Darrell. ' I'm afraid of letting people know, because of what would happen to me, and how it would make Mother and Daddy feel. I'm a coward, but I daren't tell. I never knew I was a coward before ! '

She suddenly thought of Mary-Lou, whom she had so

often called a coward. Poor Mary-Lou—now she knew how *she* felt when she was afraid of something. It was a horrible feeling. You couldn't get away from it. How *could* she have sneered at Mary-Lou and taunted her? It was bad enough to feel afraid of something without being taunted about it.

Darrell felt very sad and very humble. She had started the term in such high hopes and spirits. She was going to be top! She was going to shine in everything and make her parents proud of her! She was going to find a fine girl for a friend. And she hadn't done any of those things.

She had got a low place in the form. She hadn't found herself a friend. She had been hateful to little Mary-Lou who had so shyly and eagerly offered her friendship—and now she had done something wicked and didn't dare to say anything about it!

Darrell was certainly down in the dumps that day and nobody could rouse her out of them. Miss Potts wondered if she was sickening for something and kept a sharp eye on her. Mary-Lou was worried, and hovered round hoping to be able to do something. And for once Darrell was kind to her and did not snap at her to send her away. She felt grateful for Mary-Lou's liking and sympathy.

Two doctors came to see Sally that day! The news went round North Tower House. 'She's *fearfully* ill! But it's nothing infectious so we're not in quarantine. Poor Sally. Tessie says she had to go and see the Head this morning and she heard Sally groaning in the San. rooms above!'

How Darrell wished her mother was there that day! But she couldn't remember where her parents had gone to, though they had told her. She had forgotten in the excitement of yesterday. She sat down in a rocky corner by the sea, and thought things out.

She couldn't be a coward any longer, because it would

be worse to stay at Malory Towers and know she was a coward than it would be to leave, knowing she had been brave enough to own up. But whom should she tell?

'I'd better write and tell Sally's mother,' she thought. 'She's the one that's nearest to Sally. I'll write and tell her all about the quarrel, and how it happened and everything. I'll have to tell her, too, how Sally says she hasn't got a sister. That's all very queer, but maybe Mrs. Hope will understand it. Then Mrs. Hope can do what she likes—tell the Head, I expect! Oh, dear! But I shall feel better when it's done.'

She left her seat by the sea and went back to North Tower. She got out her writing pad and began to write. It was not an easy letter to compose, but Darrell always found writing easy, and she poured out everything to Mrs. Hope—about the quarrel and what led up to it, and all about Sally not wanting to speak to Mrs. Rivers, and how unhappy she seemed to be. She was quite surprised to find how much she seemed to know about Sally!

She felt better immediately she had finished the letter. She didn't read it through, but stuck a stamp on the envelope and posted it at once. Mrs. Hope would get it the very next morning!

Then another rumour ran through North Tower. 'Sally's taken a turn for the worse! A specialist is coming to see her! Her people have been telegraphed for! They're coming tomorrow!'

Darrell could not eat anything at all that day. It was the longest day she had ever known. Mary-Lou, scared by Darrell's stricken face, kept close by her—and Darrell welcomed her and felt comforted. Mary-Lou had no idea why Darrell looked so miserable, and didn't dare to ask her. She forgot the many sneers and taunts that Darrell had thrown at her for her weakness and feebleness; she only wanted to help.

The other girls did not notice anything much. They
went for walks, bathed, lay about in the sun, and had a
happy, lazy Sunday. Miss Potts still kept an eye on Darrell.
What *could* be the matter with her ? Was it Sally's illness
that was worrying her ? No, it couldn't be. She hadn't
been at all friendly with Sally. Nobody had, for that
matter.

Bed-time came at last. Matron had no more news of
Sally, except that she was no better. No one was allowed
to see her, of course. Matron had been quite shocked
because Darrell had begged to go and see her for a moment
or two !

Darrell lay in bed, thinking. The third- and fourth-
formers came up to bed. The fifth-formers came and
then the sixth. Then Matron, Mam'zelle and Miss Potts
retired too, and Darrell heard lights clicking out. It was
late. It was dark outside. Everyone was asleep except
Darrell.

' I simply can't lie here thinking and thinking ! ' said
Darrell to herself desperately, and she flung off her covers.
' I shall go mad ! I shall get up and go into the Court !
The roses will smell sweet there, and I shall get cool and
perhaps be able to go to sleep ! '

She slipped on her dressing-gown and went quietly out
of the room. Nobody stirred. She crept down the wide
stairs and out into the Court. And then, in the stillness
of the night, she heard the sound of a car purring up the
hill to Malory Towers ! It stopped outside. Whoever
could it be, so late at night ?

Darrell glanced up at the windows of the San. There
were bright lights there. Sally couldn't be asleep, or the
lights would be dimmed. What was going on now ? Oh,
dear, if only she knew !

Darrell slipped through the archway that led from the
Court to the drive. Yes, a car stood there, a dark shape,

silent now and empty. Whoever had come in it had gone into Malory Towers. Darrell crept round to the door that led into the Head's building. Someone had left it open ! She pushed it and went inside. Now she would find out what was happening !

17   A WONDERFUL SURPRISE

THERE was a little light burning in the hall. The Head Mistress's rooms were in darkness. She was evidently upstairs in the San. Darrell crept upstairs. There were bright lights everywhere, and a good deal of bustle. What was happening to poor Sally ?

Darrell couldn't understand what was going on. Sally must be very ill to have so many people bothering about her like this in the middle of the night ! Darrell's heart felt very heavy. She didn't dare to go any farther in case someone saw her. But she felt she *must* stay where she was. She must get to know *some*thing ! She couldn't possibly go back to bed without finding out what was happening. If only, only she could help !

She sat down on a window-seat, and drew the heavy curtains round her, straining her ears to catch a word from any of the people bustling about from one of the San. rooms to another. That was Matron's voice—the matron of North Tower ! And that was the other Matron's voice, very crisp and sharp, giving an order. And that was a man's voice. Darrell held her breath and listened to the mysterious voices and noises, but she couldn't hear a word.

Oh, what would they all say if they knew that she, hot-tempered, wicked little Darrell was at the bottom of all this fuss and worry and bother ? Darrell pulled the curtain round her head and wept great tears that soaked into the heavy silk.

She sat there for about half an hour. Then, quite suddenly, and without meaning to, she fell fast asleep ! Lost in the heavy curtains, she slept, tired out.

She did not know how long she slept. She awoke again later, hearing noises. She sat up, wondering where in the wide world she was ! Then she remembered. Of course —she was near the San. She had come to find out what was happening to Sally.

At once all the fear and anxiety closed round her once again. She felt lonely and lost, and wanted her mother. She clutched the curtains round her as she heard voices coming near. Was it doctors ? Nurses ? Perhaps the Head Mistress herself ?

And then Darrell's heart almost stopped beating ! Some one was going by the window-seat where she sat, someone who spoke in a voice she knew and loved !

' She'll be all right,' said the voice. ' Just got her nicely in time ! Now . . .'

Darrell sat as if she was turned to stone, listening to that well-known voice ! It couldn't be ! It couldn't be ! It *couldn't be* her own father's voice !

She suddenly found herself able to move. She thrust the curtains aside and looked between them. She saw her father walking along with the Matron, talking earnestly. Yes, it was, it really was her father.

' DADDY ! ' squealed Darrell, forgetting absolutely everything except the fact that there was her father, whom she thought was miles away, walking along the passage just near her. ' Daddy ! Oh, Daddy ! Stop, here's Darrell ! '

Her father stopped as if he was shot ! He couldn't believe his ears ! Darrell leapt down from the window-seat and flung herself on him like a small thunderbolt. She clung to him and began to cry.

She thrust the curtain aside and looked through

'What's the matter, darling?' said her father, amazed. 'Why are you here?'

Miss Grayling came up, astonished and rather disapproving. 'Darrell! What are you here for, child? Mr. Rivers, you had better come into my room downstairs, please.'

Carrying Darrell in his arms, her father followed Miss Grayling downstairs, with Matron clucking behind like an astonished hen. Darrell clung to her father as if she would never let him go. Was she dreaming? Could it be that this was really her own father, in the middle of the night? Darrell couldn't imagine how or why he was there, but it was enough that he was.

He sat down in a big armchair with Darrell on his knees. Matron disappeared. Only Miss Grayling was there, and she looked in a very puzzled manner at Darrell and her father. There was something here she didn't understand.

'You cry all you want to, then tell me what's the matter,' said Darrell's father. 'Why, we only saw you yesterday, and you were so happy! Never mind, I'm here, and I'll put everything right for you.'

'You can't!' wept Darrell. 'I've been wicked! It was my temper again. Oh, Daddy, it's all *my* fault that Sally is so ill!'

'My dear child, what *are* you talking about?' said her father, puzzled. Darrell snuggled her head into his chest and began to feel much better. Daddy could always put things right. So could Mother. What a blessing he was here tonight.

Then she raised her head, and spoke in surprise. 'But Daddy—*why* are you here? I thought you were miles away!'

'Well, I was,' said Mr. Rivers. 'But Miss Grayling telephoned to me to say that little Sally Hope had appendicitis and the surgeon they usually had was ill, so could I come straight along and do the operation. So of course

I did ! I hopped into the car, drove here, found everything ready, did the little operation, and here I am ! And
Sally will be quite all right and back again in school in
about two weeks' time ! '

A great load fell away from Darrell's heart. She could
almost feel it rolling away. Why, appendicitis was something *any*one might have ! Her father was always curing
appendicitis ! She spoke anxiously.

' Daddy—appendicitis couldn't be caused by a push—
or a fall—could it ? '

' Good gracious, no ! ' said her father. ' Sally's had this
little affair coming on for some time, there's no doubt
about that. All the term and before that, I should think.
But what makes you ask that question ? '

Then everything came pouring out—how funny and
queer and rude Sally had been—how Darrell had lost her
temper—the violent push, the fall—everything !

' And I worried and worried and worried,' said Darrell,
with a sob. ' I thought if Miss Grayling knew, she would
send me away from Malory Towers, and you and Mother
would be ashamed of me, and I couldn't sleep, so I got up
and . . .'

' What a silly little girl ! ' said her father, and kissed
the top of her head. ' Perhaps we had better take you
away from Malory Towers ourselves, and have you at
home, if you are going to think such silly things, Darrell ! '

' Oh, no—don't do that ! I love being here ! ' said
Darrell. ' Oh, Daddy—if you *knew* how different I feel
now that I know Sally was going to be ill, anyhow—it
wasn't anything to do with me, after all. But oh, dear—
I wrote to Mrs. Hope about it ! What *will* she think ? '

Then she had to tell all about the letter and what she
had said. Her father and Miss Grayling were puzzled to
hear how Sally had said she hadn't a baby sister.

' Something queer there that must be sorted out,' said

Mr. Rivers to Miss Grayling. 'Might prevent her from getting better as quickly as she ought to. When did you say Mr. and Mrs. Hope were coming?'

'Tomorrow,' said Miss Grayling. 'I'll see them and explain. Now, Mr. Rivers—would you like us to give you a bed here tonight? It's so late.'

'Oh, no!' said Mr. Rivers. 'I'm used to driving out late at night. I'll go back, thank you. And Darrell must go to bed. Now don't worry any more, darling—things are all right—and your little push didn't do Sally any harm, though probably the fall made her feel her bad tummy a little bit more. I expect she felt ill all day, poor child.'

'It wasn't a little push I gave her. It was a big one,' said Darrell.

'It makes me sad to think I've handed on to you the temper I've got myself,' said her father. Darrell tightened her arms round his neck.

'Don't worry. I'll get on top of it!' she said. 'I'll soon do what you do—keep it for worth-while things!'

'Well, good night, darling,' said her father, and kissed her. 'Go and see Sally as soon as you're allowed to. I think you'll feel better then!'

'I feel better now!' said Darrell, and slipped off his knee. Her eyes were red but she was smiling. How different she felt! All her worry was gone.

Her father went off in the darkness in his car. Miss Grayling herself took Darrell to bed and tucked her in. Darrell fell asleep even before the Head Mistress was out of the room.

And, in the San. Sally slept too, her pain gone. Matron watched over her, pleased to hear her steady, regular breathing. What a deft, quick surgeon Darrell's father was— only thirteen minutes to do the operation! Matron thought how lucky it was that he had been near enough to come.

Next morning dawned fair and bright. Darrell awoke

when the dressing-bell went, tired but happy again. She
lay and thought for half a minute. Her heart was full of
thankfulness. Sally would be all right. Her father had
said so. And he had said that Darrell hadn't had anything
to do with her illness. All her worry had been for nothing.
No—not quite for nothing. It had made a deep impression
on her. It wouldn't be nearly so difficult to keep her
temper next time. She had had a jolly good lesson!

' I wish I could do something to show I'm grateful and
thankful it's all turned out like this,' thought Darrell,
jumping out of bed. ' But there's nothing I can do. I
wonder how Sally is today.'

Sally was getting on very well indeed. When she heard
that her mother and father were coming to see her she
could hardly believe her ears.

' But is *Mother* coming ? ' she asked, time and again.
' Are you sure *Mother's* coming ? But she couldn't come
last Saturday. Is she really coming ? '

Miss Grayling received Mr. and Mrs. Hope in her big
drawing-room. Mr. Hope was a big burly man, looking
anxious. Mrs. Hope was a delicate-looking woman with
a sweet face.

' Sally is not quite ready for you to see her yet,' said
Miss Grayling. ' I am so glad to be able to tell you that
the operation was very successful and she is getting along
wonderfully well. Mr. Rivers, the surgeon, happened to
be at a hotel not far off, and we got him to do it. He is
the father of one of our girls here, Darrell Rivers.'

' Oh—Darrell Rivers,' said Mrs. Hope, and she took out
a letter from her bag. ' I had such a *queer* letter from her
today, Miss Grayling. Please read it. She appears to
think she was the cause of Sally's illness, but of course she
wasn't. But the other things she says are very worrying
to me. Could we have Darrell in to speak to us, before
I see Sally, do you think ? '

Miss Grayling read the letter and looked grave. 'There *is* something puzzling here,' she said. 'Why should Sally keep saying she has no sister, when she knows she has ?'

'I don't know,' said Mrs. Hope, sadly. 'But Sally has been queer ever since Baby Daphne came. She won't look at her or speak to her—and once, when she didn't know I was looking, I saw her pinch poor Daphne cruelly. And Sally is not a cruel child.'

'Have you any other children ?' asked Miss Grayling. Mrs. Hope shook her head.

'No,' she said. 'Sally was twelve when Daphne was born. She had been the only child for all that time. I thought she would be so pleased to have a sister. We haven't spoilt Sally, you know—but she didn't have to share us with anyone till Daphne came—and sometimes I wondered if she was—well—jealous.'

'Of course she was !' said Miss Grayling at once. 'I should think, Mrs. Hope, that Sally is very much attached to you, and resented sharing your love when the baby came. She probably didn't like to tell you so, in case you thought badly of her.'

'Oh, she never said a word to me !' said Mrs. Hope. 'She just changed, that's all. She wasn't merry and gay any more, she didn't come to us and love us as she used to do, and she seemed to hate the baby. I thought it would blow over. And then, when it didn't, I and my husband thought it would be best if Sally came to boarding school, because I wasn't very well at the time, and it was all I could do to look after the baby, without having to cope with Sally too. We did it for the best.'

'Yes, I see,' said Miss Grayling, thoughtfully. 'But, from Sally's point of view it must have seemed that you didn't want her any more, but had sent her away to make room for a baby who was taking up all your care and attention. Mrs. Hope, this jealousy of a much younger child is very common and very natural, and you mustn't blame Sally for it. Neither must you let it grow. If only you can make Sally feel you love her as much as ever you did it will be quite all right. Now—shall we have Darrell in ? '

Darrell was sent for. She came in nervously, scared of what Mrs. Hope might say. But she was soon put at her ease, and she told all she knew.

Miss Grayling turned to Mrs. Hope. ' I think it would be a good idea if we let Darrell go in to see Sally for a few minutes before you do,' she said. ' We will let her tell Sally that you have come—and we will let her say that you have left the baby behind in order to hurry as fast as possible to Sally. Will you do that, Darrell ? '

Darrell nodded. She had suddenly seen all Sally's trouble ! Why, she was jealous of her little baby sister ! So jealous that she wouldn't even admit she had got one. Poor, funny Sally. It was so lovely to have a sister. Sally didn't know how lucky she was !

' I'll tell her,' she said, eagerly. ' I'll do what I can too, when you've gone, to make Sally think it's fun to have a sister. I wanted to do *some*thing—and I shall love to do that ! '

18   DARRELL AND SALLY

DARRELL went to the San. upstairs. She had a little note with her for Matron from Miss Grayling. ' Please allow Darrell to see Sally for a few minutes before her mother comes.'

Matron, surprised and not very pleased, opened the door to let Darrell in. Darrell tiptoed in. It was a pleasant room, with three white beds in it, and a lovely view from

the big windows. Everything was creamy white and spot-
lessly clean. In the end bed lay Sally, white but bright-eyed.

' Hallo, Sally,' said Darrell. ' I've been so worried about
you. Are you better ? Did my father make you better ? '

' Yes. I do like him. He was so kind,' said Sally. ' I
did feel so awful all Saturday, Darrell. But I couldn't
tell anyone, could I ? I couldn't spoil the day.'

' I think you're very brave,' said Darrell. ' I say—guess
who's here to see you ? '

' Not my mother ? ' said Sally, her eyes shining. Darrell
nodded. ' Yes. And your father too. And do you know,
Sally, your mother has left behind your little baby sister,
so that she could come more quickly to see you ? Fancy
that ! She must think an awful lot of you, because usually
mothers can't bear to leave babies when they're small.'

Sally seemed to have forgotten that she had told Darrell
she had no sister. She reached out for Darrell's hand.
' Hasn't she brought Baby ? ' she whispered. ' Did she
leave her behind ? Really and truly ? '

' Yes, poor little thing,' said Darrell. ' She must be
feeling lonely ! I've got a little sister, too. It's lovely to
have a sister. Mine looks up to me no end and thinks
I'm wonderful. I expect yours will, too.'

Sally's ideas of sisters underwent a sudden change.
Things seemed suddenly to fall into their proper places.
She smiled gratefully at Darrell. ' You'll come and see
me when you can, won't you ? ' she said. ' And don't say
anything about—about—all my silliness, will you ? To the
others, I mean.'

' Of course not. It wasn't silliness. It was just a mistake on your part,' said Darrell. ' Why, anyone could
see by giving one look at your mother that she's a *proper*
mother—I mean the kind that would always love you,
however many children she had, or whatever you did. I
think she's a darling.'

'So do I,' said Sally, with a sigh. 'I'm sorry I was such a beast to you, Darrell.'

'And I can't tell you *how* sorry I am for having shoved you like that when you had such a pain in your tummy,' said Darrell.

'Did you shove me?' said Sally. 'I've forgotten. Look, what's Matron saying?'

Matron was beckoning for Darrell to come away. Mr. and Mrs. Hope were outside the door. Darrell said a hurried good-bye and tiptoed out. Mr. and Mrs. Hope went in, and Darrell heard Sally's low cry of joy as she saw her mother.

Darrell skipped happily down the stairs and through the hall into the Court. She ran to the building in which her own classroom was. The bell was just going for the ending of a lesson.

Darrell slipped into the first-form classroom. The girls looked up at her.

'Where *have* you been? You've been ages! You've missed half of maths., lucky pig.'

'I've been to see Sally,' said Darrell, importantly.

'Fibber! No one is allowed to see her yet,' said Irene.

'Well, I *have*. And she says my father has cured her pain and made her much better,' said Darrell, proud to have such a father. 'He came in the night. I saw him.'

'Darrell Rivers, you're making it all up,' said Alicia.

'No, honestly I'm not. It's all true,' said Darrell. 'I saw Mr. and Mrs. Hope too, and they're seeing Sally now. They are staying the night with Miss Grayling and going back tomorrow.'

'And has dear Sally found out yet whether she has a baby sister or not?' drawled Gwendoline.

Darrell felt a hot flame of temper rise up but she choked it down at once. 'That's no business of yours—and it's a pity *you* didn't have about six older sisters to sit on you hard and squash you flat,' said Darrell. 'You'd have been a bit nicer then. But probably only a bit.'

'Shhhhh! Mam'zelle coming!' hissed the girl at the door, and in came Mam'zelle, rather cross this morning because the third form had just proved extraordinarily stupid. Darrell didn't mind how cross Mam'zelle or Miss Potts were that day. She kept thinking of Sally's happiness. She wondered how she was getting on.

Sally and her mother and father were happy together. The curious wall that Sally had built up between herself and her mother had fallen away, because suddenly the jealousy was gone. Her mother had left the baby alone to come to *her*—and Sally was content. Not that she wanted Baby Daphne to be left with strangers—but it was a sign to her that her mother thought of her and loved her. Funny little Sally!

'We'll come and see you tomorrow before we go home,' said her mother, when Matron said it was time for Mr. and Mrs. Hope to go. 'And, if you *badly* want me to, I'll stay an extra day, and let Daddy go home without me.'

'No,' said Sally, with a sigh. 'Don't let's leave Baby too long! And I know Daddy would rather you went with him. I'm getting better already, Mother. I'll soon be well—and I shall feel quite different.'

Then Mrs. Hope knew for certain that Sally was her own, unselfish little girl again, and she was glad. What a good thing Darrell Rivers had written to her as she did! Now everything was all cleared up.

Darrell was allowed to go and see Sally twice a day, long before anyone else was. Sally welcomed her eagerly. Sally was so different now—no longer a prim, closed-up little person, but a friendly, eager girl, ready to talk about her home and her dogs and her garden, asking Darrell about the lessons and the games, if Mam'zelle was cross, and what Miss Potts said, and whether Gwendoline and Mary-Lou were still friends.

'You know, Sally,' said Darrell, 'when I felt so awfully frightened because I thought I'd injured you and might be sent away from here, I suddenly knew how it must feel to be like Mary-Lou—always scared of everything! And I was sorry I'd teased her so.'

'Let's be nice to Mary-Lou,' said Sally, who, with her strength returning to her, and with Darrell's friendly visits each day, felt that she could be nice even to Gwendoline! 'Tell her I'd like her to come and see me.'

Mary-Lou was overwhelmed by this message. Fancy Sally choosing *her* for one of her first visitors! Armed with a big bottle of barley-sugar she went to the San. Sally looked rather pale, but very different. Her eyes were bright, and she smiled. She welcomed Mary-Lou graciously.

They talked, and Mary-Lou blossomed a little. She was not afraid of Sally. She told her all sorts of things. Then she looked worried.

'You know, Sally, I do wish Gwendoline wouldn't keep saying horrid things about Darrell. She keeps trying to make me think that Darrell is playing nasty tricks on me. Or that Alicia is. My ink-pot was spilt yesterday all over my atlas, and Gwendoline says she's sure Darrell did it, because she saw that Darrell's fingers were all inky that day.'

'As if Darrell would do anything like *that*!' said Sally, indignantly. 'How *can* you listen to Gwendoline when she says things like that?'

'I can't stop her,' said Mary-Lou, the scared look coming into her face again. 'You see, she will keep saying that I'm her friend, and she can tell me anything.'

'*Are* you her friend?' demanded Sally.

'No. Not really. But I don't like telling her I don't want to be,' said Mary-Lou. 'Don't call me a coward. I know I am. But I can't help it.'

'Time to go, Mary-Lou,' said Matron, coming in.
'Tell Darrell she can come in half an hour's time, and
bring a simple game with her—Happy Families or something. Not Snap.'

So Darrell came, armed with Happy Families. But the
two girls didn't get beyond dealing out the cards. They
talked about Mary-Lou and Gwendoline.

'Gwendoline's poisonous,' said Sally. 'She's always
talking against you and Alicia, making out you play those
rotten tricks on Mary-Lou.'

'I wonder who does them ?' said Darrell. 'One of the
other Tower girls, do you think ? What about Evelyn
from West Tower ? She's always doing silly, teasing tricks.'

'No. I should think it might be Gwendoline herself !'
said Sally, looking at the cards in her hand.

Darrell stared at her in surprise. 'Oh, *no*,' she said.
'Why, Gwendoline and Mary-Lou are *friends*.'

'So Gwendoline says. But Mary-Lou says different,'
said Sally.

'Yes, but—*no* one could be so awful as to pretend to
be friends with someone and then to play rotten tricks on
them all the time !' said Darrell. 'It would be a disgusting
thing to do.'

'I think Gwendoline *is* disgusting !' said Sally. 'I
never could bear her. A real double-faced person, who
doesn't care tuppence for anyone in the world but herself.'

Darrell looked at Sally. 'I think you're very clever,'
she said. 'You seem to know all about people—much
more than I do. I'm sure you know more about Mary-
Lou than I do, already.'

'I like Mary-Lou,' said Sally. 'If only we could get
her to be not so scared of everything, she'd be fun.'

'But how can we ?' said Darrell, shuffling all the cards
together absent-mindedly. 'Oh, dear—look what I've done.
Never mind, it's more interesting to talk than play cards

just now. How *can* we cure Mary-Lou ? I've tried to
buck her up and make her ashamed of herself, but it doesn't
seem to do any good.'

' Can't you see that she *is* ashamed of herself already ? '
said Sally, unexpectedly. ' But being ashamed doesn't
give her any courage. Nobody can give her pluck except
her own self.'

' Well—think of a way to make her give herself pluck ! '
said Darrell. ' I bet you can't ! '

' I'll think tonight, before I go to sleep,' said Sally.
' And when you come and see me in the morning, I'll have
a plan—you see if I haven't ! '

19   SALLY'S PLAN

DARRELL went to see Sally at Break as usual the next
morning. Sally greeted her eagerly. ' Well, I've thought
of something ! It's not a *fright*fully good plan, but it will
do as a beginning.'

' What is it ? ' asked Darrell, thinking how pretty the
plain little Sally looked that morning, with colour in her
cheeks, and twinkles in her eyes.

' Well, listen. What about you pretending to be in
difficulties in the pool, when you get the chance, and yelling out to Mary-Lou to run and get the life-belt quickly
and throw it to you ? ' said Sally. ' If she does that, and
feels that she has saved you from going under, she'll be
awfully bucked. We all know how to chuck the belt into
the water. It would be quite easy for her to do.'

' Yes. It's a good idea,' said Darrell. ' I might try it
out tomorrow. I'll give the tip to the others not to throw
it to me, but to let Mary-Lou. At least, I'll tell the people

I can trust—not dear Gwendoline, for instance! Do you really think it will help Mary-Lou not to be so scared of things if she does that?'

'Well, it seems to me that Mary-Lou will never be able to face up to things unless she thinks she's got a bit of good sense and courage in her to start with!' said Sally, seriously. 'You can't possibly do anything if you *think* you can't. But you can do impossible things sometimes if you think you *can*.'

'How do you know things like that?' asked Darrell, in admiration. 'I wish *I* did!'

'Oh, it's not very difficult really,' said Sally. 'All you do is put yourself into the place of the other person, and feel like them, and then think how you could cure yourself if you were them. That sounds muddled—but I can't very well say exactly what I mean. I haven't the words.'

'Oh, I know what you mean, all right!' said Darrell. 'You do what Mother is always telling *me* to do—get into somebody else's skin, and feel what *they're* feeling. But I'm too impatient to do that. I'm too tightly in my *own* skin! You're not. I think you're clever and kind, Sally.'

Sally went red and looked pleased. She also looked rather shy. 'I'm not clever—and you know I'm not kind, by the way I behaved to Daphne,' she said. 'But it's nice that you think so, anyway! Do you think you can work the idea out all right, Darrell?'

'Oh, yes, I think so,' said Darrell. 'I'll try it tomorrow, when we're in the pool. Mary-Lou has got a bit of a cold and isn't allowed to bathe this week, so she'll be watching by the side. She can easily go and get the life-belt and fling it to me. Won't she be bucked!'

'I guess she's glad she's got a cold this week,' said Sally, with a chuckle. 'She does so hate the water! I bet she'll never learn to swim.'

'It was funny when Matron said Mary-Lou had a cold and wasn't to go in the water,' said Darrell, 'because dear

Gwendoline immediately began to sniff like anything in class, hoping Miss Potts would report it to Matron, and *she* would be told too that she mustn't bathe. She's even worse than Mary-Lou at getting into the water!'

'What happened?' asked Sally, with interest. 'Oh, I do wish I was back in school. I'd die of boredom if I hadn't got you to come and tell me things.'

'Well, Miss Potts got angry with Gwendoline's sniffs and sat on her properly,' said Darrell. 'And then Gwendoline said she was sure she had caught Mary-Lou's cold, so Miss Potts sent her to Matron—and Matron gave her a large dose of awful medicine, and was most unsympathetic—and she didn't say Gwendoline wasn't to go into the water, she said the salt in it would probably do her good. And I heard her tell Miss Potts that the only way to take Gwendoline's tales was with a pinch of salt, so she might as well swallow some in the pool!'

Sally laughed heartily. She could just picture Gwendoline's anger at having medicine for no real reason, and not getting her way after all. Darrell got up.

'There's the bell,' she said. 'I'll come back after lunch and tell you all the tit-bits. I haven't told you yet how Alicia and Betty tied thread to a pile of Mam'zelle's books on her desk, and Alicia pulled the thread and jerked off the books under Mam'zelle's very nose! I thought Irene would die of laughing. You know how she explodes.'

'Oh, yes, do come back and tell me everything,' said Sally, who looked forward to Darrell's visits more than to anything else. 'I do love hearing you talk.'

It was strange how completely different Sally seemed now. When Darrell looked back and remembered the quiet, self-contained, serious person Sally Hope had always appeared, it seemed impossible that she had turned into the laughing, eager, twinkling-eyed girl in the bed—a sensible, kindly girl with a real sense of fun.

'She's not such good fun as Alicia, of course,' said Darrell to herself, 'but she's more *trust*able, somehow. And she isn't as sharp-tongued, though she's just as clever in what she thinks about people.'

Darrell carefully thought out the plan for tricking Mary-Lou into sudden good sense and a bit of pluck. It should be quite easy. She would tell Alicia and Betty to take the others to the other end of the pool, so that she, Darrell, would be alone in the deep end. Then she would struggle and yell and pretend she had cramp.

'I'll yell out to Mary-Lou and shout, "Quick, quick, throw me the life-belt!",' she thought. 'Then surely Mary-Lou will do that, and I'll clutch it and pant and puff, and call out, "Oh, Mary-Lou, you've saved my life!" And if after that Mary-Lou doesn't have a better opinion of herself, it'll be queer. Once she knows she can really do something like that, maybe she'll pull herself together and be able to face up to some of the silly things that scare her!'

It really did seem a very good plan. Darrell let Alicia and Betty into the secret. 'It's really Sally's idea,' said Darrell. 'It's a very good one, don't you think so?'

'Well—why ever should you want to bother yourselves with that silly little baby of a Mary-Lou?' said Alicia in surprise. 'You'll never make her any better. She's hopeless.'

'But we *might* make her better,' argued Darrell, rather disappointed with the way that Alicia took the idea.

'Not much chance,' said Alicia. 'I expect what *will* happen is that Mary-Lou will be too scared stiff to do a thing, and will simply stand blubbing by the pool and let somebody else run for the life-belt. And that will make her worse than ever, because everyone will despise her.'

'Oh,' said Darrell, feeling damped. 'That would be sickening. Oh, Alicia, I didn't think of that.'

Darrell told Sally what Alicia had said. 'I quite see what she means,' she said. 'And it might make Mary-Lou worse instead of better, because everyone would laugh at her. You see, Alicia is awfully smart, Sally—we never thought of that, did we?'

'Yes. Alicia *is* very smart,' said Sally, slowly. 'But sometimes she's a bit *too* smart, Darrell. She's forgotten something important.'

'What's that?' asked Darrell.

'She's forgotten that it's *you* who are going to struggle and yell for help,' said Sally. 'Everyone knows that Mary-Lou thinks you're wonderful and would do anything in the world for you—if you'd let her. Well, here is something she *can* do—and *will* do! You see if I'm not right. Give Mary-Lou a chance, Darrell. Alicia sees her as a weak little cry-baby. But she could be something more than that, for the sake of someone she loved.'

'All right, Sally. I'll give her a chance,' said Darrell. 'But I can't help thinking Alicia is right. She really is smart, you know, and can always size people up. I wish she wasn't friends with Betty. I wish she was *my* friend!'

Sally didn't say any more. She played dominoes with Darrell and was rather quiet. Matron came and shooed Darrell away soon after that, and she had to go off to her prep.

'I'm going to try out Sally's idea on Mary-Lou,' she told Alicia. 'So you and Betty will take the others off to the shallow end, won't you, when you see Mary-Lou standing by the deep end? Then I'll yell out, and we'll see if Mary-Lou has the nerve to throw me the belt. It's not much to do!'

'It'll be too much for *her*,' said Alicia, rather annoyed that Darrell should still think of going on with the idea after she had poured cold water on it. 'Still, we'll see.'

So, the next afternoon the plan was carried out. The

first-formers went chattering down to the pool in their bathing costumes and beach-gowns. Gwendoline went too, looking sulky because the form had teased her unmercifully about her pretended cold !

Mary-Lou had not changed into her bathing-things, and was pleased. She did so hate the water ! Darrell called to her. 'You can throw pennies in for me, Mary-Lou, and watch me dive for them in the deep end ! '

'All right,' said Mary-Lou, pleased, and put some pennies into her pocket. Her cold was almost better. What a pity ! She had so much enjoyed not having to bathe !

Into the water plunged the girls. Some jumped in, some dived in. Only Gwendoline went cautiously down the steps. But even she went in quickly for once, because somebody gave her a push and down she went, spluttering and gasping. And when she arose, angry and indignant, not a single girl was near her, of course, so she had no idea at all who had pushed her. Darrell or Alicia she supposed. Beasts !

Mary-Lou was at the deep end, watching the others. At least, she watched Darrell mostly, admiring the way she swam, cutting the water so cleanly with her strong brown arms, and thrusting through the waves like a small torpedo. Mary-Lou put her hands into her pocket and felt the pennies there. It was nice of Darrell to ask her to throw them in for her. It was always nice to do anything for Darrell, even if it was only a little thing.

'Come down to the other end and let's have a race ! ' cried Alicia suddenly. 'Come on, everyone.'

'I'll just stay here for a bit and dive for pennies ! ' yelled Darrell. 'I'm puffed for racing. I'll get out of your way when you start. Hi , Mary-Lou, have you got the pennies ? '

Alicia and Betty, who were the only girls in the plan, watched what would happen. Both girls felt certain that

Mary-Lou would weep and remain rooted to the rocks when Darrell called out. She wouldn't have the nerve to rush for the life-belt!

The other girls were splashing about, getting into position for the race. Mary-Lou threw a penny into the water and Darrell dived for it.

She brought it up in triumph. 'Throw another, Mary-Lou!' she cried. Splash! In went another penny. Darrell dived again, thinking that now was the time to pretend to be in difficulties. She came up, gasping.

'Help! Help!' she cried. 'I've got cramp! Quick, Mary-Lou, the life-belt, the life-belt! Help, help!'

She threw her arms about and struggled, letting herself sink under a little. Mary-Lou stared, absolutely petrified. Alicia nudged Betty.

'Just what I thought,' she said in a low voice. 'Too much of a ninny even to get the life-belt!'

'HELP!' yelled Darrell, and two or three of the other girls, thinking she was really in trouble, swam strongly up the pool.

But somebody else reached Darrell first! There was a resounding splash, and into the water, fully dressed, jumped the scared Mary-Lou, doing her best to remember the few swimming strokes she knew. She managed to reach Darrell, and put out her arms to her, to try and save her.

Darrell, popping her head out of the water for the second time, was filled with the utmost amazement to see Mary-Lou's wet head bobbing beside her! She stared as if she couldn't believe her eyes.

'Hold on to me, Darrell, hold on to me!' panted Mary-Lou. 'I'll save you.'

THEN up came the other two or three swimmers and called out sharply. 'What's up, Darrell ? Get out of the way, Mary-Lou.'

But Mary-Lou couldn't. She had made her great effort, jumped into the water and swum a few strokes—but now her strength was gone and her clothes were weighing her down. One of the swimmers took her safely to the side, where she clutched a bar, panting, looking anxiously over her shoulder to see if Darrell was safe.

She had apparently quite recovered from the cramp, for she was swimming over to Mary-Lou with strong, quick strokes, her eyes gleaming.

'Mary-Lou ! You jumped right into the water, and you hardly knew how to swim ! You're an idiot, but you're the pluckiest idiot ever I knew ! ' cried Darrell.

Somebody helped the shivering, astonished Mary-Lou out of the pool. Miss Potts came down the cliff at that moment and was amazed to see a fully-dressed and soaking Mary-Lou scrambling out, with girls crowding round her, clapping her on the shoulder and praising her.

'What's happened ? ' said Miss Potts, in wonder. 'Did Mary-Lou fall in ? '

Eager voices told her what had happened. 'She jumped in to save Darrell ! Darrell had the cramp and yelled for the life-belt. But Mary-Lou jumped straight in to save her—and she can hardly swim ! '

Miss Potts was as astonished as everyone else. *Mary-Lou !* But Mary-Lou screamed if she saw an earwig ! What an amazing thing.

'Why didn't she throw the life-belt ? ' asked Alicia.

'It w-w-w-wasn't there,' answered Mary-Lou, her teeth

Somebody helped the shivering Mary-Lou out of the pool

chattering partly from cold and partly from excitement and shock. 'It's g-g-g-gone to be m-m-m-mended. Didn't you know ? '

No. Nobody had noticed that it was gone from its place. So Mary-Lou had not been stupid. She had known the life-belt was not there to save Darrell, and she had done the next best thing—jumped in herself. Well, who would have thought it ?

Miss Potts hurried the shivering Mary-Lou up the cliff. Darrell turned to face Alicia, her eyes shining.

'Well—who was right ? Sally or you ? Why, Mary-Lou was *brave*. It isn't as if she liked the water or even knew how to swim properly ! She was as brave, no, braver than any of us, because she must have been so afraid ! '

Alicia could be generous even when she was proved to be in the wrong. She nodded. 'Yes. She was jolly brave. I never thought she had it in her. But I bet she wouldn't have done it for anyone else but *you* ! '

Darrell could hardly wait to tell Sally. She rushed to her after tea, her face glowing. 'Sally ! Your idea was *mar*vellous ! Simply wizard. Do you know, there wasn't a life-belt there this afternoon, so Mary-Lou jumped straight into the water with all her clothes on and everything, to try and save me ! '

'Gosh ! ' said Sally, and her face too began to glow. 'I never thought of *that*—did you ? Darrell, that's marvellous. You'll be able to tackle Mary-Lou properly now.'

'What do you mean ? ' asked Darrell.

'Well—tell her how brave she is, and how no one ever guessed it, and now she knows it herself she'll be able to be brave about lots of other things,' said Sally. 'Easy ! Once you can make anyone believe in themselves, they're all right.'

'You *are* a funny, wise person,' said Darrell, admiringly. 'I never think of things like that. All right. I'll do my best, and when Mary-Lou comes to see you, you tell her a few things, too ! '

So Mary-Lou, to her enormous surprise and delight, became the heroine of the hour, for soon it had gone all up and down the school how she had jumped into the pool, fully-dressed, to try and save Darrell.

' It's no good you shrinking away into a corner any more, or screaming yourself blue in the face because you've seen a spider ! ' said Darrell. ' Now we know how brave you are, we shall expect to see a bit more of your bravery ! '

' Oh, *yes*,' said Mary-Lou, beaming. ' I'll try. Now I know I can be brave, it's different. It's when you know you can't be, that things are awful. I never, never in my life thought I would dare to jump into the deep end like that—and yet I did ! I never even thought about it. I just did it. It wasn't really brave, you know, because I didn't have to screw up my courage or anything.'

The only person who had no word of praise for Mary-Lou was Gwendoline. For one thing she was really jealous of all the fuss made of Mary-Lou. Even the teachers made quite a to-do about it, for one and all realized that this was their one chance of making Mary-Lou realize that she *could* do things if she wanted to. Gwendoline hated all the fuss—especially as it was *Darrell* that Mary-Lou had jumped in to save.

' Fancy anyone wanting to do *her* a good turn ! ' she thought, remembering the hard slaps she had once had from the angry girl. ' I'd have left her to struggle. Stupid Mary-Lou ! I suppose she will get all conceited now.'

But Mary-Lou didn't. She remained her own rather shy, quiet self, but now she had more confidence, and stood up for herself better. She had been proved and had not been found wanting. She was pleased and proud, though she did not show it, as a girl like Gwendoline would have done.

For one thing she stood up to Gwendoline better, and

this annoyed and exasperated Gwendoline intensely. And
when Sally came back into school again, as she did in two
weeks' time, she too seemed changed, and would stand no
nonsense from Gwendoline. She stood up for Mary-Lou,
and ticked Gwendoline off in a way that irritated her and
made her long to snap at Sally.

The term went on, more and more quickly now. Only
three more weeks till the holidays! Darrell could hardly
believe the time had flown by so quickly.

She was working much better now, and twice she had
been fifth from the top in her weekly marks. Gwendoline
was the only one steadily at the bottom. Even Mary-Lou
had crept up a place or two. Darrell wondered how
Gwendoline was going to persuade her parents that she
was top in everything at the end of the term, when she took
home her report. Because her report would certainly show
up Gwendoline's appalling work.

Darrell spoke to her one day about it. 'Gwendoline,
what will your mother and father say when they see on your
report how badly you've done in your form work?' she
asked, curiously.

Gwendoline looked very startled. 'What do you mean
—my report?' she asked.

'Golly, don't you know what reports are?' asked Darrell,
in surprise. 'Look, I'll show you an old one of mine.
I've got my last one here, from my old school. I had to
bring it with me to show Miss Potts.'

She showed the report to Gwendoline who stared at it in
the utmost horror. What! A list of all the subjects taken,
with their marks, and position in form, and comments on
the work done! Gwendoline could quite well imagine some
of the comments that would be on hers!

'French. Very backward and lazy.

'Maths. Does not try in the least. Could do with some
coaching in the holidays.

'Games. Disgraceful. Has no sense of sportsmanship or team-work at all.'

And so on. Poor Gwendoline. It really had never occurred to her for one single moment that her bad and lazy work would be reported in this fashion to her parents. She sank down in a chair and stared at Darrell.

'But Gwendoline, did you *never* have a report on your work before?' asked Darrell, in surprise.

'No,' said the crest-fallen Gwendoline. 'Never. I told you I had never been to school before I came here. Only my governess, Miss Winter, taught me—and she never made out reports, of course. She just told Mother how well I was getting on, and Mother believed her. I didn't know I was so backward till I came here.'

'Well, I should think your parents will get a terrific shock when they see your report!' said Darrell, heartlessly. 'I should think it will be the worst one in the school. You'll be sorry you told so many fibs to your mother and Miss Winter at half-term, when you take your report home for the holidays!'

'I shall tear it up!' said Gwendoline, fiercely, feeling that she wouldn't be able to bear the astonishment, dismay and anger of her parents when they saw her report.

'You can't,' said Darrell. 'It goes by post. Ha ha! I'm jolly glad you'll be shown up at home. Mary-Lou told me some of the idiotic things you told your mother and Miss Winter at half-term. Fancy boasting like that, when you've no more brains than a mouse, and what you have you don't use!'

Gwendoline was speechless. How *dare* Darrell speak to her like that? And HOW DARE Mary-Lou repeat to the others the things she had overheard her say to her mother at half-term? Nasty, sly, disgusting little meanie! She would jolly well pay her out. She would take her fountain-pen and stamp on it! She would—she would . . . Oh, there was no end to the things she would do to that beastly, ungrateful Mary-Lou!

' After I've been friends with her, too!' thought Gwendoline, angrily. 'There's disloyalty for you! I hate her.'

Then she began to think about her report. She felt afraid when she thought of her father reading it. That was why he had sent her away to school—because he had said she was lazy and vain and too pleased with herself. He had said some horrid things. Gwendoline tried to forget them, but they came back into her mind at odd times.

She could tell what untruths she pleased, she could boast all she liked—but if in her report there were the words ' lazy, unreliable, irresponsible, conceited, stupid '—words she knew she richly deserved—well, her boasts and fibs would all be wasted.

' Only two or three weeks more,' thought Gwendoline, frantically. ' Can I possibly make my report any better in those few weeks? I shall *have* to try! *Why* didn't I know there were school reports before? I could have worked a bit harder. Now I shall simply have to SLAVE!'

And, to the intense astonishment of Miss Potts, and the no less intense surprise of Mam'zelle, Gwendoline began to work! How she worked! She pored over her books. She wrote endless compositions and then rewrote them in her best writing. She was the most attentive one in the class.

' *What* has happened to Gwendoline?' asked Miss Potts of Mam'zelle. ' I begin to believe she has a few—just a few—brains at last!'

' I too,' said Mam'zelle. ' See this French exercise? Only one mistake! Never has this happened before to Gwendoline. She is turning over a new stalk.'

' New *leaf*, you mean,' said Miss Potts. ' Well, well, surprising things happen. There's Darrell working much better too—and Sally Hope quite a new child. And Mary-

Lou has blossomed out tremendously since she jumped into the pool.   But, Gwendoline is really the most surprising one.   She wrote me quite a passable composition yesterday, with only six spelling mistakes.   Usually she makes at least twenty.   I shall be able to put " *Can* use her brains " on her report, instead of " *Never* uses her brains ! " '

Gwendoline did not enjoy working so hard.   Darrell laughed at her, and told the others why there was such a sudden change in the lazy Gwendoline.

' She doesn't want her people to know she told such fibs to them at half-term,' she said.   ' Does she, Mary-Lou ? That's what comes of boasting, Gwendoline.   Sooner or later you have to eat your words.'

Mary-Lou laughed too.   She was much bolder nowadays, though only when Darrell or Sally were there.   Gwendoline scowled at her.   Horrid little turn-coat !

Gwendoline had her chance of paying Mary-Lou out the next day.   She went into the common room when there was no one else there—and in Mary-Lou's locker was her precious fountain-pen !   Gwendoline saw it at once.

' That's the end of *that* ! ' she said, spitefully, and threw it on the floor.   She stamped on it hard, and the pen smashed, spilling ink all over the wooden floor !

21   A SHOCK FOR DARRELL

IT was Jean who saw the smashed pen first.   She came into the common room to get a book, and stopped short when she saw the ink on the floor, and the bits and pieces of the blue pen.

' Golly ! ' said Jean.   ' Who's done that ?   What a mean trick ! '

Emily and Katherine came in. Jean pointed to the pen.
'Look,' she said. 'There's a nice little bit of spite for you.'

'It's Mary-Lou's pen,' said Katherine, in distress.
'What a mess. Who *could* have smashed it? It's not an
accident.'

Mary-Lou came in with the quiet Violet. When she
saw her pen, she stood and wailed aloud. 'Oh! Who's
done that? I had it for my birthday from Mother. And
now it's all smashed!'

All the girls gathered round. Darrell and Sally and
Irene were astonished to see such a silent circle when they
came chattering in. They joined it, and were not surprised
when Mary-Lou's wails broke out again.

'What will Mother say? She told me to take great care
of it if I took it to school.'

Alicia came whistling in, and she too was amazed to see
the smashed pen, surrounded by its pool of deep violet ink.
What a hateful thing to do to anyone!

'Who did it?' she demanded. 'It ought to be reported
to Potty. I bet it's Gwendoline—spiteful little beast.'

'Where *is* Gwendoline?' asked Katherine. Nobody
knew. Actually she was just outside the door, about to come
in and pretend to be surprised and disgusted at the broken
pen too. But, hearing the angry voices of the girls, her
heart failed her. She stood hesitating and listening.

'Look here,' said Alicia, 'there's one certain way we can
find out who did this—and we will too.'

'What's that?' asked Katherine.

'Well, whoever stamped on this pen and smashed it must
have got violet ink on the underneath of their shoes,' said
Alicia grimly.

'Oh, yes,' said the others. 'Of course!'

'That's clever of you, Alicia,' said Katherine. 'We'll
examine every pair of shoes in our North Tower lockers—
and when we see violet ink we shall know who did this.'

' I know without looking ! ' said Darrell's scornful voice.
' Nobody could have done it but Gwendoline.   There's no
one mean or spiteful enough but her ! '

Gwendoline trembled with rage and fright.   She took a
hasty look at the underneath of her out-door shoes.   Yes,
they were stained with violet ink.   Hastily she ran down the
passage, ran into the little store-room, took up a bottle of
violet ink, and raced to the cloakroom where the shoe-
lockers were.   If only she got there in time !

She did, because the others were busy clearing up the
mess before going to examine the shoes.   Gwendoline
smeared some of the violet ink on to the under-sides of one
of Darrell's shoes, then threw the bottle into a nearby cupboard.   Then she hastily took off her own stained shoes,
and stuffed them into the cupboard too.   She pulled on a
pair of slippers.

She ran out into the Court, and re-appeared at the
door of the common room, apparently quite calm and
unruffled.   Oh, Gwendoline could act very well when it
suited her !

' Here's Gwendoline ! ' cried Alicia.   ' Gwendoline, do
you know anything about Mary-Lou's pen ? '

' Pen ?   What about her pen ? ' asked Gwendoline,
innocently.

' Someone's jumped on it and smashed it,' said Sally.

' What a *beastly* thing to do ! ' said Gwendoline, putting
on a disgusted face.   ' Who did it ? '

' That's what *we* want to know,' said Darrell, feeling
infuriated with Gwendoline's smug expression.   ' And
we're going to find out, see ! '

' I hope you will,' said Gwendoline.   ' Don't glare at
me like that, Darrell.   *I* haven't done it !   Much more
likely *you* have !   I've noticed you've been jealous ever
since so much fuss was made of Mary-Lou for jumping into
the pool to rescue you ! '

Everyone gasped. How could Gwendoline have the cheek to say a thing like that? Darrell began to boil. She felt the familiar red-hot flame rising up in her. Sally saw her face and put her hand on her arm.

'Go slow, old thing,' she said, gently, and Darrell simmered down. But she almost choked in the effort not to rage back at the smiling Gwendoline.

'Gwendoline,' said Katherine, keeping her eyes on the girl's face, 'we think that whoever stamped on this pen must have violet ink on her shoes. So we mean to examine everyone's shoes, and we are sure we shall find the culprit in that way.'

Gwendoline did not change her expression at all. 'That's a very good idea!' she said, warmly. 'A very good idea indeed. I wish I'd thought of it myself. It certainly *will* tell us who the hateful person is that smashed up poor Mary-Lou's pen.'

Everyone was astonished to hear these words. A little doubt crept into the minds of the girls. Would Gwendoline be so pleased with the idea if she *had* smashed the pen? Perhaps she didn't do it after all?

'You can look at my shoes first of all, if you like,' said Gwendoline, and she turned up first one foot and then another. There was no smear of ink on them, of course.

'We shall have to examine the shoes in the lockers too,' said Katherine. 'But first, will everyone please turn up their feet for us to see?'

Everyone did, but no one had inky marks. Then, in a solemn group, the first-formers set off for the cloakroom in which their shoe-lockers were kept.

Gwendoline's shoes were examined first, because Katherine, like the rest, felt that her shoes were more likely to be marked with ink than anyone else's. But they were not.

It was one of Darrell's shoes that was smeared with the

bright-coloured ink ! Katherine pulled it out, and then stared at it in the greatest amazement and horror. She held it out in silence to Darrell.

'It's—it's *your* shoe ! ' she said. ' Oh, Darrell ! '

Darrell stared at the inky shoe speechlessly. She looked round at the silent girls beside her. Some of them turned away their eyes. Alicia met hers with a hard look.

' Well, well, who would have guessed it was our straight-forward Darrell ? ' said Alicia, flippantly. ' I wouldn't have thought it of you, Darrell.'

She turned away with a look of disgust. Darrell caught hold of her arm.

' Alicia ! You surely don't think *I* smashed the pen ! I didn't, I tell you, I didn't ! I would never dream of doing such a hateful thing. Oh, Alicia—how *could* you think I'd do it ? '

' Well—you can't deny your shoe is inky,' said Alicia. ' You've got a dreadful temper, Darrell, and I've no doubt that in a fit of spite you stamped on Mary-Lou's pen. Don't ask me why ! I haven't a temper like yours.'

' But Alicia—I'm not spiteful ! ' cried Darrell. ' You know I'm not. Alicia, I thought you were my friend ! You and Betty always let me come with you. · You can't believe a thing like this about a friend of yours.'

' You're no friend of mine,' said Alicia, and swung out of the room. ·

' There's some mistake ! ' said Darrell, wildly. ' Oh, *don't* believe I did it, please, don't believe it ! '

' *I* don't believe you did it ! ' said Mary-Lou, with tears running down her cheeks. She slipped her arm through Darrell's. ' I know you didn't. I'll stick by you, Darrell ! '

' And so will I, of course,' said Sally's soft voice. ' I can't believe you did it, Darrell, either.'

Darrell was so glad to have two friends out of the stony-eyed girls around that she could almost have wept. Sally took her out of the cloakroom. Katherine looked round at the others. Her face was puzzled and dismayed.

' I can't believe it's Darrell either,' she said. ' But—I suppose—until it's proved differently we'll have to think of her as the culprit. It's a pity, because we've all liked Darrell.'

' I never did,' said Gwendoline's malicious voice. ' I always thought she was capable of any mean trick, with that temper of hers.'

' Shut up,' said Jean, roughly, and Gwendoline shut up, well satisfied with what she had said and done.

Sally and Mary-Lou were good friends to Darrell then. They stuck by her, helped her, and stoutly defended her. Mary-Lou was openly defiant to Gwendoline. But it was all very unpleasant, and though no one had suggested a punishment for the smashing of the pen, it was punishment enough to have cool looks and cold voices always around.

Mary-Lou was very worried about the matter. It was all because of *her* pen that Darrell had got into this trouble. But she knew that it couldn't be Darrell. Like Sally, she had great faith in Darrell's natural honesty and kindness, and she was certain she could never do a mean trick to any one.

Well, then, who could have done it ? It must have been someone with a spite against both Mary-Lou and Darrell, and that person must be Gwendoline. Therefore, Gwendoline must have smeared Darrell's shoes with the ink !

But it also followed that Gwendoline's own shoes must have been inky too—and yet, when she showed them to the girls, they had been quite free from ink.

Mary-Lou lay in bed one night and frowned over the problem. How could it have been done ? Was Gwendoline there when they had planned to examine the shoes ? No, she wasn't.

But she might have been listening outside! And she would have had time to rush to the shoe-lockers, smear Darrell's shoes with ink, and take off her own, before sauntering back to the common room and joining in the conversation!

Mary-Lou sat up in excitement. She was suddenly sure that that was what had happened. She began to shake a little, as she always did when she was frightened or excited. Where could Gwendoline have hidden her shoes? Somewhere near the shoe-lockers, anyway. Would she have taken them away and hidden them in a safer place? Or might they still be there?

It was very late and very dark. Everyone had gone to bed long ago. Mary-Lou wondered if she dared to go down to the cloakroom and have a look round. She so badly wanted this hateful affair to be cleared up.

But she was so afraid of the dark! Still, she had been afraid of the water too, till she had jumped in to save Darrell. Perhaps she wouldn't be afraid of the dark either, if it was to help Darrell. She would try and see.

Mary-Lou crept out of bed. She didn't put on a dressing-gown. She simply didn't think of it. She crept down the room and out of the door. Thank goodness there was a dim light shining in the passage!

Down the passage she went, to the stairs, and down the stairs to the rooms below. She made her way to the cloak-rooms. Oh, dear, they were in pitch-darkness. Mary-Lou felt a cold shiver creeping down her back. She was frightened. In a moment she would scream. She knew she would!

'This is for Darrell! I'm doing something for somebody else and it's very important,' she said to herself, as firmly as she could. 'I shan't scream. But oh, *where's* the switch?'

She found it and pressed it down. At once the light

Mary-Lou crept down the stairs

came on and the cloakroom could be seen clearly. Mary-
Lou drew a deep breath. Now it was all right. She
wasn't in the dark any more. She felt very proud of herself for not screaming when she had so badly wanted to.

She looked at the lockers. That was Gwendoline's
over there. She went to it and took out all the shoes.
No—not one was inky. Now—where could the inky ones
be hidden ?

22   THE END OF THE TERM

MARY-LOU caught sight of the little cupboard nearby.
She knew what was kept there. Old balls, an old racket or
two, split gym shoes and all kinds of rubbish. Gwendoline's
shoes *might* be there ! She opened the cupboard door
cautiously, afraid that a spider or earwig might come out.

She peered into the dusty rubbish, and poked it about
with her finger. She pulled at an old racket—and something fell with a thud.

Mary-Lou wondered if the noise had awakened anyone
and she held her breath, shaking. But no one seemed to
have heard. She began to poke about again.

She found Gwendoline's shoes ! She found the bottle
of violet ink ! That was what had fallen down with a thud !
Mary-Lou looked at the bottle, and knew what Gwendoline
had used it for. She looked at the shoes—and there, on
the right-hand one was a broad violet mark !

With trembling hands Mary-Lou looked at the name
inside the shoe again, just to make sure. Yes—there was
the name, written in Miss Winter's small printing—Gwendoline Lacey.

'So it *was* Gwendoline ! It *was* ! I knew it wasn't

Darrell!' thought Mary-Lou, joyfully. 'I'll go straight back and wake the others. I'll tell them at once. Well— no, I won't. Perhaps Katherine would be cross if she knew I'd gone snooping round at night.'

Mary-Lou took the bottle of ink, and the shoes. She clicked off the light and stood in darkness. But did she mind? Not a bit. She didn't once think of the black darkness as she sped upstairs. Her mind was full of her grand discovery. Darrell hadn't done it! Darrell hadn't done it!

Mary-Lou was awake first in the morning. She went to Katherine's bed and shook the surprised head-girl. 'Wake up! I've something important to tell you! Wake all the others.'

The others awoke when they heard the disturbance, and sat up in bed, rubbing their eyes. Mary-Lou stood in front of the beds, and waved Gwendoline's shoes dramatically.

'Look! I've found the *real* inky shoes! And I've found with them a bottle of violet ink! See? The person who really smashed my pen hid her own shoes and smeared Darrell's with this ink to make it seem as if *she'd* done it!'

'But *whose* shoes are they?' asked Katherine, in amazement. 'And where did you get them?'

'I crept downstairs in the dark last night, and hunted in the cloakroom,' said Mary-Lou triumphantly. Everyone gaped in surprise. Mary-Lou creeping down in the dark! Why, she was terrified of the dark, everyone knew that!

'I found the shoes and the bottle in the cupboard there,' said Mary-Lou. 'And shall I tell you the name written inside? No, I won't. Have a look round the room, all of you—and you'll see whose name is written in these shoes—you can tell by her face!'

It was true. Gwendoline's face was red with shame and horror. She stared at Mary-Lou in misery and anger. So she had been found out after all! *Why* hadn't she taken those shoes and the bottle and thrown them into the sea!

'It's Gwendoline!' said the girls, in hushed voices, staring at the red-faced girl in disgust and horror. And this time Gwendoline did not attempt to deny anything. She lay down in bed with her face hidden in the pillow.

Katherine examined the shoes and the bottle. Then she walked up to Darrell's bed and held out her hand.

'Darrell, I apologize to you for thinking for one moment it was you. I didn't really—but there seemed nothing else to think. I do beg your pardon.'

'Oh—it's all right,' said Darrell, her face radiant. 'It's quite all right! I have felt pretty awful—but I did have Mary-Lou and Sally sticking up for me. Gwendoline won't have anyone!'

One by one the girls begged Darrell's pardon. Alicia was a little stiff about it, for she felt really ashamed of the hard words she had said. But then, Alicia *was* hard. She had a good many lessons to learn before she could lose her hardness and gain in sympathy and understanding of others.

'I'd like to be friends again,' she said, awkwardly. 'You come along with Betty and me as you did before, won't you?'

'Well,' said Darrell, looking round at Sally's steadfast little face beside her, 'well—I think if you don't mind, I'll stick to Sally and Mary-Lou. I wasn't always nice to them, but they did stick by me when I was in trouble—and they're my real friends now!'

'Oh!' said Mary-Lou, her face glowing. 'Thank you, Darrell!'

Sally said nothing, but Darrell felt a delighted pinch just above her elbow. She turned and smiled. She felt very happy. Now everything would be all right again till the end of the term. Good !

She saw Gwendoline lying face downwards on her bed. She was crying bitterly. In the gladness of her heart Darrell could not bear to see even her enemy in misery. She went over to Gwendoline and shook her, but not unkindly.

'Gwendoline ! I shan't say a word about this to any one and neither will the others if I ask them not to. But you've got to buy Mary-Lou a lovely pen in return for the one you smashed. See ? '

'Yes,' said Gwendoline's muffled voice. 'I will.'

And that was all that anyone got out of Gwendoline. She could not say she was sorry. She could not even say a few ashamed words when she gave Mary-Lou a really magnificent fountain-pen she had bought. She was weaker than Mary-Lou ever was, for she hadn't even the strength to conquer herself.

'She'll never be any good, Katherine, will she ? ' said Darrell one day. Katherine smiled.

'It depends how long she stays at Malory Towers,' she said. 'It's queer how the longer you stay here the decenter you get. That's what my aunt told me. She came here, too, and she told me all kinds of stories about awful girls who got all right ! '

'Not if they're like Gwendoline,' said Darrell. 'Nothing will ever alter *her*. I wish she was leaving ! '

Gwendoline wished she was, too. The last two weeks of the term were not pleasant ones for her. Nobody mentioned the affair of the fountain-pen again, but everyone thought of it whenever they saw Gwendoline, and they would not look at her, or speak to her if they could help it. They were certain, too, that it was she who had played so many horrid tricks on Mary-Lou the whole of the term.

Poor Gwendoline ! What with the girls' contempt, and

her own feeling that she must work like a slave for the rest of the term, she did not have at all an easy time. But she was only reaping what she had sowed, so she could not grumble!

Darrell was very happy for the rest of that term. She and Sally and Mary-Lou were always together. Darrell no longer wanted Alicia's friendship. Sally was her friend now, and a very satisfying friendship it was, for Sally was even-tempered and well-balanced, and Darrell was not likely to fly into tempers with Sally around!

Exams. came and went. Darrell did very well. Sally did not do so well, partly because she had missed two or three weeks of the term, and partly because she had not been allowed to take the full work of her form after her illness.

Gwendoline came out better than anyone expected. ' It just shows,' said Miss Potts, rather severely, ' it just shows, Gwendoline, what you can do if you try. Why you saved your efforts for the last two or three weeks of the term I can't imagine. Perhaps next term you will be obliging enough to work during the whole of the term!'

Gwendoline did not tell Miss Potts what had made her work so hard the last few weeks! She hoped fervently that Miss Potts would put a few nice things down on her report. What a horrid term it had been! She wished she wasn't coming back. Next term she must try and make the girls forget all she had done this term.

Darrell thought it had been a lovely term—except for Sally's illness and the two or three days when the girls had thought she had played that horrid trick on Mary-Lou. But Darrell didn't often think of those times. She was sunny-natured and liked to think of the nice things. She was sorry the term was coming to an end—but still, the hols. would be lovely!

Sally was going to stay with her in the holidays, and she was going to stay a week with Sally, too.

' You'll see my little sister,' Darrell said. ' You'll like her. She's a sport.'

' And you'll see mine, too,' said Sally, half-shyly. ' I shall have to teach her to be a sport—like you ! '

Mary-Lou wished she lived nearer either Sally or Darrell, then she might have been able to see them. Never mind, there was always next term, and the next—and the next . . . Mary-Lou had the sense to know that Sally was Darrell's real friend, and not herself—but she didn't mind. Darrell was fond of her and admired her. That was all that mattered to loyal little Mary-Lou. How surprised her mother was going to be when she found that Mary-Lou was no longer afraid of the dark !

The last day came, with all its excitement of last-minute strapping of trunks and hunting for lost keys. The school became a perfect circus, and North, South, East, and West Tower girls became all mixed up everywhere.

' Always this last day is a madness ! ' panted Mam'zelle, trying to force her way through a seething mass of excited girls. ' Darrell ! Sally ! *Will* you please let me through ? Ah, these mad English girls ! '

Miss Potts, calm and efficient even in the midst of utter confusion, handed out small bags, marked children off the list when parents fetched them in cars, found lost keys and generally remained the one sane person in North Tower. Even Matron got flustered at times, and spent ages looking for a clothes list she had carefully stuck into her belt.

The coaches came rolling up for the train-girls. ' Come on, Darrell ! ' cried Sally. ' Let's get the front seats. Where's Mary-Lou ? '

' She's going by car ! ' called Darrell. ' Hi , Mary-Lou, good-bye ! Write to me and tell me all your news. Good-bye ! '

' Come along, now ! ' cried Miss Potts, and the girls were all hustled into the coaches. ' Where's Alicia ? If she disappears again I shall really go mad. Alicia ! Get in at once, and don't get out again. Good-bye, girls. Be good—or at least, as good as you can ! And don't dare to face me next term without your health certificates ! '

' Good-bye, Potty. Good-bye ! ' yelled the girls. ' Good-bye, dear old Potty ! '

' Goodness ! ' said Darrell, who had never heard Miss Potts called Potty to her face before. ' How dare they ! '

' It's the only time we do, just when we shout good-bye ! ' said Alicia with a grin. ' She never seems to mind then. Look at her grinning all over her face ! '

Darrell leaned out of the coach. ' Good-bye, Potty ! ' she yelled. ' Good-bye—and good-bye Malory Towers ! ' she said, almost under her breath. ' I'll be glad to see you again.'

Good-bye ! Good-bye till next time. Good-bye, Darrell and Sally and the rest. We'll meet you again soon. Good luck till then !

SECOND FORM AT
MALORY TOWERS

CONTENTS

'I'VE simply loved the hols.,' said Darrell, as she got into her father's car, ready to set off to school once more. 'But I'm glad it's time for school again. I've been eight weeks away from it!'

'Well, well, how simply terrible!' said her father. 'Is your mother ready, or must I hoot? It's an extraordinary thing that I'm always the first one ready. Ah, here comes Mother!'

Mrs. Rivers hurried down the steps. 'Oh dear, have I kept you waiting?' she said. 'The telephone went at the last minute. It was Sally Hope's mother, Darrell, asking what time we shall be along to pick up Sally and take her with us.'

Sally Hope was Darrell's best friend. Mr. Rivers, Darrell's father, was motoring them both down to Malory Towers, their school in Cornwall. They were setting off very early so that they would be there before dark, and Sally was going with them.

'I hate leaving home but I just can't help being excited at going back again,' said Darrell. 'This will be my fifth term at Malory Towers, Mother—and I'm to be in the Second Form. I *shall* feel grand!'

'Well, you're thirteen now, so it's time you went up,' said her mother, settling down in the car. 'You will quite look down on the first form, won't you?—think they are mere babies!'

'I suppose I shall,' said Darrell, with a laugh. 'Well, the third form look down on *us*—so we're all kept in our places!'

'There's your little sister waving to you,' said her father, as the car slid down the drive. 'She will miss you, Darrell.'

Darrell waved frantically. 'Good-bye, Felicity!' she yelled. '*You'll* be coming to Malory Towers sometime, then we'll go together!'

The car purred out of the drive into the road. Darrell took a last look back at her home. She would not see it again for three months. She felt a little sad—but then, being a sensible girl, she cheered up at once and set her thoughts on Malory Towers. She had grown to love her school very much in the last year, and she was proud that she belonged to it. Four terms in the first form with Miss Potts lay behind her—now she had a year in the second form to look forward to.

They arrived at Sally Hope's house in an hour's time. Sally was ready for them, her school trunk and her night-case standing beside her on the steps. With her was her mother, and by them stood a toddler of about eighteen months, clutching at Sally's hand.

'Hallo, Sally! hallo, Daffy!' shouted Darrell, in excitement. 'Good, you're ready!'

The trunk was put in the boot at the back of the car, with Darrell's. The night-case was strapped on the grid. Sally's lacrosse stick was shoved in with the odds and ends, and then she got in herself.

'Want to come too!' called Daffy, her eyes full of tears as she saw her beloved Sally going away.

'Good-bye, Mother dear! I'll write as soon as I can!' called Sally. 'Good-bye, Daffy darling.'

The car slid off again, and Daffy began to howl. Sally looked a little upset. 'I hate leaving Mother,' she said, 'and now I hate leaving Daffy, too. She's lovely now—she can run everywhere, and she talks awfully well.'

'Do you remember how you hated her when she was a baby?' said Darrell. 'Now I bet you wouldn't be without her. It's fun to have a sister.'

'Yes, I was horrid to her,' said Sally, remembering.

'That was an awful first term I had at Malory Towers—I was so miserable, thinking I'd been sent away from home to make room for Daffy, the new baby. I hated you too, Darrell—isn't it queer to think of?'

'And now we're best friends,' said Darrell with a laugh. 'I say—who do you think will be head of the second form this term, Sally? Katherine's in the third form now, so she won't be. It'll be somebody else.'

'Alicia perhaps,' said Sally. 'She's about the oldest.'

'I know—but do you think she would make a good head?' said Darrell, doubtfully. 'I know she's awfully clever, and gets top marks in anything—but don't you think she's too fond of playing the fool?'

'She might stop that if she was head of the form,' said Sally. 'What Alicia wants is a bit of responsibility, *I* think. She just won't take any. You know she was asked to run the Nature Walks last term, and she wouldn't. But I can think of another reason why she wouldn't make a good head-girl.'

'What?' asked Darrell, enjoying this gossip about her school fellows.

'Well, she's rather hard,' said Sally. 'She wouldn't bother to help people if they were in trouble, she wouldn't bother herself to be kind, she'd just be head-of-the-form and give orders, and see that they were kept, and nothing else—and you do want something else in a head-girl, don't you think so?'

'Well, who do you think is fit to be head of the form?' demanded Darrell. 'What about *you*? You size people up awfully well, and you're fine when anybody's upset or in trouble. And you're so—well, so *steady*, somehow. You don't fly off the handle like I do, or get all worked up about things. I'd love you to be head.'

'I wouldn't want to be,' said Sally, 'and any way, there's no chance of it. I think *you* would be fine as head of the form, Darrell—you really would. Everyone likes you and trusts you.'

For a wild moment Darrell wondered if it was possible that she might be chosen! It was true that all the girls, except one or two, really liked and trusted her.

' But there's my temper, still,' she said, regretfully. ' Look how I flared up last term when Marigold ticked me off at tennis, thinking I was somebody else. I didn't know she'd make a mistake, of course—but just think how I yelled at her and flung my racket down and stamped off. I can't think what came over me.'

' Oh, the sun was too much for you and lots of us that day,' said Sally, comfortingly. ' You don't usually lose your temper for silly things like that. You *are* learning to keep it for things it's useful for ! Like going for that ass of a Gwendoline Mary, for instance ! '

Darrell laughed. ' Yes, she really is an idiot, isn't she ? Do you remember how silly she was over Miss Terry, that singing mistress we had last term—the one that took Mr. Young's place for two months ? I thought Miss Terry was stupid to put up with it.'

' Oh, Gwendoline will always be silly over *some*body,' said Sally. ' She's that kind. I expect she'll pick on somebody this term too, to worship and follow round. Well, thank goodness it's not likely to be *me* ! '

' I hope there'll be some new girls,' said Darrell. ' It's fun sizing them up, isn't it ?—and seeing what they're like.'

' There are sure to be some,' said Sally. ' I say— wouldn't it be funny if Mary-Lou was told to be head-girl ! '

Both girls laughed. Mary-Lou was devoted to both Sally and Darrell, though Darrell was her heroine—and the girls liked little Mary-Lou very much. But she was such a timid little thing, shrinking away from all idea of responsibility, that it was quite funny to picture her face if she was ever told she was to be head of the form.

'She'd have a blue fit and go up in smoke,' said Darrell.
'But she's *much* better now, Sally.   Do you remember how
she used to shake at the knees when she was scared ?   She
hardly ever does that now.   We've all been decent to her
and not scared her, and we've made her believe in herself—
so she's different.   She'll never be so bad again.'

It was a long, long drive to Cornwall.   The journey was
broken by picnic meals, taken by the wayside, sitting on
heather or grass.   Mrs. Rivers took the wheel of the car
once to relieve her husband.   The girls sat at the back and
talked or drowsed, as the journey lengthened out.

'Not very far now,' said Mr. Rivers, who was back at the
wheel.   'We may see some other cars on their way to the
school, too.   Look out for them.'

They soon saw one—a low red car belonging to Irene's
people.   Irene was at the back and waved violently, almost
knocking off her father's glasses, as he sat at the wheel.   The
car swerved.

'Isn't that just like Irene,' said Sally, with a grin.   'Hey,
Irene !   Had good hols. ? '

The two cars kept more or less together, and the girls
looked back at Irene's merry face.   They liked her.   She
was a clever girl, especially at music, but a real scatter-brain
otherwise, always forgetting things and losing them.   But
she was so good-humoured that nobody could be cross with
her for long.

'There's another car !   Whose is it ? ' said Sally, as a
third one came in from a side-road, complete with school
trunk at the back.   It swung away ahead of them.

'One of the bigger girls,' said Darrell.   'Looks like
Georgina Thomas.   I wonder who will be head of the whole
school this year.   Pamela's gone now.   I hope Georgina
won't.   She's too bossy for anything.'

Now they were very near the school and it suddenly came
into sight round a corner.   The girls looked at it in silence.

They both liked their school immensely and were very proud of it. They saw the great grey building, with a rounded tower at each end—North Tower, South Tower, East and West. A creeper, now turning red, climbed almost up to the roof.

'Our castle!' said Darrell, proudly. 'Malory Towers. Best school in the world.'

Soon the car swung up to the big flight of steps leading to the great front door. Other cars were in the drive, and groups of chattering girls stood about. Gay voices called across the drive.

'Hallo, Lucy! Look, there's Freda! Isn't she brown? Had good hols., Freda? You look as if you'd lived in the water, you're so brown.'

'Hallo, Jenny! Did you get my letters? You never answered one, you pig. Hey, Tessie. Look out for my night-case. Take your great feet off it!'

'Good-bye, Mother! Good-bye, Daddy! I'll write as soon as I've settled in. Don't forget to feed my pet mice, will you?'

'Get out of the way there! You'll be run over by that car! Oh, it's Betty Hill. Betty, Betty! Have you brought any tricks or jokes back with you?'

A pair of wicked eyes looked out of the window of the car, and a tuft of hair fell over a brown forehead. 'I may have!' said Betty, stepping out. 'You never know! Anyone seen Alicia? Or hasn't she come yet?'

'The train-girls haven't arrived! The train is late, as usual!'

'Darrell! Darrell Rivers! Hallo, there! And Sally. I say, let's go in and find our dormy. Come on!'

What a noise! What a tumult! Darrell couldn't help feeling thrilled. It was good to be back at school again— back at Malory Towers.

DARRELL said good-bye to her parents and they purred
off in the car.   Darrell was always glad that her father and
mother were sensible when they said good-bye.   They
didn't burst into tears as Gwendoline's mother always did.
They didn't expect her to stay close beside them and look
mournful.   They laughed and talked just as usual, promised
to come down at half-term, then kissed her good-bye, and
went, waving cheerfully.

Soon she and Sally were carrying their night-cases up the
steps into the big hall.   They had their lacrosse sticks too,
which got entangled with people's legs as the other girls
surged around and about.

Miss Potts was in the hall.   She had been their form-
mistress when they had been in the first form, and was still
their house-mistress, for she was in charge of North Tower,
in which they slept.   All the girls' bedrooms or dormitories
were in the four towers, and there was a house-mistress in
charge of each one, and also a matron.

Miss Potts saw Sally and Darrell and called them.
' Sally !   Darrell !   Take charge of this new girl for me,
will you ?   She will be in the second form with you, and
will be in your dormy.   Take her up to Matron.'

Darrell saw a tall, thin girl standing by Miss Potts, looking
nervous and scared.   Darrell remembered how lost she had
felt when she had first come to Malory Towers, and she
felt sorry for the girl.   She went up to her, Sally behind her.

' Hallo !   Come along with us and we'll look after you.
What's your name ? '

' Ellen Wilson,' said the girl.   She had a very pale face
and looked tired out.   In the middle of her forehead was

a deep line, cutting down between her eyebrows, making her look as if she was continually frowning. Darrell didn't much like the look of her, but she smiled at Ellen kindly.

'I expect you feel pretty muddled with all this row going on,' she said. 'I felt the same last year when I came. My name's Darrell Rivers. And this is my friend, Sally Hope.'

The girl gave polite little smiles and then followed silently behind them. They all made their way through the excited throng of girls.

'There's Mary-Lou!' said Darrell. 'Hallo, Mary-Lou! You've grown!'

Little Mary-Lou smiled. 'I hope so!' she said. 'I'm tired of being the smallest in the form. Who's this?'

'Ellen Wilson. New girl. Second form,' said Darrell.

'In our dormy,' added Sally. 'We're taking her to Matron. Hallo, here's Irene. Irene, we saw you nearly knock off your father's glasses in the car, when you waved to us.'

Irene grinned. 'Yes, that was the third time I'd done it. He was just getting annoyed with me. Are you going to Matron? I'll come along too.'

'Got your health certificate?' asked Sally, slyly. It was a standing joke with the girls that Irene always arrived without it, no matter how safely her mother had packed it in her night-case, or given it in an envelope to Irene to put in her pocket.

'Got yours?' said Darrell to Ellen Wilson. 'We have to hand them over at once. And woe betide you if you go down with measles or chicken pox or something if you've just handed in a certificate saying you haven't been near anyone ill! Golly, Irene, you don't *really* mean to say you haven't got yours again?'

Irene was feeling in all her pockets, with a humorous look of dismay on her face. 'Can't find it at the moment,' she said. 'Must be in my night-case. But no—Mother said she wasn't going to put it in there any more because it always disappeared. Blow ! '

' Matron said she'd isolate you next time you came without a health certificate,' said Sally. ' You'll have to be in the San. for two days till your mother sends another one. You really are an idiot, Irene.'

Feeling frantically in all her pockets, Irene followed Sally, Darrell and Ellen to North Tower, and went in with them. The second-form dormy was not far from the first-form dormy, where Darrell had slept for the last four terms. It was on the second floor and was a lovely big room with ten white beds in it, each covered with a pretty eiderdown.

The girls dumped their night-cases down in the dormy and went to look for Matron. Ah, there she was, shepherding another new girl up to the dormy. Darrell looked at the girl. She was about the same age as Darrell, and, like Darrell, had black curly hair, but cut much shorter, more like a boy. She looked rather dirty and untidy, but she had a very attractive grin, and her eyes twinkled as she looked at the other girls. She did not look nearly so lost or forlorn as Ellen.

' Ah, Sally—Darrell—here's another new girl,' said Matron, briskly. ' Take charge of her, will you ? Her name is Belinda Morris. Now—have you all got your night-cases ? And what about your health certificates ? '

' Our night-cases are there,' said Darrell, pointing to where they had dumped them on the floor. ' And here's my health certificate, Matron.'

' Where's *my* night-case ? ' said Belinda, suddenly.

' Surely you had it with you a minute ago ? ' said Matron, looking all round. ' Well, give me your certificate and then go and look for your case.'

' But it's in the case,' said Belinda, and looked vaguely round.

' You probably left it down in the hall for everyone to

fall over,' said Matron. 'You girls! Thank you, Darrell. Is this your certificate, Sally ?—and yours, Mary-Lou—and yours, Ellen. What about yours, Irene ?'

'It's a most peculiar thing, Matron,' began Irene, hunting in all her pockets again. 'You know, I *had* it when I started off this morning. I remember Mother saying . . .'

Matron stared at Irene, really exasperated. 'Irene! Don't dare to tell me you've not brought it again. You know what I told you last term. There is a rule here that girls who forget their health certificates shall be isolated until one is produced. I've never had to enforce that rule yet—but in your case I really think . . .'

'Oh, Matron, don't isolate me!' begged Irene, taking her night-case, opening it and emptying all the contents higgledy-piggledy on the floor. 'I'll find it. I will!'

The girls stood by, laughing. Really, Irene was very funny when she had lost something. Matron looked on grimly. Irene bent low over the case, hunting hard—and suddenly she gave a cry and put her hand to her chest.

'Oooh! Something's pricking me! Whatever can it be ? Gracious, something's run a sharp point right into me!'

She stood up, rubbing her chest. Then she opened the front of her coat—and the girls gave a scream of laughter.

'Irene! You donkey! You've got your health certificate pinned on to your front! You couldn't lose it if you wanted to.'

Irene looked down, pleased. 'Of course!' she said, unpinning it. 'I remember now. I *knew* I should lose it unless I really did hang on to it somehow—so I pinned it tightly to my front. Here it is, Matron. You won't have to isolate me after all!'

Matron took it, and put it with the others she had. 'A narrow squeak for you, Irene!' she said, and her plump face broke into a smile. 'You put a grey hair into my head at the beginning of every term! Now, you girls—unpack your night-cases and put out your things. The trunks won't be unpacked till tomorrow—and then each of you will have to check the clothes' list you brought with you.'

She departed, rustling stiffly in her starched apron, looking out for more returning girls, collecting lists and names and certificates, bringing order out of confusion, and welcoming back all the sixty or so girls returning to North Tower. In the other towers, three more matrons were doing the same thing. It was a real task to welcome back about two hundred and fifty girls, with their trunks, night-cases and odds-and-ends!

Belinda had wandered off to look for her night-case. Whilst the others were still putting out their things, she sauntered back, a brown suit-case in her hand. She opened it and shook out a pair of pyjamas. She stared at them in surprise.

'Golly! I didn't know I had pyjamas like this,' she said. 'And what posh bedroom slippers Mother has put in for me. For a surprise, I suppose!'

Darrell looked over her shoulder. Then she grinned. 'You'll get into trouble if you unpack any more of those things,' she said. 'They belong to Georgina Thomas! She'll be jolly wild if she finds out you've got her night case! She's probably hunting all over the place for it now. Can't you read, Belinda?'

Darrell pointed to the name marked on the collar of the pyjamas. 'Georgina Thomas'.

'Goodness, what an ass I am!' said Belinda, and stuffed all the things back untidily into the case. 'I thought it was *my* case!'

She went out of the room again, presumably to hunt once more for her lost case. Darrell grinned at Irene.

'I don't know what we're going to do if we have *two* people like you, Irene!' she said. 'One's bad enough—

but *two*! You'll drive Mam'zelle cracked between you.
And as for Miss Parker, our form-mistress—well, you know
what she is! She can't stand anything vague or careless.
We shall have some fun this term with you and Belinda in
the class together!'

Irene didn't in the least mind being teased. She was a
clever, good-humoured girl, brilliant at music, but very
thoughtless and vague over the ordinary little everyday
things. If anyone lost a grammar book it was Irene. If
anyone forgot to turn up at a special lesson, it was Irene.
And now here was another girl, Belinda, who seemed to be
just as bad. Irene very much liked the look of her, and had
already made up her mind to be friends.

Belinda soon came back again, this time, fortunately, with
her own case. She tipped everything out, and then proceeded to put her things in place, just as the others did—
pyjamas under the pillow—tooth-brush, face-flannel, tooth-
paste and sponge on a glass ledge at one end of the dormy,
where the wash-basins were. Brush and comb in their bag
inside the top drawer of the dressing-table. Then the
empty night-case was put with the pile outside in the
corridor, waiting to be taken to the box-room.

There came a great clatter up the stairs and the girls in
the dormy raised their heads. 'The train-girls! They've
come at last. Aren't they late!'

More girls clattered into the dormy. Alicia Johns came
in, her eyes bright. Behind her came Jean, the straight-
forward, sensible Scots girl. Then came Emily, a quiet girl
whose only real interest was sewing, and the most elaborate
embroidery.

'One, two, three, four, five, six, seven, eight of us,'
said Darrell, counting. 'Two more to come. Who are
they?'

'Gwendoline Mary for one, I suppose,' said Irene, with
a grimace. 'Dear Gwendoline Mary! I expect her mother

is still sobbing over letting her darling lamb go away from
her! Who's the tenth?'

'Here comes Gwendoline,' said Darrell, and the girls
heard that familiar, rather whining voice. Gwendoline was
a spoilt only child, and although Malory Towers had done
her a lot of good, the holidays always seemed to make her
worse again.

She came in—and with her was the tenth girl.
Gwendoline Mary introduced her. 'Hallo, everyone!
This is Daphne Millicent Turner, a new girl. She's in our
form and in our dormy. She travelled down in my carriage
and I'm sure she's going to be a favourite with all of us
in no time!'

3   FIRST DAY OF TERM

THIS, of course, was a silly way to introduce any new girl,
especially as every listening girl immediately felt that anyone
likely to be Gwendoline's favourite was not at all likely to be
theirs! They smiled politely at the new girl, taking her in
from top to bottom.

She was very pretty. Her golden hair curled about her
forehead, and her eyes were much bluer than Gwendoline's
large pale ones, but they were set nearer together than
Gwendoline's, giving her rather a sly look. She had beautiful white teeth, and a very charming smile.

She used it now. 'I'm so pleased to come to Malory
Towers,' she said. 'I've never been to a school before.'

'That's one thing we had in common!' said Gwendoline,
in a pleased voice. 'I didn't go to school before I came here
either.'

'It would have been better for you if you had,' said

Alicia. 'You wanted a lot of licking into shape, Gwendoline. I suppose, as usual, you were waited on hand and foot at home these hols., with your old governess and your mother telling you that you were the most wonderful girl in the world!'

Gwendoline looked annoyed. 'You don't need to be rude immediately you see me, Alicia,' she said. 'Come along, Daphne, I'll show you what to do. You are in our dormy, which will be very nice. I can show you round quite a lot. I know how I felt when I first got here and didn't know anyone.'

Daphne seemed very grateful. She had very good manners, and thanked everyone nicely whenever they showed her or told her anything. She certainly was very pretty and graceful. It was clear that for some reason Gwendoline had quite made up her mind to be her friend and helper.

'I told you she'd have to be silly about *some*body,' said Sally to Darrell, as they went downstairs to their supper. 'Well, she's welcome to Daphne. She's got too many airs and graces for me!'

'Gwendoline says that Daphne's father is practically a millionaire,' said Darrell. 'She had a nurse, a governess and her own maid before she came here!'

'Oh—so that's why dear Gwendoline is sucking up to her!' said Sally. 'I thought there must be *some*thing. Hey, Irene—you've still got your hat on! Do you particularly want to wear it at supper?'

'Oh, gosh!' said Irene, putting her hand up to her head. 'Have I forgotten to take it off? Belinda, you might have told me!'

Belinda grinned. 'I don't know that I noticed it,' she said. 'So many things strike me as odd here, at the moment. Wearing a hat to supper didn't seem to be anything out of the ordinary.'

'What a pair you'll make!' said Sally. 'Come on, Darrell, come on, Mary-Lou. We shan't get any supper if we don't hurry.'

All the girls were tired that night, and the second-formers were very glad to tumble into bed. Gwendoline had chosen the bed next to Daphne. 'If you feel homesick, just tell me,' she said to Daphne, who looked really charming in blue pyjamas, her curly hair all about her shoulders in a golden mass. Gwendoline's hair, too, was golden, but it was straight. She envied Daphne her curls.

'I expect I shall feel rather queer,' said Daphne, getting into bed. 'You see, I'm so used to lots of people round me Mummy coming to kiss me good night—and my governess popping in to see if I'm all right—and my maid folding all my things. I shall . . .'

'No more talking,' said Sally, suddenly.

Gwendoline sat up. 'You're not head of form or dormy, Sally,' she said. 'Don't give orders, then!'

'I'm not,' said Sally. 'You know the rules, Gwendoline. I'm just reminding you of them, that's all.'

Gwendoline lay down. Presently the whispering began again. Sally got cross.

'Shut up, Gwendoline. It's long past time to stop talking. We all want to go to sleep.'

'Wait till you're head and I'll obey you, but not till then!' said Gwendoline, rather anxious to show off in front of her grand new friend. 'We'll know tomorrow who's head.'

'Well, it won't be *you*,' said Alicia's malicious voice from down the room.

'Shhhh!' said Darrell, hearing a footstep. It was Matron. She came in quietly, saw the wakeful girls, and spoke kindly to them. 'Not asleep yet? Hurry up! No more talking now, of course. Good night.'

She went out. Gwendoline debated whether or not to begin whispering to Daphne again. But a tiny snore from

Daphne showed that she was asleep. So it wouldn't be any good to defy Sally—Daphne wouldn't be able to whisper back !

Soon all the girls were fast asleep. They didn't hear Miss Potts peep into the room and shut the door quietly. They didn't even hear the sixth-formers trooping upstairs later on. They were all tired out.

The dressing-bell awoke everyone with a jump. Sally sat straight up, startled. ' Oh—it's only the school bell,' she said, and laughed. ' I couldn't think what it was for a moment.'

The first day was always fun. No real lessons were done, though classes were held. Tests were given to see what the new girls knew. New books, pencils and so on were given out. A list of various duties was compiled, each girl taking her turn at them, week by week.

The new girls all had to go to see Miss Grayling, the quiet, low-voiced Head Mistress. She told the girls exactly the same as she had told Darrell the year before. ' You will all get a lot out of your years at Malory Towers. See that you give a lot back ! Be just and responsible, kind and hardworking. I count as our successes those who leave here as young women good-hearted and kind, sensible and trustable, good sound people that the world can lean on. Our failures are those who do not learn these things in the years they are here.'

Daphne, Ellen, Belinda and all the other new girls in various forms, heard these words that morning. All of them listened, impressed. Some remembered the words and never forgot them. They would be the successes. All three new girls in the second form seemed to be listening earnestly and sincerely, especially Daphne. Miss Grayling glanced at her, looking at her closely without appearing to. She knew quite a lot about Daphne Millicent Turner.

Daphne looked back, putting all her soul into her eyes.

She wanted badly to make a good impression on Miss Grayling. She smiled her charming smile, but the Head Mistress did not return it. She spoke a few more serious words and then dismissed the girls. They went silently out of the room.

'Isn't she wonderful?' said Daphne, fervently. 'Gwendoline said she'd make a real impression on me, and she has.'

Nobody appeared to care whether any impression had been made on Daphne or not. They separated and went their different ways.

This term Darrell and Sally made their way to the second-form room. They passed the door of the first-formers, the room where they themselves had sat for many terms. The door was open. A tangled crowd of small girls were choosing desks and bagging seats.

'Babies!' said Darrell, loftily. 'Just inky-fingered kids who probably don't know their twelve-times table yet.'

Two old second-formers, now third-formers, passed them in the passage. 'Hallo, kinds!' said one of the third-formers, condescendingly. 'Look out for old Nosey! She's hard on people who make too many spelling mistakes!'

Nosey was the popular name for Miss Parker, the second-form mistress. She had rather a large nose, which, so the girls said, she kept putting into things that were no concern of hers. Certainly she was a most inquisitive person when she suspected any mischief was going on, and did not rest till she had got to the bottom of it.

She was strict but sometimes she had dreamy fits when she seemed to forget the class and sit gazing into the distance. The class lived for these rare moments and then made the most of them. Darrell was sure she would not like Miss Parker nearly as much as she had liked Potty, the mistress who had taught her in the first form.

Belinda and Ellen seemed to be very keen to know all the

details about the various teachers. Darrell and Sally were pleased to supply them. Daphne, of course, went to Gwendoline for information.

'You've got to be careful of both Mam'zelles,' said Darrell. 'But most of all of Mam'zelle Rougier, the tall thin one. They've both got tempers—but Mam'zelle Dupont's temper is just a short, hot one, and Mam'zelle Rougier's is a real *bad* one!'

'And look out for Miss Carton, the history mistress, because, if you don't like history, she'll sharpen her tongue on you!' said Alicia. 'I do like it, so I'm all right. But if you don't, look out!'

The first day passed pleasantly and interestingly. The new girls were taken to see the various parts of the big school buildings, the tennis courts, and the gardens. They marvelled at the great swimming-pool hollowed out from the rocks continually filled with fresh water each tide.

'I suppose you can swim very well,' said Daphne to Gwendoline. Gwendoline hesitated and looked round. She had been boasting quite a lot to Daphne, but not in the hearing of the others. Now Darrell was too near for her to make any untruthful statement about her swimming.

'Well—not so well as the others,' she said.

'I bet you swim the best,' said Daphne, warmly. 'You're too modest!'

Darrell giggled. No one could call Gwendoline modest, surely! She was the worst boaster in the school, and sometimes could not draw the line between stupid boasting and real untruth.

Ellen said she could not swim. 'I've never had much time for games,' she said. 'But I'd like to play them well. I've had to work so hard always.'

'You must be jolly clever,' said Mary-Lou. 'You won the only scholarship offered that would take you to Malory Towers, didn't you?'

'Yes. But I don't believe I'm *really* clever,' said Ellen, the little line deepening on her forehead and giving her a worried look. 'I mean—I can work and work and work, and remember things all right—but I'm not brilliant like some girls. Some don't need to work hard at all—they're top because they're so clever, and they can't help it. I have had to work for everything. Still—I badly wanted to come to Malory Towers, and here I am, so the hard work was worth it!'

'Well, you try being good at games as well as at work,' said Sally, who was very keen on all games herself. 'You know what they say "All work and no play . . ."'

'Makes Jack a dull boy—and Ellen a dull girl!' said Ellen, with a small laugh. 'I'm afraid that's what I am, too—dull!'

Belinda loved everything about Malory Towers. Irene, who seemed to have taken her as much in tow as Gwendoline had taken Daphne, was delighted with Belinda's rapturous admiration of everything.

'Oh, the views!' cried Belinda. 'Look at that sea! Look at the colours in that swimming-pool! Where's my paint-box, quick!'

It was then that for the first time the girls discovered Belinda's talent. She could draw and paint marvellously well. Best of all, or so the girls thought, she could caricature anyone in a bold pencil or charcoal drawing, producing a comic exaggerated likeness that sent everyone into peals of laughter.

'We'll have some fun with you, Belinda!' said Irene. 'You can draw Nosey Parker—and Mam'zelle—both Mam'zelles, in fact—and Matron—and everyone. I'm glad you came. We'll certainly have some fun with you!'

ON the first day of the term Miss Parker announced who the head-girl of the form was to be. The class were all agog to hear her, and sat like mice whilst she rustled her papers and looked for her pencil.

' I am sure you all want to know who has been chosen for head-girl this term,' she said. ' Well, I will not keep you in suspense long. After a short discussion at the staff meeting we decided on—Sally Hope.'

The girls clapped and Sally blushed red. She was very pleased indeed. Miss Parker went on, glancing at her notes as she spoke.

' You may perhaps like to know what girls were in the running for the position. Darrell Rivers was, Jean Mac-Donald was another. Winnie Toms was a third.'

Everyone expected to hear Alicia's name mentioned, or Irene's. But Miss Parker did not give any more names at all. Irene didn't mind. She knew she was a scatter-brain and she didn't in the least want to be head of the form. So long as she had her music she was happy. Being head of the form might rob her of some of her practice time !

But Alicia did mind. She had been top of the form last term. She had a fine brain and an excellent memory, and although she never needed to work hard because she had these to help her, still she certainly had done well last term.

And yet she wasn't even in the running for the position of head-girl ! She bit her lips and wished she could stop herself going red.

' There's too much favouritism ! ' she told herself, fiercely. ' Just because I play the fool sometimes and upset the mistresses, they won't even consider me as head ! '

But Alicia was not altogether right. It was not playing the fool that made the staff pass over her name, but something else. It was Alicia's hardness to those she didn't like, her sneers at those less clever than herself, who needed help, not taunts. Often the staff laughed privately over Alicia's ridiculous tricks, and enjoyed them—but nobody liked her wild and unruly tongue, and the sharp things it could say.

'She'll get a lot of admiration and envy but she won't get much love or real friendship from others,' Miss Grayling had said at the staff meeting. 'As for Betty, her friend, she is clever too, but a little empty-head, compared with Alicia, who really has it in her to make good if she tried. It isn't Alicia's brain that is at fault, it's her heart!'

And so the choice had been made—Sally Hope, the steady, loyal, kindly, sensible Sally, Darrell's best friend. Sally might not be top of the form, but she would always listen to anyone in a difficulty. Sally would not do brilliantly in exams, as Alicia would—but she would always help a younger girl at games or lessons. She would be completely fair and just as head-girl of the form, and she wouldn't stand any nonsense.

Everyone in the form knew that a good choice had been made, although some of them would have welcomed a bad choice, for they didn't like Sally! Gwendoline was furious. So was Betty, who had hoped that Alicia would have been chosen. So were one or two of Betty's friends, not in Sally's dormy.

Darrell squeezed Sally's arm. 'Jolly good!' she said. 'I'm glad. Won't your mother be pleased? You'll be head of our dormy too, Sally. Sucks for Gwendoline!'

It certainly was most annoying for Gwendoline that night in bed, when Sally took command. Sally did not mean to use her new power too much or too soon, but she knew that if Gwendoline began to be silly again, she would have to make a stand at once. Gwendoline didn't understand leniency, but took advantage of it.

So, as soon as the whispering began again, after lights out, Sally spoke up.

'Shut up, Gwendoline. I told you that last night. I wasn't head of dormy then. But I am now. So shut up when I tell you.'

'Poor Daphne's homesick' began Gwendoline.

'It won't make her any better if you whisper stuff and nonsense into her ear,' said Sally.

There was a short silence. Then Belinda's voice cut through the darkness, asking a question.

'Sally! What happens if we disobey and go on whispering when the head-girl has said we're not to?'

'Nobody ever does,' said Sally, grimly. 'But I believe there is an unwritten law at Malory Towers that if anyone makes herself a nuisance at night a nice big hair-brush is chosen and a few slaps given.'

'Oh!' said Belinda, and snuggled down in bed, grinning to think of what Gwendoline would feel now. Would she whisper again or not?

Gwendoline had opened her mouth to continue her conversation with Daphne, but when she heard Belinda's question and its answer, she shut it again, shocked. How dare Sally hint such a thing to a second-former! She debated whether or not Sally was just saying it to scare her. But, remembering Sally's grim voice, she decided she wouldn't risk it. It would be too humiliating if Sally really did carry out her threat. Daphne would never respect her again!

So there was peace in the dormy, and when Matron came silently to the door, there was only the regular breathing of ten girls to be heard. Eight were fast asleep. But two were awake.

They were Gwendoline and Ellen. Gwendoline was

cross, and that always made her wakeful. Ellen was thinking about her work. She had done fairly well in the test-papers that morning, but not brilliantly. Was she really up to the second-form work here ? Oh yes, she had won that scholarship, but it wasn't brains that had done it, only hard, hard work. Was it going to be terribly hard work here to keep up with the others ? Her brain didn't seem to work so easily as it used to. Ellen was worried, and did not fall asleep till long after Gwendoline.

It took the new girls a few days to get into the way of things. Ellen and Daphne learnt their way about more quickly than Belinda, who kept turning up in the wrong classroom continually. She would go into the first-form classroom instead of in the second form, and Miss Potts got quite annoyed with her.

' Belinda ! Don't tell me you're here *again* ! ' she would say. ' Do you particularly want to work with the first form ? Of course, if you really feel that the work of the second form is . . .'

But by that time Belinda had fled, muttering hurried apologies. She would appear in her own form-room a minute or two late, giggling.

' I'm so sorry, I got lost, Miss Parker,' she would say, and subside into her seat.

' I'll look after her a bit, Miss Parker,' said Irene. But Miss Parker forbade that immediately.

' That would mean the two of you getting lost,' she said. ' You'd probably be down in the swimming-pool waiting for a diving lesson whilst we were all up here doing maths. It's time Belinda learnt to look after herself. After all, she's been here three days now ! '

' Yes, Miss Parker,' said Belinda, meekly, and began to make a little sketch of the teacher on her blotting-pad. She was always drawing, wherever she was. She kept a little sketch book in her pocket and filled it with odd drawings of the girls, the flowers on the window-sill, the view from the window, anything that caught her observant eye.

Mam'zelle Dupont, plump, short and beady-eyed, holding her lorgnettes close to her eyes, was a source of delight to Belinda, for she was so easy to draw. Nearly every girl in the class now had a neat little sketch of Mam'zelle marking her place in her French grammar. It was the ambition of the class to have, as a marker, caricatures of all the mistresses taking their different classes—Miss Carton for their history books, Miss Grayling for the scripture exercise books, Mr. Young for the school song book and so on.

Belinda had promised to do one for each girl as a marker, providing that they would tidy her drawers for her, keep her desk spick and span, and generally see that whatever she forgot, was done before she got into trouble.

'I simply can't help forgetting things,' she explained. 'I'm even worse than Irene. If I get into too many rows I get upset and can't draw. That's awful.'

'Don't worry! We'll run round you all right!' said Alicia, looking in delight at the sly drawing Belinda had done of Mr. Young the singing-master. There he was, with his funny little moustache twisted up at the ends, his bald head with the three or four hairs plastered down the middle, his too-high collar, and his eyes large behind their glasses.

'You really are a marvel, Belinda,' said Betty, looking over Alicia's shoulder at the drawing. 'What will you draw for me if I promise to take over your week of class-room duties when your turn comes?'

Thus Belinda made her bargains, and got out of all the jobs she didn't want to do! Miss Parker was amazed to find the girls doing so much for Belinda. Belinda exasperated her, with her irresponsible ways, and she couldn't think why the girls ran round her so much.

'It's queer,' she said to Mam'zelle. 'They never do

that for Irene, who is almost as bad. Do they like Belinda so much then? I can't see what there is in that silly child to make them fuss round her so much! Why, I even saw *Gwendoline* tidying out her desk for her this morning, instead of going off at Break!'

'Ah, Belinda has the artistic temperament!' said Mam'zelle. 'She has no time for such things as tidying desks and making beds. I myself have an artistic temperament, but in this so-English school, it gets no sympathy. You English, you do not like such things.'

'No, we don't,' said Miss Parker, who had heard a good many times before about Mam'zelle Dupont's artistic temperament. It usually took the form of groaning over such laborious jobs as marking papers, making out long lists and so on. Mam'zelle's artistic temperament was always at war with such tasks, and she tried in vain to hand them over to more practical people, such as Miss Potts or Miss Parker.

'We must be patient with such as Belinda,' went on Mam'zelle. 'How I have suffered because people . . .'

'Well, believe me, Belinda will suffer too, if she doesn't get rid of some of her ways,' said Miss Parker, grimly. 'I know what Miss Potts had to put up with, in Irene, the last year. She put a bit of sense into her, thank goodness, and I can deal with her. Belinda's got to toe the line too. It's a pity all the girls seem bent on doing so much for her.'

Nobody told Miss Parker the real reason, and although she tried hard to find out, she couldn't. Nobody showed Miss Parker any of the drawings either. Belinda had a malicious pencil sometimes, and just hit off the weak points in her subjects. Miss Parker's big nose always appeared in her drawings just a *little* bit bigger than life! Mam'zelle Rougier was always bonier than she really was. Mam'zelle Dupont was rounder and fatter. No, the girls certainly didn't want to show those clever caricatures to their teachers!

The only teacher who was really delighted with Belinda was Miss Linnie, the art mistress. She was young and light-hearted with a great sense of fun. She soon found out Belinda's gift for art, and encouraged her all she could.

' I'm going to enjoy myself here ! ' said Belinda to Irene. ' Miss Linnie's thrilled with me and is helping me no end. And I've got out of all the silly jobs I hate. Emily's even going to darn my stockings for me ! '

' You're lucky,' said Irene, enviously. ' I wouldn't mind swopping some of my music compositions if somebody would do jobs for *me*—but nobody wants the music I write ! But they all want your funny drawings, Belinda ! '

5   SORTING THEMSELVES OUT

THE first week went slowly by. It always did go slowly, and then after that the weeks went faster and faster. All the girls had now settled in well, and were enjoying themselves.

The weather kept fine and warm and there was still bathing to be had for those who wanted it. The tennis courts were still in use too, although the winter game of lacrosse was now being played. So there was plenty to do in spare time.

Gwendoline and Daphne had become firm friends. Gwendoline had not had a proper friend during the four terms she had been at Malory Towers and she was thrilled to have Daphne. She admired the girl's prettiness and her charming ways, and loved to hear the stories of her wealthy home.

The two girls had much in common. Neither of them

liked the water and nothing would persuade them to take a dip in the Pool.

'We have to do enough of that each summer,' objected Gwendoline, one hot day, when her form tried to get her to come along and bathe. 'We don't *have* to swim this term, so I'm jolly well not going to. Anyway, you don't really want me to come—all you want me for is to creep behind me and push me in!'

'No—we want Belinda to see you shivering in your bathing suit, putting one toe gingerly into the water!' said Alicia. 'It would make such a comical picture for our classroom wall, Gwendoline!'

'Beast!' said Gwendoline, who hated to be made fun of. She walked off with Daphne. 'Just because they like violent things like swimming and tennis and rough games, they think everyone ought to,' she said to Daphne. 'After all, you and I have never been to school before we came here, and we'll never get used to all their stupid ideas. I wish I had been born French. Then I shouldn't have had to swim if I didn't want to, or tire myself out trying to hit a silly ball over a net.'

'We have three courts at home,' said Daphne. 'Two are hard and one is soft. You see, Mother is a marvellous hostess, and she likes to give tennis parties as well as other kinds. But, of course, the ones people really love are the ones she gives on board Daddy's yacht.'

Gwendoline hadn't heard about the yacht before. She gazed enviously at her friend. Perhaps Daphne would invite her to stay one summer holidays and then she too could go on this wonderful yacht. How pleased her mother would be to know she had made such a fine friend at last!

'You must have hated coming away to school, Daphne,' she said. 'Leaving all your luxury, and having to pig it here. I don't expect you ever made your bed in your life before you came here.'

'Of course I didn't,' said Daphne, shaking back her pretty hair. 'And I bet you didn't either!'

'No, I didn't,' said Gwendoline. 'My governess Miss Winter always did things like that for me. She still does in the holidays. She's a stupid old thing but she's useful in those ways. She wasn't much good at teaching me, though. I was awfully backward when I first came here.'

Gwendoline still was! Instead of getting down to things and trying to work really hard all the term to catch up with the others, she made a great show and did very little. Her parents were almost resigned to the fact that her reports always contained the words 'Fair. Could work harder.' 'Weak. Does not use her brains enough.' 'Poor—has not tried her best.'

Her father made plenty of cutting remarks about her reports, but as her mother always sympathized with Gwendoline, and spoilt her, his remarks did no good at all, except to make Gwendoline cross. Then she would burst into tears and it would be all that Miss Winter and her mother could do to comfort her. Gwendoline knew how to turn on her tears all right.

And Daphne knew how to turn on her charming smile! It got her out of a good deal of trouble, especially with Mam'zelle Dupont, Miss Linnie the art mistress, and Mr. Young the singing master.

Mam'zelle could not resist that smile. Daphne could make it sweet, pathetic, brave, affectionate—it was extraordinary what a smile could be!

When Daphne presented a badly written French exercise to Mam'zelle, she would turn on her smile, and Mam'zelle would gaze warmly at her. Ah, the pretty child!

'I've done my best, Mam'zelle,' Daphne would say, still keeping on her smile. 'But I'm afraid it's not very good yet. You see—it's so difficult my not having been to school before.'

Then the smile would become rather pathetic, and Mam'zelle, quite overcome, would pat Daphne's arm.

'You do your best, *mon enfant*! You cannot do more! See, I will help you if you like to come to me in the evenings for extra work!'

Mam'zelle would make this generous offer, beaming all over her face. But Daphne was quick enough to deal with it at once. She would shake her head regretfully and say how sorry she was, but already she had extra work with another mistress.

Then on would come that smile again, and the blue eyes would look beseechingly at Mam'zelle.

'Do not make me do all this French work again, please, Mam'zelle,' she would say. 'I have so much to do, to catch up with the others my first term.'

And, no matter who had their French exercises to do all over again, Daphne never did. She could do anything with Mam'zelle, if only she exerted her charm and put on that ravishing smile!

Unfortunately it worked the other way with Miss Parker, Miss Potts and Mam'zelle Rougier—especially with Mam'zelle Rougier, who, as a rule, made it a habit to dislike those girls that the other Mam'zelle liked, and to like those she didn't.

She was hard on Daphne, and soon it became impossible for the girl even to try to smile at her. They both disliked one another intensely. If it had not been for the unexpected help of somebody else in the class, Daphne would have had a very bad time, and have had all her work returned from Mam'zelle Rougier.

That somebody was, surprisingly enough, Mary-Lou! Mary-Lou had become exceedingly good at French, for her mother had had a French girl to look after her in the holidays for the past year, and Mary-Lou could chatter almost as

well in French now, as she could in English, pleasing both
Mam'zelles immensely.

Mary-Lou thought Daphne was lovely. She couldn't
help gazing and gazing at her. She would never, never like
her as much as she liked Darrell and Sally, of course, but
she couldn't help warming to her prettiness and nice manners.

One day she saw Daphne almost in tears over some
returned work from Mam'zelle Rougier, who had told
Daphne that she would return it yet again if it was not
given in perfect this time. Mary-Lou went to her.

'Can't Gwendoline help you?' she asked timidly.
'She's not doing anything in particular. Shall I ask her
to come and help you?'

Daphne dabbed her eyes and turned a watery but still
charming smile on Mary-Lou. 'No, it's no good asking
Gwen. She'd help if she could. But she's not much better
than I am at French!'

'Well—I suppose you wouldn't like *me* to help you,
would you?' asked Mary-Lou, eagerly. 'I'd like to.'

'Oh, thanks awfully,' said Daphne, thrilled. 'You're
frightfully good at it, I know. Simply wizard. Look,
what have I done wrong here?'

Mary-Lou slipped happily into a seat beside Daphne and
began to explain a few things to her. Without realizing it
she had soon done the whole of the work, and Daphne
smiled to herself, and thanked Mary-Lou warmly.

'That's all right,' said Mary-Lou, shyly. She gazed at
Daphne's curling golden hair. 'You've got beautiful hair,'
she said.

Daphne was like Gwen. She loved people to admire her
and say nice things. She looked at little Mary-Lou and
quite liked her. Also she thought it would be extremely
useful if Mary-Lou would always help her with her French.

'I suppose you wouldn't give me a hand with my French
sometimes, would you?' she asked. 'I don't want any

extra coaching from either of the Mam'zelles, but I'd love to let you explain things to me. You explain very well.'

Nobody had ever asked Mary-Lou for help before in that way. She went brilliant red, and swallowed hard.

'I'd love to,' she said at last. 'Fancy *me* helping *you*! I'm the one that's usually always rushing round for help. I'd love to, Daphne.'

So, to the astonishment of the second-formers, they saw the curious sight of little Mary-Lou sitting by Daphne in the evenings at the end of the common-room, carefully explaining the mistakes made in the French exercise of the day before!

'*And* doing all the next day's work for her too!' said Darrell, in disgust. She didn't like to see the faithful Mary-Lou sitting so long with somebody else. Why, Mary-Lou had tagged along behind Darrell and Sally for terms and terms! Surely she wasn't going to make that awful Daphne her friend.

'Let her be,' said the sensible Sally. 'If she wants to help her, why not? Daphne is awful at French, but I don't blame her for not taking extra coaching from the Mam-zelles. You know how irritable Mam'zelle Rougier gets in the evening, and you know how long Mam-zelle Dupont keeps you if you do go for extra work. You're supposed to go for half an hour and she keeps you two hours!'

'I hope Daphne won't put any of her silly ideas into Mary-Lou's head,' said Darrell.

'Maybe Mary-Lou will put a few *sensible* ideas into Daphne's head,' said Sally. 'I know you're longing to interfere, Darrell. Well, don't!'

The girls soon sorted themselves out in the form, making their own friends, choosing people to sit next to and go walks with. It was nice to have a particular friend, and to have someone to confide in.

Sally had Darrell and Darrell had Sally. Irene had Belinda. The two became quite inseparable, and did one another no good. What one forgot the other certainly didn't remember! They seemed to make one another worse.

Alicia, of course, had Betty. Alicia was not as good-tempered as usual. She still smarted because she had not been made head-girl, and she was not at all nice to Sally nor as loyal to her as she should have been. Sally took no notice, but she was not very happy about it.

Gwen had Daphne, of course—and now Mary-Lou seemed to want Daphne too! How was Gwen going to feel about that?

'You needn't worry,' said Daphne to Gwen. 'I'm only using her, silly little thing! I'll let her come out with me sometimes, when you're busy, because I don't want her to think I only want her help for my French. You can use her too, Gwen. Copy my work when I've done it!'

So Gwendoline put up with Mary-Lou's company at times, and even said nothing when she went off alone with Daphne. What did it matter? Daphne was only using her!

But all the same Daphne couldn't help liking little Mary-Lou—and it was certainly a change from the silly Gwen to have good-hearted Mary-Lou trotting by her side once or twice a week!

6   THE INVISIBLE CHALK

AFTER a few weeks Alicia got restless. 'It's time we livened things up a bit!' she said to Betty. 'I know we're second-formers now and all that—but there's no reason why we shouldn't have a bit of fun. Sally's such a bore—never a joke, never a trick!'

'What shall we do?' said Betty, her wicked dark eyes gleaming. 'I've got some invisible chalk. Have you got anything?'

'Invisible chalk! You never told me!' said Alicia, her face brightening. 'What is it? Show me!'

'I've got it in my locker, in a box,' said Betty. 'The common-room will be empty now. Come along and I'll show you. It's queer stuff.'

The two girls went to their common-room. Betty opened her locker and took out a tin box. Inside, wrapped carefully in paper, was a thick slab of curious pink chalk.

'It doesn't look invisible!' said Alicia. 'What does it do?'

'Well, if you rub it on to a chair, it can't possibly be seen,' said Betty. 'And whoever sits down on it makes it warm and it leaves a bright pink patch on a dress or skirt.'

'I see,' said Alicia. 'Golly—we could rub it on the mistress's chair in our form-room—when Mam'zelle Rougier is coming perhaps.'

'I know! Let's rub it on to Mr. Young's chair, when he comes to take singing!' said Betty. 'On his piano stool! Then he'll sit down hard on it when he plays the accompaniment for our songs—and when he gets up and turns round to write on the blackboard—golly, what a scream!'

Alicia laughed loudly. 'It would be better to play it on Mr. Young than on Nosey or Mam'zelle—he won't suspect a thing—and the first form will have a share in the joke too, because they take singing with us!'

Alicia cheered up considerably after this. She and Betty

tried out the invisible chalk very carefully, and it was a great success.

Betty took a wooden-bottomed chair and rubbed the curious pink chalk all over it. 'Look,' she said, 'it doesn't show at all, Alicia. Can you see anything of it?'

Alicia looked carefully at the chair, tipping it this way and that. 'It's perfect,' she said. 'Not a thing to be seen! Funny how you can rub it on and it seems to disappear, Betty. It really is invisible. Now, you sit down on it and let me see what happens.'

Betty sat down, and remained there for a minute or two. The chalk would not work unless it was slightly warmed. As Betty was sitting solemnly there with Alicia watching her, Gwendoline popped her head in to look for Daphne. She was astonished to see Betty sitting solemnly by herself on a chair, with Alicia a little way off.

'What are you doing?' she asked curiously. 'What's happening?'

'Nothing,' said Alicia. 'Buzz off! Daphne's not here.'

'But what are you *doing*?' persisted Gwendoline, suspecting something, though she didn't know what. 'Why is Betty sitting on that uncomfortable chair in the middle of the room like that?'

'Alicia! Nosey wants you!' suddenly cried a voice, and Jean's head came round the door. 'Hurry! She's in a stew about something. Your maths paper, I should think.'

'Blow!' said Alicia, and shot off. 'Be back in a minute, Betty,' she said, and ran down the passage. Jean looked with interest at Betty sitting all alone in the middle of the common-room.

'Tired?' she asked. Betty scowled. She felt foolish. She wanted to hurl a book at Gwendoline's silly golden head, but she didn't dare to get up in case she had a nice chalky pattern on her back. She didn't want to let anyone else into the trick at the moment.

' Paralysed or something, poor thing,' said Gwendoline. ' Can't get up. Or perhaps it's rheumatism ! '

To Betty's great relief Gwendoline became tired of teasing her and went out to find Daphne. Jean gave a grin and left too. Betty got up and looked round at herself. She gave a chuckle of delight. She had a brilliant pink pattern on the skirt of her tunic. How extraordinary that the invisible chalk should act like that when it was warmed up !

Alicia came flying in. ' Does it work ? ' she cried, and giggled when Betty swung round and showed her the bright pink marks. ' Golly, it's fine ! We'll try it on old Mr. Young tomorrow ! '

' Shall we tell anyone ? ' asked Betty.

' Not a soul,' said Alicia. ' Someone's sure to give it away by giggling if we do. No—we'll let dear Mr. Young spring this surprise himself on an astonished audience ! '

Neither Betty nor Alicia did much prep that night. Potty, who was taking prep, looked with suspicion at the two plotters and wondered what was up. It was obvious that their thoughts were pleasantly and humorously engaged far elsewhere.

Potty knew the signs. She warned Miss Parker. ' Those two in your form, Alicia and Betty, are up to something, Miss Parker. Look out tomorrow. You'll have an unaccountable smell, or a curious noise, or an orgy of book-dropping or something.'

' Thanks,' said Miss Parker, grimly. ' I'll watch out.'

But she could see nothing out of the way in her first lesson, or in her second one either. The girls worked much as usual. Only Alicia and Betty seemed restless. But then they often were, especially Alicia, whose quick mind often chafed at the slower rate of the others.

The lesson before Break was singing. Just before the

second lesson was finished Betty put up her hand. ' Please, Miss Parker, it's my turn to get things ready for Mr. Young in the singing-room. May I go ? '

Miss Parker glanced at the clock. ' Yes. You have about four minutes.'

Betty flashed a quick grin at Alicia and went demurely to the door. Once outside she raced down the corridor and made her way to the singing-room. No one was there. Mr. Young was always a minute or two late, thank goodness !

Betty flew to the piano stool. It was the round leather-topped kind, that could be screwed round and round. Betty took out her piece of pink chalk and rubbed it vigorously all over the top of the round stool.

She was sure there was not a single spot unchalked, though, of course, she could not see anything of what she had done at all. It certainly was invisible chalk !

Then she quickly sent the stool spinning round till it was too low for Mr. Young. If ever it was too low or too high he had a little habit of sitting on the stool and going round and round with it till it had reached the height he liked. If only he did that today it would give the chalk a wonderful chance of getting properly on to him !

Betty stacked the music ready and cleaned the blackboard. Then there came the sound of feet and the first form marched into the room under the sharp eye of Miss Potts.

Then came the second form. Alicia's eyes were bright. Betty grinned at her and winked. Then she went to hold the door for the two mistresses to go out and for Mr. Young to come in.

In he trotted, a dapper little man in a well-brushed black suit and a too-high collar. He smoothed his pointed moustache and bowed politely to the girls.

' Good morning, young ladies.'

' Good morning, Mr. Young,' they chorused, and rustled

their song-sheets. The lesson began. Mr. Young took some blackboard drill for five minutes, explaining various notes and signs. Then he went to the piano.

Betty nudged Alicia and held her breath. But, most annoyingly, Mr. Young did not sit down. He struck a few notes with one hand, standing facing the girls as he did so, his baton raised.

'Exercises, please,' he said. 'I wish to see your mouths well open, and to hear the sound coming from the Back of the Throat.'

Mr. Young set great store on the 'Back of the Throat'. It was always coming into everything, exercises, songs and sight-reading. 'Back of the Throat' was his one unfailing motto.

Now he stood, instead of sitting, and conducted the exercises. Alicia was in agonies of disappointment. Suppose he didn't sit down at all? Probably the next person then to sit down would be the accompanist of the mistress who taught dancing—and she always wore a brightly coloured frock so that the chalk wouldn't show at all! What a waste!

But Mr. Young did sit down eventually, of course. He had a new song to teach to the girls, and, as always, he wanted to play the whole thing through two or three times before he taught it, so that the girls could catch the lilt and swing and tune of it.

So down he sat. Aha! That stool was once more too low! Mr. Young twirled himself vigorously round on it till it was the right height. The girls giggled. Mr. Young could never realize how funny he was, twirling round lightly on that little stool.

'Now I will play you your new song,' said Mr. Young. 'You may sit to listen to it. You will hear when the chorus comes, for I will sing it to you.'

Off he started, tumty-tum-ti-tum, his hands flying up

and down, and then his voice booming out at the chorus.
Alicia and Betty winked at one another. The chalk ought
to be working now !

Three times Mr. Young played the song and then he got
up. ' Did you like it ? ' he asked, and the girls chorused
loudly. ' Oh, *yes*, Mr. Young ! '

Mr. Young turned towards the blackboard and picked
up a piece of white chalk. At once the girls saw that he
was smeared with the brightest imaginable pink at the back !
They stared in delight.

' Look at Mr. Young ! What's he rubbed against ? Oh,
do look ! '

Soon the class was in a state of giggle and Mr. Young
glared round.

' Silence, please ! What behaviour is this today ? '

There was a momentary silence, but as soon as the
unfortunate singing-master turned back to the board again
more giggles broke out. Then Irene gave one of her
terrific explosions.

Mr. Young flung the chalk down on the floor. He
looked as if he was about to stamp on it, and probably
he would have done so if the door hadn't suddenly opened,
and Miss Grayling appeared. She had someone with
her.

' Oh, excuse me for interrupting your class, Mr. Young,'
she said. ' But could you just have a word with Mr.
Lemming about the piano here ? '

Mr. Young had to swallow his annoyance and explain
what was wrong with the piano. In doing so he turned
his back to Miss Grayling who eyed his patch of brilliant
pink with the utmost astonishment. The girls were as
quiet as mice now, and Alicia and Betty felt distinctly
anxious.

Miss Grayling turned to Sally, the head of the second
form. ' Will you go to the hall and fetch the clothes brush

there?' she said. 'Poor Mr. Young has brushed against something.'

Sally flew off and fetched the brush. Mr. Young was surprised to hear Miss Grayling's remark. He looked over his shoulder trying to see himself.

'Is it paint?' he asked in alarm. 'I do hope not! Oh—only chalk! How in the world did it get there?'

7   'OY!'

SOON the offending pink chalk had been vigorously brushed away by Mr. Lemming, who then proceeded to sit down on the piano stool himself to try out some of the bass notes, which had gone wrong. Alicia and Betty watched breathlessly. Most of the girls, guessing that some trick was being played, watched eagerly too.

They were well rewarded when Mr. Lemming rose from the stool. He was wearing a long black overcoat and on it was a wonderful pattern of bright pink. Mr. Young stared at it in amazement.

'Ah, you have it too!' he cried. 'See, Miss Grayling, Mr. Lemming has brushed up against something also. I will soon put him right.'

In spite of being under Miss Grayling's eye the girls began to giggle. Miss Grayling looked very puzzled.

'Your coat was quite all right when we came along here,' she said to Mr. Lemming. 'I am sure I should have noticed it if you had brushed against anything so violently pink as this. In any case there is no wall as pink as this chalk! Whatever can have happened?'

She walked to the stool and looked at it very closely.
Alicia and Betty hardly dared to breathe.   But the invisible
chalk lived up to its name and Miss Grayling did not see
a sign of it.   It did not occur to her to sit down and see
if the same thing happened to her.   Still feeling puzzled
she took Mr. Lemming out of the room, and the lesson
proceeded again.

Not until the end of it did poor Mr. Young sit down on
that stool again.   When he got up, behold!   He was as
pretty a sight as before, and the girls stuffed their hankies
into their mouths trying not to explode with mirth.   Mr.
Young noticed nothing this time.   He walked pompously
to the door and gave the girls the quick little bow he always
kept for them.

'Good morning, young ladies!'   And out he went,
showing his patch of brilliant colour.   As he went the bell
for Break rang, and the girls tore into the Court, longing
to give way to their pent-up laughter.

'Alicia!   You had something to do with it!   *What*
was it?'

'Oh, it was marvellous!   When he turned round to the
blackboard I thought I should die!'

'Betty!   Do tell!   Was it your trick?   How did you
do it?   I looked at the stool and there wasn't a thing to
be seen!'

'That reminds me,' said Betty to Alicia with a grin.
'I must get a wet cloth and rub it over the stool.'   She
disappeared, and the girls surged round Alicia, begging her
to tell them the secret.

Meanwhile Mr. Young was walking down one of the
long corridors, quite unaware of his beautiful decoration.
Mam'zelle Dupont happened to come out of a room just
behind him, and stared disbelievingly at the extraordinary
sight.   She raced after him.

'Monsieur Young!   Ha, Monsieur Young!'

' The chalk ought to be working now! '

Mr. Young was scared of both Mam'zelles. He hastened his steps. Mam'zelle ran more quickly.

'Monsieur, Monsieur, attendez, je vous prie! Wait, wait. You cannot go out like that! It is terrible!'

Mr. Young swung round, annoyed. 'What is it? What's terrible?'

'This! This!' said Mam'zelle, and tapped him smartly on the chalk. A cloud of it flew off at once. Mr. Young was horrified at being tapped so familiarly by Mam'zelle and amazed at the cloud of chalk that flew from his person. He wriggled himself round to try and see it, remembering what Mr. Lemming's coat had been like.

'I will attend to you,' said Mam'zelle, out of the kindness of her heart, and caught hold of his arm. She hurried him to a hall-stand, took up a brush there, and with extremely vigorous strokes she removed the chalk from his clothes.

He was angry and not at all grateful. 'Twice it has happened this morning,' he said angrily to Mam'zelle and actually shook his fist in her face as if she was the culprit. She backed away, alarmed. Mr. Young snatched up his hat and went off, muttering to himself.

'He is not polite, that man,' said Mam'zelle to herself. 'I do him a kindness, and he puts his fist into my face. I will never speak to him again.'

The only girl who had seen this episode in the hall was Darrell, and she hurried to the others with the tit-bit. 'I was going past the end of the hall and I saw Mam'zelle banging at Mr. Young for all she was worth with the clothes brush,' she panted. 'He was so angry! Oh, do let's do it again, Alicia. It's a gorgeous trick!'

It is always a mistake to play the same trick twice running, and Alicia knew it. But she could not resist the temptation to try it on Mam'zelle Dupont.

'Shall we?' she asked Betty, and Betty nodded in glee. The girls crowded round to see the queer invisible chalk.

They chuckled and laughed when they thought of the singing-lesson, and they let the first-formers into the secret too.

Altogether the trick cheered up everyone considerably, and the thought that they would play it once more gave them something to look forward to.

' Who can rub it on the mistress's chair before the French lesson this afternoon ? ' demanded Betty. ' Alicia and I can't. We've no chance of being in the room. Who is room monitor ? '

' I am,' said Darrell. ' I'll do it ! Give me the chalk ! What do you do ? Just rub it over the chair ? '

Ten minutes before afternoon school Darrell slipped into the second-form classroom. It was her job that week to tidy the bookshelves, clean the blackboard and see that the chalk was handy and the duster there.

It took her only a minute to do these things. Then she went to the chair that stood behind the desk and took the chalk from her pocket. She was about to rub it over the seat of the chair when a mischievous idea struck her.

Couldn't she write something short so that a word would appear on Mam'zelle's skirt, and send everyone into fits ? It would have to be a short word.

' I'll write " OY ! " ' said Darrell to herself, in glee. ' I'll have to write it backwards, so that it will come off on Mam'zelle the right way round.'

So, very painstakingly she rubbed the chalk on the seat of the chair in the form of the two letters O and Y. Oy ! Fancy going about with that written on you ! How all the girls would yell.

The bell went for lessons. Darrell slipped the chalk into her pocket and went to her place. She giggled when the rest of the form came in.

' Did you do it ? Did you have time ? ' whispered

the girls. Darrell nodded. Then in came Mam'zelle, appearing to be in quite a good temper, and the door was shut.

Mam'zelle sat down at once. She had very tiny feet and did not like standing. The girls watched eagerly. When would she stand up ? Darrell could hardly wait for her to turn her back to the class. What would they say when they saw what she had written on the chair !

Jean was called to the blackboard to write something. ' Do it all wrong ! ' hissed Darrell. ' Then Mam'zelle will get up to correct it.'

So, much to Mam'zelle's surprise, the usually careful Jean made ridiculous mistakes in the French words she wrote down, and appeared to be quite unable to put them right, despite Mam'zelle's exasperated instructions. At last, thoroughly annoyed, she dismissed Jean to her seat, and got up to put the mistakes right herself.

The class saw her back view at once, and gasped. Written across her tight-fitting skirt in bright pink letters was the word ' OY ! ' Even Darrell was surprised to see it so clearly, and suddenly felt very uncomfortable. It was one thing to make a patch of pink appear on somebody's clothes —it could easily be explained away—but how could the word ' OY ! ' be explained ? It was quite impossible.

The class gaped at Mam'zelle's back view. They were absolutely taken aback. They didn't know whether to giggle or to be alarmed.

' Darrell ! You idiot ! Suppose she goes walking up the corridor in front of all the other mistresses with that written on her skirt ! ' hissed Alicia. ' Really, you might have more sense.'

The thought of the other mistresses seeing Mam'zelle's ' OY ! ' really alarmed the form. Miss Parker would certainly not approve. She would consider it most disrespectful.

But how to get it off ? That dreadful pink ' OY ! ' flashed

back and forth as Mam'zelle wrote on the board, turned
to the class to explain, and wrote again.

'I'll tell Mam'zelle she's got some dust or something on
her skirt and I'll brush it off,' promised Darrell, in a whisper.
'At the end of the lesson.'

But she had no chance to, for Mam'zelle walked off in
a hurry, remembering that she was late for the first form,
next door. And the first-formers had the surprise of their
lives when they saw Mam'zelle's pink ' OY ! ' flashing at
them every other minute !

They couldn't keep back their giggles and Mam'zelle
grew more and more furious. 'What is there so funny
about me this afternoon ?' she demanded. 'Is my hair
untidy ? Is my face black ? Are my shoes not a pair ?'

'No, Mam'zelle,' said the first form, almost helpless with
trying to stop their laughter.

'I am not funny and I do not feel funny,' said Mam'zelle,
severely. 'But I shall soon do some funny things. Ah,
yes ! I shall soon say " One hundred lines of French
poetry from you, please, and from you and you ! " Aha !
I shall soon be very funny ! '

With that she swung round to the blackboard and the
' OY ! ' flashed again. The first form clutched one another
in agonies of suppressed laughter.

But all the same they had the sense to grab Mam'zelle
before she went out of the room. 'We'll have to get that
off her before she goes,' said Hilda. 'Or else the second-
formers will get into awful trouble. I expect they meant
to brush it off somehow and didn't have the chance.'

So, before Mam'zelle left the first-form room, Hilda
politely offered to brush down her skirt, as it was all dusty
with chalk.

'Tiens ! ' said Mam'zelle, looking down at it. 'This
blackboard chalk ! It is not good for dresses. Thank you,
Hilda, *vous êtes gentille !* You are kind.'

She stood like a lamb whilst Hilda assiduously brushed her skirt back and front, and got rid of the pink ' OY ! ' Then she walked out of the room. The second-formers, who had finished their lesson, were watching for her, hoping to brush her down themselves before she went off to the little room she shared with Miss Potts.

With great relief they saw that Mam'zelle's skirt was now spotless. They went back into their form-room and sank down into their chairs.

' Thank goodness ! ' said Alicia. ' We might have got into a first-class row over that. Potty or Nosey would certainly have reported it if they'd seen that " OY ! " You know how annoyed the mistresses get if they think we've been really disrespectful, Darrell. You were an idiot. I suppose Sally put you up to it. Fine head of form she is ! '

' Shut up ! ' said Darrell, annoyed with herself and every-one else too. ' Sally had nothing to do with it. I just didn't think, that's all ! '

8   THE TERM GOES ON

THE affair of the invisible chalk was talked about for days afterwards. Some of the upper school got to hear about it, and secretly wished they too could have seen Mam'zelle's ' Oy ! ' Those in the know grinned at Darrell when they met her, and whispered ' Oy ! ' into her ear !

It seemed as if everyone thought that the whole idea was Darrell's, and Alicia and Betty were annoyed about it. Why should Darrell get all the credit, when all she had done was to make that word appear on Mam'zelle's skirt, and risk getting the whole of the form into very serious trouble ?

The two of them cold-shouldered Darrell, and Darrell retaliated by ignoring them as much as she could. She knew that Alicia was still sore about not being head-girl, and was not being nice to Sally. Darrell was loyal, and she was not going to have that if she could help it !

Alicia's tongue grew wild and sharp again. Darrell, knowing that Alicia was trying to make her lose her temper, grew red with suppressed rage, but said nothing. She mustn't lose her temper, she mustn't ! If she did she would begin to shout, she might even throw something at Alicia—and then she would put herself in the wrong immediately. So she looked as if she was going to burst, but didn't.

And it was very bad for her. Sally tried to calm her down, but that made Darrell worse.

'Don't you see that it's because you're my friend that I get so wild with Alicia ? ' Darrell would say. ' She could say all she liked about me, I wouldn't care—but it's hard to sit and listen to things about *you*, Sally. All because she's jealous. She just says them because she knows I've got a temper and want to stick up for you.'

'Well, for goodness' sake don't go and fall into her trap,' said the sensible Sally. ' That would be idiotic. She and Betty would have the laugh over you easily.'

So poor Darrell had to grit her teeth and say nothing when Alicia and Betty had one of their cross-talk conversations to bait her.

'*Dear* Sally ! ' Alicia would say. 'Always so good— and yet so dull. The Perfect Head-Girl. Don't you think so, Betty ? '

'Oh, I do so agree with you,' Betty would say, with a smile that infuriated Darrell. ' Think what a good example she is to us all—dear, conscientious Sally. Really, I feel

overcome with shame at my faults when I see Sally sitting
so prim and good in class. Not a joke, not a smile. *Such*
a model for all of us ! '

' What *should* we do without her ? ' Alicia would go on,
glancing slyly at Darrell to see if she was at bursting-point
yet. If Darrell got up and went away, the two counted
it as a victory for them—but poor Darrell knew quite well
that if she stayed much longer, her mouth would open
and she would say things she would regret bitterly afterwards.

So Darrell's temper was not too good those days. And
there was someone else whose temper was not good either.
And that was Ellen's.

She had been quite even-tempered, though rather worried-
looking for the first few weeks. And then suddenly she
became really irritable. She snapped at the girls, and the
little cleft in her forehead deepened until it seemed as if
she was always frowning.

Jean tried to find out if anything was the matter. Sally
had tried, but Ellen seemed to think that Sally was just
being a good head-girl, trying to set her right and stop
her being so irritable. So she snapped at Sally, and the
head-girl, surprised and hurt, said no more.

' Funny girl ! ' she said to Darrell. ' I don't understand
her. She's won a scholarship to Malory Towers which
must mean she's terribly clever—and she works as hard
or harder than any of us do—and yet she's never top, or
even in the first three or four ! I suppose she's cross about
that and gets bad-tempered. I don't like her.'

' Neither do I,' said Darrell. ' She's not worth bothering
about, Sally. Leave her alone.'

' Oh, I think she's worth bothering about,' said Sally.
' Everybody is. I'll ask Jean to have a word with her.
She sits next to her in class.'

Jean was a very forthright girl, with little imagination,
and usually went at things in the way a tank might, crush-

ing all resistance, insisting on knowing what she wanted
to know. But for some reason she did not tackle Ellen
quite in this way. She sat next to her in class and she
slept next to her in the dormy—so she had had plenty of
opportunity of hearing Ellen's unconscious sighs and little
groans when she was hard at work—or when she was trying
to go to sleep!

She knew that Ellen often lay awake at night, and she
guessed that Ellen was worrying about something. It
couldn't be her work, surely—no scholarship girl needed
to worry about work! As far as she had seen, all scholarship girls found work very easy indeed.

Jean was a kindly girl, though sometimes much too blunt
in her speech and ways. She tried to think how to get
at Ellen. There didn't seem any way except by asking her
straight out what was the matter, and couldn't it be put
right?

But that just wouldn't do. Ellen would snap at once,
as she did to Sally. So, for once, Jean gave the matter
some thought, and did not act as clumsily as she usually
did.

Ellen had no friend. She did not encourage anyone at
all, not even the quiet Emily. Jean set herself out to be
friendly in unobtrusive ways. She would never be able to
force out of Ellen what was the matter—but perhaps she
could persuade the girl to trust her enough to want to tell
her! This was really a very praiseworthy idea on Jean's
part, for it was seldom that the blunt Scots girl bothered
herself to go to a lot of trouble in her dealings with people.

But she was rather proud that Sally had asked her to
try her hand at Ellen, as she herself had failed. So,
although Ellen did not realize it at the time, Jean set herself
out to be kind and helpful in all kinds of little ways.

She helped Ellen to hunt for ages for her gym shoes
which were lost. She sympathized when the photograph

of Ellen's parents got broken, and offered to get some glass cut for the frame, when next she went to the shops. She helped her to dry her hair when she washed it. Just little things that nobody, not even Ellen at first, noticed very much.

But gradually Ellen grew to trust this shrewd Scots girl. She told her when she had a very bad headache, although she refused to go to Matron and tell her too. She stopped snapping at Jean, though she still snapped at everyone else —except Mary-Lou. It would need a very hard-hearted, bad-tempered person to snap at little Mary-Lou!

There were some evenings when Ellen was quite unbearable. ' Really, anyone would think she suffered from what my mother calls " Nerves ",' said Alicia, one evening. ' Jumps at any little thing, takes things the wrong way, snaps like a bad dog—look at her now, scowling at her work-basket as if it had bitten her ! '

If anyone passed too close to Ellen and knocked her elbow, she would jump and snap ' Look out ! Can't you see where you're going ? '

If anyone interrupted her reading, she would slam her book down on the table and glare at the offender. ' Can't you see I'm reading ? There isn't a quiet place in the whole of this beastly house ! '

' You're not reading,' Darrell would say. ' You haven't turned a page since you took up your book ! '

' Oh—so you've been watching me, have you ? ' Ellen would say, and her eyes would suddenly fill with tears. Then she would go out of the room and slam the door.

' Isn't she awful ! Scratches like a cat ! '

' I wish she'd won a scholarship to somewhere else ! '

' Always pretending to read and study and yet she slides down lower every week ! Hypocrite, I call her ! '

' Och, she's not a happy girl ! Maybe she hasn't settled down here yet ! ' That was Jean, of course, and Sally would flash her a glance of approval. Jean certainly had an uphill task with Ellen, but she was persevering with it !

The weather was bad just then, and there was no lacrosse, and not even a walk, for the country round about was deep in mud. The girls grew restless, penned up indoors, and the teachers decided that, bad weather or not, there had better be a School Walk the next day.

Everyone groaned. The rain poured down. The sky was black and lowering. The lacrosse fields were half under water. Whatever would the country lanes be like ? The sea was an angry grey-green, and the wind was so high on the cliff that no girl was allowed up there in case she was blown over.

Gwendoline and Daphne grumbled the loudest of all. Gwendoline developed a persistent sniff in class, hoping that Miss Parker would think she had a cold and let her off the walk. But Miss Parker had been warned by Potty of Gwendoline's sniffs, and was not sympathetic.

' If you sniff any more, you can go and do it outside the door,' she said. ' If there's one thing I cannot bear, it's somebody sniffing. It's disgusting, it's unnecessary, and in your case, it is probably put on, Gwendoline.'

Gwendoline glared. Why were there no school teachers like her old governess at home, Miss Winter ? She always rushed for a thermometer at once, if Gwendoline so much as cleared her throat, and would never, never dream of making her go out for a walk in such terrible weather !

She did not dare to sniff again, and was annoyed at Darrell's grins. Daphne looked at her sympathetically. Not that she cared whether Gwendoline had a cold or not, but it was the thing to do—Gwendoline simply lapped up sympathy.

Daphne herself tried other tactics to get out of the walk. She had no intention at all of wading through miles of mud. She went to Mam'zelle Dupont with her exercise book that evening. She put on her sweetest smile and knocked at the door of the little room which Miss Potts shared with Mam'zelle. She hoped fervently that Potty wasn't there. Potty always seemed to be irritated by Daphne's presence.

Fortunately Potty wasn't there. 'Ah, it is you, *ma petite* Daphne!' cried Mam'zelle, welcoming her favourite with a smile almost as charming as Daphne's. 'You have something to say to me? You do not understand something, is it not?'

'Oh, Mam'zelle, I'm in such a muddle over these tenses,' said Daphne. 'I really do feel that I ought to have a little extra coaching in them, if you could possibly spare the time. I do so badly want to get my French better.'

'But it has been much better lately, my dear child!' cried Mam'zelle, beaming, not knowing that little Mary-Lou had been doing most of Daphne's French for her. 'I am pleased with you.'

Daphne turned on her smile again and Mam'zelle's heart melted still further. Ah, this pretty Daphne! She put her arm round her. 'Yes, yes, of course I will give you a little extra coaching,' she said. 'We shall soon put these tenses right. You can stay now, *ma petite*?'

'No, not now, Mam'zelle,' said Daphne. 'But I could give up that lovely country walk tomorrow, if you would be good enough to take me then. It's the only spare time I have.'

'The good child—to give up the walk that you English girls so dearly love!' cried Mam'zelle, who thought that all walks were an extremely silly invention. 'Yes, I can take you then. I will tell Miss Parker. You are a good girl, Daphne. I am pleased with you!'

'Thank you, Mam'zelle,' said Daphne, delighted, and gave Mam'zelle a ravishing smile as she went triumphantly out of the room.

MISS PARKER was surprised and annoyed when she heard that Daphne was not to go with the class on their long walk. She looked crossly at Mam'zelle.

'But why this sudden desire for French on Daphne's part?' she said. 'She's just the type of girl that needs a jolly good long walk—yes, and a muddy one too. Shake some of her airs and graces off her! Give her the extra lesson another time, Mam'zelle.'

But Mam'zelle was obstinate. She did not like Miss Parker, with her big nose. She pursed up her small mouth and shook her head. 'I cannot take Daphne any other time. It is good of the girl to give up a nice walk to improve her French.'

Miss Parker made a disbelieving noise that irritated Mam'zelle at once. 'She wants to get out of the walk, you know that perfectly well, Mam'zelle. It's foolish to give her her way like that! Daphne gets her way too easily, and I don't like some of her methods. Too underhand for me!'

Mam'zelle stood up for her favourite, and began to exaggerate. 'Miss Parker! If you knew how much that girl wanted to go for her walk! Ah, to splash through the autumn lanes! Ah, to sniff the sea air after being cooped up so long! Daphne has sacrificed her pleasure, and she should be praised for that, not blamed. She will be hard at work with me whilst you are all enjoying yourselves out in the lovely air.'

'Well, she wouldn't take Mam'zelle Rougier in quite so easily as she takes *you*,' said Miss Parker, beginning to lose her temper. '*She* sees through her all right!'

Mam'zelle began to bristle. 'I will have a word with Mam'zelle Rougier,' she began. 'I will have two, three, four words. She shall not say things about Daphne, who is getting so much better at French!'

'Let's drop the subject,' said Miss Parker, feeling heartily tired of Daphne. 'Go and have it out with Mam'zelle Rougier if you like. I don't care! Except that I feel Daphne has got the better of us, I'm glad not to have her with us on the walk, moaning and groaning, dragging her feet along!'

Daphne could not resist telling everyone of the way she had managed to get out of the walk. Gwendoline wished she had been sharp enough to do the same. The others were frankly disgusted with the hypocritical little trick.

'Fancy doing all that just to get out of going for a walk!' said Darrell. 'It'll be fun, splashing through the puddles in our Wellingtons. Well—if you *want* to spend the afternoon doing French verbs, good luck to you! That's just like you, somehow, Daphne.'

But, the walk didn't come off after all! The wind blew itself into a gale, and Miss Parker decided that it must be put off. The girls were just putting on their macs and Wellingtons when she came to the cloakroom to tell them. Daphne had already taken her French book to Mam'zelle.

'Girls! I'm sorry! But the wind has become a perfect gale!' said Miss Parker, appearing suddenly in the cloak-room. 'The walk is off. But to make up, we'll all go into the gym and have an afternoon of riotous games, shall we? And I'll get Matron to let us have a picnic tea in there, to make a change, if some of you will carry in the stuff.'

The girls cheered. An afternoon of jolly games—racing round, competing with one another, laughing, yelling—and ending up with a picnic tea on the floor. That certainly would be a change!

Matron came up to scratch too—she provided four super chocolate cakes for a treat, as well as two pots of golden honey. The girls were thrilled.

'What about Daphne, Miss Parker?' said Mary-Lou, remembering that Daphne was with Mam'zelle. 'Shall I go and fetch her?'

'Idiot!' said Alicia, under her breath. 'Fancy reminding Miss Parker of Daphne! Serve her right to miss all this! I'll tell Mary-Lou what I think of her in a minute!'

Miss Parker looked down at Mary-Lou's anxious face, and wondered for the twentieth time why Mary-Lou bothered about Daphne when she had Darrell and Sally for friends.

'Oh, Mary-Lou, no, you mustn't disturb Daphne!' said Miss Parker, clearly, so that all the listening girls heard quite well. 'She badly wanted to have this extra coaching, Mam'zelle tells me, and was quite willing to forgo the walk. She would be willing to forgo the games and picnic too, I am sure. We mustn't disturb her. When a girl shows herself to be as studious as that it would be a pity to spoil it all.'

Mary-Lou was the only one who did not see the sly humour of Miss Parker's words. The others did immediately, and a roar of laughter broke out. Miss Parker smiled too.

'Sucks for Daphne!' said Alicia. 'Serves her jolly well right!'

They had a gay and riotous afternoon, and got thoroughly tired and dusty. Then they sat down to an enormous tea, demolishing bread and butter and honey and the four chocolate cakes in no time.

Daphne appeared just as the last piece of cake was eaten. She had had an extremely boring afternoon, for Mam'zelle Dupont had taken her at her word and had given her some very, very thorough coaching in the French verbs. She

had made poor Daphne repeat them after her scores of
times, she had corrected her pronunciation conscientiously,
she had even made her write them out.

Daphne wished heartily she had never suggested such a
thing. She had thought that she would have had a nice
cosy time with Mam'zelle, talking about herself. But
although Mam'zelle was fond of Daphne and quite taken
in by her, she was determined to do her duty as regards
coaching the girl. So she kept poor Daphne's nose to the
grindstone, and when Daphne faintly protested, saying that
she thought she had bothered Mam'zelle enough and the
girls would be back from their walk now, surely, Mam'zelle
pooh-poohed the idea at once.

'We shall hear the girls come back,' she said, not knowing
that they had never gone out. 'As soon as we hear them,
you shall go down to join them, *ma petite*, and you will
enjoy your tea, I am sure. A good conscience makes us
enjoy our food well.'

When Mam'zelle, puzzled by the non-appearance of the
girls back from their walk, sent Daphne down to see what
had happened, the girl could have burst into tears when she
saw the empty plates, the cake all gone, and the happy faces
of the second-formers in the gym.

'You mean pigs!' she cried. 'You didn't go out after
all! And you've had tea without me!'

'We couldn't disturb you at your extra French lesson,'
grinned Alicia. 'Dear Miss Parker quite agreed it would
be a pity to spoil it for you, as you were so anxious to have
it.'

Daphne glared at Gwendoline. '*You* might have come
for me,' she said. 'You could easily have slipped off and
fetched me!'

'The only person who tried to get you was Mary-Lou,'
said Sally. 'She actually went up to Miss Parker and
suggested that she should go and get you. Mary-Lou

doesn't think that extra French is preferable to walks or games.'

Daphne looked at Mary-Lou and felt warm towards her. Not even Gwendoline, her friend, had tried to get her out of that awful French lesson to join the games. But Mary-Lou had. Mary-Lou had thought loyally of her.

'Thanks, Mary-Lou,' said Daphne, and turned a rather watery smile on her. 'I won't forget that. That was decent of you.'

From that time the selfish, boastful, untrustworthy Daphne was nice to Mary-Lou, not only because the smaller girl helped her so much with her French but because she really liked her and admired her. Perhaps never before had Daphne really liked anyone for themselves.

Mary-Lou, of course, was delighted. She had quite fallen under Daphne's spell, and was too simple to see the faults in the girl's character. She was very happy to be with her, and delighted to help her whenever she could. She did not even see that the help she gave almost amounted to making Daphne cheat, for many an evening she did practically the whole of Daphne's prep for her.

Gwendoline began to be jealous of Mary-Lou, for she sensed that Daphne was really beginning to like her very much. But Daphne always laughed when Gwendoline spoke to her about it.

'You *know* I'm only using her!' she said. 'Don't be a mutt, Gwen. You're my friend and I don't want anybody else. I've nothing whatever in common with Mary-Lou—— She's a silly little simpleton, a stupid little mouse!'

It was a good thing that Mary-Lou did not hear these remarks, for she would have been shocked and hurt. She was very glad to feel that Daphne really did like her. She often lay in bed thinking of the girl's beautiful hair and lovely smile. She wished she was as charming as that. But she wasn't, and never would be.

Daphne did not forgive the others for being mean enough not to warn her, when they knew the walk was off. She was even a little cold to Gwendoline about it, and Gwendoline, fearful of losing her grand friend's liking, made haste to lick her boots again, listening to all Daphne's tales with most satisfactory attention.

Sally heard Daphne one evening. She was sitting near the curtain in the common-room and the two girls, Gwen and Daphne, did not see her.

'Didn't I ever tell you about the time my mother gave a party on board our yacht, and I sat next to the Prince at supper?' began Daphne.

'Were you allowed to sit up to supper?' said Gwendoline. 'And whatever did you find to say to a prince?'

'Oh, well—he seemed to admire my hair and talked to me a.·fully nicely,' said Daphne, beginning to embroider her tale as usual. 'I stayed up till one o'clock that night. The yacht was lovely. It had little lights all over it, and people on land said it looked beautiful—like a ship in a fairy-tale.'

'What were you dressed in?' asked Gwendoline.

'Oh—a frilly frock with little pearls all over it and my pearl necklace. It's worth hundreds of pounds,' said Daphne.

Gwendoline gasped. 'Where is it?' she said.

'Oh, I'm not allowed to bring anything like that to school,' said Daphne. 'Mother's very strict about things of that sort, you know. I haven't any jewellery here—or grand dresses—or anything you haven't got.'

'No. I've noticed that—I think it's very sensible of your mother,' said Gwendoline.

Sally had got tired of all this grand talk. She slipped off the window-sill. 'It's a pity your mother didn't supply you with your own lacrosse stick, and another pair of shoes, and plenty of writing-paper,' she remarked. 'Then you wouldn't have to keep borrowing from everyone else ! A little less yacht, and fewer cars—and more envelopes and a book of stamps would be better for you, Daphne ! '

Daphne looked haughtily at Sally. ' Mind your own business ! ' she said. ' I was talking to Gwen.'

' It *is* my business ! ' persisted Sally. ' You are always borrowing from one or other of us—and you never pay back ! As you're so rich, you ought to use some of your plentiful pocket-money to buy the things you lack ! '

' Beast ! ' said Daphne, as Sally went out of the room. ' She's jealous of me, I suppose—just because *her* people aren't as well-off as mine ! '

10   THE TWO MAM'ZELLES

HALF-TERM came and went. Sally and Darrell went out together with Darrell's parents and had a lovely time. To Gwendoline's disappointment Daphne's parents did not visit her, so there was no chance of being asked out to meals with Daphne, or going off in a magnificent car.

' I wanted to see your mother,' said Gwendoline. ' She looks so lovely in her photo.'

On Daphne's dressing-table stood a photograph of a very beautiful woman, in a flowing evening gown, with gleaming jewels round her lovely neck. Everyone had admired it.

' You aren't much like your mother, all the same,' said Darrell, critically, to Daphne. ' She's got wide-set eyes— and yours are rather near together. And your nose isn't the same.'

'Everybody isn't always like their mother,' said Daphne.
'I take after my father's family, I suppose.   I have an aunt
who is very, very beautiful.'

'And I suppose you are considered to resemble her,
Daphne?' said Jean, in her quiet, amused voice. 'What
it is to have beautiful and distinguished relatives! I have
a plain mother, who's the kindest darling on earth—and
quite an ugly father—and all my aunts are as plain as I
am! But I don't care a bit. They're jolly good fun, and
I like the whole lot.'

Gwendoline asked Daphne if she would like to go out
with her at half-term, and Daphne accepted graciously.
Mrs. Lacey, Gwendoline's mother, was very struck with
the beautiful girl and her charming smile.   As for Miss
Winter, the governess, who always most faithfully came to
see her darling Gwen every half-term, she could hardly
take her eyes off her, which annoyed Gwendoline very much.

'Such a nice friend for you, dear,' said Mrs. Lacey to
Gwendoline. 'Such beautiful manners! And how rich
her people must be to own a yacht and all those cars.
Wouldn't it be nice if you could go and stay with them?'

'Ssh, Mother,' said Gwendoline, afraid that Daphne
would hear.   But Daphne was far too busy charming poor
Miss Winter.   She played up to Gwendoline very well too,
remarking on her friend's brilliance, her clever comments
in class, and what a favourite she was with the teachers.

Mrs. Lacey listened with pride and pleasure. 'Well,
you never told me these things in your letters, Gwen darling,' she said, fondly. 'You're too modest!'

Gwendoline felt a little embarrassed and began to hope
that Daphne wouldn't lay it on too thickly—if she did, her
mother would expect a wonderful report, and Gwendoline
knew perfectly well there was no hope of that.

Belinda and Irene went out together, both forgetting their
hats, and both returning without their gloves.   They went

with Belinda's parents, who appeared to be as bad as Belinda herself, for they lost the way when bringing the girls back to Malory Towers, and turned up over an hour late; much to Miss Parker's annoyance. She could not bear the time-table to be played about with. But neither Belinda nor Irene noticed her cold manner as they went noisily into the room to report their return to her.

Alicia and Betty had gone out together, of course, and had come back full of giggles. Apparently one of Alicia's brothers had been in the party, and had related with much gusto all the tricks that he and his class had been up to that term.

To everyone's surprise Jean had asked the bad-tempered, irritable Ellen to come out with her ! Ellen had refused at first, rather ungraciously—and then had unexpectedly said she would. But it had not been a very pleasant outing, for Ellen had been rather silent and had not tried in any way to be pleasant to her hosts. She seemed sunk into herself, and Jean was sorry she had asked her.

'You might have been a bit more cheerful, Ellen,' she said, as they came into the school again. 'You hardly spoke and you didn't laugh once, even when my father made some quite good jokes ! '

'Well, don't ask me out again then,' said Ellen, snappily, and turned away. Jean caught the gleam of tears in her eyes. Funny girl ! So touchy that nobody could say a word to her without getting their head bitten off ! Jean was beginning to be tired of her efforts to be nice to Ellen.

'Now we can look forward to Christmas ! ' said Darrell, with satisfaction. 'Half-term's over.'

'We've got those awful French plays to mug up now,' groaned Alicia. 'Whatever possessed the two Mam'zelles to think up such a horrible thing for the second form to do ? Who wants to see us perform French plays ? '

Each form had to produce some sort of entertainment at the end of the term. It was the lot of the second form to learn two French plays, one chosen by Mam'zelle Dupont, the other by Mam'zelle Rougier.

It was over the choosing of the girls to play the different characters in these plays that the two Mam'zelles almost came to blows.

In one play there was a Princess—the Princess True-Heart. In the other there was an angel—the Angel of Goodness. Mam'zelle Dupont wanted her favourite, Daphne, to play both parts. She pictured the pretty, golden-haired girl as the Princess—ah, how wonderful she would look! And as an angel! Truly Daphne was made for the part of an angel!

But Mam'zelle Rougier unfortunately had quite different ideas. 'What! You would choose that imbecile of a Daphne to play two good parts like that!' scoffed Mam'zelle Rougier. 'She could never learn half the words—and her pronunciation is AB—OM—IN—ABLE! You know it. I will not have that girl in a good part.'

'Ah, but she will look the parts to perfection!' cried Mam'zelle Dupont, sweeping her arms wide part to emphasize her words. 'She looks a real Princess—and when she smiles, it is truly the smile of an angel.'

'Bah!' said Mam'zelle Rougier, rudely. 'She is one of your favourites, your little pets. Now Sally would do well in one of those parts—she would learn well and her pronunciation is good. Or Darrell. Or even Mary-Lou would be better than Daphne, for she at least speaks French as it should be spoken.'

'You are mad!' cried Mam'zelle Dupont. 'As if any of those girls could play such parts as these. I insist on Daphne playing the parts.'

'Then I shall not have anything to do with the plays,' said Mam'zelle Rougier, stiffly. 'It is always a mistake to do as you do, Mamzelle Dupont, and have favourites—and when it comes to forcing them on me, it is finished!'

'I do not have favourites!' said Mam'zelle Dupont, untruthfully, tapping her foot on the ground. 'I like all the girls just the same.'

Mam'zelle Rougier snorted disbelievingly. 'Then you are the only one who thinks so,' she said. 'Good day, Mam'zelle. I cannot stand arguing here, talking nonsense about such girls as Daphne.'

She swung round and walked off stiffly, holding her thin bony body like a stick. Plump little Mam'zelle Dupont stared after her angrily. Favourites, indeed! How dared Mam'zelle say things like that to her? Never would she speak to Mam'zelle Rougier again. Never, never, never! She would leave Malory Towers. She would go back to her beloved France. She would write to the newspapers about it. Mam'zelle Dupont made a noise like the growling of a dog, and startled Miss Potts considerably as she came in at the door.

'Don't you feel well, Mam'zelle?' she said, rather alarmed at Mam'zelle's red face and glaring eyes.

'I do not feel at all well. I have been insulted,' said Mam'zelle Dupont. 'I am not to be allowed to choose the girls in my own plays. Mam'zelle Rougier objects to my choosing the pretty, charming Daphne for the Princess. She will not even allow me—me, Mam'zelle Dupont—to give her the part of the Angel of Goodness!'

'Well, I must say I agree with her,' said Miss Potts, sitting down and arranging her papers. 'Daphne always seems a double-faced little creature to me.'

'You too are in the plot against me!' said Mam'zelle, going all dramatic, and working herself up into a tearful rage. 'You too! Ah, these cold English people! Ah, these . . .'

Miss Potts was very glad indeed to hear a knock at the

door at that moment. She didn't like dealing with Mam'-zelle in these moods. Matron came in, smiling. 'Can I have a word with you, Mam'zelle ?' she asked.

'No, you cannot,' said Mam'zelle, fiercely. 'I am upset. My heart it beats so—and so—and so. But I tell you this—I will choose what girl I wish for my plays. Ah-h-h-h !'

And, making a noise like a dog again, Mam'zelle walked angrily from the room, leaving Matron quite stupefied. 'Whatever is she talking about ?' she asked Miss Potts.

'Oh, she's had some sort of upset with the other Mam'-zelle,' said Miss Potts, beginning to add up marks. 'They get across one another at times, you know. But this appears to be more serious than usual. Well, they'll have to sort out their own tangles !'

Mam'zelle Dupont and Mam'zelle Rougier took it in turns to train the girls in the two French plays. Mam'zelle Dupont put Daphne into the two principal parts each time she took the play, much to the girl's gratification. But, equally promptly, Mam'zelle Rougier relegated her to a minor part the next day and put Sally and Darrell into the principal ones. It was most muddling.

Neither Mam'zelle would give way. The quarrel appeared to be deadly and serious. They looked the other way when they met. They never spoke to one another. The girls thought it was a great joke, but on the whole they took Mam'zelle Dupont's part, for they liked her much the better of the two. They did not approve of her choice of Daphne for the principal parts, but that couldn't be helped.

Belinda, intrigued by the quarrel, did a masterly set of caricatures of Mam'zelle Rougier, taller and bonier than ever. She drew her with a dagger in her hand, stalking poor Mam'zelle Dupont. She drew her hiding behind a bush with a gun. She drew her pouring poison into a tea-cup to present to her enemy.

The girls giggled over the pictures. Alicia was very struck by them. A wicked idea came into her head.

'Belinda! Mam'zelle Dupont would adore these pictures! You know what a sense of humour she has. She ought to see them. Put them on her desk tomorrow afternoon, just before she takes French translation—and watch her face when she opens the book!'

'I bet we shan't have any French translation tomorrow afternoon once she sees the pictures!' giggled Betty, and the others agreed.

Belinda bound the pictures neatly into a book. She had put no name to them, but they were so cleverly drawn that anyone could see at once that they were meant to represent the two Mam'zelles. 'I'll pop it on the desk just before the afternoon class,' she said. 'And you can jolly well all of you do my prep for me tonight, to repay me for getting you off your French translation tomorrow!'

Alicia whispered something to Betty. Betty looked startled and then grinned broadly. Alicia had just told her something interesting. 'It isn't Mam'zelle Dupont who's taking us tomorrow. It's Mam'zelle Rougier! Watch out for fireworks!'

11   A SHOCK FOR THE SECOND FORM

THE book of drawings was placed on the classroom desk in good time. The girls stood in their places, excited, waiting for Mam'zelle to come. How she would roar at the pictures! How she would enjoy the joke against her enemy, Mam'zelle Rougier!

Alicia was holding the door. It had been quite by chance that she had heard that the lesson was to be taken by Mam'-zelle Rougier instead of Mam'zelle Dupont. She hugged herself secretly when she thought of the bombshell she had prepared. It would pay back Mam'zelle Rougier for many a sharp word she had given Alicia!

Quick footsteps came down the passage. The girls stiffened. Somebody came in at the door and went to the desk—but it wasn't the Mam'zelle they had been expecting. It was, of course, the other one. Mam'zelle Rougier seated herself and addressed the class.

'Asseyez vous, s'il vous plait!'

Some of the girls forgot to sit down, so overcome with horror were they to think that Mam'zelle Rougier was sitting there with that book of caricatures right under her nose. Mam'zelle rapped on her desk.

'Are you deaf? Sit!'

They sat. Belinda stared beseechingly round. She caught Alicia's satisfied grin and felt angry. So Alicia had known that Mam'zelle Rougier was coming instead of Mam'-zelle Dupont—and had used her as a cat's paw to play a very dangerous trick. Everyone knew what Mam'zelle Rougier's temper was like. She would probably go straight to the head!

Belinda didn't know what do do. Darrell saw how alarmed she was, and did a bold thing. She got up and walked to Mam'zelle's desk, and put her hand on the book.

'I'm sorry this was left here by mistake, Mam'zelle,' she said, politely. She almost got away with it. But not quite. The girls stared breathlessly.

'Wait a moment,' said Mam'zelle Rougier. 'Books left on the desk must not be removed without permission. What is this book?'

'Oh—only a—a sketch-book,' said Darrell, desperately. Mam'zelle glanced round the silent class. Why were they all looking and listening so intently? There was something curious here.

She took up the book and opened it. Her glance fell on the picture of herself stalking Mam'selle Dupont with a dagger. She stared at it incredulously. There she was in the picture, tall, thin, bony—positively evil-looking—and with a dagger too!

She turned over a page. What! Here she was again—with a gun. Ah, no, this was too much! She turned another page and another. Always she saw herself there, unkindly caricatured, pursuing poor Mam'zelle Dupont, who had been given a most amiable look, and was obviously the heroine, whilst she, Mam'zelle Rougier, was the villain!

'This is unbelievable!' said Mam'zelle, under her breath, almost forgetting Darrell, who stood petrified nearby, and all the other waiting girls. Belinda was very pale. What bad luck! Whatever would happen now? Oh, why had she been such an idiot as to let Alicia lead her into this silly trap—just to make Alicia and Betty enjoy seeing her well ticked-off.

Mam'zelle became aware of the girls again. She snapped at Darrell and made her jump. 'Go back to your place.'

Darrell fled thankfully. Mam'zelle looked round the class, raking them with cold, angry eyes.

'Who has done this? Who has committed the insult of placing this book beneath my eyes?'

Sally spoke up at once. 'We're all in it, Mam'zelle. But we didn't mean *you* to see the book. We meant it for Mam'zelle Dupont. We didn't know you had changed over lessons today.'

This was unfortunately the worst possible thing that Sally could have said. Mam'zelle shot to her feet at once, her eyes stony.

'What! You meant to give this to Mam'zelle Dupont! You meant her to laugh at me with you! Is that what she

does behind my back ? Ah, how glad I am to know how
she behaves, this shameful Frenchwoman ! She shall know
of this ! I go to Miss Grayling at once—this very minute ! '

The class sat in horrified silence. It had not occurred
to them that it might be insulting to Mam'zelle Rougier to
show the book of comical drawings to Mam'zelle Dupont.
Belinda felt faint.

' Mam'zelle ! Don't go to Miss Grayling. I . . .'

But the class were not going to let Belinda take the blame.
Even Alicia looked scared now. Many of the girls spoke
at once, drowning poor Belinda's faint voice.

' Mam'zelle, we're sorry. Don't report us ! '

But Mam'zelle, swept by a cold fury, was already departing
out of the door. The girls looked at one another in real
horror.

' Alicia—*you knew* Mam'zelle Rougier was coming this
afternoon instead of Mam'zelle Dupont,' said Belinda.
' I saw you wink at Betty. You *knew* ! And you used me
to play one of your nasty tricks ! I'd never have shown
those pictures to Mam'zelle Rougier, and you know it.'

Alicia was truthful, whatever her faults were. She did
not deny it. ' I didn't know she'd make such a fuss,' she
said, rather feebly.

' Alicia, you're a beast ! ' said Darrell, feeling a hot flame
working up inside her. ' You might have thought what
serious trouble you'd get Belinda into. You, you . . .'

' Leave me to deal with this,' said Sally's quiet voice
behind her. ' Don't get all worked up, Darrell. I'll deal
with Alicia.'

' Oh, will you ? ' said Alicia, spitefully. ' Well, you
won't. If you think you're going to tick me off, you're
not, Miss Head-of-the-Form, Good-Girl-of-the-School,
Sally Hope.'

' Don't be silly,' said Sally, in disgust. ' I can't think
what's come over you lately, Alicia. You are always trying

' This is unbelievable! ' said Mam'zelle

to make things difficult for me.   I'm going down to the
Head myself, this very minute—and you're to come too,
Belinda.   We'll try to get things put straight before they
go too far.'

'You'll put the whole blame on to me, of course!' said
Alicia, scornfully.   'I know you!   Get Belinda out of
trouble and me into it!'

'I shan't say anything about you,' said Sally.   'I'm not a
sneak.   But I'd think a lot better of you if you came along
with us, and explained your part in the affair!'

'I don't care what you think of me,' said Alicia, getting
angry.   'I'm not going to tag along at your heels and say
"Please, I did it!"   You're not going to make me do anything I don't want to do!'

'I'm not going to try,' said Sally.   'Come on, Belinda,
let's go before it's too late.'

Poor Belinda, looking frightened out of her life, went
along the passage and down the stairs and out into the
Court.   They made their way to the Head Mistress's
rooms.

'Oh, Sally—it's awful!' said Belinda, all her high
spirits and light-heartedness gone.   'Mam'zelle was so
fierce.   And those pictures were rather beastly, some of
them.'

When the girls knocked on the door of the Head Mistress's drawing-room, they heard voices inside.   Miss
Grayling was there, and Mam'zelle Rougier—and Miss
Linnie the art mistress.   She had been called in to see if
she could tell them who had done the clever and malicious
drawings.

'Belinda Morris, of course!' she said, after a glance.
'There's no girl in the school as clever as she is at sketching.
She'll be a first-class artist one of these days.   My word—
these *are* clever!'

'Clever!' snorted Mam'zelle.   'They are wicked, they

are disrespectful, they are bad, bad, bad ! I demand that you punish this girl, Miss Grayling. I demand that the whole class shall be severely punished too.'

Just at that moment Sally knocked at the door. ' Come in ! ' said Miss Grayling, and the two girls entered.

' Well ? ' said Miss Grayling. Sally swallowed hard. It was all very difficult—especially as Mam'zelle was glaring at her so fiercely.

' Miss Grayling,' she began, ' we're very, very sorry about this.'

' What is it to do with you ? ' asked Miss Grayling. ' I thought Belinda did the pictures ? '

' Yes, I did,' said Belinda, in a low voice.

' But it was the whole class who wanted to put them on the desk—and let Mam'zelle Dupont see them,' said Sally. ' But—Mam'zelle Rougier came instead, and she saw them. I'm very sorry about it.'

' But why should you picture Mam'zelle Rougier pursuing her friend in such a murderous manner ? ' asked the Head, looking through the book. ' I don't see why that should interest or amuse Mam'zelle Dupont.'

There was a silence. Then Mam'zelle Rougier spoke stiffly. ' We are not friends, Mam'zelle Dupont and I.'

And before Miss Grayling could stop her, Mam'zelle had poured out her grievance over the plays. Miss Grayling listened gravely. Then she turned to the girls.

' Then do I understand that one day the chief characters are played by Sally and Darrell, and the next day by Daphne ? ' she asked.

Sally said yes, that was what had happened. Mam'zelle Rougier suddenly looked rather ashamed. It occurred to her that she and Mam'zelle Dupont had been very silly, and had allowed their private quarrel to muddle up the play and make things awkward for the girls.

She wished she had thought twice about taking the book down to the Head. No wonder the girls had put the quarrel into those stupid drawings—but why did they make her the villain and Mam'zelle Dupont the heroine? Ah, that was not nice!

'You didn't know, then, that Mam'zelle Rougier was going to take the class instead of Mam'zelle Dupont?' said the Head, suddenly. Sally hesitated a fraction of a second. Alicia had known—and Betty too. But she, Sally, hadn't known, nor had any of the others.

'I didn't know that, of course, Miss Grayling,' she said.

'Did anyone know?' persisted the Head. Sally did not know how to answer. She did not want to tell tales, but she could not very well say nothing. Belinda broke in.

'Yes, someone knew—and that someone used me for a cat's paw. I'd never, never have shown those drawings to Mam'zelle Rougier. I won't tell who it was—but do believe me when I say I wouldn't have hurt Mam'zelle Rougier's feelings for anything. It was just a joke.'

'Yes, I see that,' said Miss Grayling. 'An unfortunate joke, of course, but still a joke. A joke that was played on the wrong person and caused anger and distress. As I see it, quite a lot of people are to blame in this.' She glanced at Mam'zelle Rougier, who grew rather red. 'There was a quarrel, it seems, to start with. Without that, possibly all this would not have occurred. You two girls may go now. I will discuss with Mam'zelle what punishment is fitting for you all.'

In silence Belinda and Sally went out of the door. Miss Linnie came with them. Mam'zelle Rougier was left behind, as Miss Grayling had made her a sign to stop.

'Belinda, you're an idiot,' said Miss Linnie.

'I'll never draw anyone again!' said Belinda, dismally.

'Oh, yes you will!' said Miss Linnie. 'But you'll probably draw kinder pictures in future. Don't be too clever, Belinda—it always lands you into trouble sooner or later !'

12   MAM'ZELLE DUPONT
PUTS THINGS RIGHT

UPSTAIRS something was happening. Mam'zelle Dupont had come past the door of the second form, and had found it open. On looking in, she had found, to her surprise, that Mam'zelle Rougier had apparently deserted her form and left the girls alone. More surprising still, the girls were sitting as quiet as mice—and what long faces !

'What is the matter, *mes petites* ?' cried Mam'zelle, her little beady eyes ranging over the silent class. 'What has happened ?'

Mary-Lou, thoroughly upset by everything, gave an unexpected sob. Mam'zelle turned to her. Mary-Lou was one of her pets, for Mary-Lou could chatter French perfectly.

'What is wrong, then ! Tell me ! Am I not your friend ! What is this that has happened ?'

'Oh, Mam'zelle—an awful thing has happened !' burst out Mary-Lou. 'Belinda did some pictures of you and Mam'zelle Rougier. Nice ones of you but awful ones of Mam'zelle Rougier—and we didn't know Mam'zelle was coming instead of you this afternoon—and we put the book on the desk for *you* to see, and . . . and . . .'

'Ah ! Mam'zelle Rougier, she saw them instead, and she has gone blue in the face, and she has taken Belinda and poor Sally to Miss Grayling !' cried Mam'zelle. 'Ah, this bad-tempered woman ! She cannot see a joke.

I, I myself will go to see Miss Grayling. I will tell her one, two, three things about Mam'zelle Rougier ! Ah-h-h ! '

And off went Mam'zelle Dupont, scuttling along on her high heels like a harassed rabbit. The girls looked at one another. What an afternoon !

Mam'zelle did not meet Belinda and Sally, for they went different ways. Just at the moment that she knocked at Miss Grayling's door, Sally and Belinda walked into the classroom, looking rather gloomy. They reported what had happened.

' So you did split on me after all,' said Alicia, in disgust.

' We didn't even mention your name,' said Belinda. ' So you needn't be afraid, Alicia.'

' I'm not afraid ! ' said Alicia. But she was. She hadn't been in Miss Grayling's good books lately and she knew it. She didn't want to be hauled over the coals for this now. But she didn't like the girls' scornful glances.

' Mam'zelle Dupont's gone off to join the merry family now,' said Darrell. ' I wonder what is happening.'

Mam'zelle Dupont had swept into the Head's drawing-room, startling both Miss Grayling and Mam'zelle Rougier. Miss Grayling was just getting an account of the quarrel between the two French mistresses from a rather shame-faced Mam'zelle Rougier, when the other Mam'zelle swept in.

She saw the book of drawings at once and picked them up. She examined them. ' Ah, là, là ! This Belinda is a genius ! Ha ha !—look at me here, Miss Grayling—did you ever see such a plump rabbit as I look ? And oh, Mam'zelle Rougier, what are you doing with that dagger ? It is marvellous, wonderful ! But see here ! I am to be poisoned ! '

Mam'zelle Dupont went off into peals of laughter. She wiped the tears from her eyes. ' You do not think it is funny ? ' she said in astonishment to the other mistresses.

'But look—look—here I am to be shot with this gun. As if my good friend Mam'zelle Rougier would do such a thing to me! Ah, we quarrel sometimes, she and I, but it matters nothing! We are two Frenchwomen together, *n'est ce pas*, Mam'zelle Rougier, and we have much to put up with from these bad English girls!'

Mam'zelle Rougier began to look a little less frigid. Miss Grayling looked at one or two of the pictures and allowed herself to smile. 'This one is really very funny, Mam'zelle Dupont,' she said. 'And this one, too. Of course, the whole thing is most disrespectful, and I want you both to say what punishment we must give the class —and especially, of course, Belinda.'

There was a silence. 'I feel,' began Mam'zelle Rougier, at last, 'I feel, Miss Grayling, that perhaps Mam'zelle Dupont and I are a little to blame for all this—our stupid quarrel, you know—naturally it intrigues the girls—and . . .'

'Ah, yes, you are right!' cried Mam'zelle Dupont, fervently. 'You are quite, quite right, my friend. It is we who are to blame. Miss Grayling—we demand no punishment for the bad, bad girls! We will forgive them.'

Mam'zelle Rougier looked a little taken aback. Why should Mam'zelle Dupont forgive them? They hadn't drawn *her* unkindly! But Mam'zelle Dupont was rushing on in her headlong way.

'These pictures, they are more funny than bad! It is a tease, a joke, is it not? We do not mind! It was our stupid quarrel that started it. But now, now we are friends, are we not, Mam'zelle Rougier?'

Mam'zelle Rougier could not say no to that. Swept away in spite of herself, she nodded. Mam'zelle Dupont gave her two sudden and exuberant kisses, one on each cheek. Miss Grayling was much amused.

'That Belinda!' said Mam'zelle Dupont, looking at the drawings again. 'Ah, what a clever child. One day,

maybe, Miss Grayling, we shall be proud of these drawings !
When Belinda is famous, Mam'zelle Rougier and I, we
shall look together with pride on these pictures, and we
shall say, " Ah, the little Belinda did these for us when
she was in our class ! " '

Mam'zelle Rougier said nothing to this. She was feeling
that she had been made to do all kinds of things she hadn't
meant to do. But she couldn't go back on what she had
said now. That was certain.

' Well, perhaps you would go back to your classes now,'
suggested Miss Grayling. ' And you will tell the girls,
and set their minds at rest ? Belinda must apologize, of
course. But I think you'll find she will do that without
any prompting.'

The two Mam'zelles departed, arm-in-arm. The girls
they met stared at them in surprise, for everyone knew
that the two had been bitter enemies for the last week or
so. They went up to the second form, who stood in silence,
glad to see Mam'zelle Dupont looking so cheerful, and the
other Mam'zelle not quite so sour as usual.

Mam'zelle Dupont set their minds at rest. ' You have
been bad girls. Very bad girls. Belinda, you let your
pencil run away with you. I am shocked ! '

She didn't look shocked. Her beady black eyes twinkled.
Belinda stood up.

' I want to apologize,' she said, rather shakily, ' to both
of you.'

Mam'zelle Rougier didn't see any necessity for Belinda
to apologize to Mam'zelle Dupont, but she didn't
say so. She accepted the apology as graciously as she
could.

' And now for punishment,' said Mam'zelle Dupont, in
a stern voice, but still with twinkling eyes, ' for punishment
you will pay better attention to your French lessons than
you have ever done before. You will learn well, you will

translate marvellously, you will be my best pupils. Is
that not so ? '

' Oh, *yes*, Mam'zelle,' promised the girls fervently, and,
for the time being at any rate, even Gwendoline and Daphne
meant it ! Mam'zelle Rougier went. Mam'zelle Dupont
took over the five remaining minutes of the lesson.

' Please,' said Darrell, at the end, ' Mam'zelle, will you
tell us who *is* to take the chief parts in the French plays
we're doing ? It's so muddling not knowing. Perhaps
you and Mam'zelle Rougier have settled it now.'

' We have not,' said Mam'zelle Dupont, ' but I, I am
generous today. I will let the poor Mam'zelle Rougier
have her way, to make up to her for the shock you have
given her this morning. I will not take Daphne for the
chief parts. You, Darrell and Sally, shall have them. That
will please Mam'zelle Rougier and put her into such a good
mood that she will smile on you all ! '

Daphne was not too pleased about this. She looked at
Mam'zelle, rather hurt. All the same, it was a good thing,
she thought, because how she was EVER going to learn
all that French talk in the play she really didn't know ?
Perhaps it would be just as well if she didn't have the chief
parts, after all. She would look hurt, but be very sweet
and generous about it !

So, looking rather stricken, she spoke to Mam'zelle.
' It's just as you like, Mam'zelle. I *had* been looking
forward to swotting up my parts for you—but I hope I'm
generous enough to give them up to others without a fuss ! '

' The kind girl ! ' said Mam'zelle, beaming. ' I will make
it up to you, Daphne. You shall come to me and we will
read together a French book I loved when I was a girl.
Ah, that will be a treat for both of us ! '

The class wanted to laugh when they saw Daphne's
horrified face. Read a French book with Mam'zelle ! How
dreadful. She would have to get out of that somehow.

The affair of the drawings had three results. Alicia was sulky, because she felt she had come out very badly in the matter, and she knew that Sally and Darrell and some of the others didn't think very much of her because of it. The two Mam'zelles were firm friends now, instead of enemies. And Daphne was now given a very minor part indeed in the plays, where she would not appear as someone beautiful, but only as an old man in a hood. She was very much disgusted.

'Especially as I've written and told my people all about my fine parts,' she complained. 'It's a shame.'

'Yes, it is,' said Gwendoline. 'Never mind, Daphne— you won't have to do all that swotting now!'

Jean came up with a box at that moment. She jingled it under their noses. 'Have you got your games sub., you two? We're collecting it today. Five bob each.'

'Here's mine,' said Gwendoline, getting out her purse.

'Yours, please, Daphne,' said Jean. Daphne took out her purse. 'Blow!' she said. 'I thought I had ten shillings, but there's only a sixpence. Oh, yes—I had to buy a birthday present for my governess last week. Gwen, lend me the money till I get some from home, will you?'

'She lent you two bob last week,' said Jean, jingling the box again. 'I bet you didn't pay her back! And you borrowed sixpence off me for church collection, let me tell you. Why don't you keep a little book showing your debts?'

'What do little sums like that matter?' said Daphne, annoyed. 'I'll be getting pounds and pounds on my birthday soon. Anyway, I can pay back this week. My uncle is sending me thirty shillings.'

'Well, I'll, I'll lend you five bob till then,' said Gwendoline, and put a ten-shilling note into the box. Jean turned to Darrell and collected her money. She went to Ellen and jingled the box under her nose.

'Five bob, please, Ellen.'

'Don't do that under my nose!' said Ellen, jumping. 'What is it you want? Five shillings? Well, I haven't got it on me just now. I'll give it to you later.'

'You said that last time,' said Jean, who was a most persistent person when it came to collecting money. 'Go on—get it, Ellen, and then the collection will be finished.'

'I'm working,' said Ellen, annoyed. 'Take the thing away. I'll give you the five shillings soon.'

Jean went off, also annoyed. Daphne spoke in a low voice to Gwendoline. 'I bet she hasn't got the five bob to give! She won a scholarship here, but I don't believe her people can really afford to keep her at a school like this!'

Ellen didn't quite hear what was said but she knew it was something nasty, by Daphne's sneering tone. She flung down her book. 'Can't *any*body work in this place!' she said. 'Stop your whispering, Daphne, and take that smile off your silly face!'

13   POOR ELLEN!

'REALLY!' said Daphne, as Ellen walked out of the room and banged the door. 'What awful manners that girl's got! What's the matter with her?'

Nobody knew. Nobody guessed that Ellen was getting more and more worried about her work. She knew that the end of term tests were coming along, and she wanted to come out well in them. She must! So she was working hard every minute, and she had begun to feel at last that she would be able to face the tests and do well.

But that evening she did not feel very well. Her throat hurt her. Her eyes hurt her, especially when she moved them about. She coughed.

Surely she wasn't going to be ill! That would put her terribly behind in her work. It would never do. So Ellen dosed herself with cough lozenges, and gargled secretly in the bathroom, hoping that Matron would not notice anything wrong.

Her eyes were too bright that evening. Her usually pale cheeks were red. She coughed in prep. Miss Potts, who was taking prep, looked at her.

'Do you feel all right, Ellen?' she asked.

'Oh, quite all right, Miss Potts,' said Ellen, untruthfully, and bent her head over her book. She coughed again.

'I don't like that cough,' said Miss Potts. 'I think perhaps you had better go to . . .'

'Oh, Miss Potts, it's only a tickle in my throat,' said Ellen, desperately. 'Perhaps I'd better get a drink of water.'

'Well, go then,' said Miss Potts, still not quite satisfied. So Ellen went. She leaned her hot head against the cool wall of the cloakroom and wished miserably that she had someone she could confide in. But her snappiness and irritability had put everyone against her—even Jean. Jean had tried to be nice—and Ellen hadn't even bothered to go and get the games subscription for her.

'I don't know what's come over me lately,' thought the girl. 'I used not to be like this, surely. I had plenty of friends at my other school. I wish I'd never left there. I wish I'd never won a scholarship!'

She must go back. Her throat still hurt her and she slipped a lozenge into her mouth. Then she went back to the classroom, trying to walk firmly, though her legs felt rather wobbly.

She had a high temperature and should have been tucked up in bed. But she wasn't going to give in. She must do her work. She mustn't get behind. She must do well in the tests, whatever happened.

She tried to learn some French poetry, but it buzzed round and round in her head. She began to cough again.

'Oh, shut up,' said Alicia, in a whisper. 'You're putting it on to get Potty's sympathy!'

That was so like Alicia! She didn't like people who coughed or sniffed or groaned. She had no sympathy to spare for those who needed it. She was a healthy, strong, clever girl, who had never been ill in her life, and she scorned stupid people, or those who were delicate and ailing, or in trouble. She was hard, and it didn't seem as if she was getting any kinder. Darrell often wondered how she could so badly have wanted Alicia to be her friend when she had first come to Malory Towers!

Ellen looked at Alicia with dislike. 'I can't help it,' she said. 'I'm not putting it on.' She sneezed and Alicia gave an exclamation of disgust.

'Don't! Go to bed if you're as bad as all that!'

'Silence!' said Miss Potts, annoyed. Alicia said no more. Ellen sighed and tried to concentrate on her book again. But she couldn't. She was glad when the bell went and she could get up and go out into the cooler air. She was hot and yet she shivered. Oh, blow, she certainly was in for a cold. Perhaps it would be better tomorrow.

She tried to stuff some food down her throat at supper-time, in case Miss Parker noticed she wasn't eating anything. But Miss Parker did not often take any notice of Ellen. She was usually a quiet girl, with a name for bad temper, and Miss Parker was not at all interested in her, though sometimes surprised that her work was not better.

It was Sally who noticed that Ellen seemed ill that night. She heard her quick, rather hoarse breathing and looked at her in concern.   She remembered how Ellen had coughed in prep.   Poor Ellen—was she feeling simply awful, and not wanting to make a fuss ?

Sally was both sensible and kind.   She went to Ellen and took her hot hands.   ' Ellen !   You're not well !   Let me go with you to Matron, silly ! '

The little act of kindness made the tears start to Ellen's eyes.   But she shook her head impatiently.

' I'm all right.   Leave me alone !   Just got a headache, that's all.'

' Poor old Ellen,' said Sally.   ' You've got more than a headache.   Come along to Matron.   You ought to be in bed ! '

But Ellen wouldn't go.   It was not until Jean came up and sympathized with her that she broke down and confessed that yes, she really did feel awful, but she couldn't possibly go to bed with all that work to do before the tests ! ' I must do well, you see,' she kept saying.   ' I must.' The tears ran down her cheeks as she spoke, and she suddenly shivered.

' You won't do any good by keeping up when you should be in bed,' said Jean.   ' Come along.   I'll keep you well posted in what we do in lessons, I promise you !   I'll make notes for you and everything ! '

' Oh, will you ? ' said poor Ellen, coughing.   ' All right then.   If you'll help me to catch up, I'll go and see Matron now.   Perhaps just one day in bed will put me right.'

But one day was certainly not going to put Ellen right ! She was very ill and Matron put her to bed in the San. at once.   Ellen was so thankful to be there that she couldn't help crying.   She was ashamed of herself, but she couldn't stop the tears.

' Now don't you worry,' said Matron, kindly.   ' You should have been in bed days ago by the look of you !

Silly child! Now you just lie still and enjoy a week in
bed.'

A week! Ellen started up in horror. She couldn't
possibly miss a week's work. She stared at Matron in
dismay. Matron pushed her back.

'Don't look so horrified. You'll enjoy it. And as soon
as you feel like it, and your cold is not infectious, you can
choose a visitor.'

'Poor Ellen's really ill,' said Jean, as she went back to
the others. 'I don't know what her temperature is, but
I saw Matron's face when she took it, and it must be pretty
high.'

'She coughed like anything in prep tonight,' said Sally.
'I felt sorry for her.'

'Well, Alicia didn't,' said Gwen, maliciously. 'She told
her to shut up! Dear, kind Alicia!'

Alicia glared. She was always making sharp remarks
about Gwen—but this time Gwen had got one back at *her*
—and Alicia didn't much like it.

'Oh, we all know that Alicia can't bear to give a little
sympathy out,' said Darrell, unable to stop herself. She
had felt annoyed with Alicia lately, because she had been
so offhand with Sally. Also she had thought that Alicia
should certainly have owned up that it was she who had
known Mam'zelle Rougier was going to take the lesson
instead of Mam'zelle Dupont. She had made Belinda get
into a row, when she could have prevented it.

Alicia, too, was ashamed of this now. But it was too
late to do anything about it. There was no point in owning
up now that the matter was closed. But she kept kicking
herself for not doing so at the right time. She had been
too obstinate.

She was sorry too that she had been hard on Ellen that
evening—but how could she know she was really ill? She
hadn't any time for that silly Ellen, always snapping and

snarling at everyone! Let her be ill! A good thing if she *was* away from the class for a while. *She* wouldn't miss her!

Ellen felt very ill for four days, then she felt a little better. Her temperature went down, and she began to take a little more interest in things. But alas! her old worry came back immediately she was well enough to think clearly!

Those tests! She knew that on the result of the tests depended her place in form. And it was very important that she should be top or nearly top. Her father and mother were so very proud that she had won the scholarship to such a fine school. They were not well-off, but they had told Ellen they would do anything they could to keep her at Malory Towers, now that she had won the right to be there by her own hard work.

The uniform had been so expensive. Even the train fare was expensive. It was a good thing she had been able to get a lift down in somebody's car. Mother had bought her a new trunk and a new suit-case. More expense. Oh, dear—was it really a good thing to win a scholarship to a school like Malory Towers if you had to count your pennies? Perhaps it wasn't.

Then another thought struck her. She had had to have the doctor. That would be another expense on the bill. And all the time she was losing her school work, and would do badly her first term. Her parents would be bitterly disappointed.

So Ellen worried and worried. The Matron and the Nurse couldn't think why she did not throw off her illness as quickly as she should. Every day she begged to be allowed to get up, but Matron shook her head. ' No, you can't, dear. You're not quite right yet. But would you like a visitor now? You can have one if you like.'

' Oh, yes. I'd like Jean, please,' said Ellen at once.

Jean had promised to take notes for her. Jean would tell her all about the lessons she had missed. Jean was dependable and reliable.

So Jean came to see her, bringing a pot of honey. But it was not honey that Ellen wanted. She hardly even glanced at it.

'Did you bring the notes you said you would make for me?' she asked, eagerly. 'Oh, Jean—didn't you?'

'Good gracious me—what do you want notes of lessons for already?' demanded Jean, in astonishment. 'You're not even up!'

'Oh, I do, I do,' said Ellen. 'You promised, Jean. Well, bring them next time. You tell me all the lessons you've had now.'

Jean screwed up her eyes and tried to remember. She thought Ellen queer to want to talk about lessons instead of games or fun. She began to tell Ellen.

'Well, in maths. we did those new sums again. I can bring you some to show you. And in French we learnt that long piece of poetry on page sixty-four. I can recite some of it if you like. And for geography we learnt . . .'

Matron bustled up. 'Jean! Ellen mustn't hear a word about lessons yet! She mustn't start worrying her head about work. She couldn't help missing it, and Miss Parker and Mam'zelle will quite understand that she will be a bit behind when she comes back.'

Ellen stared at her in consternation. 'But, Matron! I *must* know it all. I must! Oh, do let Jean tell me. And she's going to bring me some lesson notes she's made for me too.'

'Well, she certainly mustn't. I forbid it,' said Matron. So that was that. Ellen took no more interest in Jean's conversation. She lay back, desperate. She'd be near the bottom now! How unlucky she was!

NOBODY missed Ellen very much. She hadn't any of Darrell's high spirits or friendliness, none of Alicia's mischief or fun, she hadn't even the shyness and timidity of Mary-Lou, that made her missed when she wasn't there.

'You don't much notice Mary-Lou when she's there under your nose—but you do miss her when she's not,' said Darrell once. And that was true.

Darrell was missing Mary-Lou quite a lot these days, for Mary-Lou was attaching herself firmly to Daphne. Nobody could quite understand it. Nobody believed that Daphne wanted Mary-Lou's friendship—she only wanted her help in French. Even when Darrell pointed out that it was almost cheating for Mary-Lou to do such a lot for her, she would hardly listen.

'I can't do much to help anybody,' said Mary-Lou. 'It's only in French that I'm really good—and it's so nice to help somebody who wants it. And besides--Daphne does really like me, Darrell!'

'Well, so do I like you, and so does Sally,' said Darrell, really exasperated to think that Mary-Lou should attach herself to such a double-faced person as Daphne.

'Yes, I know. But you only put up with me out of the kindness of your heart!' said Mary-Lou. 'You've got Sally. You let me tag along behind you like a nice puppy —but you don't really want me, and I couldn't possibly help you in any way. But I *can* help Daphne—and though I know you think she's only using me for her French, she's not.'

Darrell was certain that Daphne only put up with Mary-Lou because of the French—but she wasn't quite right.

Daphne was very fond of Mary-Lou now. She couldn't quite think why, because it wasn't like her to be fond of anyone—but Mary-Lou was so unobtrusive, so shy, so willing to help in any way. 'She's like a pet mouse, that you want to protect and take care of!' thought Daphne. 'You can't help liking a mouse.'

She poured out her tales of wealth to Mary-Lou, and Mary-Lou listened in the most gratifying manner. The younger girl was proud that someone as grand as Daphne should bother to notice her and talk to her and tell her things.

Ellen was away from school eleven days and had worried terribly the last six or seven because Jean had not been allowed to bring her lesson-notes or to tell her about the lessons. Now she came back, pale, a little thinner, with an obstinate look in her eyes. She was going to catch up somehow! If she had to get up at six in the morning, and learn her lessons under the sheets by means of a flashlight, she would!

She asked Miss Parker if she would be kind enough to give her extra coaching in what she had missed. Miss Parker refused in a kindly manner.

'No, Ellen. You're not up even to your ordinary work at the moment, let alone taking extra coaching. I shan't expect much from you, nor will anyone else. So don't worry.'

Ellen went to Mam'zelle Dupont and even to Mam'zelle Rougier. 'I do so want to know what I've missed so that I can make it up,' she said. 'Could you give me a little extra coaching?'

But neither of the Mam'zelles would. 'You are not yet quite strong, *mon enfant*!' said Mam'zelle Dupont, kindly. 'No one will expect you to do brilliantly now this term. Take things more easily.'

So poor Ellen was quite in despair. Nobody would help

her! They all seemed to be in a league against her—Matron, Doctor, Miss Parker, the two Mam'zelles.

And in ten days' time the tests began! Ellen usually liked exams, but she was dreading these. She couldn't think how it was that the girls joked about them so light-heartedly.

Then an idea came to her—a bad idea, that at first she put away from her mind at once. But it came back again and again, whispering itself into her mind so that she had to listen to it.

' If you could perhaps see the test-papers before they were given out! If you could read the questions and know what you were going to be asked! '

Ellen had never cheated in her life. She had never needed to for she had good brains and she knew how to work hard. People didn't cheat if they could do as well or better without cheating! Ah, but when you couldn't, when something had gone wrong, and you didn't know your work—would you cheat then if it was the only way to gain a good place?

It is not often that a test like that comes to a person with good brains, who has always scorned cheating—but now it came to Ellen. It is easy not to cheat if you don't need to. Is it easy not to cheat if you *do* need to? When that test comes, you will know your character for what it is, weak or strong, crooked or upright.

Ellen could no longer push the thought out of her mind. It was always there. Then one day she was in Miss Parker's room and saw what she thought was a test-paper on her desk. Miss Parker was not in the room. It needed only a moment to slip round and look at the paper.

Ellen read swiftly down the questions. How easy they were! Then, with a shock she saw that they were questions set for the first form, not the second. Her heart sank.

Before she could look for the second-form questions and

see if they were there she heard Miss Parker's footsteps and slipped round to the other side of the desk. She must never let anyone guess that she was thinking of doing such a dreadful thing.

Ellen was always slipping into Miss Parker's room, or Miss Potts' room after that. She chose times when she knew they would not be there. She even went through Miss Parker's desk in the second-form room one morning after school hoping to find something there in the way of test questions.

Alicia found her there and looked surprised. 'What *are* you doing?' she said. 'You know we're not supposed to go to that desk. Really, Ellen!'

'I've lost my fountain pen,' mumbled Ellen. 'I wondered if perhaps Miss Parker had . . .'

'Well, even if she *had* got it, you shouldn't go sneaking in her desk,' said Alicia, scornfully.

Then another time Darrell found her in Miss Potts' room, standing at Mam'zelle's empty desk, running her fingers through the papers there. She stared in surprise.

'Oh—er—Mam'zelle sent me here to find a book for her,' said Ellen, and was shocked at herself. She had always heard that one sin leads to another, and she was finding out that this was true. She was trying to cheat—and that made her tell untruths. What next would it be!

'Well, I must say Ellen isn't much improved by being away for nearly a fortnight,' said Betty, one evening in the common-room, when Ellen had snapped someone's head off, and gone out sulkily. 'She's just as snappy as ever—and she doesn't look a bit well yet.'

'Bad temper's her trouble,' said Alicia. 'I'm fed up with her. Always frowning and sighing and looking miserable!'

Gwendoline came in, looking bothered. 'Anyone seen my purse? I'm sure I put it into my desk, and now it's gone.   And I put a ten-shilling note in it only this morning, because I wanted to go out and buy something !   Now I can't ! '

' I'll help you to look for it,' said Daphne obligingly, and got up.   ' I bet it's still in your desk somewhere ! '

But it wasn't.   It was most annoying.   Gwendoline screwed up her forehead and tried in vain to think if she had put it anywhere else.

' I'm sure I didn't,' she said at last.   ' Oh, how sickening it is.   Can you lend me some money, Daphne ? '

' Yes.   I've got my purse in my pocket,' said Daphne. ' Anyway I owe you some.   I meant to have paid you before. I got some money yesterday from my uncle.'

She felt in her pocket and then looked up, a dismayed expression on her face.   ' It's gone !   There's a hole in my pocket !   Blow !   Wherever can I have dropped it ? '

' Well, I must say you're a pretty pair ! ' said Alicia. ' Both of you losing your purses—just when they are full of money too !   You're as bad as Irene or Belinda ! '

Belinda had lost a half-crown only the day before, and had crawled all over the form-room floor looking for it, much to Mam'zelle's amazement.   She hadn't found it and had demanded her games subscription back from Jean. She hadn't got it, however, for Jean maintained that once the money had gone into her box, it was no longer the giver's—it belonged to the Games' secretary, or the school, or whatever fund it was meant for.

The two purses didn't turn up.   It was annoying and rather mysterious.   *Two* purses—full of money.   Gwendoline looked at Daphne and lowered her voice.   ' You don't think somebody's taken them, do you ?   Surely there couldn't be anyone in our form that would do a thing like that ! '

Alicia was very curious about the purses.   Into her mind slid the memory of seeing Ellen going through the mistress's

Ellen was rummaging through Miss Parker's desk

desk in the second-form room.   Why should she do that?
She had said she had lost her fountain pen—but she hadn't,
because Alicia had seen her using it at the very next lesson.
Well, then . . .

Alicia determined to keep an eye on Ellen.   If she was
doing anything dishonest or underhand it ought to be
reported to Sally.   It was tiresome to think that Sally would
have the right to hear about it and settle whether or not
it should go before Miss Parker.   Alicia felt the usual stab
of jealousy when she thought of Sally as head-girl.

Ellen didn't know that Alicia was keeping an eye on
her, but she did know that she was suddenly finding it
very difficult to be alone, or to go into either Miss Parker's
room, or Miss Potts' room, or even the form-room when
nobody else was there.   Alicia always seemed to pop up
and say:

'Hallo, Ellen! Looking for somebody? Can I help
you?'

Daphne borrowed as usual from somebody, but Gwendoline didn't.   Gwendoline had been taught not to borrow,
and she had written to ask her people to send her some
more money to get on with.   Daphne borrowed some from
Mary-Lou and then offered half of it to Gwendoline.

'Oh *no*,' said Gwendoline, a little shocked. 'You can't
lend other people's money to me, Daphne! I know you
borrowed that from Mary-Lou. Why don't you do as
I'm doing and wait till you get some more from your
people? That's the worst of being as rich as you are—
I suppose you just simply don't understand the value of
money!'

Daphne looked a little surprised, for this was the first
time she had ever had any kind of criticism, even slight,
from her faithful Gwendoline.   Then she slipped her arm
through her friend's.

'I expect you're right!' she said. 'I've always had as

much money as I wanted—I don't really know the value of it. It's the way I've been brought up. Don't be cross, Gwen.'

'I don't know what would happen to you if you were ever in real need of money!' said Gwendoline. 'You *would* be miserable without your yacht and your cars and your servants and your beautiful house! How I wish I could see them all!'

But Daphne did not say, as Gwen always hoped she would, 'Well, come and stay with me for the holidays!' It rather looked as if Gwendoline would not be seeing her grand friend during the Christmas holidays, or attending parties and pantomimes with her. It rather looked as if she would have to put up with her own home and adoring mother and worshipping governess!

15   A DREADFUL EVENING

IT was the day before the tests were to begin. Some of the girls were swotting up hard, feeling rather guilty because they hadn't paid as much attention to their work as they ought to have done. Betty Hill was poring over her books. So was Gwendoline. And, as usual, poor Ellen had her nose between the pages of a book, trying to cram into a short time what could only be learnt slowly and in peace.

Miss Parker was quite worried about Ellen. The girl gave her a strained attention in class, and yet her work was only fair. It wasn't for lack of trying, Miss Parker knew. She supposed it must be that Ellen was not very fit after her illness.

Ellen knew that the test-papers were ready. She had heard Miss Parker talking about them. As for Mam'zelle, in her usual tantalizing manner she had shaken her test-paper in front of her class, and cried ' Ah, you would like to know what I have set you, would you not ! You would like to know what are these difficult questions ! Now the first one is . . .'

But she never did say what the first one was, and the class laughed. Anyway, Mam'zelle Dupont was never so strict over tests as Mam'zelle Rougier, who set the most difficult questions and expected them to be answered perfectly—and then groaned and grumbled because nearly all the girls failed to get high marks !

It was Ellen's last chance that day to try to see the papers. If only that irritating Alicia wouldn't always keep hanging around ! The thought occurred to Ellen that Alicia might be spying on her—but she dismissed it at once. Why should she ? Nobody in the world save Ellen herself knew that she wanted to see the test-papers.

She hung about in the passage outside Miss Parker's room for a long time that evening. But there was never any chance of going in without being seen. Somebody always seemed to be going by. It was astonishing how many girls went this way and that way past Miss Parker's door.

Then, most annoyingly, the only time that the passage was really empty was when Miss Parker herself was in the room. She was there with Miss Potts. Ellen could quite well hear what they were saying.

She bent down by the door as if she was re-tying her shoe-lace.

' The second form haven't done too badly this term,' she heard Miss Parker say to Miss Potts. ' They seem to have benefited by the year they spent with you ! Most of them can use their brains, which is something ! '

'Well, I hope they do well in the tests,' said Miss Potts. 'I always take an interest in their first tests when they go up to the second form for the first time. Having had the girls for three or four terms I can't lose my interest in them quickly. I suppose Alicia or Irene or Darrell will be top. They've all got good brains.'

'Have a look at the questions,' said Miss Parker, and Ellen actually heard the rustling of the test-papers being handed over to Miss Potts. How she longed to see them!

There was a silence as Miss Potts read them. 'Yes. A bit stiff, one or two of them—but if the girls have paid attention, they ought to do them all quite well. What about the French papers?'

'Mam'zelle's got them in her room,' said Miss Parker. 'I'll take these along to her and give them to her. She takes the second form first thing tomorrow and can take the papers there with her.'

Ellen's heart leapt. Now she knew where the papers would be that night! In Mam'zelle's room. And that was not very far from the dormy. Could she—dare she—get up in the night and go and peep at them?

A girl came round the corner and almost knocked Ellen over. It was Alicia.

'Gracious, it's you, Ellen! You were lounging about here when I came up—and now I come down and you're still here! What on earth are you doing?'

It's no business of yours!' said Ellen, and walked off. She went to the common-room and sat down. She had to work things out. Dare she creep out in the middle of the night and hunt for the papers? It was a very, very wrong thing to do. But oh, if only she had been well all the term, and had been able to work and use her brains properly, she could easily have been top or near the top. It wasn't her fault that she would be near the bottom.

So she sat and reasoned with herself, trying to persuade herself that what she was doing wasn't really so bad as it looked. She was doing it to save her parents from being so disappointed. She couldn't let them down. Poor Ellen! She didn't stop to think that her parents would much rather see her honestly at the bottom, than dishonestly at the top!

Alicia was growing quite certain that it was Ellen who had taken the money. If not, why in the world was she always sneaking about by herself, listening outside doors, and doing such peculiar things? Neither of the purses had turned up. Nor had Belinda's half-crown. Another purse and more missing money had not been traced either, and Emily had reported that her gold bar brooch, which her god-mother had given her the term before, had also gone.

Emily was very tidy and careful and never lost things like Belinda or Irene. When Alicia heard her talking about her lost brooch in the common-room, she made up her mind to tell the others what she thought. Ellen, as usual, was not there. 'Out sneaking round somebody's door, I expect!' thought Alicia.

'I say,' she said, raising her voice a little. 'Sally! I've got something to say about all these mysterious disappear-ances. I don't exactly want to accuse anyone—but I've been watching somebody lately, and they've been doing rather peculiar things.'

Everyone looked up in surprise. Sally looked round the common-room. 'Are we all here?' she said. 'Yes— wait though—Ellen isn't. We'll get her.'

'No, don't,' said Alicia. 'It would be as well not to.'

'What do you mean?' said Sally, puzzled. Then her eyes widened. 'Oh—you don't mean—no, Alicia, you don't mean that it's Ellen you've been watching! What has she been doing that's so peculiar?'

Alicia told how she had watched Ellen and seen her

sneaking about in the passages, apparently waiting for a
room to be empty. She related how she had found her
going through Miss Parker's desk. Everyone listened,
amazed.

'I wouldn't have thought it of her!' said Daphne, in a
disgusted voice. 'What a thing to do! I never did like
her. There's no doubt she took my purse and Gwen's—
and Emily's brooch, and goodness knows how many things
besides.'

'You're not to say that till we've proved something,' said
Sally, sharply. 'We've no definite proof yet—and only
Alicia, apparently, has seen Ellen sneaking about.'

'Well,' said Darrell, reluctantly, 'Sally, I noticed something once too. I found Ellen in Miss Potts' room, going
through some things on her desk.'

'How dreadful!' said Daphne, and Gwen echoed her.
Jean said nothing. She had been more friendly with Ellen
than anyone else, though she had never been able to like
her very much—but it seemed to her that Ellen was not
quite the type of girl to become a thief. A thief! How
terrible it sounded. Jean frowned. Surely Ellen couldn't
be that!

'I don't think I believe it,' she said, slowly, in her clear
Scots voice. 'She's a queer girl—but I don't think she's
queer in that way.'

'Well, I bet she never gave you her games subscription!'
said Alicia, remembering how Ellen had refused to go and
get it.

'She did, the next time I asked her,' said Jean.

'Yes—and I bet it was after one of the purses had disappeared!' exclaimed Betty. Jean was silent. Yes, that
was true. Ellen had not given up her subscription until the
purses had gone. Things looked very black for Ellen.

'What are we to do?' said Darrell, helplessly. 'Sally,
you're head-girl. What are you going to do?'

' I'll have to think about it,' said Sally. ' I can't decide this very minute.'

' There's nothing to decide ! ' said Alicia, with scorn in her voice. ' She's the thief. Well, tackle her with it and make her confess ! If you don't, I shall ! '

' No, you mustn't,' said Sally at once. ' I tell you, we've none of us got real proof—and it's a bad, wicked thing to do to accuse somebody without definite proof. You are not to say a word, Alicia. As head-girl I forbid you.'

Alicia's eyes sparkled wickedly. ' We'll see ! ' she said, and at that very moment who should come into the room but Ellen ! She sensed hostility as soon as she came in and looked round, half-scared.

The girls stared at her silently, rather taken-aback at her sudden appearance. Then Sally began to talk to Darrell and Jean turned to Emily. But Alicia was not going to change the subject, or to obey Sally either !

' Ellen,' she said, in a loud clear voice, ' What do you find when you go sneaking about in empty rooms and looking through desks ? '

Ellen went pale. She stood perfectly still, her eyes glued on Alicia. ' What—what do you mean ? ' she stammered at last. Surely, surely nobody had guessed that she was looking for the exam papers !

' Shut up, Alicia ! ' said Sally, peremptorily. ' You know what I said.'

Alicia took no notice. ' You know jolly well what I mean, don't you ? ' she said to Ellen, in a hard voice. ' You know what you take when you creep into an empty room or go through somebody's desk or locker or drawer ! Don't you ? '

' I've never taken anything ! ' cried Ellen, a hunted look on her face. ' What should I take ? '

' Oh—perhaps purses with money in—or a gold brooch

or two,' drawled Alicia. 'Come on—own up, Ellen. You look as guilty as can be, so why deny it ? '

Ellen stared as if she could not believe her eyes. She looked round at the quiet girls. Some of them could not look at her. Mary-Lou was crying, for she hated scenes of this kind. Sally looked angrily and hopelessly at Alicia. It was no good stopping things now. They had gone too far. How dared Alicia defy her like that !

Darrell was angry, too, but her anger was partly directed at Ellen, whom she too thought looked exceedingly guilty. She was angry that Alicia had defied Sally, the head-girl— but after all—if Ellen was guilty, it was surely better that it should all be cleared up immediately ?

'Do you mean that—that you think I've been stealing your things ? ' asked Ellen at last, with a great effort. 'You can't mean that ! '

'We do,' said Alicia, grimly. 'Why else should you snoop round as you do ? And why go through Miss Parker's desk ? Can you give us a good explanation of that ? '

No. Ellen couldn't. How could she say that she was hunting for the exam papers because she wanted to cheat. Oh, if once you started doing something wrong there was no end to it ! She put her hands up to her face.

'I can't tell you anything,' she said, and tears made her fingers wet. 'But I didn't take your things. I didn't.'

'You *did*,' said Alicia. 'You're a coward as well as a thief. You can't even own up and give the things back ! '

Ellen stumbled out of the room. The door shut behind her. Mary-Lou gave an unhappy sob. 'I'm so sorry for her ! ' she said. 'I can't help it ! I am ! '

THERE was a silence, only broken by Mary-Lou's sniffs. Most of the girls were upset and horrified. Alicia looked rather pleased with herself. Sally was tight-lipped and angry. Alicia looked at her and smiled maliciously.

' Sorry if I've upset you, Sally,' she said, ' but it was time we had it out with Ellen. As head-girl you should have done it yourself. As it was, you left it to me ! '

' I did not ! ' said Sally. ' I forbade you to say anything. We shouldn't have accused Ellen—I know it's not right till we've got proof. And I wanted to think of the best way of doing it—not in front of everyone, that's certain ! '

Darrell felt uncomfortably that Sally was right. It would have been best to wait a little, and think about it and then perhaps for Sally to have spoken with Ellen alone. Now the fat was in the fire ! Everyone knew. Whatever would Ellen do !

' Well, all I can say is I'm grateful to Alicia for bringing the matter to a head,' said Daphne, shaking back her shining curls from her forehead. ' Perhaps our belongings will be safe now.'

' You ought to be loyal to Sally, not to Alicia,' flared up Darrell.

' Don't let's argue any more,' said Sally. ' The thing's done now, more's the pity. There's the supper-bell. For goodness' sake, let's go.'

They went soberly down to the supper-table. Ellen was not there. Jean asked about her.

' Shall I go and fetch Ellen, Miss Parker ? ' she said.

' No. She's got one of her headaches and has gone early

to bed,' said Miss Parker. The girls exchanged looks. So Ellen couldn't even face them again that evening.

'Guilty conscience,' said Alicia to Betty, in a voice loud enough to reach Darrell and Sally.

Ellen was in bed when the form went up at their bed-time. She lay on her side, her face in the pillow, perfectly still. 'Pretending to be asleep,' said Alicia.

'Shut up,' said Jean, unexpectedly, in a low voice. 'You've done your bit already, Alicia Johns! We'll have no more jeering tonight, Hold your tongue.'

Alicia was taken-aback and glared at Jean. Jean glared back. Alicia said no more. Soon the girls were in bed and the lights were put out. They stopped talking at once. Sally had insisted that the rules were to be kept, and the girls respected her and kept them.

One by one they fell asleep. Daphne was one of the last to sleep, but long after she was asleep too, somebody else was wide awake. That was Ellen, of course.

She had gone to bed early for three reasons. One was that she really had got 'one of her headaches'. Another was that she didn't want to face the girls after their accusing faces. And the third was that she wanted to think.

She had hardly been able to believe her ears when the girls had accused her so unjustly. Ellen had not taken anything. She was completely honest in that way, however much she might have made up her mind to cheat over the exam. A thief! Alicia had called her that in front of everyone. It wasn't fair. It was most cruel and unjust!

But was it altogether unjust? After all, the girls, two of them at least, had seen her snooping round and had seen her going through Miss Parker's desk and looking through things on Miss Potts' desk too. It must seem to them as if such behaviour meant dishonesty—and it did mean dis-honesty, though not the kind they accused her of.

'What am I doing! How can I cheat like this! How

can I be such a sneak and do such dreadful things!' Ellen suddenly cried in her mind. 'What would Mother think of me! But oh, Mother, it's all because of you and Daddy that I want to do well. Not for myself. Surely it isn't so wrong if I cheat to please my parents, and not to please myself?'

'It *is* wrong,' said her conscience. 'You know it is! See what your foolishness has led you into! You have been accused of something terrible—all because you were trying to do something wrong, and hadn't even done it!'

'I shan't cheat. I won't think of it any more,' Ellen decided suddenly. 'I'll do badly in the papers and explain why to Mother. I will, I will!'

Then the girls came up and she heard Alicia's spiteful remark. 'Pretending to be asleep.' In a flash she remembered her unkind accusations, her sneering words, and she remembered too how all the girls seemed to be against her and to believe she was wicked and bad.

Anger crept through her. How dared they accuse her wrongly, without any real proof at all? They all thought her bad, and nothing would convince them that she wasn't, she was sure. Very well, then, she *would* be bad! She *would* cheat! She'd get up in the middle of the night and go and find those papers. She knew where they were— in Mam'zelle's room.

Ellen lay there in the darkness, her mind going over everything again and again. She felt defiant and obstinate now. She was labelled 'Bad' by the girls. Then she *would* be bad. She'd enjoy it now! She would read those exam papers, and then she would look up all the answers, and she would surprise everyone by coming out top with practically perfect marks! That would make them all sit up!

She had no difficulty at all in lying awake until she was sure that the staff had gone to bed. Her eyes looked straight up into the darkness, and her head felt hot. She clenched her fists when she thought of Alicia's scornful face.

At last she thought it would be safe to get up. She sat up in bed and looked round. The moon was up and a ray pierced the darkness of the room. There was no move·ment anywhere, and all she could hear was the regular breathing of the other girls. She slid out of bed. She put her feet into her bedroom slippers and pulled her dressing-gown round her. Her heart was beating painfully.

She crept out of the room. She knocked against one of the beds on the way and held her breath in case she awoke the girl asleep there. But there was no movement.

She made her way down the moonlit passage, and down the stairs to Mam'zelle's room, the one she shared with Miss Potts. It was in darkness. Mam'zelle had gone to bed long ago.

Ellen went to the window to make sure that the curtains were tightly drawn. She did not want anyone to see even a crack of light there at that time of night. They were thick curtains and shut out the moonlight. Then she shut the door and switched on the electric light.

She went to the desk. It was untidy as usual, for Mam'-zelle Dupont, unlike Mam'zelle Rougier, could never keep her books and papers in neat order. Ellen began to go through the papers on top of the desk.

She went through them twice. The exam papers were not there! Her heart stood still. Surely they must be there. Perhaps they were *in* the desk. She hoped it was not locked. She had seen Mam'zelle lock it sometimes.

She tried it. Yes—it *was* locked. What a blow! Mam'zelle must have locked the test-papers up! Ellen sat down, her knees shaking with the suspense. Then her eyes caught sight of a key lying in the pen-tray. She snatched it up. She fitted it into the desk—and it opened !

How like Mam'zelle to lock the desk carefully and leave the key in the pen-tray!

With trembling hands Ellen looked through the vast collection of papers there. In a corner, neatly banded together by Miss Parker, were the second-form test-papers!

With a thankful sigh Ellen took them up. She was just about to look carefully through them when she heard a sound. Her heart almost stopped! In a trice she slipped to the door and switched off the light. Then she shut the desk quietly and went over to the door to listen.

The sound came again. What was it? Was it somebody walking about? She would have to be very careful if so. She stuffed the papers into the big pocket of her dressing-gown and held them there. She had better get out of Mam'zelle's room if she could, because if anyone found her there she would get into very serious trouble.

Upstairs, in the dormy, just after Ellen had crept out, Darrell awoke. It was her bed that Ellen had bumped into, and she had not awakened immediately. But she sat up half a minute after Ellen had gone out of the room, wondering what had awakened her.

She was just about to settle down again when she noticed Ellen's empty bed. The moon was sending a bright ray down on it—and there was no lump there to show that Ellen was lying asleep. It was flat and empty!

Darrell stared at the empty bed. Where was Ellen? Was she ill again? Or—was she doing a bit more snooping to see if she could find anything valuable?

Darrell looked across at Sally. She ought to tell Sally and let her deal with it. Alicia had already interfered enough, and she, Darrell, ought to let Sally say what was to be done about the empty bed, if Ellen didn't come back very quickly.

Ellen didn't come back. Darrell waited impatiently for some minutes and then decided to try to find her. She wouldn't wake Sally. She was full of curiosity and wanted to follow Ellen herself. It seemed an exciting thing to do in the middle of the night!

She put on her slippers and dressing-gown. She went out of the room, treading quietly in her soft slippers. She stood in the passage and listened. She could hear nothing.

She padded down the passage and came to the stairs. Perhaps Ellen was going through the desks in the second-form room—or even in the first form! She went quietly down the stairs. She came to the first-form room, which had its door shut. Darrell opened it. The room was in darkness and she shut the door again. It made a little click.

She went to the second-form room and opened the door there. She thought she heard something and switched on the light quickly. She could see no one there. She switched off the light again and was about to shut the door when she thought she heard a sound. She quickly switched the light on again—and then, over by the cupboard she saw a movement! Just as if someone had pulled the door to very quickly.

Darrell's heart beat. Was it Ellen in there? Or somebody else? She wouldn't like it at all if it was a burglar. But it must be Ellen. She had gone from her bed and was nowhere to be seen. She must be there, in the cupboard, hiding.

Darrell went swiftly to the cupboard and gave the door a sharp tug. It came open—and there, crouching in the cupboard, scared and trembling, was Ellen! She had slipped out of Mam'zelle's room and gone into the second-form room when she had heard Darrell coming. She had hidden in the cupboard, as still as a mouse.

Darrell looked in amazement at her. 'Come out!' she said. 'You bad girl, Ellen! Have you been stealing something again?'

'No,' said Ellen, and came out. She held on to the test-papers in her pocket, and Darrell noticed the action.

'What have you got there?' she demanded. 'Show me! Quick! You're hiding something.'

'I'm not! I'm not!' cried Ellen, forgetting all about being quiet. Darrell tried to snatch Ellen's hand away from her pocket, and Ellen, afraid, lashed out at Darrell with her other hand. It caught her on the face.

Then Darrell lost her temper! She flew at Ellen, shook her fiercely, and slapped her hard on the cheek! Ellen fell over the legs of a desk and dragged Darrell down with her. She struggled and Darrell pummelled her well. 'You wicked girl!' shouted Darrell. 'Coming out and stealing things! You give me what you've taken!'

Ellen suddenly went limp. She could not struggle any longer. Darrell was able to drag her up and make her take her hand away from her pocket. She pulled out the packet of papers roughly. The band broke and they scattered all over the floor. Ellen covered her face and began to sob loudly.

Darrell stared at the papers and picked one or two up. 'So you cheat too, do you?' she said, in a scornful voice. 'Tomorrow's exam papers! Ellen Wilson, what sort of a girl are you? A thief and a cheat! How dare you come here to Malory Towers?'

'Oh, put the papers back and don't let anyone know!' sobbed Ellen. 'Oh, don't tell anyone!'

'I'll certainly put the papers back,' said Darrell, grimly. 'But as for not telling anyone, that's absurd!'

She dragged Ellen to the door. 'Where did you find the papers? In Mam'zelle's desk. We'll put them back there then.'

She put them back, and then, with trembling fingers, Ellen locked the desk again. They went up to the dormy. All the girls were still asleep.

Crouching in the cupboard was Ellen

'Tomorrow,' said Darrell, 'I shall tell Sally, Ellen. And she will decide what is to be done about you. I expect you'll be expelled. Now get into bed and try to go to sleep!'

17   RUMOURS AND TALES

NOBODY heard the two girls coming back. No one guessed that Darrell and Ellen had been out of their beds and back again. Darrell, furious and excited, lay awake for some time, debating whether or not to wake Sally there and then and tell her what had happened.

'No, I won't,' she decided, reluctantly. 'It would only wake all the others, and I must get Sally alone and tell her.'

She suddenly fell asleep, and, tired out with excitement, slept very soundly indeed. But Ellen could not sleep at all. This was nothing new for her. Most nights she did not sleep until the early hours of the morning. Now she lay on her back in bed, quite stunned by all the night's happenings. But gradually she ceased to worry about them for a bigger trouble came upon her. Her headache grew so bad that she thought her head must surely burst! Red hot hammers seemed at work inside it and at last the girl grew really frightened.

What was happening to her? Was she going mad? Was this what it felt like? She lay perfectly still with her eyes closed, hoping that the pain would die down. But it didn't. It got worse.

At last it was so bad that she began to moan softly. The thought of kind, comforting Matron came to her. Matron!

Matron had been kind to her in the San. She would be kind now. Ellen felt that if she could only have one small bit of kindness from someone she would feel better.

She sat up painfully, her head spinning round. The moon was now shining fully into the dormy. She could see all the white beds with their eiderdowns slipping off, or neatly pulled up. The girls lay in various positions, fast asleep.

Ellen got out of bed slowly, because any quick movement made her head hurt unbearably. She forgot about her dressing-gown, she forgot about her slippers. She made her way slowly to the door as if she was walking in her sleep. She passed out of it like a little ghost in pyjamas.

How she found her way to Matron's room she never remembered. But Matron suddenly awoke from sleep to hear a soft knocking at her door that went on and on.

'Come in!' she cried, 'Who is it?' She switched on the light. But nobody came in. The soft knocking went on and on. Matron was puzzled and a little alarmed.

'Come in!' she called again. But nobody came. Matron leapt out of bed and went to the door, a sturdy figure in a voluminous nightdress. She flung the door open—and there stood poor Ellen, drooping like a weeping willow tree, her hand up as if she was still knocking at the door.

'Ellen! What's the matter, child? Are you ill?' cried Matron and pulled her gently into her room.

'My head,' said Ellen, in a tired whisper. 'It's bursting, Matron.'

It didn't take Matron long to deal with Ellen. Seeing that the girl was in great pain, and that she could hardly even open her eyes, Matron soon had her in a warm and comfortable bed in a little room opening off her own. She gave her medicine and a hot drink. She put a comforting hot-water bottle in beside her. She was kind and gentle and spoke in a very low voice so as not to jar Ellen's aching head.

'Now you go to sleep,' she said. 'You'll feel better in the morning.'

Ellen did fall asleep. Matron stood by the bed and looked down at her. She was puzzled. There was something wrong with this girl. She was worrying secretly about something, and she had been doing worrying before, when she was in the San. Perhaps it would be better for her to go home for a while.

In the morning Darrell woke up with the others when the dressing-bell went. She sat up, remembering all the excitement of the night. She glanced at Sally. She must somehow get her alone.

Then Sally gave an exclamation. 'Where's Ellen? Her bed's empty!'

Everyone looked at Ellen's empty bed. 'Perhaps she got up early,' suggested Emily. 'We'll see her at break-fast-time.'

Darrell felt a bit worried. Had Ellen got up early? Where was she?

Ellen was not at breakfast, of course. The girls looked at the empty place, and Darrell felt distinctly uncomfortable. Surely—surely Ellen hadn't run away in the night and not come back! Mam'zelle was taking breakfast that day and Darrell spoke to her.

'Where's Ellen, Mam'zelle?'

'She is not coming to breakfast,' said Mam'zelle, who knew nothing more than that. Miss Parker had told her hurriedly as she passed her in the corridor. 'I do not know why. Perhaps she is ill.'

Now Alicia began to feel uncomfortable too. She remembered how she had accused Ellen so bitterly the day before. Where *was* Ellen? She too began to wonder if the girl had run away home.   She ate her porridge rather silently.

The next piece of news came from a first-former, Katie. She had heard Miss Parker talking to Miss Potts, and had caught a few words.

' I say !   What's up with Ellen Wilson ? ' she demanded. ' I heard Nosey tell Potty that she was going to be sent home ! What's she done ? '

Sent home !   The second-formers looked at one another. Did that mean that the staff had found out about Ellen— had perhaps discovered she had been stealing ?   And she was to be expelled !   Good gracious !

' She's either been found out by one of the mistresses, or else she's gone and confessed,' said Alicia, at last.   ' We'd better not say too much about what we know.   It's not much to the credit of the school.   I expect it will be all hushed up.'

' Do you mean that you really think Ellen is being sent away—expelled from the school—because she stole those things ? ' said Daphne, looking suddenly white.   ' Surely she won't ! '

' She jolly well will,' said Betty, and there was such scorn in her voice that Daphne looked quite startled.   ' And a good thing too !   Fancy having that kind of girl at Malory Towers ! '

Darrell was bewildered by the turn things had taken. Now she didn't know whether to report the happenings of last night or not.   If Ellen was to be sent home for stealing, then there didn't seem much point in telling anyone that she, Darrell, had caught her cheating—taking the test-papers to look at before the test.   Because certainly Ellen wouldn't take the tests now, and why blacken her name even more, now that she was apparently being sent off in disgrace ?

Darrell was a generous girl, even to those she considered

her enemies.   She thought over the night before.   She had
certainly given Ellen a good deal of punishment for cheating !
She felt rather hot when she remembered how she had
slapped Ellen's face, pummelled her and knocked her down.
That was her temper again, of course.   Sally wouldn't have
done a thing like that.   Sally would have dealt with the
whole thing in a dignified, calm way, and would have made
Ellen show her the test-papers without a lot of undignified
rough behaviour that ended in both girls rolling on the
floor !

' I don't manage things very well, somehow,' thought
Darrell, rubbing her nose with her hand.   ' I just go off the
deep end with a splash !   I fly off the handle, I go up in
smoke !   Well, what am I going to do ?   Tell Sally or
not ? '

She decided not to.   There didn't seem any point at
all in complaining about Ellen, and making her character
still worse if she was really going to be sent home.   So
Darrell held her tongue, a thing that not many of the second
form would have done in the circumstances, for most of them
dearly loved a gossip.

Still, there was plenty of gossip in the second form
about Ellen.   Everyone seemed to take it for granted that
somehow or other it had been found out by the staff that
Ellen had taken the purses, money and brooch and possibly
other things as well, and was being expelled for that.

Curiously enough, one of the girls who seemed most distressed about this was Daphne.   ' But surely they won't
expel her without some proof ? ' she kept saying.   ' Sally,
Darrell, you said to Alicia yesterday that there was no real
proof that Ellen had stolen anything.   What will happen
to Ellen ?   Will another school take her ? '

' I don't know.   I shouldn't think so,' said Alicia.   ' She's
finished !   Serve her right ! '

' Don't be so hard,' said Jean.   ' Don't think I'm standing up for her—I'm not. But you always sound so hard and unmerciful, Alicia.'

' Well, I was right yesterday when I accused Ellen, wasn't I ? ' demanded Alicia. ' You were all so soft you didn't want to have it out with her ! Good thing I did.'

The second form decided to say nothing about Ellen to the staff. If Miss Grayling was going to expel the girl, she would want to keep it quiet. So the less said the better.

So, rather to Miss Parker's surprise, nobody asked about Ellen at all. ' Curious, this lack of interest,' she thought, and she said nothing either. The girls had no idea at all when or if Ellen had gone home, though somebody passed round a rumour that a car had been seen in the drive that morning. Perhaps it had come to fetch Ellen !

It hadn't. It was the doctor's car. He had been called in to examine the girl, and he had spoken gravely to Matron and Miss Grayling. ' There's something here I don't understand. Is the child worried about anything ? Is there anything wrong at her home ? Has anything upset her at school ? '

Neither Matron nor the Head Mistress could give the doctor any information. As far as they knew there was nothing wrong at Ellen's home, and there had been no upset in her form. Miss Parker was called in and she too said that as far as she knew Ellen had not been in any trouble in any class, except for mild tickings-off for not doing work up to standard.

' We think, Ellen,' said Miss Grayling gently, when the doctor had gone, ' we think you should go home when you feel well enough. That would be the best place for you now.'

She was startled by Ellen's response to this suggestion. The girl sat up and pushed back her hair in a despairing way. ' Oh, no, Miss Grayling ! Don't expel me ! Please don't ! '

'Expel you!' said the Head, in amazement. 'What do you mean?'

Ellen had broken into sobs and Matron came hurrying up at once, making signs to Miss Grayling to go. 'She mustn't be excited in any way,' she whispered. 'So sorry, Miss Grayling, but I think you'd better go. I'll deal with her now.'

Miss Grayling, very puzzled indeed, went quietly out of the room. Why should Ellen think she was going to be expelled? There was something here that needed looking into.

It took Ellen a long time to calm down. She really thought that Miss Grayling's suggestion of going home meant that she was telling her she was to be sent away from Malory Towers—expelled in disgrace. Perhaps Darrell had been to her and told her about the cheating? Or perhaps Alicia had told her that they all believed she had been stealing, and Miss Grayling had decided to expel her because of that. Ellen didn't know. She began to worry all over again and Matron was alarmed at the quick rise in her temperature.

Some of the second-formers were upset at the thought that Ellen might have been already expelled, and had been sent home without even saying goodbye. Mary-Lou especially was upset. She hadn't liked Ellen very much, but she was very sorry for her. She spoke to Daphne about it at Break.

'Daphne, isn't it awful? What will poor Ellen say to her parents when she gets home? Do you think she will have to tell them herself that she's been sent away for stealing?'

'Don't!' said Daphne. 'Don't let's talk about it, Mary-Lou. Look, we've got about ten minutes, haven't we? I've got a most important parcel to send off this morning, and I can't find any string anywhere. Be a dear and get me some. I've got the brown paper.'

Mary-Lou sped off, wondering what the important parcel was. She couldn't seem to find any string at all. It was astonishing, the total lack of any string that morning! When at last she got back to Daphne, the bell went for the next lesson.

'Haven't you got any string ?' said Daphne, disappointed. 'Oh, blow! Well, I'll see if I can find some after the morning lessons, and then I'll slip down to the post with the parcel this afternoon. I've got half an hour in between two lessons, because my music mistress isn't here today.'

'Is it so very important ?' asked Mary-Lou. 'I could run with it for you, if you like.'

'No. You'd never get there and back in time,' said Daphne. 'It's a long way by the inland road. You could manage it by the coast road, but there's such a gale again today you'd be blown over the top! I'll go in between lessons this afternoon.'

But she couldn't go after all, with her 'important parcel', whatever it was, for the music mistress turned up, and Daphne was called away to her lesson. She left the parcel in her desk.

'Oh dear!' she said at teatime, to Gwen and Mary-Lou. 'I did so badly want to take my parcel to the post—and I had to have my music-lesson after all—and now I've got to go to Miss Parker after tea for a returned lesson, and after that there's a rehearsal for that silly French play.'

'What's so urgent about the parcel ?' asked Gwen. 'Somebody's birthday ?'

Daphne hesitated. 'Yes,' she said. 'That's it. If it doesn't go today it won't get there in time!'

'Well, you'll have to post it tomorrow,' said Gwen. Mary-Lou looked at Daphne's worried face. What a pity she, Mary-Lou, couldn't take it for her. She always liked doing things for Daphne, and getting that charming smile in return.

She began to think how she might do it. 'I'm free at seven, after prep,' she thought. 'I'll have half an hour before supper. I could never get to the post-office and back if I take the inland road—but I could if I took the coast road. Would I dare to—in the dark and rain?'

She thought about it as she sat in afternoon school. 'People don't mind what they do for their friends,' she thought. 'They dare anything. Daphne would be so thrilled if I went to the post and got her birthday parcel off for her. How kind she is to want it to get there on the day. Just like her. Well—if it isn't too dark and horrible, I might run along tonight for her. I mustn't tell anyone though, because it's against the rules. If Sally got to know, she'd forbid me!'

So timid little Mary-Lou planned to do something that even not one of the seniors would do on a dark, windy night—take the coast road on the cliff, whilst a gale blew wildly round!

18   MARY-LOU

AFTER prep that night Mary-Lou scuttled back to the second-form room, which was now empty except for Gwendoline, who was tidying up.

Mary-Lou went to Daphne's desk. Gwendoline looked at her jealously. 'What do you want in Daphne's desk? I can take her anything she's forgotten. I wish you wouldn't suck up to her so much, Mary-Lou.'

'I don't,' said Mary-Lou. She opened the desk-lid and fished for the brown-paper parcel, now neatly tied up with string. 'I'm going to the post with this for Daphne. But don't go and split on me, Gwen. I know it's against the rules.'

Gwendoline stared at Mary-Lou in surprise. '*You* breaking the rules!' she said. 'I don't believe you ever did that before. You're mad to think you can get to the post and back in time.'

'I shall. I'm taking the coast road,' said Mary-Lou, valiantly, though her heart failed her when she said it. 'It's only ten minutes there and back by that road.'

'Mary-Lou! You must be daft!' said Gwendoline. 'There's a gale blowing and it's dark as pitch. You'll be blown over the cliff as sure as anything.'

'I shan't,' said Mary-Lou, stoutly, though again her heart sank inside her. 'And, anyway, it's only a small thing to do for a friend. I know Daphne particularly wants this parcel to go today.'

'Daphne isn't your friend,' said Gwendoline, a flare of jealously coming up in her again.

'She is,' said Mary-Lou, with such certainty that Gwendoline was annoyed.

'Baby!' said Gwendoline, scornfully. 'You're too silly even to see that Daphne only uses you because you can help her with her French. That's the only reason she puts up with you hanging round her. She's told me so.'

Mary-Lou stood looking at Gwendoline, the parcel in her hand. She felt suddenly very miserable. 'It's not true,' she said. 'You're making it up.'

'It *is* true!' said Gwendoline, spitefully. 'I tell you Daphne has said so herself to me heaps of times. What would a girl like Daphne want with a mouse like you! You're just useful to her, that's all, and if you weren't so jolly conceited you'd know it without being told!'

Mary-Lou felt as if it must be true. Gwendoline would never say such a thing so emphatically if it wasn't. She picked up the parcel, her mouth quivering, and turned to go.

' Mary-Lou ! You don't mean to say you're going to bother with that parcel after what I've just told you ! ' called Gwendoline, in surprise. ' Don't be an idiot.'

' I'm taking it for Daphne because I'm *her* friend ! ' answered Mary-Lou, in a shaky voice. ' She may not be mine, but if I'm hers I'll still be willing to do things for her.'

' Stupid little donkey ! ' said Gwendoline to herself, and began to slam books back on to shelves and to make a terrific cloud of dust with the blackboard duster.

She didn't tell Daphne that Mary-Lou had gone off into the darkness with her parcel. She was feeling rather ashamed of having been so outspoken. Daphne might not like it. But after all it was nearly the end of the term, and there would be now no need for Mary-Lou to help Daphne. She would probably be glad to be rid of Mary-Lou when she no longer needed her help with her French.

Half-past seven came and the supper-bell rang. Girls poured out of the different rooms and went clattering down to the dining-room. ' Oooh ! Coffee tonight for a change ! And jammy buns and rolls and potted meat ! '

They all sat down and helped themselves, whilst Miss Parker poured out big cups of coffee. She glanced round the table. ' Two empty chairs ! Who's missing ? Oh, Ellen, of course. Who's the other ? '

' Mary-Lou,' said Sally. ' I saw her just after prep. She'll be along in a minute, Miss Parker.'

But five minutes, ten minutes went by and there was no sign of Mary-Lou. Miss Parker frowned.

' Surely she must have heard the bell. See if you can find her, Sally.'

Sally sped off and came back to report that Mary-Lou was nowhere to be found. By this time Gwendoline was in a great dilemma. She and she only knew where Mary-

Lou was. If she told, she would get Mary-Lou into trouble. Surely she would be back soon? Maybe she had had to wait at the post-office!

Then she suddenly remembered something. The post-office shut at seven! It wouldn't be any use Mary-Lou trying to post a parcel there, because it would be shut. Why hadn't she thought of that before? Then what had happened to Mary-Lou?

A cold hand seemed to creep round Gwendoline's heart and almost stop her breathing. Suppose—suppose that the wind had blown little Mary-Lou over the cliff? Suppose that even now she was lying on the rocks, dead or badly hurt! The thought was so terrible that Gwendoline couldn't swallow her morsel of bun and half-choked.

Daphne thumped her on the back. Gwendoline spoke to her in a low, urgent voice.

'Daphne! I must tell you something as soon after supper as possible. Come into one of the practice-rooms where we shall be alone.'

Daphne looked alarmed. She nodded. When supper was finished she led the way to one of the deserted practice-rooms and switched on the light. 'What's the matter?' she asked Gwendoline. 'You look like a ghost.'

'It's Mary-Lou. I know where she went,' said Gwendoline.

'Well, why on earth didn't you tell Miss Parker then?' asked Daphne, crossly. 'What *is* the matter, Gwen?'

'Daphne, she took your precious parcel to the post just after seven o'clock,' said Gwendoline. 'She took the coast road. Do you think anything's happened to her?'

Daphne took this in slowly. 'Took my parcel to the post? What*ever* for! At this time of night, too.'

'She went all soppy and said that although it meant her going out in the dark and the wind, she'd do it because you were her friend,' said Gwendoline.

'Why didn't you stop her, you idiot?' demanded Daphne.

'I did try,' said Gwendoline. 'I even told her that you were *not* her friend—you only found her useful for helping you with your French, as you've often and often told me, Daphne—and you'd think that would stop anyone from going off into the dark on a windy night, wouldn't you, to post a silly parcel?'

'And didn't it stop her?' said Daphne, in a queer sort of voice.

'No. She just said that she would take it for you because she was *your* friend,' said Gwendoline, rather scornfully. 'She said you might not be her friend, but she was yours, and she'd still be willing to do things for you.'

Gwendoline was amazed to see tears suddenly glisten in Daphne's eyes. Daphne never cried! 'What's up?' said Gwendoline in surprise.

'Nothing that you'd understand,' said Daphne, blinking the tears away savagely. 'Good heavens! Fancy going out on a night like this and taking the coast road—just because she wanted to take that parcel for me. And the post-office would be shut too! Poor little Mary-Lou! What can have happened to her?'

'Has she fallen over the cliff, do you think?' asked Gwendoline.

Daphne went very white. 'No—no, don't say that!' she said. 'You can't think how awful that would be. I'd never, never forgive myself!'

'It wouldn't be *your* fault if she did,' said Gwendoline, surprised at this outburst.

'It would, it would! You don't understand!' cried Daphne. 'Oh, poor kind little Mary-Lou! And you sent her out thinking I didn't like her—that I only just used her! I *do* like her. I like her ten times better than I like you! She's kind and generous and unselfish. I know I did use her at first, and welcomed her just because she could help me—but I couldn't help getting fond of her.   She just gives everything and asks nothing ! '

' But—you told me heaps of times you only put up with her because she was useful,' stammered Gwendoline, completely taken aback by all this, and looking very crestfallen indeed.

' I know I did !   I was beastly.   It was the easiest thing to do, to keep you from bothering me and nagging me about Mary-Lou.   Oh, I shall never, never get over it if anything has happened !   I'm going after her.   I'm going to see if I can find her ! '

' You can't ! ' cried Gwendoline, in horror.   ' Hark at the wind !   It's worse than ever ! '

' If Mary-Lou can go out into that wind to post a stupid parcel for me, surely *I* can go out into it to find her ! ' said Daphne, and a look came into her pretty, pale face that Gwendoline had never seen before—a sturdy, determined look that gave her face unexpected character.

' But, Daphne,' protested Gwendoline, feebly, and then stopped.   Daphne had gone out of the little music-room like a whirlwind.   She ran up to the dormy and got her mackintosh and sou-wester.   She tore down to the cloak-room and put on her Wellingtons.   Nobody saw her.   Then out she went into the night, flashing on her torch to see her way.

It was a wild night, and the wind howled round fiercely. It took Daphne's breath away as she made her way to the coast road up on the cliff.   Whatever would it be like there ! She would be almost blown away.

She flashed her torch here and there.   There was nothing to be seen but a few bent bushes, dripping with rain.

She went a little farther and began to call loudly and desperately.

' Mary-Lou !   Mary-LOU !   Where are you ? '

The wind tore her words out of her mouth and flung them
over the cliff.   She called again, putting her hands up to
her mouth.   ' Mary-Lou !   MARY-LOU !   MARY-
LOU ! '

And surely that was a faint call in answer.   ' Here !
Here !   Help me ! '

19   A HEROINE!

DAPHNE stood quite still and listened.   The cry came
again on the wind, very faint.   ' Here !   Here ! '

It seemed to come from somewhere in front.   Daphne
struggled on against the wind, and then came to a place
where the cliff edge swung inwards.   She followed the edge
round cautiously, not daring to go too near, for the wind
was so strong.   Still, it seemed to be dying down a little
now.

She suddenly heard Mary-Lou's voice much nearer.
' Help !   Help ! '

Daphne was afraid of being blown over the cliff if she
went too near the edge.   But the voice seemed to come
from the edge somewhere.   Daphne sat down on the wet
ground, feeling that the wind would not then have so much
power over her and began to edge herself forward, holding
on the tufts of grass when she could.

She came to where the cliff had crumbled away a little,
and made a series of ledges, going steeply down to the sea.
She crawled to this place, lay flat down and shone her light
over the broken cliff.

And there, a few feet below, was poor Mary-Lou, clinging

for dear life to a ledge, her white face upturned to the glare of the torch.

'Help!' she called again, feebly, seeing the torch. 'Oh, help me! I can't hold on much longer!'

Daphne was horrified. She could see that if Mary-Lou did leave go, she would hurtle down to the rocks a long way below. Her heart went cold at the thought. What could she do?

'I'm here, Mary-Lou!' she called. 'Hold on. I'll fetch help.'

'Oh—Daphne! Is it you! Don't go away, Daphne. I shall fall in a minute. Can't you do something?'

Daphne looked down at Mary-Lou. She felt that it would not be the slightest use leaving her and going for help for it was clear that Mary-Lou might leave go at any moment. No, she must think of something else and do it at once.

She thought of her mackintosh belt, and her tunic belt. If she tied those both together and let them down, Mary-Lou might hold them and drag herself up. But would they reach?

She undid her mackintosh belt and took off her tunic belt with fingers that fumbled exasperatingly. All the time she kept up a comforting flow of words to Mary-Lou.

'I'll save you, don't you worry! I'll soon have you up here! I'm making a rope with my belts and I'll let it down. Hold on, Mary-Lou, hold on, and I'll soon save you!'

Mary-Lou was comforted and held on. She had been so frightened when the gale took her and rolled her over and over to the edge of the cliff. How she had managed to hold on to the tufts of grass she didn't know. It had seemed ages and ages till she heard Daphne's voice. Now Daphne was here and would rescue her. Whatever Gwendoline had said, Daphne was her friend!

Daphne lay down flat again. She found a stout gorse

bush behind her and she pushed her legs under it till her feet found the sturdy root-stem growing out of the ground. Heedless of scratches and pricks, she wound her two feet firmly round the stem, so that she had a good hold with her legs and would not be likely to be pulled over the cliff by Mary-Lou.

A frantic voice suddenly came up to her. 'Daphne! This tuft of grass is giving way! I shall fall! Quick, quick.'

Daphne hurriedly let down the rough rope, made of her two belts. Mary-Lou caught at it and looped the end firmly round her wrists. Daphne felt the pull at once.

'Are you all right?' she called, anxiously. 'You won't fall now, will you?'

'No. I don't think so. My feet have got quite a firm hold,' called back Mary-Lou, much reassured by the belt round her wrists. 'I shan't pull you over, shall I, Daphne?

'No. But I don't think I'm strong enough to pull you up!' said Daphne, in despair. 'And the belts might break and let you fall. I don't see that we can do anything but just hang on to each other till somebody finds us.'

'Oh, poor Daphne! This is awful for you,' came back Mary-Lou's voice. 'I wish I'd never thought of taking that parcel.'

'It was kind of you,' said Daphne, not knowing how to get the words out. 'But you're always kind, Mary-Lou. And Mary-Lou, I'm your friend. You know that, don't you? Gwen told me the beastly things she said. They're not true. I think the world of you, I do really. I've never been fond of anyone before.'

'Oh, I knew Gwen told me untruths, as soon as I heard your voice and knew you'd come to look for me,' said Mary-Lou, out of the darkness. 'I think you're a heroine, Daphne.'

'I'm not,' said Daphne. 'I'm a beastly person. You simply don't know how beastly.'

'This is a funny conversation to be having on a cliff-side in a stormy night, isn't it ? ' said Mary-Lou, trying to sound cheerful. 'Oh dear—I am so sorry to have caused all this trouble. Daphne, when will people come to look for us ? '

'Well, only Gwen knows I've come out,' said Daphne. 'If I don't come back soon, surely she will tell Nosey Parker, and they'll send out to look for us. I do hope she'll have the sense to tell someone.'

Gwendoline had. She had felt very worried indeed about first Mary-Lou and now Daphne. When Daphne had not come back after half an hour, Gwendoline had gone to Miss Parker. She told her where Mary-Lou had gone and that Daphne had gone to look for her.

'What! Out on the coast road at night! In this weather! What madness ! ' cried Miss Parker, and rushed off to Miss Grayling at once.

In two or three minutes a search-party was out with lanterns, ropes and flasks of hot cocoa. It was not long before the two girls were found. Miss Grayling gave an agonized exclamation as she saw them. 'They might both have been killed ! '

Daphne's arms were almost numb with strain when the search-party came up. They saw her lying flat on the ground, her legs curled tightly round the stem of the prickly bush, holding the two belts down the cliff-side—and there, at the other end, holding on for dear life, was Mary-Lou, the sea pounding away far below her.

A rope was let down to Mary-Lou, slipped right over her head, and tightened over arms and shoulders. Another one looped tightly round her waist. Daphne got up thankfully, her legs almost asleep, and Miss Parker caught hold of her. 'Steady now ! Hold on to me ! '

Mary-Lou was pulled up safely by a hefty gardener. She

lay on the ground, crying with relief. The gardener undid
the ropes and lifted her up. 'I'll carry her,' he said.
'Give her a drink, Mam, she's freezing!'

Both girls felt glad of the hot cocoa. Then, holding on
to Miss Parker, Daphne staggered back to school, followed
by the gardener carrying Mary-Lou, and then by the rest
of the party.

'Put both girls to bed,' Miss Grayling said to Matron.
'They've had a terrible experience. I only hope they don't
get pneumonia now! Daphne, you saved little Mary-
Lou's life, there's no doubt about that. I am very proud
of you!'

Daphne said nothing at all, but, to Miss Grayling's
surprise, hung her head and turned away. She had no
time to puzzle over this, but helped Matron to get Mary-
Lou undressed and into bed. Both girls were soon in warm
beds, with hot food and drink inside them. They each felt
extremely sleepy, and went off to sleep quite suddenly.

The second-formers were in bed, worried and sleepless.
Gwen had told them about Mary-Lou going off, and
Daphne following her to see if she could find her. They
knew that a search-party had gone out. All kinds of
horrible pictures came into their minds as they lay in bed
and listened to the wind.

They talked long after lights out. Sally did not forbid
them. This was not a usual night—it was a night of
anxiety, and talking helped.

Then, after a long time, they heard Miss Parker's quick
footsteps coming along the corridor. News! They all
sat up at once.

She switched on the light and looked round at the seven
waiting girls. Then she told them the story of how Mary-
Lou and Daphne had been found, and how Daphne, by her
ingenious idea, had saved Mary-Lou. She described how
she had laid herself down on the wet ground, her feet curled

round the gorse bush stem, and had held the belts down to Mary-Lou until help came.

'Daphne's a heroine!' cried Darrell. 'I never liked her—but, Miss Parker, she's been marvellous, hasn't she! She's a real heroine!'

'I think she is,' said Miss Parker. 'I did not guess that she had it in her. She's in bed now, in the San., but I think she'll soon be all right again. We'll give her three cheers and a clap when she comes back to class.'

She switched off the light and said good night. The girls talked excitedly for a few minutes more, thankful that they knew what had happened. Fancy Daphne turning out like that! And doing it for Mary-Lou! Why, Gwen had always said that Daphne only put up with Mary-Lou because she helped her with her French.

'Daphne must be fond of Mary-Lou,' said Darrell, voicing what everyone thought. 'I'm glad. I always thought it was mean to use Mary-Lou and not really like her.'

'I wonder what became of the parcel,' said Belinda 'Mary-Lou can't have posted it, because the post-office was shut. I bet nobody thought of the precious parcel.'

'We'll go and hunt for it tomorrow,' said Sally. 'I say—what a small dormy we are tonight—only seven of us. Ellen gone—and Daphne and Mary-Lou in the San. Well, thank goodness they're there and not out on the cliff.'

The wind rose to a gale again and howled round North Tower. The girls snuggled down closer into the beds. 'I do think Daphne was brave,' said Darrell, 'and I can't *imagine* how timid little Mary-Lou could possibly have dared to go out in this gale. *Mary-Lou* of all people.'

'People are queer,' said Irene. 'You simply never can tell what a person will do from one day to the next.'

'You never said a truer word!' chuckled Darrell.   'To-day you put your French grammar away in the games cup-board and tried to put your lacrosse stick into your desk—and goodness knows what you'll do tomorrow.'

20   AN ASTONISHING PARCEL

IT was difficult to do tests in the midst of so much excite-ment.   The story of Mary-Lou and Daphne ran through the school and everyone talked about it.   The two girls did not appear in school that day, because Matron was keeping them quiet.   They neither of them seemed any the worse for their adventure.

Before afternoon school Darrell, Sally, Irene and Belinda set off up the cliff-path to look for the parcel.   The wind had completely died down and it was a lovely day, one of Cornwall's best.   The sky was as blue as a cornflower, and the sea picked up the colour and made the view a really beautiful one, as the girls walked up the coast-path.

'Look—that must be where Mary-Lou was blown over,' said Darrell, pointing to where the cliff had crumbled. 'And see—surely that's the gorse bush Daphne wound her legs round.   Golly, she must have been scratched!'

The girls stood and looked at the place where Mary-Lou and Daphne had had their frightening adventure.   Sally shivered, thinking of what it must have been like in the dark night, with the wind howling round and the sea pounding on the rocks below.

'It's horrid to think of,' she said.   'Come on—let's hunt

about for the parcel. Mary-Lou must have dropped it somewhere near here, I should think.'

They began to look. It was Darrell who found the parcel, lying wet and torn in the grass some little way off.

' I've got it ! ' she shouted, and ran to pick it up. ' Oh, it's all coming to pieces. The paper is pulpy, and the contents are coming out ! '

' Better take off the paper and carry the things inside home in our hands,' said Sally. So Darrell stripped off the wet, pulpy paper and shook out the contents. They fell on the grass.

They were rather queer. The girls looked at them, lying there. There were four purses of different sizes and shapes. There were three boxes, the kind that brooches or lockets are sold in by jewellers—little leather boxes with a catch you had to press to open them.

Darrell picked one up and pressed it. It shot open— and a little gold bar brooch gleamed inside. She looked at it, bewildered, then passed it to Sally.

' Isn't that Emily's brooch—the one she lost ? '

' It's got her name behind it if it is,' said Sally, in a sober voice. She took out the brooch and looked at the back of the little gold bar.

' Yes—it's Emily's,' she said. ' Her name is there.'

Sally opened another of the boxes. It contained a little gold necklace, plain and simple.

' Katie's ! ' said Irene at once. ' I've seen her wearing it ! Good gracious—how did these come to be in the parcel ? Is it the right parcel we've found ? '

Sally picked everything up from the grass. Her face looked very serious. ' It's the right parcel,' she said. ' Look—these purses belong to people we know. That's Gwen's. And that's Mary-Lou's. And that's surely Betty's.'

The four girls looked at one another in bewilderment.

They looked at the contents in bewilderment

'If this was the parcel that Mary-Lou was posting for
Daphne, how was it Daphne put all these things into it?'
said Sally, voicing what everyone was thinking.

'Could she have got them from Ellen?' said Darrell,
puzzled. 'We all know Ellen must have taken them.
Wherever did she get them from? Is she doing it to shield
Ellen, or something?'

'We'll have to find out,' said Irene. 'Sally, we'd better
take the parcel to Miss Grayling. We can't keep this to
ourselves.'

'No, we can't,' said Sally. 'We'll go back at once.'

They went back, saying very little, puzzled and solemn.
Here were the stolen things, the things they had accused
Ellen of taking—Daphne had somehow got hold of them and
for some extraordinary reason was sending them away—and
Mary-Lou had almost lost her life in trying to post them,
and had been rescued by Daphne! It was all most complicated.

'I think it's all very mysterious,' said Belinda. 'I can't
make head or tail of it. It's a pity Ellen's been expelled,
or we might go to her and show her what we've found.'

The girls had no idea that Ellen was still at Malory
Towers. What with one rumour and another they were
all firmly convinced she had been sent home!

The bell was ringing for afternoon school as they got in.
They caught Miss Parker as she was going to the second
form and asked her for permission to go and see Miss
Grayling.

'We've found the parcel that Mary-Lou went to post
and we think we ought to hand it over to Miss Grayling,'
explained Sally.

'Very well. Don't be too long,' said Miss Parker, and
went on her way. The four girls went to Miss Grayling's
part of the buildings and knocked at her door.

'Come in!' said her low voice, and they opened the door

and went in. She was alone. She looked up in surprise when she saw four girls. Then she smiled, for she liked all of them, even harum-scarum Belinda.

'Please, Miss Grayling, we found the parcel that Mary-Lou went to post for Daphne,' said Sally, coming forward. 'And here are the things that were inside it. The paper was so wet that we had to take it off.'

She placed the purses and the boxes down on the Head Mistress's desk. Miss Grayling looked at them in surprise. 'Were *these* inside!' she said. 'Are they all Daphne's then? I understand that it was Daphne's parcel.'

There was an awkward pause. 'Well, Miss Grayling, they are things belonging to us girls,' said Sally, at last. 'We missed them at various times. Some of the purses had money in when they were taken. They are empty now.'

Miss Grayling suddenly looked quite different. A stern expression came into her eyes, and she sat up straight. 'You will have to explain a little better, Sally,' she said. 'Am I to understand that these were stolen at some time from one or other of you this term?'

'Yes, Miss Grayling,' said Sally, and the others nodded.

'You think Daphne took them?' said Miss Grayling, after a pause. The girls looked at one another.

'Well,' said Sally at last, 'we did think Ellen had taken them, Miss Grayling. We knew she had been expelled, you see—and we thought . . .'

'Wait!' said Miss Grayling, in such a sharp tone that the four girls jumped. 'Ellen *expelled*! Whatever do you mean? She is in the San. under Matron's eye. She went to her two nights ago with a blinding headache, and we are keeping her under observation to try to find out what the matter is.'

The girls were absolutely taken aback. Sally went brilliant red. She oughtn't to have believed those rumours!

But she had wanted to believe them, because she didn't like Ellen. The girls couldn't find a word to say.

Miss Grayling eyed them sharply. 'This is most extraordinary!' she said at last. 'I simply cannot understand it. What made you think Ellen should be expelled? And why did you think she had taken these things? She is surely not that type of girl at all. As you know, she won a scholarship here by means of very hard work and she came with a most excellent report as regards character from her last head mistress.'

'We—we thought she had taken them,' began Sally. 'At least, I said we ought not to accuse her till we had definite *proof*—but, but . . .'

'I see. You actually accused the unfortunate girl to her face, I suppose? When was this?'

'The evening before last, Miss Grayling,' said Sally, trying to avoid the Head Mistress's eyes, which had suddenly become gimlets, and were boring into her.

'The evening before last,' said Miss Grayling. 'Ah, that explains matters. It must have been because of that that Ellen got so upset, and was overcome by that fearful headache and went to Matron. And somehow you thought she had been expelled—goodness knows why—some silly rumour, I suppose, fostered by you because you wanted to believe it! You may have done serious damage to an innocent girl.'

Darrell swallowed once or twice. She was remembering how she had attacked Ellen that night in the second-form room. Certainly Ellen had been cheating—but Darrell had called her a thief and said unforgivable things to her. She looked at Miss Grayling and knew that she must tell her what had happened between Ellen and herself. It was because of *that*, she felt sure, that Ellen had been ill that night. Oh dear—how things did begin to go wrong once you were silly yourself!

'Can I say a word to you alone, please, Miss Grayling,' said Darrell, desperately. 'It's something the others don't know about, but I think I'd better tell you.'

'Wait outside the door for a minute or two,' ordered Miss Grayling, nodding at Sally, Belinda and Irene. 'I haven't finished with you yet.'

They went outside and shut the door, feeling surprised. Whatever had Darrell got to tell Miss Grayling? She might at least have told them too!

Darrell poured out the story of how she had followed Ellen that night and caught her in the second-form room cupboard, clutching the test-papers in her hand.

'And I called her a cheat, which she was,' said Darrell, 'and I called her a thief, too, and told her I'd tell Sally in the morning and it would be reported and she would be expelled. And I suppose it worried her so much that she got that awful headache and went to Matron. And I never knew, and we all thought that somehow you must have found out she was a thief and had expelled her quietly, without making a fuss.'

'Well, really!' said Miss Grayling, when this outpouring had come to an end. 'The things that go on in this school that nobody knows about! It's incredible. Do you actually mean to tell me, Darrell, that you and Ellen were fighting together on the floor of the second-form room in the middle of the night? That is not at all a thing to be proud of.'

'I know,' said Darrell. 'I'm awfully sorry about it now. But I just saw red, Miss Grayling—and lost my temper. I can't bear cheats.'

'It's very strange,' said Miss Grayling, thoughtfully. 'Ellen is a scholarship girl, and I have never known such a girl have any need to cheat. I can't believe that Ellen was cheating. If she was, there is some reason for it that must be found out. Don't any of you like Ellen, Darrell?'

Darrell hesitated. 'Well—she's so nervy and snappy and irritable, Miss Grayling. She snaps if we jerk the table, she shouts at us if we interrupt her reading. She's terribly bad-tempered. I think Jean likes her more than any of us do. She's been awfully patient with her.'

'I wish I'd known all this before,' said Miss Grayling. 'Now I know why Ellen was so upset when I suggested sending her home. I thought possibly she might feel better and happier at home—and she must have thought I was really meaning to expel her, because somebody had come to me and told me she was stealing or cheating. Poor Ellen. I think she has over-taxed that brain of hers and this is the result.'

Darrell stood silent. She felt that Miss Grayling was not very pleased with her. 'I'm sorry for what I did,' she said, trying to blink back the tears. 'I know I keep on and on saying I'll never lose my temper again or lose control of myself. You won't believe me any more.'

'I shall go on believing you and trusting you every single time,' said Miss Grayling, turning her deep-blue eyes on Darrell and smiling. 'And one day you'll be strong enough to keep your promise. Probably when you are in the sixth form! Now tell the others to come in again.'

They came in. Miss Grayling addressed them gravely. 'What Darrell told me I think it is better not to repeat to you for my own good reasons. I think she should not repeat it to you either. I will just say this—Ellen is not the thief, you may be absolutely certain of that.'

'Not the thief!' said Sally. 'But—we all thought she was—and Alicia accused her to her face . . . and . . .'

Sally had let Alicia's name slip without thinking. Miss Grayling drummed on her desk with a pencil. 'Oh—so Alicia did the accusing, did she?' she said. 'Then she has something to feel very guilty about. I think that that public accusation brought Ellen's trouble to a head. Sally,

you are head-girl of the form. I leave it to you to show
Alicia that a little more kindness and a little less hardness
would be very much more admired by me, by you and
everyone else.'

'Yes, Miss Grayling,' said Sally, feeling extremely guilty
herself. 'But Miss Grayling—who *was* the thief?'

'It couldn't possibly have been Daphne,' said Irene.
'Nobody who did what Daphne did last night could possibly
be so mean. Why, Daphne's a heroine! Everyone says
so!'

'And you think that if someone does a brave deed quite
suddenly, then he or she could never do a mean one?'
asked Miss Grayling. 'You are wrong, Irene. We all
have good and bad in us, and we have to strive all the time
to make the good cancel out the bad. We can never be
perfect—we all of us do mean or wrong things at times—
but we can at least make amends by trying to cancel out the
wrong by doing something worthy later on. Daphne has
done quite a bit of cancelling, I think—but her heroic deed
doesn't mean that she can never do a small, mean one.'

'Is she the thief then?' asked Sally, incredulously.

'That is what I mean to find out,' said Miss Grayling.
'If she is, she shall tell you herself, and you shall judge her.
Now go back to your classroom. I am going to see Daphne
in the San. And by the way, Ellen could see someone
today. What about Jean? You said she liked Ellen more
than any of you did. Tell her to go and see Ellen after tea
and be nice to her.'

'Can she tell her we know she's not the thief?' asked
Darrell, anxiously. 'And oh, Miss Grayling—could I see
her for a few minutes too, by myself?'

'Yes,' said Miss Grayling. 'But no more fighting,
Darrell, or Matron will deal very promptly with you indeed!'

AND MISS GRAYLING

MISS GRAYLING made her way to the San. She spoke to Matron, who nodded. 'Yes, Daphne is quite all right now. She has just got up.'

The Head Mistress told Matron to take Daphne into the next room, where they would be alone. Daphne went, helped along by Matron, and sat down in an arm-chair, wondering rather fearfully what the visit was about. Miss Grayling looked so serious.

'Daphne,' said the Head, 'these things were found in the parcel that Mary-Lou went to post for you. You had packed them up yourself. Where did you get them ? And why did you want to send them away ? '

She suddenly tipped the purses and the little boxes on to Daphne's knee. The girl stared at them in absolute horror. She went very pale and opened her mouth to speak. But no words came.

'Shall I tell you where you got them from ? ' said Miss Grayling. 'You took them out of desks and lockers and drawers. You spent the money, Daphne. You did, in fact, exactly what you have done in two other schools, which have quietly intimated to your parents that they would rather have you removed. But they did not tell your parents why.'

'How did you know ? ' whispered Daphne, her once pretty face white and haggard.

'It is the custom at Malory Towers to get a confidential report of any new girl's character from her previous head mistress,' said Miss Grayling. 'We do not, if we can help it, take girls of bad character, Daphne.'

'Why did you take me then?' asked Daphne, not daring to meet the Head's eyes.

'Because, Daphne, your last head mistress said that you were not *all* bad,' said Miss Grayling. 'She said that perhaps a fresh start in a fine school like this, with its traditions of service for others, for justice, kindliness and truthfulness, might help you to cancel out the bad and develop the good. And I like to give people a chance.'

'I see,' said Daphne. 'But I'm worse than you think, Miss Grayling. I haven't only stolen—I've told lies. I said I'd never been to another school before, because I was afraid the girls might get to know I'd been sent home twice from schools. I pretended my people were very rich. I—I had a photo on my dressing-table that wasn't my mother at all—it was a very grand picture of a beautiful woman . . .'

'I know,' said Miss Grayling. 'The staff were warned about you, but not the girls. I have heard many things that made me sad, Daphne, made me think that you did not deserve the chance you had been given. Your greatest drawback is your prettiness—you want to make people admire you, you want to make them think you come of handsome, distinguished parents, from a wealthy home— you have to have envy and admiration, don't you? And because your parents are not as grand as you feel they ought to be, with you for a daughter, and cannot afford to give you as much pocket-money and pretty things as the others, you take what you want—you steal.'

'I'm no good,' said Daphne, and she looked down at her hands. 'I know that. I'm just no good.'

'And yet you have done a very brave thing,' said Miss Grayling. 'Look at me, please, Daphne. The girls admire you today—they call you a heroine. They want to cheer you and clap you. You have plenty of good in you!'

Daphne had raised her head and was looking at Miss Grayling. She flushed. 'I'm to blame for what happened to Mary-Lou,' she said. 'When I heard that Ellen had been expelled for stealing the things I had really stolen myself, I was afraid. I was too much of a coward to own up—but I thought if the empty purses and the boxes were found, my finger-prints would be on them and I'd be found out. So I thought I'd send them away by post, to a made-up address. And Mary-Lou knew I was anxious to get the parcel off and that's how she met her accident.'

'I see,' said Miss Grayling. 'I wondered why you sent away the things, Daphne. It is a great mercy that you found Mary-Lou when you did. Otherwise your foolishness and wrong-doing might have caused a great tragedy.'

'I suppose you will be sending me home, Miss Grayling,' said Daphne, after a pause. 'My parents will have to know why. They will guess there is some serious reason. They don't pay my fees you know, they couldn't afford to. My godmother does. If *she* knows about this, she will stop paying for my education; I shall have spoilt my whole life. Am I to be sent away, Miss Grayling?'

'I am going to let the girls decide that,' said Miss Grayling, gravely. 'That is, if you are brave enough to let them, Daphne. I want you to go to the second form and tell them the whole story. Confess everything to them and see what they say.'

'Oh, I can't,' said Daphne, and covered her face with her hands. 'After all I've said—and boasted! I can't!'

'Well, you have the choice,' said Miss Grayling, getting up. 'Either I send you home without any more ado—or you put yourself in the hands of your school fellows. It is a hard thing to do, but if you really want to make amends, you will do it. You have some good in you. Now is your chance to show it, even if it means being braver than you were last night!'

She left Daphne and went in to see Ellen. She sat down by her bed. 'Ellen,' she said, 'Daphne is in great trouble. The others will know soon and I have come to tell you myself. It has been discovered that it was she who took all that money and the jewellery that was missing.'

It took a moment for this to sink into Ellen's mind. Then she sat up. '*Daphne!* But the girls thought it was I who took them! They accused me. They'll never believe it was Daphne.'

'They will,' said Miss Grayling, 'because I rather think Daphne herself is going to tell them! And now, Ellen, tell me—what made you take those test-papers the other night? You are a scholarship girl with brains—you did not need to cheat.'

Ellen lay down again suddenly. She was overcome with shame. How did Miss Grayling know? Had Darrell told everyone then? Of course she had.

'Nobody knows except Darrell and myself,' said Miss Grayling. 'Darrell told me, but told no one else. So you need not worry. But I want to know why you did it. There is something you are worrying about, Ellen, and these headaches of yours won't go until you are at peace with yourself and have lost whatever worry it is you have.'

'I *did* need to cheat,' said Ellen, in a small voice. 'My brain wouldn't work any more. And I got these headaches. I knew I wouldn't even pass the tests—and the girls that night accused me of being a thief, which I wasn't—and I got all hopeless and thought that I might as well be a cheat if they all thought I was a thief!'

'I see,' said Miss Grayling. 'But why wouldn't your brain work any more?'

'I don't know,' said Ellen. 'Because I'd worked it a bit too hard, I expect, when I went in for the Scholarship. You see, Miss Grayling, I'm not really very brilliant. I get good results because I slog so—I go on and on, working and studying, where perhaps a real Scholarship girl can get better results with half the work. I worked all through the hols. too.   I was tired when I got here—but I did so badly want to do well my first term.'

' Did it matter so much ? ' asked Miss Grayling, gently.

' Yes,' said Ellen.   ' I didn't want to let my people down. They've had to pay out more than they can afford really for my uniform and things.   They're so proud of me.   I *must* do well.   And now I've ruined everything.'

' Not quite ! ' said Miss Grayling, feeling very much relieved to find that simple overwork was at the root of Ellen's trouble, and worry about what her family would think.   ' I shall write your parents a letter to tell them that you have worked very hard and done well, but that you are over-strained and must have a real holiday when it comes. By next term you will be quite fresh again, and you will have forgotten all this and be ready to rush up to the top of the form ! '

Ellen smiled at the Head, and the little worried cleft in her forehead disappeared like magic.   ' Thank you,' she said gratefully.   ' I'd like to say a lot more, but I can't.'

Miss Grayling popped in to have a word with Mary-Lou, and then went back to her own quarters.   So many girls— so many problems—so much responsibility in putting things right, and getting the best out of every girl !   No wonder Miss Grayling had more grey hairs than she should have had.

22   DAPHNE OWNS UP.
THE END OF TERM

IMMEDIATELY after tea that day the second form were told by Miss Parker that they were to go to their common-room and wait there.

'Why ?' asked Belinda, in surprise.

'You'll see,' said Miss Parker. 'Go along now. Some-one is waiting there for you.'

They all went, and rushed pell-mell into the common-room, wondering what the mystery was. Mary-Lou was there, looking a little scared, wrapped in her dressing-gown. Matron had carried her down.

And Daphne was there, fully dressed! The girls rushed at her. 'Daphne! You're a heroine! Daphne! Well done! You saved Mary-Lou's life!'

Daphne did not answer. She sat there and looked at them, rather white in the face, and did not even smile.

'What's the matter ?' asked Gwendoline.

'Sit down, all of you,' said Daphne. 'I've got something to say. Then I shall go away and you won't see me again.'

'Good gracious! Why all this melodrama ?' asked Jean, disquieted by Daphne's tragic voice.

'Listen,' said Daphne. 'You've got to listen. I'm the thief. I took those things. I've been sent away from two schools already for much the same thing. Miss Grayling knew that, but she wanted to give me another chance. So I came here. I told you lies—especially Gwen. We haven't a yacht. We haven't three or four cars. I told you I'd never been to school before because I didn't want any-one to find out I'd been expelled. I hadn't enough money to pay for some of the subs. Jean wanted, and how could I say that, when you all thought my father was a millionaire? So I took money and purses. And I took jewellery too, because I like pretty things and haven't nearly enough myself.'

She paused. The faces round her were shocked and horrified. Gwendoline looked as if she was about to faint. Her grand friend with her millionaire father! No wonder Daphne had never asked her to stay for the holidays. It was all lies.

'You all look shocked. I knew you would be. Miss Grayling said I was to come and confess to you myself, and you would judge me. I can see you judging me now. I don't blame you. I've judged myself, too, and I hate myself! I let you accuse Ellen wrongly, I let you . . .'

'And I fell into the trap and accused Ellen!' said Alicia, in a shamed voice. 'You are a beast, Daphne. You could have stopped me. I shall never forgive myself for doing that to poor old Ellen.'

There was a long pause. Then Sally spoke. 'Is that all, Daphne?'

'Isn't it enough?' said Daphne, bitterly. 'Perhaps you want to know why I got the wind up and sent away those things in a parcel, which poor Mary-Lou took for me. Well, when the rumour went round that Ellen was expelled for thieving, I was scared those purses and things might be discovered, with my finger-prints on. I know the police always look for prints. So I thought I'd better pack them up, put a false address on and send them away through the post. Then nobody would trace them to me. And because of that idiotic idea, Mary-Lou nearly got killed.'

'Yes—and because of that, you came out after me, and risked your own life for me!' said Mary-Lou's soft voice. She got up and went to Daphne. 'I don't care what the others say. I'll stick by you, Daphne. I don't want you to go. You won't ever take things again here now, I know. There's more good in you than bad.'

'Well, I'm sure I don't want to have anything more to do with her,' said Gwendoline, in a disgusted voice. 'If my mother knew . . .'

'Shut up, Gwendoline,' said Darrell. 'I'm sticking by Daphne too. I've done some pretty awful things this week myself, though I can't tell you what. And I think this— whatever wrong Daphne has done this term is cancelled out completely by her courage last night! We thought her deed was brave and noble then—and what she has just told us now doesn't make it any less brave or noble.'

'I agree with you,' said Sally. 'She's cancelled out her wrong with a right, as far as I'm concerned. And what's more, it wanted courage to come and face us all like this. You've got plenty of that, Daphne. If we stick by you and help you, will it make any difference to you ? I mean—will you stop any underhand ways and mean tricks ? '

'Do you mean that ? ' said Daphne, a sudden hope making her face shine. 'What about the others ? '

'I'm with Sally and Darrell,' said Jean.

'So am I,' said Belinda, and Irene nodded too. Emily thought for a moment and added her word as well.

'Yes, I'll agree,' she said. 'I think you've behaved terribly badly, Daphne—and terribly well too. At any rate you ought to have a chance to make good.'

'You, Alicia ? ' said Sally. Alicia had been very silent for the last few minutes. She was overcome with remorse about Ellen. She raised her eyes.

'It seems to me that I need to have a chance given to me to make good, as much as Daphne,' she said, shamefacedly. 'I've been worse than any of you.'

'You have been very hard and merciless, Alicia,' said Sally. 'You jeer at me for wanting to get proof before we accuse people, and for wanting to be fair and kind—but it's better in the end.'

'I know,' said Alicia. 'I do know that. I'm sorry. I've disliked you because you were head-girl instead of me this term, Sally. I've been a perfect idiot. I'm not the one to judge Daphne. I'll follow your lead, you may be sure.'

'Well, it seems as if it's only Gwendoline who is standing out,' said Sally, turning to the sulky-looking girl. 'Poor Gwendoline ! She's lost her grand friend and can't get over it. Well, we'll go and tell Miss Grayling that we are all agreed on the matter except Gwendoline. We want to give Daphne another chance, and we don't want her to go.'

'No, don't do that,' said Gwendoline, alarmed at the thought of appearing small and mean to Miss Grayling. 'I agree too.'

'And you agree, Daphne?' said Sally, looking at the quiet girl in the chair.

'Thank you, Sally. With all my heart,' said Daphne, and turned her head away. It was a great moment in her life—the forking of the ways. It was up to her to take the right way and she knew it. If only she was strong enough to!

A timid hand touched her arm. It was Mary-Lou. 'Come back to Matron now,' she said. 'She told us we were to, as soon as the meeting was over. I'll help you up the stairs.'

Daphne smiled for the first time, and this time it was a real smile, a sincere one, not turned on for the sake of being charming. 'You're the one that needs helping up!' she said. 'Come on, or Matron will be hounding us out of here.'

Jean went to see Ellen—a very different Ellen. Things seemed to be clearing up magically. 'I feel miles better now,' said Ellen. 'I'm not doing any more real lessons this term, Jean, and no work at all in the hols. I shan't snap and snarl any more either. I've lost that awful headache that made me so jumpy. It suddenly went after I'd had a talk with Miss Grayling. It was most extraordinary.'

'You're lucky to be in bed just now,' said Jean. 'The tests are simply awful. You should have seen the maths one, Ellen. Honestly I could only do half the sums. But the French one, set by Mam'zelle Dupont, was wizard.'

What with one thing and another, the week of tests passed very quickly and then it was the last week of all. Mistresses began to look harassed as the task of adding up marks, correcting papers, making out reports, grew heavier and heavier.   Mam'zelle Dupont worked herself up into a frenzy because she had lost her beautifully added-up marks list, and begged Miss Parker to do it for her again.

Miss Parker wouldn't.   'I've enough worries of my own,' she said.   'You're as bad as Belinda, Mam'zelle.   She managed to answer a history test when all the rest of the class were doing a geography paper.   Don't ask me how. That girl is the worst scatter-brain I ever saw in my life. How she got hold of a history paper when I had given out geography tests . . .'

'But why didn't she point out the mistake to you ?' asked Mam'zelle, astonished.

'She said she didn't even *notice* that the questions were history ones,' groaned Miss Parker.   'These girls !   They will be the death of me.   Thank goodness there are only two more days till the end of term !'

Only two more days.   But what hectic ones !   Packing things, looking for things, losing things, exchanging addresses, tidying cupboards, stacking books, cleaning paint-pots . . . all the thrilling little things that come at the end of term, and add to the excitement of going home.

'It's been a queer sort of term,' said Darrell to Sally. 'Don't you think so, Sally ?   I'm not very pleased with some of the things I've done.   You've been fine, though. You always are.'

'Rubbish !' said Sally.   'You don't know how many times I've hated Alicia for defying me.   You don't know lots of things about me !'

'I've enjoyed this term though,' said Darrell, remembering everything.   'It's been interesting.   Ellen and her snappiness—and the way we all thought wrong things about her—and now it's all come right and she's quite different and she and Jean are as thick as thieves together !'

'And then Daphne,' said Sally, the word 'thieves'

bringing her to mind. 'That was an extraordinary affair, wasn't it, Darrell ? I'm glad we gave her a chance. Isn't it funny the way she's dropped that silly Gwendoline Mary and taken Mary-Lou for her friend ? '

'Jolly good thing,' said Darrell. 'Mary-Lou may be a timid little thing—but she's sound at heart. And it's much better for her to have a friend of her own than go tagging after us all the time. But I shall always like little Mary-Lou.'

'Gwendoline looks sour these days,' said Sally, nudging her friend as Gwendoline went by alone. 'Nobody's darling now ! '

'Won't do her any harm,' said Darrell, hard-heartedly. 'She'll soon be Mother's darling and Miss Winter's darling, and have her bed made for her and everything done ! Dear darling Gwendoline Mary. She didn't come very well out of the Daphne affair, did she ? '

'No, she didn't. Perhaps she'll be better next term,' said Sally, doubtfully. 'Oh, my goodness, what *is* Belinda doing ? '

Belinda shot by with a work-basket in her arms, from which trailed yards and yards of wool and cotton. It wound itself round people's ankles and legs and at last forced her to stop.

'Get off my cottons ! ' she yelled indignantly. 'You're holding me up ! '

'Oh, Belinda—you'll always be an idiot ! ' cried Darrell, unwinding some red wool from her right ankle. 'Go away ! I'm getting a forest of cotton round me. Belinda, don't forget to bring back a whole lot of funny sketches after the hols.'

'I will ! ' said Belinda, with a grin. 'And what about Alicia thinking up a new trick for next term. Hie, Alicia, we've thought of some holiday prep for you ! Make up some super tricks for next term, see ? '

'Right ! ' called Alicia. 'I will. You can bank on

that ! Better than the "Oy !" on Mam'zelle's back, Darrell ! '

' Oy ! What is an Oy ? ' demanded Mam'zelle Dupont, bustling up. ' An " OY !" on my back ? What is this you have done to me now ? '

She screwed herself round, trying to see what an oy was, and the girls screamed with laughter.

' It's all right, Mam'zelle. It's not there now.'

' But what *is* an oy ? ' demanded Mam'zelle. ' I shall ask Miss Parker.'

But Miss Parker was not interested in Mam'zelle's ' oys '. She was only interested in getting the girls safely away on holiday. Then she could sit down and breathe in peace.

And at last they were really off. Cars swung into the drive. The train-girls went off singing. Belinda rushed frantically back for her suit-case, which she had as usual forgotten.

' Good-bye, Malory Towers ! ' yelled the girls. ' Good-bye, Potty ! Good-bye, Nosey ! Good-bye, Mam'zelle Oy ! '

' They're gone,' said Mam'zelle. ' Ah, the dear, dear girls, how I love to see them come—and how I love to see them go ! Miss Parker, you must tell me, please. What is this " Oy " ? I have never heard of it.'

' Look it up in the dictionary,' said Miss Parker, as if she was speaking to her class. ' Four weeks of peace, blessed peace. I can't believe it ! '

' They will soon be back, these bad girls,' said Mam'zelle. And she was right. They will !

THIRD YEAR AT
MALORY TOWERS

CONTENTS

1 A NEW GIRL FOR MALORY TOWERS

DARRELL was busy helping her mother to pack her clothes to take back to boarding-school. Her little sister Felicity was watching, wishing that she too was going with Darrell.

'Cheer up, Felicity!' said Darrell. 'You'll be coming back with me in September. Won't she, Mother?'

'1 hope so,' said her mother. 'Miss Grayling said she thought she would have room for her then. Oh, Darrell, surely you don't want all those books! They make your trunk so heavy.'

'Mother, I do!' said Darrell. 'And do let me take back my roller-skates. We're allowed to skate round the courtyard now. It's such fun.'

'All right,' said Mrs. Rivers. 'But it means unpacking half the trunk, because they must go at the bottom. Oh dear—did we mark your new bedroom slippers?'

'No!' groaned Darrell. 'Felicity, be a darling and mark them for me. Matron absolutely goes off the deep end if she finds anything not marked.'

Felicity darted off to get a pen. She was eleven and Darrell was fourteen. How she longed to go to Malory Towers too! According to Darrell it was the finest school in the kingdom!

'1 wish we hadn't got to call for that new girl,' said Darrell, bent over her trunk. 'What's her name now, Mother? I keep forgetting it.'

'Zerelda,' said her mother. 'Zerelda Brass.'

'Golly!' said Darrell. 'Zerelda! Whatever will she be like?'

'Oh, all right, I expect,' said Mrs. Rivers. 'She's American, you know. But her English grandmother has asked her over here for a year, and she's to go to Malory Towers. It's a marvel they were able to take her at short notice like that. '

'What's she like?' asked Darrell. 'Have you seen her?'

'No. Only a photograph,' said Mrs. Rivers. 'She looked about twenty there! But she's only fifteen, I think. '

'Fifteen! Then she won't be in my form,' said Darrell. 'She'll be in one higher up. Mother, isn't it a shame Sally's in quarantine for mumps? She'll be late coming back. '

Sally Hope was Darrell's best friend at school. Usually they arrived together at Malory Towers, for either Darrell's father or Sally's drove them down together in their cars. But this time Sally would be late because of the mumps quarantine.

'You'll have to write and tell her everything,' said Mrs. Rivers. 'Oh, thank you, Felicity—you've marked the slippers beautifully. Have you put in your bed-jacket, Darrell? Oh yes, there it is. Well, now we're really getting on. Where's the list? I'll just run down it and see if we have left anything out. '

'If Sally hadn't been in quarantine we wouldn't have had to call for Zerelda,' said Darrell. 'There wouldn't have been room. Mother, I have a feeling she will be awful. Whatever shall we talk about to her all the way down to Cornwall?'

'Good gracious—can't you talk about Malory Towers?' said her mother. 'You seem to be able to talk about it for hours on end at home. '

At last the packing was all done. Then there was the usual hunt for the key of the trunk, which always disappeared regularly each holiday.

'Have you signed my health certificate, Mother?' asked Darrell. 'Where is it? In my night-case? Right. I wonder if Irene will have got hers safely this term?'

Felicity giggled. She loved hearing about the harum-scarum Irene who always started off safely with her health certificate, and could never find it when she arrived.

Darrell's father was driving her mother and Darrell down to Malory Towers the next day. They had to start early, so all the packing was done the day before. All that Darrell had to do the next day was to go round the house and garden with Felicity and say good-bye to everything, even the hens!

'I shan't have to say good-bye to you in September, Felicity,' said Darrell. 'Well, good-bye, now, and just see you get on well in games this term, so that I can be proud of you when you come to Malory Towers!'

They were off at last, purring away down the road to the West Country. It was a lovely day in January, cold and sunny. Darrell pulled the rug round her. She was sitting alone at the back of the car. Her mother was in front. Soon they would come to Zerelda's house and then Darrell would have her at the back with her.

Zerelda lived in a big house about fifty miles along the way. Her grandmother had been a great friend of Mrs. Rivers' mother, and it was really Darrell's Gran that had asked Mrs. Rivers if she could fetch Zerelda and take her down to the school with Darrell.

'I think it would be so nice if she and Darrell could have a good long talk about the school,' said Darrell's Granny. 'Zerelda is sure to feel a bit queer, going to a school in a different country.'

But Darrell didn't feel very pleased about it. She was disappointed that they couldn't fetch Sally, her friend, and somehow she didn't like the sound of Zerelda. Was it the unusual name? Or was it that she felt her mother didn't altogether like the sound of Zerelda either? Anyway, they would soon see!

'Here's Notting,' said Mr. Rivers, seeing the name on a signpost. 'This is where we call for the American, isn't it?'

'Yes,' said Mrs. Rivers, looking at a card in her hand. 'Turn to the right by the church. Go up the hill. Turn to the right again at the top and you will see a big white house. That's where Zerelda is living.'

They soon drew up at a big white house, almost a mansion. A butler opened the door. Then a smart, little old lady came running out, the friend of Darrell's Granny.

'This *is* kind of you!' she said. 'Zerelda! Are you ready? Here they are.'

No Zerelda appeared. Mrs. Rivers said they wouldn't come in and have coffee, as they wanted to be at the school before dark.

'If Zerelda is ready, we'll set off straight away,' said Mr. Rivers. He felt a little annoyed. Where was this Zerelda? She ought to have been ready and waiting! He went to the back of the car and got ready a strap for the luggage.

'Zerelda! Come at once!' called her grandmother. She turned to the butler. 'Do you know where Miss Zerelda is? Oh dear, where can she be?'

It was some minutes before Zerelda appeared. And when she did arrive Darrell couldn't think that it *was* Zerelda! She suddenly saw a tall, willowy person come down the stairs, with glinting hair the colour of brass, arranged in a big roll on the top of her head, with curls cascading over her shoulders.

Darrell stared. Who was this? She looked like somebody out of the films. And, good gracious, she had lipstick on surely?

It couldn't be Zerelda. This girl looked about twenty. She came forward with a lazy smile.

'Oh! Zerelda! Where were you?' said her grandmother. 'You've kept us waiting.'

'Sorry,' drawled Zerelda. Her grandmother introduced her to the Rivers family. Mr. Rivers looked impatient. He hated to be kept waiting—and he didn't like the look of this Zerelda much!

Neither did Darrell. In fact, she felt quite alarmed. Zerelda must be seventeen or eighteen at least! Whatever would they talk about in the car?

'You'd better put on your school hat,' said her grandmother, handing it to Zerelda.

'What! Wear that terrible thing!' said Zerelda. 'Gee, Gran'ma, I never shall!'

Darrell didn't dare to say that she would certainly have to. She was quite tongue-tied. Zerelda seemed really grown-up to her. It wasn't only her looks, and the way she did her hair—it was her self-confident manner, and her grown-up way of talking.

She slid gracefully into the seat by Darrell. 'Now, Zerelda, you remember you're going to an English school, to learn a few English ways,' said her grandmother, at the window of the car. 'Oh dear, wipe that lipstick off your mouth. I've told you again and again it won't do here. You seem to think you're eighteen, but you're only a schoolgirl. Now mind you ... '

Mr. Rivers, feeling that talk between Zerelda and her grandmother would probably go on for some time, put in his clutch and revved up the car. 'Good-bye!' said Mrs. Rivers, feeling that they might stay there for ever if she didn't firmly say good-bye.

The car moved off. Zerelda's grandmother was left still talking at top speed in the drive. Mr. Rivers heaved a sigh of relief, and looked at his wife out of the corner of his eye. She looked back. Darrell caught the look and felt a little comforted. Daddy and Mother thought the same about Zerelda as she did!

'Have you got enough rug?' Darrell asked politely.

'Yes, thanks,' said Zerelda. There was a silence. Darrell racked her brains to think what to say.

'Would you like me to tell you something about Malory Towers?' she asked Zerelda at last.

'Go ahead, honey,' said Zerelda, rather sleepily. 'Spill the beans. What's our class-teacher like?'

'Well—you won't be in my class, because you're fifteen, aren't you?' said Darrell.

'Nearly sixteen,' said Zerelda, patting the big roll on the top of her head. 'No, I guess I won't be in your class. You're not very big are you?'

'l'm as big as anyone else in my form,' said Darrell, and she thought to herself that if she wore her hair in the same ridiculous way as Zerelda did, she too would look tall.

She began to talk about Malory Towers. It was her favourite subject, so her voice went on and on, telling about the great school with its four big towers, one at each end— the courtyard in the middle—the enormous pool in the rocks, filled by the sea each tide, where the girls bathed in the summer-time.

'And in each tower are the dormies where we sleep, and our common-rooms—the rooms we play about in, you know, when we're not in class,' said Darrell. 'Our house-mistress is Miss Potts. By the way, which tower are you in?'

There was no answer. Darrell looked in angry indignation at Zerelda. She was fast asleep! She hadn't heard a single word of all that Darrell had been telling her! *Well*!

2 BACK AT SCHOOL AGAIN

DARRELL was so annoyed with Zerelda for falling asleep whilst she told her all about her beloved Malory Towers that she made up her mind not to say another word when Zerelda deigned to wake up.

She took a good look at the American girl. She was certainly very striking-looking, though her mane of hair was not really a very nice shade of gold. Darrell thought that Brass was a good surname for Zerelda. Her hair did look brassy! Darrell wondered if it had been dyed. But no, surely nobody would let her do that. Perhaps girls grew up more quickly in America though?

'It's a pity she's coming to Malory Towers,' thought Darrell, looking closely at Zerelda's beautifully powdered face, with its curling eye-lashes and rosy cheeks. ' She just won't fit. Though Gwendoline will love her, I expect ! But Gwendoline Mary always does lose her silly heart to people like Zerelda ! '

Mr. Rivers looked back at the sleeping Zerelda and gave Darrell a comradely grin. She smiled back. She wondered what Zerelda's father and mother could be like ; she thought they must be pretty queer to have a daughter like Zerelda.

Then she gave herself a little shake. ' She may be quite nice really. It may just be because she comes from a country that lets its girls grow up sooner than ours do, ' thought Darrell. She was a very fair and just girl and she made up her mind to give Zerelda a chance.

' Though thank goodness she'll be in a higher form, as she's nearly sixteen, ' thought Darrell. ' 1 shan't see much of her. I hope she's not in North Tower. Oh dear—whatever would Miss Potts think of her if she was ! '

She thought of the downright Miss Potts. She thought of plump, sensible Matron who never stood any nonsense from anyone. And she thought of the mistress who took the third form, in which Darrell had already been for a term.

' Miss Peters ! Gracious ! She'd have a fit if Zerelda was in her form ! ' thought Darrell, seeing the mannish, hearty-voiced Miss Peters in her mind's eye. ' It's really almost a pity she won't be in my form. I'd love to see Miss Peters deal with Zerelda ! '

Darrell was tired when they at last reached Malory Towers. They had stopped twice on the way for meals, and Zerelda had awakened, and talked in a gracious, grown-up manner to Mr. and Mrs. Rivers. Apparently she thought England was ' just wunnerful'. She also thought that she, Zerelda, could teach it a few things.

Mrs. Rivers was polite and friendly, as she always was to everyone. Mr. Rivers, who had no patience with people like Zerelda, talked to Darrell and ignored the American girl.

'Say, isn't your father wunnerful?' said Zerelda to Darrell, when they were speeding on their way again. 'Those great eyes of his—and the black beetling brows? Wunnerful!'

Darrell wanted to giggle. She longed to tell her father about his 'black beetling brows' but there was no chance.

'Tell me about this school of yours,' said Zerelda, sweetly, thinking that Darrell was rather silent.

'I've told you already,' said Darrell, rather stiffly, 'but you must have been bored because you went to sleep.'

'Say, isn't that just too bad?' said Zerelda, apologetically.

'There's no time to tell you anything, anyway,' said Darrell, 'because here we are!' Her eyes shone as they always did when they saw Malory Towers again for the first time.

The car swept up to the front door. It always seemed like the entrance to a castle, to Darrell. The big drive was now crowded with cars, and girls of all ages were rushing about, carrying bags and lacrosse sticks.

'Come on,' said Darrell, to Zerelda. 'Let's get out. Golly, it's grand to be back! Hallo, Belinda! I say, Irene, got your health certificate? Hallo, Jean. Heard about Sally? She's in quarantine. Sickening, isn't it?'

Jean caught sight of Zerelda getting out of the car, and stared as if she couldn't believe her eyes. Zerelda still had no hat on, and her hair cascaded down her shoulders, and the roll on top glinted in a ray of late sunshine.

'Golly—who's that? Some relation of yours?' said Jean.

Darrell giggled. 'No, thank goodness. She's a new girl!'

'No! My word, what does she think she's come to Malory Towers for? To act in the films?'

Darrell darted here and there among her friends, happy and excited. Her father undid the trunks, and the school porter carried them in. Darrell caught sight of the label on Zerelda's trunk. 'North Tower'.

'Blow! She's in our tower after all,' she thought. 'Hallo, Alicia! Had good hols.?'

Alicia came up, her bright eyes gleaming. 'Super!' she said. 'My word—who's that?'

'New girl,' said Darrell. 'I know how you feel. *l* couldn't take my eyes off her either when I first saw her. Unbelievable, isn't she?'

'Look—there's our dear Gwendoline Mary having a weep on Mother's shoulder as usual!' said Alicia, her attention caught by the sight of Gwendoline's mother, who was dabbing away tears as she said good-bye to Gwendoline.

'There's Miss Winter, Gwendoline's old governess, too,' said Darrell. 'No wonder poor Gwen never gets any better—always Mother's Darling Pet. We get some sense into her in term-time, and then she loses it all again in the hols.'

Gwendoline caught sight of Zerelda and stared in surprise. A look of great admiration came over her face. Alicia nudged Darrell.

'Gwendoline's going to worship Zerelda. Look! Don't you know that expression on her face? Zerelda will have at least one willing slave!'

Gwendoline said something to her mother and her governess. They both looked at Zerelda. But it was plain that neither of them liked the look of her as much as Gwendoline did.

'Good-bye, darling,' said her mother, still dabbing her eyes. 'Write to me heaps of times.'

But Gwendoline Mary was not paying much attention. She was wondering if anyone was looking after Zerelda. Could she possibly go up to her and offer to show her round? Then she saw that Darrell was with her. Darrell would soon push her off if she went up, she knew.

Zerelda stood looking round at all the bustle and excitement. She was dressed in the same brown coat, brown stockings and shoes as the others, and yet she managed to look quite different. She didn't seem to notice the curious glances thrown at her.

Darrell, seeing her father and mother about to go, rushed over to them to say good-bye.

'It's so nice to see you plunging into everything so happily as soon as you're back,' said her mother, pleased to see how gladly everyone greeted Darrell. 'You are no longer one of the smaller ones, Darrell—you seem quite big compared to the first- and second-formers now!'

'I should think so! Babies!' said Darrell, with a laugh. 'Good-bye, darlings. I'll write on Sunday as usual. Give Felicity my love and tell her Malory Towers is as nice as ever.'

The car moved off down the drive. Darrell waved till it was gone. Then she felt a punch on the back and turned to see Irene there. 'Darrell! Come along to Matron with me. I can't find my health certificate.'

'Irene! I don't believe you,' said Darrell. 'Yes, I'll come. Where's my night-case? Oh, there it is. Hie, Gwendoline, look out with that lacrosse stick of yours. That's twice you've tripped me up.'

Darrell suddenly remembered Zerelda. 'Oh golly! I've forgotten Zerelda. She's going to be in North Tower too. I'd better get her or she'll be feeling absolutely lost. I know how I felt when I came here first—everyone laughing and ragging and talking and I didn't know a soul!'

She set off towards Zerelda. But Zerelda did not look at all lost or bewildered. She looked thoroughly at home, with a tiny smile on her red mouth as if she was really rather amused by everything going on around her.

Before Darrell could reach her someone else spoke to Zerelda.

'Are you a new girl? I believe you are in North Tower. If you'd like to come with me I'll show you round a bit.'

'Gee, that's kind of you,' said Zerelda, in her slow drawl.

'Look,' said Darrell, in disgust. 'There's Gwendoline Mary all over her already! Trust *her*! She just adores

8

anyone like Zerelda. Zerelda, come with us. We'll take you to
Matron.'

'I'll look after her, Darrell,' said Gwendoline, turning
her large pale-blue eyes on Darrell. 'You go and look for
Sally.'

'Sally's not coming back yet,' said Darrell, 'she's in
quarantine. I'll look after Zerelda. She came down with
us.'

'You can *both* take me around,' said Zerelda, charmingly,
and smiled her slow smile at Gwendoline. Gwen slipped
her arm through Zerelda's and took her up the steps into the
hall.

Alicia grinned. 'Let's hope dear Gwen will take her off our
hands for good,' she said. 'But I suppose she'll be in a much
higher form. She looks about eighteen!'

The groans of Irene attracted their attention. 'Oh, Irene! I
simply don't believe you've lost your health certificate again,'
said Darrell. 'Nobody could possibly lose it term after term as
you do.'

'Well, I have,' said Irene. 'Do come to Matron now and
stand by me.'

So they all went to find Matron. Darrell and Alicia gave up
their health certificates. Matron looked at Irene.

'I've lost it, Matron,' said Irene. 'The worst of it is I don't
even remember having it today! I mean, I usually remember
Mother giving it to me, anyhow—but I don't even remember
that this time. My memory's getting worse than ever.'

'Your mother came to see me not ten minutes ago,' said
Matron, 'and she gave me your certificate herself. Go away,
Irene, or you'll make me lose it too!'

Gwendoline brought Zerelda to Matron. Matron stared as if
she couldn't believe her eyes. 'Who's this? Oh—Zerelda
Brass. Yes, you're in North Tower. Is this your health
certificate? She's in your dormy, Gwendoline. Take her there—
and—er—get her ready to go down for a meal.'

Darrell grinned at Alicia, and Alicia winked back. Matron wouldn't be quite so polite about Zerelda tomorrow.

'Come on,' said Alicia. 'Let's go and unpack our night-cases. l've heaps to tell you, Darrell!'

3   THE FIRST EVENING

'ANY more new girls coming, have you heard?' Darrell asked Alicia.

'Yes, one. Somebody called Wilhelmina,' said Alicia. 'She's coming tomorrow. One of my brothers knows one of *her* brothers. When he heard she was coming here, he whistled like anything and said, "Bill will wake you up all right!"'

'Who's Bill?' said Darrell.

'Wilhelmina, apparently,' said Alicia, taking the things out of her night-case. 'She's got seven brothers! Imagine it! *Seven*! And she's the only girl.'

'Golly!' said Darrell, trying to imagine what it would be like to have seven brothers. She had none. Alicia had three. But seven!

'l should think she's half a boy herself then,' said Darrell.

'Probably,' said Alicia. 'Blow, where's my toothbrush? l know I packed it.'

'Look—there's Mavis!' said Darrell. Alicia looked up. Mavis had been a new girl last term. She had not been a great success, because she was lazy and selfish. She had a beautiful voice, pure and sweet, but curiously deep—a most unusual voice that was being well trained.

Mavis was proud of her voice and proud of the career she was going to have. 'When l'm an opera-singer,' she was always saying, 'l shall sing in Milan. I shall sing in New York. When I'm an opera-singer, I shall ...'

The others got very tired of hearing about Mavis's future career. But they were most impressed with her strong, deep voice, that could easily fill the great school hall. It was so rich and sweet that even the little ones listened in delight.

'But the worst of Mavis is that she thinks she's just perfect because she's got such a lovely voice,' Jean had complained a dozen times the term before. Jean was head-girl of the third form, and very blunt and forthright. 'She doesn't see that she's only just a schoolgirl, with duties to do, and work to get through, and games to play. She's always thinking of that voice of hers—and it's wonderful, we all know that. But what a pity to have a wonderful voice in such a poor sort of person!'

Darrell hadn't liked Mavis. She looked at her now. She saw a discontented, conceited little face, with small dark eyes and a big mouth. Auburn hair was plaited into two thick braids.

'Mavis is all voice and vanity and nothing else,' she said to Alicia. 'I know that sounds horrid, but it's true.'

'Yes,' said Alicia, and paused to glance at Mavis too. 'And yet, Darrell, that girl will have a wonderful career with that voice of hers, you know. It's unique, and she'll have the whole world at her feet later on. The trouble is that she knows it now.'

'I wonder if Gwendoline will still go on fussing round her, now she's seen Zerelda?' said Darrell. Gwendoline, always ready to fawn round anyone gifted, rich or beautiful, had run round Mavis in a ridiculous way the term before. But then Gwendoline Mary never learnt that one should pick one's friends for quite different things. She was quite unable to see why Darrell liked Sally, or why Daphne liked little Mary-Lou, or why everyone liked honest, trustable Jean.

'Where's Betty?' asked Darrell. 'I haven't seen her yet.' Betty was Alicia's best friend, as clever and amusing as Alicia, and almost as sharp-tongued. She was not in North Tower, much to Alicia's sorrow. But Miss Grayling, the Head Mistress, did not intend to put the two girls into the same house. She was sorry they were friends, because they were too alike, and got each other into trouble continually because of their happy-go-lucky, don't-care ways.

'Betty's not coming back till half-term,' said Alicia, gloomily. 'She's got whooping-cough. Imagine it—six weeks before she can come back. She's only just started it. I heard yesterday.'

'Oh, I say—you'll miss her, won't you,' said Darrell. 'l shall miss Sally too.'

'Well, we'll just have to put up with each other, you and l, till Betty and Sally come back,' said Alicia. Darrell nodded. Alicia amused her. She was always fun to be with, and even when her tongue was sharpest, it was witty. Alicia was lucky. She had such good brains that she could play the fool all she liked and yet not lose her place in class.

'But if *I* do that, I slide down to the bottom at once,' thought Darrell. 'I've got quite good brains but I've got to use them all the time. Alicia's brains seem to work whether she uses them or not!'

Mary-Lou came up. She had grown a little taller, but she was still the same rather scared-looking girl. 'Hallo!' she said. 'Wherever did you pick Zerelda up, Darrell? l hear she came down with you. How old is she? Eighteen?'

'No. Nearly sixteen,' said Darrell. 'l suppose Gwendoline is sucking up to her already? Isn't she the limit? l say, what do you suppose Miss Potts will say when she sees Zerelda?'

Miss Potts was the house-mistress of North Tower, and, like Matron, not very good at putting up with nonsense of any sort. Most of the girls had been in her form, because she taught the bottom class. They liked her and respected her. A few girls, such as Gwendoline and Mavis, feared her, because she could be very sarcastic over airs and graces, or pretences of any sort.

Darrell felt rather lost without Sally there to laugh with and talk to. She was glad to walk downstairs with Alicia. Belinda came bouncing up.

'Where's Sally? Darrell, I did some wizard sketching in the hols. I went to the circus, and I've got a whole book of circus sketches. You should just see the clowns!'

'Show the book to us this evening,' said Darrell, eagerly. Everyone loved Belinda's clever sketches. She really had a gift for drawing, but, unlike Mavis, she was not forever thinking and talking of it, or of her future career. She was a jolly school girl first and foremost, and an artist second.

'Seen Irene?' said Alicia. Belinda nodded. Irene was her friend, and the two were very well-matched. Irene was talented at music and maths, but a scatterbrain at everything else. Belinda was talented at drawing, quite fair at other lessons, and a scatterbrain almost as bad as Irene. The class had great fun with them.

'Seen Zerelda?' asked Darrell, with a grin. That was the question everyone asked that evening. 'Seen Zerelda?' No one had ever seen a girl quite like Zerelda before.

At supper that night there was a great noise. Everyone was excited. Mam'zelle Dupont beamed at the table of the third-formers of North Tower.

'You have had good holidays?' she enquired of every-one. 'You have been to the theatre and the pantomime and the circus? Ah, you are all ready to work hard now and do some very very good translations for me. *N'est-ce pas?*'

There was a groan from the girls round the table. 'No, Mam'zelle! Don't let's do French translations this term. We've forgotten all our French!'

Mam'zelle looked round the table for any new face. She always made a point of being extra kind to new girls. She suddenly caught sight of Zerelda and stared in amazement. Zerelda had done her hair again, and her golden roll stood out on top. Her lips were suspiciously red. Her cheeks were far too pink.

'This girl, she is made up for the films!' said Mam'zelle to herself. 'Oh, *là là*! Why has she come here? She is not a young girl. She looks old—about twenty! Why has Miss Grayling taken her here? She is not for Malory Towers.'

Zerelda seemed quite at home. She ate her supper very composedly. She was sitting next to Gwendoline, who was trying to make her talk. But Zerelda was not like Mavis, willing to talk for hours about herself. She answered Gwendoline politely enough.

'Have you lived all your life in America? Do you think you'll like England?' persisted Gwendoline.

'l think England's just wunnerful,' said Zerelda, for the sixth time. 'l think your little fields are wunnerful, and your little old houses. I think the English people are wunnerful too.'

'Wunnerful, isn't she?' said Alicia, under her breath to Darrell. 'Just wunnerful.'

Everyone had to go early to bed on the first night, because most of the girls had had long journeys down to Cornwall. In fact, before supper was over there were many loud yawns to be heard.

Zerelda was surprised when Gwendoline informed her that they had to go to bed that night just about eight o'clock. 'Only just tonight though,' said Gwendoline. 'Tomorrow the third-formers go at nine.'

'At *nine*,' said Zerelda, astonished. 'But in my country we go when we like. I shall never go to sleep so early.'

'Well, you slept in the car all right,' Darrell couldn't help saying. 'So you must be tired.'

They all went to the common-room after supper, chose their lockers, argued, switched on the wireless, switched it off again, yawned, poked the fire, teased Mary-Lou because she jumped when a spark flew out, and then sang a few songs.

Mavis's voice dominated the rest. It really was a most

remarkable voice, deep and powerful. It seemed impossible that it should come from Mavis, who was not at all well-grown for her age. One by one the girls fell silent and listened. Mavis sang on. She loved the sound of her own voice.

'Wunnerful!' said Zerelda, clapping loudly when the song was ended. 'Ree-markable!'

Mavis looked pleased. 'When I'm an opera-singer,' she began.

Zerelda interrupted her. 'Oh, that's what you're going to be, is it? Gee, that's fine. I'm going in for films!'

'Films! What do you mean? A film-actress?' said Gwendoline Mary, her eyes wide.

'Yes. I act pretty well already,' said Zerelda, not very modestly. 'I'm always acting at home. I'm in our Dramatic Society, of course, and last year at college I acted Lady Macbeth in Shakespeare. Gee, that was ...'

'Wunnerful!' said Alicia, Irene and Belinda all together. Zerelda laughed.

'I guess I don't say things the way you say them,' she said, good-naturedly.

'You'll have a chance to show how well you can act, this very term,' said Gwendoline, remembering something. 'Our form's got to act a play—"Romeo and Juliet". You could be Juliet.'

'That depends on Miss Hibbert,' said Daphne's voice at once. Daphne had already imagined herself in Juliet's part. 'Miss Hibbert's our English mistress, Zerelda, and ...'

'Bed, girls,' said Miss Potts' voice at the door. 'Eight o'clock! Come along, everyone, or you'll never be up in the morning!'

4 ZERELDA GOES INTO THE FOURTH

IT was fun settling in the next day. The girls rushed into the third form classroom, which overlooked the courtyard and had a distant view of the sea.

'Zerelda's to go to the fourth form classroom,' said Jean, looking round for the American girl. 'She's not with us after all.'

'I didn't think I would be,' said Zerelda. 'I'm much older.'

Jean looked at her. 'Zerelda,' said Jean, 'I'd better give you a word of advice. Miss Williams, the fourth form mistress, won't like your hair-style—or your lipstick either. You'd better alter your hair and rub that awful stuff off your lips before you go to the fourth form. Anyway, they'll rag you like anything if you don't.'

'Why should I do what you tell me?' said Zerelda, on her dignity at once. She thought a great deal of her appearance and could not bear to have it remarked on by these proper little English girls.

'Well, I'm head-girl of this form,' said Jean. 'That's why I'm bothering to tell you. Just to save you getting into trouble,'

'But Zerelda's hair looks lovely,' said Gwendoline, who always resented having to have her own hair tied neatly, instead of in a golden sheet over her shoulders.

Nobody took the slightest notice of Gwendoline's bleating.

'Well, thanks all the same, Jean, but I'm not going to make myself into a little pig-tailed English schoolgirl,' said Zerelda, in her lazy, rather insolent drawl. 'I guess I couldn't look like you, anyway. Look at you all, plain as pie! You ought to let me have a try at making you up—I'd soon get you some looks!'

Daphne, who fancied herself as very pretty, laughed scornfully.

'Nobody wants to look a scarecrow like you! Honestly, if you could see yourself!'

'1 have,' said Zerelda. '1 looked in the glass this morning!'

'When you're in Rome, you must do as Rome does,' said Jean, solemnly.

'But I'm not in Rome,' said Zerelda.

'No. It's a pity you aren't!' said Alicia. 'You'll wish you were in three minutes' time when Miss Williams catches sight of you. Go on into the classroom next door for goodness' sake. Miss Williams will be along in half a minute. So will our teacher, Miss Peters. She'd have a blue fit if she saw you.'

Zerelda grinned good-humouredly, and went off to find her classroom. As she got to the door Miss Williams came hurrying along to the fourth-formers. She and Zerelda met at the door.

Miss Williams had no idea that Zerelda was one of her form. The girl looked so grown-up. Miss Williams blinked once or twice, trying to remember who Zerelda was. Could she be one of the new assistant mistresses?

'Er—let me see now—you are Miss Miss—er ... Miss ...' began Miss Williams.

'Zerelda,' said Zerelda, obligingly, thinking it was a queer thing if the mistresses all called the girls 'Miss'.

'Miss Zerelda,' said Miss Williams, still not realising anything. 'Did you want me, Miss Zerelda?'

Zerelda was rather astonished. 'Well—er—not exactly,' she said. '1 was told to come along to your class. I'm in the fourth form.'

'Good heavens!' said Miss Williams, weakly. 'Not—not one of the girls?'

'Yes, Miss Williams,' said Zerelda, thinking that the teacher was acting very queerly. 'Say, haven't I done right? Isn't this the classroom?'

'Yes,' said Miss Williams, recovering herself all at

once. 'This is the fourth form room. But you can't come in like that. What's that thing you've got on the top of your head?'

Zerelda looked even more astonished. Had she got a hat on by mistake? She felt to see. No, there was no hat there.

'There's nothing on my head,' she said.

'Yes, there is. What's *this* thing?' said Miss Williams, patting the enormous roll of hair that Zerelda had pinned there in imitation of one of the film-stars.

'That? Oh, that's a bit of my hair,' said Zerelda, wondering if Miss Williams was a little mad. 'It really *is* my hair, Miss Williams. I've just rolled the front part up and pinned it.'

Miss Williams looked in silence at the roll of brassy coloured hair and the cascades of curls down Zerelda's neck. She peered at the too-red lips. She even looked at the curling eye-lashes to make sure they were real and not stuck on.

'Well, Zerelda, I can't have you in my class like this,' she said, looking very prim and bird-like. 'Take down that roll of hair. Tie it all back. Clean your lips. Come back to the room in five minutes.'

And with that she disappeared into the form room and the door was shut. Zerelda stared after her. She patted the roll of hair on top. What was the matter with it? Didn't it make her look exactly like Lossie Laxton, the film-star she admired most of all?

Zerelda frowned. What a school! Here were a whole lot of girls, all growing up fast, and not one of them knew how to do her hair, not one of them looked smart—'and I bet they're all as stupid as owls,' said Zerelda, out loud.

She decided to go along and do something to her hair. That prim and proper Miss Williams might say something to the Head. Zerelda had been very much impressed with Miss Grayling and the little talk she had had with her. What had Miss Grayling said? Something about learning to be good-hearted and kind, sensible and trustable, good, sound women the world could lean on. She had also said that Zerelda might learn something from her stay in England that would help her afterwards—and that Zerelda, if she was sensible and understanding, might also teach the English girls something.

'Well, I don't want to get on the wrong side of Miss Grayling from the word go,' thought Zerelda, as she went to find her dormy. 'Where's this bedroom of ours? I'll never find my way about in this place.'

She found the dormy at last and went in to do her hair. She looked at herself in the glass. She was very sad at having to take down that beautiful roll of hair. It took her ages to put it there each morning. But she unpinned it and brushed it out. She divided it into two, and pinned it back, then tied her mane of hair with a piece of ribbon so that it no longer fell wildly over her shoulders.

At once she looked younger. She rubbed the red from her lips. Then she looked at herself. 'You look plain and drab now, Zerelda,' she said to herself. 'What would Pop say? He wouldn't know me!'

But Zerelda didn't look plain and drab. She looked a young girl, with a natural, pleasant youthful face. She went slowly to find her classroom. She was not sure whether she had to knock at the door or not. Things seemed to be so different in an English school—more polite and proper than in an American school. She decided to knock

'Come in!' called Miss Williams, impatiently. She had forgotten all about Zerelda. Zerelda went in. She now looked so completely different that Miss Williams didn't recognize her!

'What do you want?' she asked Zerelda. 'Have you come with a message?'

'No,' said Zerelda, puzzled. 'I'm in the fourth form, aren't I?'

'What's your name?' said Miss Williams, looking for her list of names.

Zerelda was now quite certain that Miss Williams was mad. 'l told you before,' she said. 'I'm Zerelda.'

'Oh, good gracious—so you are,' said Miss Williams, looking at her keenly. 'Well, who would have thought your hair would make such a difference! Come and sit down. That's your place over there.'

The fourth form were mystified and amused. They were all keen hard-working fifteen-year-olds, who were to work for their School Certificate that year.

'Let me see—how old are you, Zerelda?' said Miss Williams, trying to find Zerelda's name on her list.

'Nearly sixteen,' said Zerelda.

'Ah then—you will probably find the work of this form rather easy,' said Miss Williams. 'But as it's your first term in an English school, that's just as well. There will be many different things for you to learn.'

Zerelda looked round at the fourth-formers. She thought they looked too clever for words. How serious they were! She wished she was back in the third form with Alicia, Darrell, Belinda and the rest. They had all seemed so jolly and care-free.

The third form were busy making out time-tables and lists of duties. Books were given out. Miss Peters, tall, mannish, with very short hair and a deep voice, was in charge. The girls liked her, but sometimes wished she would not treat them as though they were boys. She had a hearty laugh, and a hearty manner. In the holidays she rode practically all the time, and was in charge of the riding-teams on Saturday mornings at Malory Towers.

'l really wonder she doesn't come to class in riding-breeches,' Alicia had said often enough to the third form, making them giggle. 'I'm sure she hates wearing a skirt!'

'Shall I put a set of books for the new girl, Wilhelmina Robinson?' asked Jean, who was in charge of the books. 'When is she coming, Miss Peters?'

''This morning, I believe,' said Miss Peters. 'She and her brothers have been in quarantine for something or other. I think Miss Grayling said she would be arriving this morning. By car, I suppose.'

After Break the third form went to the sewing-room for half an hour, and it was from there that they saw the arrival, the quite astonishing arrival, of Wilhelmina Robinson.

They suddenly heard the clatter of horses' hooves outside— a tremendous clatter. Alicia went to the window at once, wondering if there was a riding-lesson for anyone. She gave an exclamation.

'I say! Just look here! Whoever is it?'

All the class crowded to the window. Miss Donnelly, the gentle, sweet-tempered sewing-mistress, protested mildly. 'Girls, girls! What are you doing?'

'Miss Donnelly, come and look,' said Alicia. So she went to the window. She saw a girl on a big black horse, and with her were seven boys, ranging in age from about eight to eighteen, each of them on horseback! There was a great deal of laughter, and stamping and curveting and cries of 'Whoa there!'

'Golly! It must be Wilhelmina!' said Darrell. 'And her seven brothers! Don't say that her brothers are coming to Malory Towers too!'

'Well! What a way to arrive!' said Gwendoline Mary. 'Galloping up like that on horseback! What a peculiar family Wilhelmina's must be!'

5 THE ARRIVAL OF WILHELMINA

UNFORTUNATELY the bell for the next class rang at that moment and the third-formers could not see what happened next. Would Miss Grayling come out to the horse-riders? How would Wilhelmina enter the Towers? Darrell imagined her riding up the steps and into the hall!

'Golly! Fancy riding to school like that,' said Alicia. 'I suppose she's going to keep her horse here. One or two girls do do that already. Bringing all her seven brothers too! What a girl!'

Nobody had been able to see clearly what Wilhelmina had looked like. In fact, it had been difficult to tell her from the boys, as they had all been in riding-breeches. The third-formers went to their classroom, discussing the new arrival excitedly. Wilhelmina promised to be a Somebody!

'I shall be scared of her,' said Mary-Lou.

'Don't be silly,' said Mavis, who was always very scornful of Mary-Lou. 'Why should you be scared of her? I just hate tomboys, and I'm sure she's one. She'll think of nothing but horses and dogs, and she'll smell of them too. People always do when they're mad on animals.'

'Miss Peters doesn't,' said Darrell.

'Oh, Miss Peters!' said Mavis. 'I'll be glad when I'm out of her class. She's too hearty for anything!'

Darrell laughed. Miss Peters was rather hearty and loud-voiced. But she was a good sort, though not at all sympathetic to people like Mavis. Neither had she much patience with Alicia or Betty when they played any of their idiotic tricks. In fact, she had looked with such disfavour on tricks in class that poor Alicia and Betty had almost given up playing any.

Wilhelmina didn't turn up in the classroom that morning, but Jean found Matron waiting for her in the passage when the third form went out to get ready for dinner. With her was somebody who, except for the school tunic, looked exactly like a boy!

'Jean,' said Matron, 'you're head-girl of the third, aren't you? Well, look after Wilhelmina for me, will you, and take her down to dinner? She couldn't come yesterday because she wasn't out of quarantine. Here you are, Wilhelmina—this is Jean, head-girl of your form.'

'Hallo,' said Wilhelmina and grinned a boyish grin that showed big white teeth set very evenly. Jean looked at her and liked her at once.

Wilhelmina had hair cropped almost as short as a boy's. It curled a little, which she hated. Her face was boyish and square, with a tip-tilted nose, a big mouth, and big, wide-set eyes of hazel-brown. She was covered with freckles from forehead to firm little chin.

'Hallo,' said Jean. 'I saw you arrive—on horseback, didn't you?'

'Yes,' said Wilhelmina. 'My seven brothers came with me. Mummy was awfully cross about that. She wanted me to go in the car with her and Daddy—but we got our horses and shot off before they started!'

'Good gracious!' said Jean. 'Did you really? Have you each got a horse?'

'Yes. We've got big stables,' said Wilhelmina. 'Daddy keeps racehorses too. I say—I've never been to boarding-school before. Is it awful? If it is I shall saddle Thunder and ride away.'

Jean stared at Wilhelmina and wondered if she meant all this. She decided that she didn't. She laughed and pulled Wilhelmina along to the cloakroom, because she had to wash ink off her hands before dinner. Miss Potts would be sure to spot them if she didn't!

' Malory Towers is a jolly fine school, ' said Jean.' You'll like it. '

' Shall I be able to ride Thunder each day ? ' asked Wilhelmina, staring round the big cloakroom where girls were chattering and laughing as they washed. ' I tell you, I wouldn't have come if they hadn't let me bring Thunder. I shall have to look after him too, even if it means missing some of my lessons. He would hate anyone else looking after him. '

' Haven't you ever been to school before ? ' asked Belinda, who had been listening to all this with interest.

' No. I shared the tutor that three of my brothers had, ' said Wilhelmina. ' There wasn't a school near at all. We live miles out in the country. I expect I shall be at the bottom of the form. '

Belinda liked this outspoken girl. ' I bet you won't, ' she said, and cast her eye round to see if Gwendoline was about. Yes, she was. ' Not while Gwendoline Mary is in the form, anyway ! '

' Don't be beastly, ' said Gwendoline, cross at having fun poked at her in front of a new girl.

' It will all seem a bit queer to you at first, ' said Jean. ' If you've been even to a day school before it helps—but never to have been to school at all—well, you're sure to feel a bit strange, Wilhelmina. '

' I say—would you mind very much if I asked you something ? ' said Wilhelmina, staring hard at Jean.

' What ? ' said Jean, wondering what was coming. The others came round to listen. Wilhelmina looked round at them all.

' Well, ' she said, ' I've never in my life been called Wilhelmina. Never. It's a frightful name. Everyone calls me Bill. After all, people call William Bill for short, don't they ? So my brothers said they'd call me Bill, short for Wilhelmina ! If you all start calling me Wilhelmina I shall be miserable. I shan't feel I'm myself. '

In the usual way if a new girl asked for a nickname, she would have been laughed at, or told to think again. Nicknames were only given when people knew you well and liked you. Gwendoline Mary opened her mouth to say this but Belinda spoke first.

'Yes. We'll call you Bill. It suits you. Wilhelmina's a nice name for some people, but not for you. You really *are* a Bill. What do you say, Darrell and Jean?'

'Yes,' they agreed at once. They couldn't help liking this sturdy, freckled girl with her short hair and frank smile. She *was* Bill. They couldn't possibly call her anything else.

'Well, thanks awfully,' said Bill. 'Thanks *most* awfully. Now I can forget I was ever christened Wilhelmina.'

Mavis and Gwendoline Mary looked as if they didn't approve of this at all. Why should a new girl get a nickname at once, just because she wanted it? Daphne looked disapproving too. How could any girl want a boy's name? And how could anyone like to wear her hair as short as Wilhelmina and get so many freckles? Why, Daphne couldn't bear it if she got so much as a single freckle!

Zerelda came into the cloakroom, her hair still done properly, without the big roll on the top of her head. Jean looked at her.

'Gracious, Zerelda! You do look different—about ten years younger! I bet Miss Williams was mad with you, wasn't she?'

'She was mad all right,' said Zerelda. 'Really queer, I mean! I'm quite scared of her. I'd rather have your Miss Peters. I say—who in the big wide world is this?'

She stood and stared in the utmost wonder at Bill, who looked back, quite unabashed. The two took in one another from top to toe.

'Are you a boy or a girl?' enquired Zerelda. 'Gee, I wouldn't know!'

'My name's Bill,' said Bill with a grin. 'Short for Wilhelmina. What's yours?'

'Zerelda. Short for nothing,' said Zerelda. 'Why do you wear your hair like that?'

'Because I couldn't bear to wear it like yours,' retorted Bill.

Zerelda stared at Bill again as if she really couldn't believe her eyes.

'I've never seen a girl like you before,' she said. 'Gee, you're wunnerful! Gee, I think all you English people are wunnerful!'

'Anyone would think you hadn't got an English mother,' said Darrell. 'You've lived with her all your life, haven't you? You always sound as if you have never met anyone English before.'

'My mother's as American as anyone,' said Zerelda. 'I don't know why she's gotten it into her head to send me to England. She's forgotten she was ever English. I'd like to take you back to America with me, Bill. Why, nobody would believe you were real, over there! Gee. you're just ...'

'WUNNERFUL!' chorused everyone, and Zerelda laughed.

A bell rang. 'Dinner!' yelled Belinda. 'I'm starving. Rotten breakfasts we get here!'

'Rotten!' agreed everyone. They had all eaten big plates of porridge and milk, scrambled eggs, and toast and marmalade, but it was always agreed that the food was 'rotten'—unless, of course, an outsider dared to criticize the food, and then it suddenly became 'too wizard for words'.

They tore down to the dining-room. Zerelda went to sit with the third-formers, having put up rather a poor show in the fourth form that morning, and feeling rather small—but Miss Williams called her over.

'Zerelda! This is your table now. Let me look at your hair.'

Zerelda submitted to Miss Williams' close examination, glad that she had not put any red on her lips. How dare Miss Williams treat her like a kid of six? She felt angry and annoyed. But she soon cheered up when she saw the steaming dishes of stew, surrounded with all kinds of vegetables. Gee, she liked these English meals. They were—no, not wunnerful—what was the word the others used—yes, they were wizard !

Darrell wrote to Sally that night and told her about Bill and Zerelda.

> You'll like Bill (short for Wilhelmina), [she wrote]. All grins and freckles and very short hair, mad on horses, has seven brothers, says just exactly what she thinks, and yet we don't mind a bit.

She bit her pen and then went on.

> But, oh my, *Zerelda* ! She thinks she's going to be a film-star and says she's 'wunnerful' at acting. You should have seen the way she did her hair—and the way she made up her face ! We thought we were going to have some fun with her and take her down a peg or two, but she's not in our form after all. She's nearly sixteen so she's gone into the fourth. I bet Miss Williams had a fit when she saw her walking into her classroom this morning. Sally, do hurry up and come back. Betty isn't back yet either, so Alicia and I are keeping each other company, but I'd so *much* rather have you. You steady me ! Alicia doesn't. She makes me feel I'm going to do idiotic things. I hope I'll last out till you come back !

Somebody put their head in at the door. ' Hey, is Wilhelmina here ? Matron wants her. Wilhelmina ! '

Nobody stirred. ' Wilhelmina ! ' said the voice again. ' Hey, you, new girl ! Aren't you Wilhelmina ? '

Bill put down her book hastily. ' Golly, yes, so I am ! ' she said. ' I quite forgot. I really must tell Matron to call me Bill. '

She went out and everyone laughed. ' Good old Bill ! I'd like to see Matron's face when she tells her to call her Bill ! ' said Belinda.

6 BILL AND THUNDER

AFTER a few days it seemed to Darrell as if she had been back at school for weeks. The world of home seemed very far away. She thought pityingly of her sister Felicity at her day school. Why, Felicity didn't even *guess* what it was like to be at a proper boarding-school, where you got up all together, had meals together, planned fun for every evening, and then all rushed off to bed together.

Wilhelmina, or Bill, had been rather silent those first two or three days. Darrell wondered if she was homesick. As a rule the happy, normal girls did not mope and pine—life was so full and so jolly at Malory Towers that there simply wasn't time for anything of that sort.

All the same, she thought Bill looked a bit serious. 'Not homesick, are you?' she asked, one morning when she was walking down one of the corridors with Bill.

'Oh no. I'm horse-sick!' said Bill, surprisingly. 'I keep on and on thinking of all our horses at home that I love so much—Beauty and Star and Blackie and Velvet and Midnight and Miss Muffet and Ladybird, and ...'

'Good gracious! However do you remember all those names?' said Darrell, in surprise.

'I couldn't possibly forget them,' said Bill, solemnly. 'I'm going to like Malory Towers, I know that, but I simply can't help missing all our horses, and the thunder of their hooves and the way they neigh and nuzzle—oh, you can't understand, Darrell. You'll think me silly, I know. You see, I and three of my brothers used to ride each morning to their tutor—four miles away—and we used to go out and saddle and bridle our horses—and then off we'd go, galloping over the hills.'

'Well, you couldn't do that all your life long,' said Darrell, sensibly. 'And anyway, you'll do it in the hols. again. You're lucky to have been able to bring Thunder with you here.'

'That's why I said I'd come to Malory Towers,' said Bill. 'Because I could bring Thunder. Oh dear, Darrell—it's been the week-end so far, when there weren't lessons—I'm just dreading to think what will happen when I have to go to classes and perhaps shan't see Thunder all day long. It's a pity Miss Peters wouldn't let him stand at the back of the classroom. He'd be as good as gold.'

Darrell gave a squeal of laughter. 'Oh, Bill—you're mad! Golly, I'd love to have Thunder in the classroom too. I bet he'd neigh at Mam'zelle, and she'd teach him to whinny in French!'

'She wouldn't. She doesn't like horses. She told me so,' said Bill. 'She's scared of them. Imagine that, Darrell! I shouldn't have thought there was anyone in the world silly enough to be frightened of a horse.'

Most of the third-formers had been out to the stables to see Bill's wonderful horse. Actually he didn't seem very wonderful to Darrell, who didn't know a great deal about horses, but she did think he was lovely the way he welcomed Bill, whinnying in delight, pushing his big velvety nose into the crook of her arm, and showing her as plainly as possible that he adored every bit of his freckled little mistress.

Mavis, Gwendoline, Daphne and Mary-Lou would not go near him. He was a big black horse, and they all felt certain he would kick or bite. But the others loved him.

Zerelda was not scared of him, and she admired him very much. 'Gee, he's wunnerful,' she said. 'But what a pity you've got to get yourself up in those awful breeches to ride him, Wilhelmina.'

Bill scowled. She hated to be called by her full name. 'I suppose you'd ride him in flowing skirts, with your hair down to your waist—and rings on your fingers and bells on your toes!' she retorted. 'All the way to Banbury Cross.'

Zerelda didn't understand. She didn't know the old English nursery rhyme. She smiled her lazy smile at Bill.

'You're wunnerful when you scowl like that,' she said.

'Shut up,' said Bill, and turned away. She was puzzled by Zerelda and her grown-up ways—and even more puzzled by her good humour. Zerelda never seemed to take offence, no matter how much anyone laughed at her or even jeered, as Mavis did very often.

She made the others feel small and young and rather stupid. They felt uncomfortable with her. She really did seem years older, and she deliberately used a grown-up manner, jeering gently at their clothes, their 'hair-do's' as she called them, their liking for getting hot and muddy at games, and their complete lack of interest in the lives and careers of film-stars.

But she was generous and kind, and never lost her temper, so it was difficult really to dislike her. Gwendoline, of course, adored her. She quite neglected Mavis for Zerelda, which annoyed that conceited young opera-singer immensely.

The first full week of school began on the next day, Monday. No more leniency from the mistresses, no more slacking from the girls, no more easy-going ways. 'Work, now, work for everyone!' said Miss Peters. 'It's not a very long term but you must work hard and show good results even if we are a week or two short.'

The third form did not have only the third form girls from North Tower but the third-formers from other towers too, so it was a fairly big form. The standard was high, and Miss Peters was strict.

Mavis had been in Miss Peters' black books the term before, because of her poor work. But as it had been her first term, she had not been too hard on her. But now she, like everyone else, was getting tired of Mavis's parrot-cry, 'when I'm an opera-singer' and she was quite determined to make Mavis a good third-former, opera-singer or not.

'You'd better look out, Mavis,' said Gwendoline, catching a certain look in Miss Peters' eye that morning as she studied Mavis. 'I know that look! You'll have to work this term, and forget your voice for a bit!'

'When I want your advice I'll ask for it,' said Mavis. 'I'm not scared of our hearty Miss Peters, if you are! I'm not going to slave and make myself miserable at Malory Towers for Miss P. or anyone else. Waste *your* time, if you like—you'll never have a career, or be Somebody!'

Gwendoline was very hurt. Like many silly, weak people she had a great idea of herself, and was so continually spoilt at home that she really did think herself wonderful.

'If you're going to say things like that I shan't be friends with you,' she whispered.

'Go and tag round Zerelda then,' said Mavis, forgetting to whisper softly enough.

'Mavis! That's enough whispering between you and Gwendoline,' said Miss Peters' loud voice. 'One more whisper and you can stay in at Break.'

Bill couldn't seem to settle down that first Monday morning at all. She stared out of the window. She seemed very far away. She paid no attention at all to what Miss Peters was saying.

'Wilhelmina!' said Miss Peters at last. 'Did you hear *any*thing of what I have just said?'

Everyone turned to look at Bill, who still gazed out of the window, a dreamy expression on her small square face.

'*Wilhelmina*!' said Miss Peters, sharply. 'I am speaking to you.'

Still Bill took no notice at all. To the girls' amusement and surprise she suddenly made a little crooning noise, as if she was quite by herself and there was nobody else in the room at all!

Miss Peters was astonished. The girls giggled. Darrell knew what Bill was doing. She had heard that funny little crooning noise before—it was the noise Bill made to Thunder, when he nuzzled against her shoulder!

'She must be pretending she's with Thunder!' thought Darrell. 'She's in the stables with him. She's not here at all.'

Miss Peters wondered if Wilhelmina was feeling all right. She spoke to her again. 'Wilhelmina, are you deaf? What's the matter?'

Gwendoline gave Bill a poke in the back and made her jump. She looked round at Gwendoline crossly, annoyed at being so rudely awakened from her pleasant day-dreams. Gwendoline nodded violently towards Miss Peters.

'That'll do, Gwendoline,' said Miss Peters. 'Wilhelmina, will you kindly give me your attention. I've been speaking to you for the last few minutes.'

'Oh, sorry! Have you really?' said Bill, apologetically. 'Perhaps you kept calling me Wilhelmina, though? If you could call me Bill I should always answer. You see ... '

Miss Peters looked most disapproving. What an extraordinary girl!

'In future, Wilhelmina, please pay attention to all I say, and I shall not need to address you by any name at all!' she said. 'As for calling you Bill—please don't be impertinent.'

Bill looked astonished. 'Oh, Miss Peters! I wasn't being impertinent. I'm sorry I wasn't listening to you. I was thinking about Thunder.'

'Thunder!' said Miss Peters, who had no idea that Bill had a horse called Thunder. 'Why should you think about thunder on a lovely sunny day like this? I think you are being very silly.'

'But it's just the day to think of Thunder!' said Bill, her eyes shining. 'Just think of Thunder, galloping over the hills and ... '

Everyone tried to suppress giggles. They knew perfectly well that Wilhelmina was talking about her horse, but poor Miss Peters looked more impatient than ever.

'That's enough, Wilhelmina,' she said. 'We'll have no more talk of thunder or lightning, or ... '

'Oh, how did you know that my brother George's horse was called Lightning?' said Bill in delight, honestly thinking that Miss Peters was talking of horses.

But now Miss Peters felt certain that Wilhelmina was being silly and rather rude. She gazed at her coldly.

'Have you got your book open at page thirty-three?' she asked. 'I thought you hadn't! How do you think you are going to follow this lesson if you haven't even got the right page?'

Bill hastily found page thirty-three. She tried to put all thoughts of Thunder out of her mind. She made a soft clicking noise, and Alicia and Irene grinned at one another.

'Horse-mad!' whispered Alicia, and when Miss Peters' back was turned, Alicia rocked to and fro as if she was on a trotting horse, sending the class into fits.

Darrell hugged herself in delight. It was lovely to be back at school again, lovely to sit in class and work, and giggle and hear Miss Peters ticking off this person and that. She missed Sally very much, but Alicia was fun.

'I'll beg her to play one of her tricks,' thought Darrell. 'We haven't had any *real* fun in class for terms and terms!'

7   IN THE THIRD FORM COMMON-ROOM

IT was sunny but cold the first week or two of that Easter term. The girls squabbled over getting the seats by the radiator in the common-room. Gwendoline, Mavis and Daphne were the ones that complained most of the cold—but they were the ones who took as little exercise as they could, so of course they always got chilblains and colds.

Bill didn't seem to feel the cold at all. She was still tanned, although it was early in the year. Darrell and Alicia liked the cold, and they loved rushing out to play lacrosse in the afternoons.

'They went out ten minutes before the others to practise catching. Gwendoline couldn't understand it, and she and Mavis became friends again in sympathizing with each other over the cold, and jeering at Alicia and Darrell for being so hardy.

Zerelda, of course, being a fourth-former, was now not very often able to be with any of the third-formers, so Gwendoline had had to give up any idea of being her best friend. Zerelda did not seem to be very happy in the fourth form, Darrell thought. She often came slipping into the third form common-room in the evening—saying she wanted to borrow a book or a gramophone record—and then stopping to talk to Darrell and the others.

'Got a special friend yet?' Darrell asked her one evening.

Zerelda twisted one of her curls carefully round her finger and then shook it back into its proper place.

'No,' she said. 'Stuck-up things, the fourth form! They seem to think I don't pull my weight. And they think the end of the world has come because I don't want to try and get into the third match-team for lacrosse!'

'Well, you're so tall, you could do well in the team,' said Darrell, considering her. 'You ought to be able to take some fine catches. Can you run?'

'Run! I don't *want* to run!' said Zerelda, astonished. 'As for that games captain—what's her name—Molly Ronaldson—well, I ask you, did you ever see such a girl? Big as a horse and just about as clumsy! Shouts and dances about on the field as if she had gone mad!'

Darrell laughed. 'Molly Ronaldson is one of the finest games captains we've ever had. We've won more matches with her than ever before. She's got an absolute genius for picking the right people for the match-teams. My goodness, if I could get into one of the teams I'd be so thrilled I wouldn't be able to sleep at night.'

'Is that so?' said Zerelda, in her slow drawl, looking quite astonished. 'Well, maybe I wouldn't sleep at night if I had spots on my face like Gwendoline goes in for, or if I broke one of my nails—but I'd not lose my beauty sleep for any game in the world!'

'You're a queer person, Zerelda,' said Darrell. She looked at her earnestly. 'You're missing all the nicest years of your life—I mean, you just won't let yourself enjoy the things most English girls of your age enjoy. You spend hours over your hair and your face and your nails, when you could be having fun at lacrosse, or going for walks, or even messing about in the gym.'

'Messing about in the gym! That's another thing I can't understand your liking!' said Zerelda. Gwendoline, who had come up to join in the conversation, nodded her head in agreement.

'I can't understand that either,' she said in a prim voice. 'It's a pity gym is compulsory, and games too. I wouldn't bother much about them if they weren't.'

'Only because, dear Gwendoline, you're so jolly bad at them that you make a fool of yourself every time you go into the gym or on the games field,' said Alicia, maliciously. 'Zerelda's different. I bet she'd be good at them—but she thinks that all that kind of thing is beneath her.'

Any other girl would have resented this, but Zerelda only grinned. Gwendoline, however, flared up at the unkind sneer at *her* games and gym performances, and scowled angrily at Alicia.

'Nice little scowl you've got, Gwen,' said Belinda, appearing suddenly with her sketch-book. 'Do you mind if I draw you like that? It's such a *lovely* scowl!'

Gwendoline scowled still more and flounced away. She knew Belinda's clever pencil and dreaded it! She didn't want her scowl to be drawn and passed round the common-room, accompanied by delighted giggles. Belinda shut her book and looked disappointed in rather an exaggerated manner.

'Oh, she's gone! And it was such a lovely scowl! Never mind—I'll watch out for it and draw it another time.'

'Beast!' said Gwendoline, under her breath and went to sit by Mavis. She knew she would have to look out for Belinda and her pencil now! Once Belinda wanted to draw something she didn't rest till she had done so!

'You'd better go back to the fourth form common-room now,' said Jean to Zerelda. 'The fourth-formers won't like it if you begin to live with us! We're rather beneath their notice, you know. And, after all, you *are* a fourth-former, Zerelda.'

'I know. I wish I wasn't,' said Zerelda, getting up.

'Aren't the fourth form girls "wunnerful" then?' said Alicia, with a grin.

Zerelda shrugged her shoulders and went out gracefully. 'If she'd think of something else besides her looks and the way she's going to act, and being grown-up, and would put herself out to play games decently and take some interest in her work, the fourth form wouldn't make her feel out of things,' said Jean, with her usual common sense. 'But what's the good of telling Zerelda that? She simply doesn't belong to the school at all.'

Irene drifted in, looking for something. She hummed a lively little tune. 'Tumty-ta-ti-tumty-ta-ti-too!' She had just composed a gay dance, and was very pleased about it. The girls looked at her and grinned at one another.

'Where are you off to at this time of the evening, Irene?' asked Alicia.

Irene looked surprised. 'Nowhere,' she said. 'I'm just looking for my music-book. I want to write down my new tune. Tumty-ta-ti-tumty-ta-ti-too!'

'Yes, very nice,' said Alicia, approvingly. 'But why have you got your hat and cloak on if you aren't going anywhere?'

'Oh, good gracious, have I?' said Irene, in dismay. She looked down at her cloak and felt her hat on her head. 'Blow!

When did I put these on ? I did take them off, didn't I, when we came back from the walk this afternoon ? '

'Well, you didn't have them on at tea-time or Miss Potts would have said something ! ' said Alicia. 'You really are a chump, Irene. '

' Oh, yes, I know now what must have happened, ' said Irene, sitting down in a chair, still with hat and cloak on. 'I went up to get a clean pair of stockings—and I was thinking of my new tune—and I must have taken my hat out instead of my stockings, and put it on—and then put on my cloak too. Blow ! Now I shall have to go and take them off and find my stockings—and I do want to write down that tune. '

' I'll take them up for you and find your stockings, ' said Belinda, who knew that Irene wouldn't be able to do anything sensible till she had written down her tune.

' *Will* you ? Angel ! ' said Irene, and pulled off her hat and cloak. Darrell laughed. Belinda was as much of a scatterbrain as Irene. It would be a wonder if she got as far as the cupboard to put away Irene's things—and ten to one that she wouldn't remember the stockings !

Belinda disappeared with the hat and cloak. Irene began to hum her tune again. Mavis sang it in her lovely rich voice.

' Fine ! ' said Irene, pleased. 'You make it sound twice as good, Mavis. One day I'll write a song for that voice of yours. '

' I'll sing it in New York, ' said Mavis, graciously. 'And that should make you famous, Irene, if *I* sing one of your songs ! When I'm an opera-singer, I ... '

'When you're an opera-singer, Mavis, you'll be even more conceited than you are now, ' said Alicia's sharp voice, 'which sounds impossible I know, but isn't. '

'Jean ! Can't you stop Alicia saying such beastly unfair things ? ' protested Mavis, red with annoyance. 'I'm *not* conceited. Can I help having a voice like mine ? It's a gift, and I shall make it a gift to the whole world too, when I'm grown up. '

'Alicia's tongue *is* getting a bit sharp,' said Jean, 'but you do rather ask for sharp things to be said to you, Mavis.'

Mavis was silent and cross. Gwendoline began to sympathize with her, for she too hated Alicia's hard hitting. Mary-Lou, darning a stocking in a corner, hoped that she would not come in for a flick of Alicia's tongue!

'Where's Belinda?' said Darrell. 'She's an awful long time getting those stockings for you, Irene.'

'So she is,' said Irene, who had now completely forgotten about her stockings. 'Blow! If she doesn't bring them soon, I'll have to go and fetch them myself. I simply must put a clean pair on for supper.'

Mam'zelle came bustling in, tip-tapping on her small feet in their high-heeled shoes. She held a hat and cloak in her hand.

'Irene!' she said, reproachfully, 'these are yours! Three times already have I cleared up your things from this place and that place. Now this time I have almost fallen down the stairs because of your hat and cloak!'

Irene stared in surprise. 'But—where were they?' she asked.

'On the stairs—lying for me to fall over,' said Mam'zelle. 'l see them on the stairs as I come down, and I say to myself, "What is this? Is it someone taken ill on the stairs!" But no, it is Irene's cloak and hat once more. l am very displeased with you, Irene. You will take an order-mark!'

'Oh *no*, Mam'zelle!' said Irene, distressed. Order-marks counted against the whole form. 'Mam'zelle, I'm really very sorry.'

'One order-mark,' said Mam'zelle, and departed on her high heels.

'Blow Belinda!' said Irene. 'What possessed her to put them on the stairs?'

Belinda came in at that moment. She was greeted by a volley of remarks. 'We've got an order-mark because of you, idiot!

What did you do with Irene's things? Mam'zelle found them on the stairs!'

'Golly!' said Belinda, dismayed. 'Yes, I remember. I was going up the stairs with them, and I dropped my pencil. I chucked the things down to find it—and must have forgotten all about them. I *am* sorry, Irene.'

'It's all right,' said Irene, solemnly putting on her hat and cloak. 'I'll take them up myself now—and I'll jolly well *wear* them so that *l* can't leave them lying about either!'

She disappeared for a long time. The bell rang for supper. There was a general clearing-up, and the girls got ready to go to the dining-room.

'Where's Irene now?' said Jean, exasperated. 'Honestly she ought to be kept in a cage then we'd always know where she was!'

'Here she is!' said Darrell, with a shout of laughter. 'Irene! You've still got your hat and cloak on! Oh, you'll make us die of laughing. Quick, Alicia, take them off her and rush upstairs with them. She'll get another order-mark if we don't look out.'

8 A BAD TIME FOR ZERELDA

DURING the first two or three weeks of term poor Zerelda had a very bad time. Although she was older even than the fourth-formers, and should therefore have found the work easy, she found, to her dismay, that she was far behind them in their standard of work!

It was a blow to Zerelda. After all her posing, and grown-up ways, and her manner of appearing to look down on the others as young and silly, it was very humiliating to find that her maths, for instance, were nowhere near the standard of maths in the fourth form!

'Have you never done these sums before?' asked Miss

Williams, in astonishment. 'And what about algebra and geometry? You don't appear to understand the first thing about them, Zerelda.'

'We—we don't seem to do our lessons in America the same way as you do them here,' said Zerelda. 'We don't bother so much. I never liked algebra or geometry, so I didn't worry about them.'

Miss Williams looked most disapproving. Was America really so slack in its teaching of children, or was it just that Zerelda was stupid?

'It isn't only your maths,' she said at last. 'It's almost everything, Zerelda. Didn't you ever study grammar in your school?'

Zerelda thought hard. 'Maybe we did,' she said at last. 'But I guess we didn't pay much attention to the teacher who taught grammar. I guess we played about in her lessons.'

'And didn't you do any history?' said Miss Williams. 'I realize, of course, that the history you would take would not be quite the same as ours—but Miss Carton, the history mistress, tells me that you don't know a single thing even about the history of your *own* country. America is a great country. It seems a pity to know nothing of its wonderful history.'

Zerelda looked troubled. She tried to think of something her school had really worked at. What had she taken real interest in? Ah—there was the dramatic class!

'We did a lot of Shakespeare, Miss Williams,' she said. 'Gee! I just loved your Shakespeare. He's wunnerful. I did Lady Macbeth. You should have seen me trying to wash the guilt off my hands.'

'Yes. I can quite imagine it,' said Miss Williams, drily. 'But there's a little more to education than being able to act Lady Macbeth. Zerelda, you will have to work very very hard to catch up the work of your form. I am willing to give you extra coaching, if you would like it, and Mam'zelle, who is very

distressed at your French, says she also will give you some of her
free time. '

Zerelda was really alarmed. Gee, wasn't it enough to have all
these classes and games, and be expected to attend each one
and be serious over the work, without having to do a whole lot
of extra study ? She looked so very alarmed that Miss Williams
laughed.

'Well, Zerelda, I won't burden you with extra work just yet,
if you'll really make an effort and try to give your attention to
your school work and not—er—*quite* so much attention to
your face, shall we say—and nails—and hair ?'

Zerelda was annoyed. She was going to study to be a famous
film-star, so what was the use of all this algebra and history
stuff ? Just waste of time for a girl like her ! She had good brains,
she knew she had—it was just that American schools and
English were so different. They had different standards. Life
was easier in America.

She looked down at her long, beautifully polished nails and
well-kept hands. She felt that Miss Williams had shamed her
and made her feel small. Zerelda couldn't bear that ! She was
better than any of these tough little English girls any day ! They
didn't know a thing really !

So she looked stubborn and said nothing. Miss Williams
gathered up her papers, thinking that Zerelda was really a very
difficult girl.

'Well, that's all for now, ' she said, briskly. 'I shall expect
much better work from now on, Zerelda—and please do think
of the other fourth-formers too. You know that returned work
means an order-mark, which counts against the whole form.
You have got far too many. '

Zerelda thought that order-marks were very silly. She wouldn't
have minded at all getting twenty or thirty a week ! But the other
fourth-formers minded very much.

The head-girl, Lucy, spoke to Zerelda about it. 'Look here,
Zerelda, can't you stop getting order-marks ? There are two

half-holidays given this term, but any form getting over forty order-marks has the holiday withheld. The form will be pretty wild if you make them miss their half-holiday, I can tell you!'

So, what with some serious talks from Miss Williams and some tickings-off from Lucy, and from Ellen, a serious, scholarship girl who had gone up from the third form into the fourth, and was very pleased about it, poor Zerelda had rather a bad time.

'There doesn't seem time to do anything!' she thought to herself, as she polished her nails that night. 'I simply must take care of my hair—and it takes ages to curl it properly and set it—and I can't let my complexion go—or my nails. I don't have a minute to myself. But I simply must do something about the work. For one thing, I feel as if I'm letting America down! I can't bear these English girls to be so much better at everything than I am!'

So Zerelda really did try with the work. But her pride would not let her cast off her posing and her grown-up ways. She no longer really looked down on the English girls, but she was still going to show them that she, Zerelda, was far, far above them in all the ways that mattered!

Zerelda had hoped that she would be able to show her ability for acting in the play the fourth form were going to perform. But, alas! for her, it was a French play, and Zerelda's French did not please Mam'zelle at all.

'*C'est terrible!*' cried Mam'zelle Dupont, and the other Mam'zelle for once agreed with her. Both of them were astonished at Zerelda and her ways, and spent a few pleasant half-hours telling each other of 'Zerelda, *cet enfant terrible,*' that terrible girl.

When Zerelda had been awarded fifteen order-marks, had three lessons out of every six returned, and had one day given in no prep. at all because she said she couldn't do any of it, Miss Williams went to Miss Grayling.

'Zerelda Brass isn't up to the fourth form,' she told Miss Grayling. 'She's making them furious because of the order-marks she's getting. The trouble is they know what a lot of time she wastes over her appearance, and they think if she gave a bit more time to her work, it would be better all round. I've told her this myself, of course. I don't think she's a bad girl at all, Miss Grayling—only silly, and brought up with quite the wrong ideas. What are we to do?'

'Do you think extra coaching would help?' asked Miss Grayling. 'She is nearly sixteen, you know. She ought to be well up to School Certificate standard. She had quite a good report from America.'

'No. I don't think extra coaching would help at all,' said Miss Grayling. 'It would worry her too much. She simply isn't up to the fourth form—and I really doubt if she's up to third form standard either! The trouble is she's got such a great opinion of herself, and appears to look down on the others. They resent it.'

'Of course they do,' said Miss Grayling. 'And quite rightly.' She said nothing for a minute. She felt a little disappointed. She had hoped that the American girl would be good for the English girls, and that the English girls would help the American. But apparently it hadn't worked out that way.

'She must go down into the third form,' said Miss Grayling at last. 'I know it is a humiliation and that Zerelda will feel it a disgrace—but somehow I feel that won't do her any harm. Send her to me.'

'Thank you, Miss Grayling,' said Miss Williams, and went out, really relieved to think that Zerelda would no longer be her responsibility. She would now erase all those order-marks that Zerelda had unfortunately got for her form. They would be pleased. They were a good hard-working form, and Miss Williams was proud of them. She was glad to get rid of a girl who had brought them nothing but disgrace.

'But she's not really a *bad* girl,' thought Miss Williams, who was very fair-minded. ' She's just not up to standard in any way. She'll be better in the third form. '

She sent Zerelda down to Miss Grayling. Zerelda, who would have laughed at the thought of being scared of any teacher, when she first came to Malory Towers, actually found her heart thumping away hard as she went to find Miss Grayling in her pleasant drawing-room.

She went in and stood in front of the Head Mistress's desk. Miss Grayling put down her pen and looked at Zerelda, noting her brassy golden hair, done more neatly now, but still carefully set, her brilliantly polished nails, her carefully powdered face.

' Zerelda, I have sent for you because I think you are not up to the standard of the work in the fourth form, ' said Miss Grayling, going straight to the point, as she always did. Zerelda flushed bright red.

' l am sorry about this because you are really above their average age, ' said Miss Grayling. ' But I think that it will be too difficult for you to cope with extra work, and also l am afraid that the fourth form, which is a School Certificate form, will not take kindly to quite so many order-marks as you have been producing for them. '

Zerelda blushed an even brighter scarlet, and was angry to feel herself going so red. What did she care about the silly fourth form ?

' Therefore I think you will do better if you go into the third form, ' said Miss Grayling. ' They don't take life—or lessons— quite so seriously as they will when in the fourth form—so you should be happier there, and able to work better. '

Zerelda was shocked. To go down into a lower form ! What a disgrace ! True, she liked the third-formers, and didn't get on with the fourth form girls—but she didn't want to slide down a whole form ! Whatever would her people say—and her English grandmother would be amazed.

' Oh, Miss Grayling—gee, I wouldn't like that, ' said Zerelda, in distress. She undid a button and did it up again, then undid it, not knowing what she did.

'Don't pull that button off, Zerelda,' said Miss Grayling. 'I think you'll soon settle down quite well in the third form. You can go there tomorrow. I will tell Miss Peters. Move all your things tonight.'

'But, Miss Grayling—don't make me do that!' begged Zerelda, feeling very small and disgraced, and not liking it at all. 'This is all new to me, this English school—and the work too. You see ...'

'Yes, I quite see all that,' said Miss Grayling. 'It's partly because of that that I think life would be easier for you in the way of work, if you go into a lower form. I am convinced you will not get on at all in a higher form. But, Zerelda—don't slide down any further, will you? You belong to a great country, and you are her only representative here. Be a good one if you can. And I think you can.'

This was the one thing that could touch Zerelda. Gee. she stood for America, didn't she! She was living in England, but she was a bit of America. All right, she'd go down into the third form, she'd not even make a fuss. And if the girls teased her, she'd just show them she didn't care! But—she would try to get on with the work all right. Certainly she wouldn't slide down any further!

'You may go, Zerelda,' said Miss Grayling, and Zerelda went. Miss Grayling watched her as she went gracefully out of the door. If only she could see herself as a proper little schoolgirl and not as Zerelda, the promising film-star, how nice she might be!

9 ON THE LACROSSE FIELD

MISS GRAYLING sent for Miss Peters and told her that Zerelda was to come into her form.

'That will be hard for her,' said Miss Peters. 'Not the work, I mean—though I don't think Zerelda will find even third form work easy—but the disgrace.'

'Sometimes hard things are good for us,' said Miss Grayling, and Miss Peters nodded. After all, the girls didn't come to Malory Towers only to learn lessons in class—they came to learn other things too—to be just and fair, generous, brave, kind. Perhaps those things were even more important than the lessons!

'I don't know if you think it would be a good thing to say something to the third-formers before Zerelda appears in their classroom,' said Miss Grayling. 'You have one or two there—Gwendoline, for instance—who might not be very kind. A word or two beforehand might be as well.'

'Yes. Just as well,' said Miss Peters. 'Well, I don't expect an easy time with Zerelda, Miss Grayling. She's got such queer ideas about things—spends all her time on her appearance, you know—I've not much use for that kind of girl.'

'No,' said Miss Grayling, thinking that probably it would be good for Zerelda to have the hearty Miss Peters over her for a little while. 'Well—there's plenty of good in the girl —she seems very good-humoured, and I like her smile. Just say a few words to your form, but don't make a big thing of it.'

So, to the third form's intense surprise, Miss Peters said the 'few words' to them that afternoon in class.

'Oh, by the way,' she said, 'we are to have an addition to our form. Zerelda Brass is coming to us.'

Gwendoline drew in her breath sharply, and looked round with a triumphant expression. But she was not crowing over Zerelda's humiliation. She was delighted to think that the American girl would now be approachable—actually in her form, and in her common-room! Gwendoline could dance attendance on her all she pleased. She would be her friend.

Miss Peters read Gwendoline's face wrongly. 'Gwendoline! I hope you will not delight in another girl's inability to follow the work of a higher form. I think ... '

' Oh, Miss Peters! ' said Gwendoline, a most hurt expression on her face, ' as if I would do anything of the sort. I *like* Zerelda. I'm *glad* she'll be in our form. I shall welcome her. '

Miss Peters didn't know whether to believe this or not. She disliked and distrusted Gwendoline. She decided to give her the benefit of the doubt.

' It would be just as well not to discuss the matter with Zerelda if she would rather say nothing about it, ' she said. She cast a sharp look at Alicia. She knew Alicia's sarcastic tongue. Alicia looked back at her. She didn't mean to jeer at Zerelda—but at the back of her sharp-witted mind she knew that Zerelda's disgrace would be a nice little weapon to taunt her with, if she gave herself too high-and-mighty airs.

After the afternoon class there was half an hour's lacrosse practice. The third-formers streamed out, Gwendoline last as usual, with Mavis running her close. They were the despair of the games mistress. All the girls began to talk about Zerelda.

' Golly! Fancy being chucked out of a form like that! ' said Irene. ' Poor old Zerelda. I bet she feels awful. '

' I should think she feels too ashamed for anything, ' said Mary-Lou. ' I know how I should feel. I shouldn't want to look anyone in the face again! '

' I bet the fourth form are glad, ' said Jean. ' Ellen told me they had got more order-marks because of Zerelda than they've

ever had before! Let's hope she doesn't present *us* with too
many. We haven't done too badly so far—except when Irene
and Belinda leave their brains behind! '

'l think we all ought to be very nice to Zerelda,' announced
Gwendoline. 'l think we ought to show her we're glad she'll be
in our form.'

Mavis looked at Gwendoline sourly. She knew quite well
that once Zerelda appeared, she, Mavis, would lose
Gwendoline's very fickle friendship. Nobody else had any time
for Mavis. Gwendoline wasn't much of a friend, but at least she
was somebody to talk with, and whisper to.

'Well,' said Darrell, 'Zerelda's got her faults, but she's jolly
good-tempered and generous—and I vote we welcome her and
show her we're glad to have her.'

So, feeling rather virtuous and generous-hearted, the third-
formers made up their minds to be very nice to Zerelda, and
ease her disgrace as much as they could.

They pictured her slinking into their form room the next day,
red in the face, hanging her head, almost in tears.

Poor Zerelda! She would be glad of their welcome.

'Darrell! Darrell Rivers! Come over here and I'll give you
some catches,' called the games mistress. Darrell ran up. She
was a swift runner and loved lacrosse. How she longed to be in
one of the match-teams. But it was hard for a third-former to
be in a school team unless she was very big and strong.

'You catch well, Darrell!' called the games mistress. 'One
of these days you'll get into a match-team. We could do with
a good runner and catcher in the third match. team.'

Darrell glowed with pride. Oh! If only she *could* be in the
match-team. How pleased her mother and father would be—
and how she would boast to Felicity. 'l was in the match-team
when we went to play Barchester. I was on the wing because I'm
so fast. And I shot a goal!'

She pictured it all as she ran to take another catch. Suppose
she practised very hard indeed every minute she could? Should

she ask Molly Ronaldson for extra coaching? Molly always said she was willing to give the juniors any tips if they were keen enough to come and ask for them.

But Molly was seventeen and Darrell was only fourteen. Molly seemed a very high-up, distant, rather grand person to Darrell, who hadn't really a very high opinion of herself.

She saw Molly as she was going off the field, hot and happy. She screwed up all her courage and went up to the big, sturdy girl shyly.

'Please, Molly—could I just ask you something? I do so want to be in one of the match-teams one day. Do you think there might be a *possible* chance if I do extra practice at catching—and—and if you could give me any tips?'

As red as a beetroot Darrell stared at Molly, the famous games captain. Molly laughed and clapped Darrell on the back.

'Good kid!' she said. 'I was only saying to Joan yesterday how you were coming on, and a spot of extra coaching would do you good. I'll send you the times I give extra practice to possible match-team players, and you can come along any of the times you're free.'

'Oh, *thank* you, Molly,' breathed Darrell, hardly able to speak for joy. 'I'll come every time I can.' She ran off, her face glowing. Molly had actually spoken to Joan about her! She had noticed her, had seen that she was coming on well. Darrell felt so happy that she leapt along like a deer, colliding with Mam'zelle round a corner, and almost knocking her over.

'Now, what is this behaviour?' said Mam'zelle, tottering on her high heels and clutching wildly at the wall. 'Darrell! What are you thinking of, to come round the corner like a wild beast?'

'Oh, Mam'zelle—*sorry*!' cried Darrell, happily. 'Honestly I didn't mean it. Oh, Mam'zelle, Molly Ronaldson is going to give me extra coaching at lacrosse. Think of it! I might be in the third match-team one day!'

Darrell ran straight into Mam'zelle

Mam'zelle was just going to remark that not for anything would she rejoice at that big Molly giving Darrell coaching at that extraordinary game lacrosse, when she saw Darrell's shining eyes. She had a soft spot for Darrell, and she smiled at her.

'I am very glad for you, *ma petite*!' she said. 'It is indeed a high honour. But do not go round the corner and knock your poor Mam'zelle over in this way again. You have made my heart go patter-pit!'

'Pitter-pat, you mean, Mam'zelle,' said Darrell, and ran off laughing.

She told the others what Molly had said. They were most impressed, all except those who disliked games. No one of the third form had ever been in a match-team, though one or two steady ones, such as Jean, had tried very hard. So had Sally.

'What with Bill rushing off to her horse every single minute, Irene rushing off to try out her new tune on the piano, Mavis trilling her voice, and now you, Darrell, racing off to practise catching from dawn to dusk, the third form will soon have a nice empty common-room,' said Alicia, a little jealous of Molly's notice of Darrell.

'Zerelda will be there to make up!' said Darrell. 'I don't expect she'll mind our company there—she was always slipping into our common-room till you stopped her, Jean.'

Zerelda came to the third form classroom the next day, carrying her pencil-box and paint-box, which she had forgotten to take to the form room the night before. She walked in looking quite unconcerned.

The third-formers immediately began to be nice. 'Here, Zerelda—wouldn't you rather have this desk till Sally comes back?' said Darrell. 'It's got a nice position.'

'No, Zerelda. You come and sit by me,' said Gwendoline. 'I should like that.'

Alicia looked keenly at Zerelda. Zerelda looked exactly the

same as ever ! She didn't hang her head, she didn't look upset, she wasn't even red in the face.

'l don't believe she cares a bit!' thought Alicia. But Zerelda did. She cared terribly. It was very hard indeed to walk into the classroom of a lower form, knowing that everyone had been told that she had been sent down.

She wished they wouldn't try and be kind to her like this. It was nice of them, but she hated to think they were being nice because they were sorry for her.

'Keep your chin up, Zerelda!' she said to herself. 'You're American. Fly the Stars and Stripes! Make out you don't mind a bit.'

So, appearing quite unconcerned, she took the desk she had put her things in the night before, put in her pencil-box and paint-box, and began to look for the book she would need for the first lesson.

The third-formers felt a little indignant. They had so virtuously and generously decided to welcome Zerelda, and help her not to mind what they considered to be a great disgrace—and *she* didn't seem to mind at all. She was exactly the same as usual, speaking in her slow drawl, fluffing up her hair, appearing even more sure of herself than ever.

Darrell felt rather annoyed. She considered that Zerelda ought to have shown a little more feeling. She didn't stop to think that Zerelda might be putting on a show of bravery, and that was all. Underneath it all the girl was miserable, ashamed and feeling very small.

Miss Peters came in briskly as usual. Mary-Lou shut the door. Miss Peters swept keen eyes round the class. 'Sit!' she said, and they sat. That keen glance had taken in Zerelda—but Miss Peters saw what the others did not see—a rather panic-stricken heart under all Zerelda's brave show. A hand that shook slightly as she picked up a book—a voice that wasn't quite so steady as usual.

'She feels it all right,' thought Miss Peters. 'But she's not going to show it. Well, she's got plenty of pluck. Let's hope she'll learn that she's not so important a person as she thinks she is. If we got right down to the real Zerelda, we might find somebody worth knowing! We *might*. I still don't know!'

The lesson began. Zerelda concentrated hard. She forgot her hair, her nails, her clothes. She really *worked* for about the first time in her life!

10   BILL AND MISS PETERS

MOST of the third-formers were now almost settled in to their term's work. Alicia, however, was restless, missing Betty and not finding that Darrell quite made up for her old friend. Darrell was steady and loyal and natural—but she hadn't Betty's witty tongue, nor her daredevil ways. Still she was better than anyone else. Alicia hoped that Sally wouldn't be back till Betty came!

Bill was restless too. Bill had got the idea that Thunder was pining for the other horses at home, and she was always disappearing to be with him.

'How you do coddle that horse!' said Alicia, in disgust. 'I wonder he puts up with it.'

Miss Peters was always pouncing on Bill for dreaming in class. Bill's standard of work was very uneven. She was brilliant at Latin, which she had taken continually with her brothers. She knew very little French, much to Mam'zelle's despair. She didn't know much maths because her brothers' tutor had devoted all his time to them at this subject and had not bothered much about her.

'He didn't think we did much maths in a girls' school,' explained Bill. 'But I do know my tables, Miss Peters.'

'I should hope so!' groaned Miss Peters. 'You will simply have to have extra coaching at maths, Wilhelmina.'

'Oh, I can't,' said Bill. 'I spend every minute of free time with Thunder.'

Miss Peters had known for some time now that Thunder was Bill's horse. She had seen him and admired him, much to Bill's delight. She had also marvelled at Bill's magnificent horsemanship. The girl rode as if she and her horse were one. She was never happier than when she was out riding with the others, galloping over the lovely country that lay behind Malory Towers.

But she was annoyed because she was only allowed to ride out with the others for company. She was not allowed to take Thunder out alone.

'But I do at home,' she protested loudly. 'I've gone off by myself every day for years and years and years. It's silly not to let me. What harm can I come to? I'm with Thunder all the time.'

'Yes, I know all that,' explained Miss Peters, patiently, for the twentieth time. 'But you are not at home now, you are at school, and you have to do as the others do, and keep their rules. We can't have one rule for you and one rule for them.'

'I don't see why not,' said Bill, obstinately. She often sounded rude, because she was so much in earnest, and Miss Peters sometimes lost patience with her.

'Well, you are not running this school, fortunately,' said Miss Peters. 'You must do as you are told. And, Wilhelmina, if you insist on being silly about these things, I shall forbid you to see Thunder for two or three days.'

Bill was dumbfounded. She stared at Miss Peters as if she couldn't believe her ears. She went red to the roots of her hair.

'But I couldn't *not* see Thunder,' said Bill, trying to speak patiently. 'You don't understand, Miss Peters. Though you *ought* to understand because you're so fond of horses yourself.'

'I dare say,' said Miss Peters, equally patiently. 'But I'm not top-heavy about them, as you are—I mean, I don't think, dream, smell and ride horses every minute of the day and night as you do. Do be sensible, Wilhelmina. I'm putting up with quite a lot from you, you know, and it's time you pulled yourself together, and thought a little less of Thunder, and a little more of other things.'

But that was just what Bill couldn't do, as the other third-formers soon found out. She wouldn't go for extra practice at lacrosse. She wouldn't go for a nature walk. She wouldn't even take on any of her extra duties in the common-room, which everyone had to do in turn. She got Mary-Lou to do them for her instead.

Mary-Lou was so gentle and kindly that she would do anything for anybody. Jean was very cross when she found Mary-Lou doing the flowers in the common-room instead of Bill.

'Why are you doing this?' she demanded. 'You can see on the list it's Bill's week.'

'I know, Jean,' said Mary-Lou, scared at Jean's sharp tone. 'But Bill did so badly want to go and give Thunder an extra grooming today. He got so muddy yesterday.'

'I'm getting tired of Bill racing off to the stables, never joining in anything the third form does, and getting other people to do her duties,' said Jean. 'I shall talk to her about it.'

But she made no more impression on Bill than Miss Peters had done. Bill had spent her life with horses. She had, as Miss Peters said, thought, dreamt, smelt, groomed, ridden horses all her life, and she just didn't want to do anything else.

She would have been excellent at lacrosse if she had practised. She was magnificent at gym, daring, supple and with a wonderful sense of balance. The gym mistress was delighted with her, and sang her praises to everyone.

Bill could turn 'cart-wheels' as easily as any clown in a circus, going over and over on hands and feet till the others were giddy with watching. She could fling herself in the air and turn a complete somersault. The gym mistress forbade anyone else to try and do it.

'You'll only damage yourselves,' she said. But nobody else really wanted to turn somersaults in the air!

Bill could also walk on her hands, and the others often made her perform to them in the evening when she could not go to the stables. Bill was good-natured and natural, and didn't get her head in the least turned by all the praise and acclamation given to her for her performances in gym or common-room.

Zerelda watched and marvelled. She could not imagine how any girl could want to do such extraordinary things. She thought Bill was decidedly mad, but she couldn't help liking her. In fact, most of the girls liked her very much indeed, though they were annoyed and exasperated when she wouldn't join in with them over anything.

Belinda did some beautiful drawings of Thunder. She was very good at drawing animals, and when Bill saw them she exclaimed in delight.

'Belinda! They're simply marvellous! Please, please give them to me!'

'No,' said Belinda, tucking them away into her portfolio. 'I shall keep them with my collection of animal drawings.'

'Well, Belinda, do some specially for *me*,' begged Bill. 'Oh, Belinda, you might. I'd have them all framed and stood on my dressing-table.'

'Gosh, Bill, you've got about six different photographs of horses there now,' said Belinda. 'You've no room for a picture of Thunder.'

'I have! I should put him right at the very front,' said Bill. 'Belinda, *will* you do me some drawings of Thunder? I'll do anything for you if you will.'

'Fibber!' said Belinda. 'The only person you'll do anything for is Thunder. You wouldn't lift a finger to do anything for Miss Peters or for anyone in the third form and you know it. '

Bill looked taken aback. ' Am I really as bad as that? ' she asked, anxiously. ' Is that what you all think of me? '

' Of course, ' said Belinda. ' Why, you don't even take on your own duties. I heard Jean ticking you off for that—but Mary-Lou's going on doing them just the same. So you can't have a drawing of Thunder, my dear Bill, because if you do you'll only go and stand and gaze devotedly at him all the evening when you can't go to the stables, and that will make us crosser than ever. '

Belinda paused to take breath. Bill looked as if she was going to fly into a temper. Then her sense of fairness came to her help.

' Yes. You're right, Belinda. I don't like you being right, but you are, ' she said, honestly. ' I probably *should* keep flying upstairs to look at Thunder's picture if I had a really good one. And I'm sorry about making Mary-Lou do my duties after Jean had told me about it. I'll tell her I'll do them all next week to make up. '

' Right, ' said Belinda. ' I'll draw you a fine picture of Thunder, with you on his back, if you like, if you keep your word. But—I shall jolly well take it away if you start being silly, because I'm only going to *lend* it to you till I see if you'll keep your promise. '

Bill laughed. She liked Belinda. She liked Irene, too. They both did the maddest, silliest things, but they were fun, and you could always trust them to do the decent thing. She longed for a picture of Thunder—she only had a very bad photograph of him. Now she was going to get a lovely drawing!

Jean quite thought that it was a belated result of her ticking-off that made Bill offer to do Mary-Lou's duties the next week. She was pleased.

Belinda kept her word and gave Bill a beautiful picture of Thunder, done in black charcoal, with Bill on his back in her riding-breeches and a yellow jersey. Bill was absolutely thrilled. She made Mary-Lou walk into the village with her to try to get it framed at once. She couldn't buy a frame there, so she took one of the horse-photographs out of its frame on her dressing-table and put Thunder's picture in it, neatly trimmed to fit.

Everyone admired it. 'Now you remember, Bill, it's not yours *yet*,' Belinda warned her. 'It's only lent. The very next time you dodge out of duties or third form activities you'll find that picture gone!'

But although Bill was better from that day in trying to do some of the things her form thought she ought to do, she still didn't get on very well with Miss Peters. She *would* sit and gaze out of the window, she *would* forget that her name was Wilhelmina, she would day-dream and not pay any attention to either Mam'zelle or Miss Peters.

Mam'zelle complained bitterly. 'This girl is not even polite! I say to her, "Wilhelmina, do not dream," and she does not even bother to hear me and answer. I say to reply to me. Never, never will she learn any French—except for "*Le cheval*"! Miss Peters, the only time I get that girl to turn round to face me is when I say suddenly the name of her horse. "Thunder!" I say, and she turns round at once. She is mad that girl. All English girls are mad, but she is the most mad.'

Miss Peters began to punish Bill in the way she resented and hated most. 'Here is a returned maths lesson,' she said to Bill. 'Do it please, and until you have brought it to me again you must not go to see Thunder.'

Or she would say, 'Wilhelmina, you have paid no attention in class this morning. You will not go to the stables at all today.'

Bill was angry and resentful—and disobedient! She was not going to stop seeing Thunder for anyone in the world. Least of all for Miss Peters! And so, to Jean's disgust, she ignored Miss Peters' punishments and slipped off to see Thunder whenever she liked.

Miss Peters did not even dream that Bill would disobey.

Thunder was nuzzling into her hand for sugar

'One of these days she'll find out, Bill,' said Alicia. 'Then you'll be for it! You really are an idiot.'

What with Bill and her horse, Zerelda and her ways, Irene and Belinda with their feather-brains, and Mavis and her opera-singing, Miss Peters considered that she had the most trying form in the school. 'And all from North Tower too!' thought Miss Peters. 'Really, I'm sorry for Miss Potts, their house-mistress. They must drive her mad! Now I wonder when Wilhelmina is going to bring me that returned geography lesson. She won't go to see that horse of hers till she does!'

But Miss Peters was wrong. At that very minute Bill was in the stable and Thunder was nuzzling into her hand for sugar!

11   ALICIA HAS A PARCEL

THE days flew by. It was still very cold and Gwendoline and Mavis complained bitterly, as they huddled near the fire in the common-room, or sat almost on top of the radiators.

'You should rush about a bit more in gym or on the lacrosse field,' said Darrell, whose face was a rosy-pink with good health and happiness. She had gone out to the field every moment she could spare to have coaching from Molly. She was getting very good! She knew she was. Molly had praised her catching and said it was excellent.

Gwendoline looked at Darrell with her usual scowl. She really felt miserable in the cold weather, for she came from an overheated home and could not get used to the fresh-air atmosphere of school. It annoyed her to see Darrell without a single chilblain, and to watch her race out happily into the frosty air for her lacrosse practice.

Belinda came slipping up behind Gwendoline, who was quite unaware that she was scowling. Belinda's quick pencil set to work. Mavis nudged Gwen.

'Look out! Here's Belinda again!'

Gwen turned round quickly, trying to smooth the scowl off her face—but it was difficult to feel angry and yet not scowl!

'Go away, Belinda! I don't want you to draw me!' she said, peevishly. 'I wish you'd leave me alone. I hate the way you come slinking up—I call it really sly.'

'Oh no!' said Belinda. 'I'm just interested in you, that's all. You have such a *lovely* scowl—the ugliest in the whole school, I should think. Do, do scowl again, Gwen, and let me draw it.'

Gwen stopped herself from scowling, but it was a very great effort. Belinda grinned.

'Poor Gwendoline Mary—so annoyed, that it makes her want to scowl more fiercely than ever—but she won't! Well, never mind—I'll watch for the next time.'

She went away, and everyone laughed. Gwen's eyes filled with easy tears. She could always cry at any moment. How hateful Belinda was. Gwen thought she really must go and scowl at herself in the mirror, then she would see what was so unique about it. It probably was no worse a scowl than Mavis's or Bill's—but that horrid Belinda thought it was a fine way to tease her.

Darrell came in after her lacrosse practice, glowing and beaming. 'I say, girls! What do you think? I may be a reserve for the third match-team! Only the third reserve—but it's something!'

'What's a reserve?' asked Zerelda, thinking it must be something marvellous, judging by Darrell's shining eyes.

'Well—if three girls fall out from the next match-team, I'd take the place of the third one,' explained Darrell.

'Third reserves never play,' remarked Alicia. 'Everybody knows that. So don't hope too much, Darrell.'

'I'm not,' said Darrell. 'Alicia, I do wish you would get a bit of coaching too. Molly's fine—takes no end of trouble.'

'That fat, clumsy Molly!' murmured Zerelda, in her lazy drawl. 'Gee—I just can't bear to look at her!'

It was silly of Zerelda to say things like that. It made Darrell
and Jean and the rest of the keen lacrosse players annoyed.
What did it matter what Molly looked like ? She was a splendid
games captain, and had won more matches than had been won
for years by Malory Towers !

'She may be fat, but she's not clumsy—she's a fast runner
and very powerful, ' said Darrell, stoutly.

'I'll say she is ! ' said Zerelda. 'I met her running down the
stairs the other day, and I thought there was an earthquake
coming. But it was only her great feet pounding on the stairs.
You can keep your Mollies ! I don't want them. All brawn and
no brains or charm ! '

'And you, I suppose, are all charm, and no brains ? ' said
Alicia's smooth, malicious voice. 'How nice ! Well, America
can keep her Zereldas. They're not much good here ! '

Zerelda flushed scarlet and bit her lip. The others held their
breath, expecting an outburst. But it didn't come.

'I guess I asked for that, ' said Zerelda, stiffly, and she got up.
She said no more, but went out of the room as gracefully as
ever.

Nobody said anything. They felt uncomfortable. It wasn't
right to taunt a girl when they had all decided to be nice to her—
but on the other hand Zerelda was really very annoying and
deserved to be ticked off.

'Where's Bill ? ' asked Darrell, to change the subject.

'Where do you suppose ? ' said Belinda. 'Giving titbits in the
stable. '

'Well, I wish she wouldn't, ' said Jean. 'It's absolutely flat
disobedience, and she'll get into a terrific row if she's found out.
I've argued with her and rowed her and told her to obey Miss
Peters in case something worse happens—but she simply won't
listen. I might as well talk to a stone wall. '

'She says Thunder isn't well, ' said Mary-Lou.

'Imagination ! ' scoffed Alicia. 'She just says that so that she
can go and see him without *too* guilty a conscience. '

'No. I am sure she really *does* think Thunder isn't well,' said Mary-Lou, in her gentle voice. 'She's very worried about him.'

'Well, why doesn't she ask Miss Peters to get the vet. to him?' said Irene.

'Because if she does Miss Peters will want to know how she knows he's not well,' explained Mary-Lou. 'And then the fat will be in the fire!'

'And there will be a sizzling noise and Miss Peters will go up in smoke!' said Belinda, taking out her pencil to draw Miss Peters going up in smoke.

Somebody put their head in at the common-room door. 'Hey there! Parcel post is in—and there's a parcel for you, Alicia.'

'Thanks,' said Alicia, and got up to go and get it. 'Hope it's some chocolates from my godmother. She usually sends me a box each term.'

She disappeared. Belinda finished her drawing and handed it round. Everyone yelled with laughter. Miss Peters was floating upwards, enveloped in smoke, and lightning was flashing from the smoke.

'Lovely!' said Darrell. 'I wish I could draw like you. I can't do anything like that! You're lucky, Belinda.'

'Yes, I am,' said Belinda, taking back her drawing, and adding a few more strokes. 'Don't know what I should do if I couldn't draw. I'd be miserable! Well, so would Irene be miserable if she couldn't have her music!'

'And I should be very very miserable without my voice,' said Mavis at once.

'Yes. You'd be ten times more miserable than either Irene or Belinda,' said Jean. 'And I'll tell you why. Because you just wouldn't be anything without your voice, Mavis! After all, Irene is good at maths, and she plays quite a good game of lacrosse, and she's always ready to have a bit of fun—like Belinda, who's pretty fair at everything besides being gifted at drawing But you're nothing but a Voice! Take that away and I don't believe anyone would know you were here ! '

' I can't help having a voice that overpowers the rest of me, ' said Mavis, complacently. ' It's not my fault if I seem all Voice to you. When I'm an opera-singer I shall ... '

This was the signal for everyone to begin talking at the tops of their voices. It didn't matter what they said, they just talked to drown Mavis's familiar parrot-cry. As they talked they laughed to see her annoyed face, its small dark eyes gleaming spitefully.

Well—she didn't care ! Wait till she was a bit older—then she would show the others what a gift like hers meant. She would sweep the whole world to rapture over her unique voice. Her family and her singing teachers marvelled at her voice, and were never tired of predicting a wonderful career. She could wait for that, even if it meant putting up with commonplace people like the third-formers !

Alicia came in with her parcel. ' It's not from my godmother, ' she said, ' so don't crowd round me too hopefully. It's from Sam. '

Sam was one of her brothers, a scamp if ever there was one. The third-formers were never tired of hearing of his escapades.

' Is it some sort of joke to play, do you think ? ' asked Darrell, eagerly. ' Alicia, you haven't played a trick for ages. I do hope it's a good one ! '

Alicia opened the parcel. Out fell a small box. Belinda picked it up and looked at it. Something was written on the lid.

' Sneeze, Boys, Sneeze ! '

' Whatever does it mean ? ' said Darrell, thrilled. ' Let's open the box. '

' Well, look out then, ' said Alicia, shaking out a letter from her brother. ' Don't spill the contents. They may be valuable ! '

Darrell opened the box. It was full of little white pellets, round and flat, about half an inch in diameter. ' Whatever are they?' said Darrell. 'And why the funny label on the box—"Sneeze, Boys, Sneeze!"?'

Alicia was reading Sam's letter and chuckling. 'Listen to this,' she said. 'Sam really is a scamp. These pellets have been made by one of the boys in his form—he's a bit of an inventor in his way. What you do is to put a pellet on a shelf, damp it with a solution of salt water, and then leave it. In half an hour it sends off a kind of vapour that gets up people's noses and makes them sneeze terrifically!'

Everyone laughed. 'Sam says he did it to his drawing master,' said Alicia, chuckling again, 'And he sneezed forty three times. The boys counted. What a joke!'

'Let's play it on Miss Peters!' said Darrell, thrilled. 'Oh, do let's!'

The idea of hearing the hearty Miss Peters sneezing forty-three times was very tempting. Alicia read Sam's letter to the end.' He says on no account must we use more than one pellet at a time, because the effects are very bad if too much vapour gets up anyone's nose. And he says the pellet-vapour only floats outab out four feet—so if we do play the trick on Miss Peters, she will start sneezing her head off—but we shan't sneeze at all!'

'It sounds an absolutely super trick,' said Darrell. '*Really* super! Alicia, we *must* play it. I should die of laughing to see Miss Peters sneezing like that. She has such a very terrifically loud sneeze—almost louder than anyone else's in the school.'

'Well—we mustn't begin to giggle too soon or giggle too much in case Miss Peters smells a rat,' said Alicia. 'Though l don't see how she can. After all, *she* will be the only one who sneezes.'

Everyone felt really thrilled. A trick on Miss Peters! Very few third-formers had ever dared to play jokes on her, for she was sharp, and so swift with punishment that usually nobody dared to annoy her too much. But this trick was surely foolproof!

'When can we play it? Tomorrow?' asked Darrell.

'No. Wait till we've got a test in maths or something,' said Alicia. 'Then, if Miss Peters sneezes too much, we shan't have the test!'

12   THE DAYS GO BY

THE next excitement was that Sally came back! Darrell was overjoyed. She hugged Sally, and they both began to talk at once.

'It's good to be back! I did hate not coming at the beginning of the term!'

'Oh, Sally, I have missed you! There's lots to tell you.'

'You wrote awfully good letters. I'm longing to see Bill and Zerelda. Wasn't it a shame missing everything!'

Everyone was pleased to see Sally back—everyone that is, except Alicia. Alicia had got used to having Darrell for her companion and friend. Now she would have to share her with Sally—and she might not even be able to *share* her! Darrell might not want to bother with Alicia, with Sally back again.

So Alicia greeted Sally rather coolly, and made quite a show of being friendly with Darrell, hoping that Darrell would still want her for a friend. But Darrell forgot all about Alicia for a few days, she was so pleased that Sally was back.

There was so much news to exchange, so much to discuss. Sally marvelled at Zerelda and her ways, and heard two or three times all about how she had been taken from the fourth form and put into the third. She marvelled at Bill too and her prowess in the gym and on horseback. She thought Mavis and her voice were more difficult than ever to put up with. She was amused at the way Gwendoline followed Zerelda around and was not taken much notice of!

'Oh, Darrell—you don't *know* how good it is to be back

again!' said Sally, happily. 'I kept on and on thinking of you all—working in class—joking with Mam'zelle Dupont, and being ticked off by Mam'zelle Rougier—and playing lacrosse, and having fun in the gym, and roasting chestnuts by the fire in the common-room. I was absolutely home-sick for school!'

'Well, now you're back again at last,' said Darrell. 'I chummed up with Alicia whilst you were away, Sally. Betty's in quarantine for whooping-cough and isn't back yet, so she was on her own and so was I.'

Sally didn't very much like the idea of Darrell being friends with Alicia. She felt jealousy creeping up in her. Jealousy was one of Sally's failings. She had conquered it for some time—but it came slipping into her heart again now when she saw how friendly Alicia was with Darrell. She didn't like it at all.

So Sally was as cool with Alicia as Alicia was cool with Sally, and Darrell was surprised and grieved about it. She had hoped that once Sally had settled in, she and Sally and Alicia might be companions till Betty came back. It didn't seem to Darrell to be quite fair to throw off Alicia entirely, as soon as Sally came back.

Darrell told Sally about Alicia's proposed trick. Sally didn't seem to think it a good trick to play at all!

'It's silly to play a trick like that on Miss Peters,' she said. 'For one thing, she'll guess it's a trick and will deal out awful punishments—and for another thing I don't much like those tricks that make people have sneezing fits. I think they're a bit dangerous.'

'Oh, Sally!' said Darrell, really disappointed. 'I thought you'd be so thrilled. Don't be so prim and solemn! I believe it's just because it's *Alicia's* trick you don't like it!'

Sally was hurt. 'All right—if you like to think things like that of me, you can,' she said. 'I suppose you think I'm jealous of Alicia. Well, I'm not. I can quite see why you like her so much—jolly, witty, amusing—all the things I'm not!'

Now it was Darrell's turn to look hurt. 'You're silly, Sally, '
she said. 'Yes, you are ! You know you're my friend and I only
went with Alicia and Alicia with me because you and Betty were
away. Don't spoil things, Sally. '

'All right. I'll try not to, ' said Sally, with an effort. But
jealousy is a very hard thing to fight and an even harder thing
to defeat. Try as she would Sally could not stop herself from
being a little spiteful about Alicia, and she was so cool to her
that Alicia, tickled to see her jealousy, began to play up to
Darrell even more.

'Oh dear ! ' sighed Darrell to herself one afternoon as she ran
out for a lacrosse practice, 'why is it that Alicia is always so
specially nice to me in front of Sally—and why has Sally changed
so much ? She *is* jealous, I know—but does jealousy change
people such a lot ? '

Darrell wasn't at all jealous herself. It was not in her
nature, so she couldn't really understand Sally's feelings.
She saw both sides very clearly. Sally didn't like Alicia
and wanted Darrell's entire friendship. Alicia didn't see why
she should give up Darrell's companionship completely just
because Sally had come back. Why not a threesome till Betty
returned ?

'Well, I shan't think about *either* of them ! ' said Darrell, as
she caught the lacrosse ball very deftly, spun round and sent it
cleanly and swiftly to another player. So she didn't bother
about anything except giving her whole attention to the fun of
running and catching and throwing.

Molly Ronaldson was really pleased with her. It was not only
Darrell's swiftness and deftness that made her pleased, but the
girl's keenness. She had never missed a practice, she had come
out in the coldest weather and the bitterest winds. She was a
Good Sport—and Molly Ronaldson had no higher praise for
anyone than that.

'Darrell Rivers, count yourself as third reserve for the third
match-team, ' she said, as she went off the field with Darrell.

' I'll put the notice up on the board this evening. There's always a chance you might play in a match, so keep up your practice. In this term there's such a lot of illness and people often fall out by the dozen. '

' Oh, Molly—*thank* you ! ' said Darrell, finding it quite difficult to speak, she was so overcome. ' I won't let you down— I'll not miss a single practice, even if it snows ! I say, I do think it's super of you ! '

' No, it isn't really, ' said Molly. ' I'm thinking of the *team*. You're good enough—so in you go—as reserve first, with a faint chance of playing in a match later on. '

Darrell rushed indoors, walking on air. Luckily she didn't collide with Mam'zelle round the corner this time. All she did was to bump into a bunch of fourth-formers, who scattered in alarm at her headlong rush.

' Darrell Rivers ! Are you mad ? ' said Lucy.

' No ! Well, perhaps I *am* a bit ! ' said Darrell. ' I'm third reserve for the third match-team ! Molly's just told me. '

' That's jolly good, ' said Ellen. ' Congratulations ! Lucky thing ! I'll never be in any match-team, and I'm a fourth-former. '

Everyone seemed pleased and clapped Darrell on the back. She rushed to the third form common-room to break the news there. Most of the girls were there, sitting about, reading, playing games or sewing. They looked up as Darrell burst in.

' Here comes the hurricane ! ' said Alicia, with a grin. ' Shut the door, for goodness' sake, Darrell. There's an icy blast blowing round my legs already. '

Darrell slammed the door. ' Girls, I'm third reserve ! ' she announced. ' Molly's putting it up on the notice board tonight. '

Alicia, who had been a little annoyed at Darrell's success at lacrosse that term, made up her mind to be pleased about it this time. It wouldn't do for her to be sour over this and Sally to be sweet ! So she leapt up, thumped Darrell on the back, and yelled congratulations as if there had never before been anyone in the reserve.

She would hardly let Sally get near Darrell. Jean was pleased too, and Irene and Belinda came round to marvel. Even Mary-Lou added her bit, and Zerelda smiled and looked pleased, though secretly she wondered how anyone could possibly be so thrilled about such a peculiar thing. Altogether it was quite a triumph for Darrell, and she basked in the admiration with delight.

Sally was cross to see how pleased Alicia apparently was, and how Darrell welcomed her delight. 'Oh dear!' she thought, 'I am getting horrid! I can't even make myself say all the nice things to Darrell I'd like to say, just because Alicia got there first!'

Darrell was rather surprised that Sally didn't seem as pleased as she had expected her to be. 'Aren't you glad, Sally?' she asked anxiously. 'It's an honour for the third form, you know. Do say you're pleased!'

'Of course I'm pleased!' said Sally. 'It's—it's fine. You've done jolly well, Darrell.'

But she didn't sound very whole-hearted about it and Darrell felt faintly disappointed. Never mind! Alicia was thrilled—and so were the others. Perhaps Sally was still feeling a bit out of things, having come back so late in the term.

The next excitement was a notice put up on the board, next to the notice about Darrell, to say that Miss Hibbert, the English mistress, was going to start rehearsals for 'Romeo and Juliet'. All third-formers were to go to the art-room to be tried out for parts.

'Blow!' said Gwendoline, who didn't like Miss Hibbert because she had so often ticked her off for being affected and silly in her acting. 'I was hoping she had forgotten about the play. It's such a waste of time.'

'Oh no, it isn't,' said Zerelda, who had brightened up very

much at the notice. ' Acting is marvellous ! That's a thing I really *can* do. I did Lady Macbeth over in ... '

' Yes, we know you did, ' interrupted Daphne. ' We ought to know by now, anyway ! You tell us often enough. '

' I suppose you fancy yourself in one of the chief parts, Daphne ? ' said Alicia. ' What a disappointment you'll get ! Anyway, if Zerelda's so good, she'll play Juliet—if she can get rid of that American drawl ! '

Zerelda looked alarmed. ' Do you think my way of speaking will stop me having a good part ? ' she asked.

' Well—I can't imagine Shakespeare's Juliet talking with a pronounced American accent, ' said Alicia. ' Still—if you act the part well enough I don't see why you shouldn't get it ! '

Zerelda had been rather subdued lately, but now she came to life again, with the hope of starring in ' Romeo and Juliet' ! She paid a tremendous lot of attention to her appearance and spent as much time as she dared in front of her looking-glass. She also tried to get rid of her American drawl !

This amused the class very much. Zerelda had never made the slightest attempt before to speak in the English way and had laughed at the English accent and called it silly. Now she badgered everyone to tell her how to pronounce the words the way they did.

' Well, try to say "won*d*erful" with the D in the middle, instead of "wunnerful", for a start, ' said Darrell. ' And say "twen*t*y-four" with the T in the middle, instead of "twe*nn*y-four". And couldn't you say "stop" instead of "starp" and "shop" instead of "sharp" ? Or can't you hear the difference ? '

Zerelda patiently tried to master the English way of speaking, much to Miss Peters' astonishment. She had felt quite pleased with Zerelda's efforts to keep up with the work of the form, but she was still annoyed with the girl's constant attention to her hair and appearance. Nor did she like Zerelda's still grown-up air, and her habit of appearing to look down on the others just because they were school-girls.

'Now I'll show them all!' thought Zerelda, studying the part of Juliet with great attention. 'Now they'll see what I mean when I say I'm going to be one of the greatest of all film-stars!'

13   ZERELDA'S UNFORTUNATE REHEARSAL

MISS HIBBERT took a great deal of trouble in producing the school plays. She gave her time to each form in turn, and really achieved some excellent results. This term it was the third form's turn. They were to give the play towards the end of the term. They were thankful not to be doing French plays. Both the Mam'zelles took a hand in producing those, and as they had quite different ideas about acting, it was a little trying for the actors.

'Does Miss Hibbert choose the characters the first time?' asked Zerelda.

'Oh no—she tries us all out in almost every part several times,' said Darrell. 'She does that for two reasons—she says that in that way she really does find the right actor for every part—and we all get to know every part of the play and work better as a team.'

'Gee, that's wunnerful—I mean, wonderful,' said Zerelda. 'I've been studying Juliet's part. It's a lovely one. Would you like to hear me do some of the lines?'

'Well—I'm just going out to my lacrosse practice,' said Darrell. 'Sorry! Look—ask Alicia. She's got nothing to do this period.'

But Alicia was not going to admire Zerelda's Juliet. She got up hastily. 'Sorry! I've got to go to a meeting, Zerelda. But I'm sure you'd be just wunnerful!'

'I'll hear you, Zerelda,' said Gwendoline, glad of an

opportunity to please the American girl. 'Let's go into one of the empty music-practice-rooms, where you won't be disturbed. It will be lovely to see you act. I'm sure you must be awfully good. As good as—what's the star you like so much—oh yes, Lossie Laxton!'

'Well, maybe I'm not up to her standard yet,' said Zerelda, fluffing up her hair in the way Lossie did on the films. 'Okay, Gwen—we'll go to a practice-room.'

But they were all full, and music sounded from each of them, with the exception of one at the end. Irene was there, poring over a music score.

'I say, Irene,' said Gwen, going in, 'can you ...'

'Go away,' said Irene, fiercely. 'I'm busy. Can't you see?'

'Well, you're not needing the piano, are you?' said Zerelda. 'Can't you do your work, whatever it is, somewhere else?'

'No, I can't. I shall want to try it out on the piano in a minute,' said Irene. 'Go away. Interrupting me like that!'

Zerelda was surprised. She had never seen Irene so annoyed before. But Gwendoline had. She knew that Irene could not bear to be disturbed when she was concentrating on her music, whether it was writing it out, or playing it on the piano.

'Come on,' she said to Zerelda. 'Let's go.'

'Yes. GO!' said Irene, with a desperate expression on her face. 'You've stopped me just when it was all coming beautifully. Blow you both!'

'Well, really, Irene, I do think you might let us use this room if you're only playing about with pencil and paper,' began Zerelda. 'I want to recite some lines of Juliet and ...'

Then Irene went quite mad. She threw her music, her pencil and her music-case at the alarmed Zerelda. 'You're daft!' she shouted. 'Give up my music-hour for your silly acting! Oh yes, I know you're going to be a wonderful film-star, parading about in marvellous clothes, thinking of third-rate things if ever you *do* have a thought in your head—but what's all that compared to music! I tell you I'm ... '

But Zerelda and Gwen did not wait to hear any more. They saw Irene looking round for something else to throw and as there was a vase of flowers on the little mantelpiece Gwen thought the sooner they went out of the room the better.

' *Well*! ' said Zerelda. ' If that doesn't beat all! Irene's mad! '

' Not really, ' said Gwen. ' It's only when she feels sort of inspired, and music comes welling up into her mind and she has to write it down. She's got the real artistic temperament, I suppose. '

' Well, so have I, ' said Zerelda at once. ' But I don't go mad like that. I wouldn't have believed it of her. '

' She can't help it, ' said Gwendoline. ' It's only when she's interrupted. Look—there's Lucy going out of one of the practice-rooms. We can have that one if we're quick! '

They slipped into the room that Lucy had just left. Gwendoline sat down, ready to listen for hours if she could please Zerelda and make her feel really friendly towards her. Zerelda struck a lovesick attitude and began.

> ' Wilt thou be gone? It is not yet near day ;
> It was the nightingale and not the lark,
> That pierced the fearful hollow of thine ear ;
> Nightly she sings on yon pomegranate-tree ;
> Believe me, love, it was the nightingale. '

Gwendoline listened with a rapt and admiring expression on her face. She had no idea at all whether Zerelda was good or not, but that made no difference to her praise.

' It's marvellous! ' she said, when Zerelda at last stopped for breath. ' However have you learnt such a lot? My goodness, you do act well. And you really look the part, Zerelda, with your hair and all. '

' Do I? ' said Zerelda, pleased. She always enjoyed herself when she was acting. ' I know what I'll do. I'll shake my hair loose. And I'll wrap this tablecloth round me. No—it's not big enough. The curtain will do ! '

To Gwendoline's amusement Zerelda took down the blue curtain and swathed it round herself over her brown school tunic. She undid her brilliant hair and shook it all over her shoulders. She decided to put the tablecloth round her too. Ah—now she felt more like Juliet. Holding her hands out pathetically in front of her she began another speech. It sounded really a little queer because Zerelda tried very hard to speak in the English way but kept lapsing into her usual drawl, so that the whole effect was rather funny.

Gwendoline wanted to laugh but she knew how offended Zerelda would be. The American girl paraded up and down, declaiming her speeches most dramatically, the blue curtain dragging behind her like a train, her hair almost hiding one eye.

Someone looked in. It was Bessie, a second-former. She had come to practice. But seeing two third-formers there, she fled. Then a fourth-former came. She was not scared of third-formers, but was very much astonished to see Zerelda and her strange raiment.

' I've got to practise, ' she said, coming in. ' Clear out. '

Zerelda stopped indignantly. ' Clear out yourself ! ' she said. ' Gee, of all the nerve ! Can't you see I'm rehearsing ? '

' No, I can't, ' said the fourth-former. ' And wait till a mistress sees you in that curtain—you'll be for it, Zerelda Brass. Clear out now, both of you. I'm late already. '

Zerelda decided to go all temperamental like Irene. She caught up her book of Shakespeare's plays and threw it at the fourth-former. Most unfortunately at that moment Matron came by, and, as she always did, glanced into the practice-rooms to see that each girl there was practising. She was filled with astonishment to see somebody wearing a curtain and a tablecloth, with hair all over her face, throwing a book at a girl about to sit down at the piano.

She opened the door sharply, making everyone jump. 'What's all this? What are you doing? Oh, it's *you*, Zerelda. What on earth have you got the curtain round you for? Are you quite mad? And what has happened to your hair? It looks a hundred times worse than usual. Janet, get on with your practising. Gwendoline, you shouldn't be here when a fourth-former is practising. As for you, Zerelda, if I see any more tempers like that, I shall report you to Miss Grayling! Throwing books at one another indeed! A third-former too! You'll go down into the first form if you behave like that!'

The girls couldn't get a word in, for Matron fired all this off at top speed. She pushed Janet firmly down on the stool, shooed Gwendoline out as if she was a hen, and took Zerelda firmly by the shoulder.

'You'll just come with me and let me find out if you've torn the cloth or the curtain,' she said. 'If you have you'll sit down in my room under my eye and mend it. And while I think of it— if you don't darn your stockings better than you have been doing, I shall have to ask you to come to me for darning lessons.'

Angry and embarrassed, poor Zerelda had to walk down the corridor after Matron, trying to take the curtain and cloth away from her shoulders and waist, and wishing she could tie her hair back.

But Matron would give her no time to rearrange or tidy herself. This stuck-up, affected American girl had annoyed Matron so often—now Matron was getting a bit of her own back! Let everyone see Zerelda in this rumpled, ridiculous state!

And most unfortunately for Zerelda they met a whole batch of giggling second-formers, who stared at Zerelda in delighted amazement.

'What's she done? Where's Matron taking her? Doesn't she look *awful*!' poor Zerelda heard the twelve-year-olds say. She blushed miserably and looked round for Gwen. But Gwen had gone. She knew Matron in this mood, and she wasn't going to go near her if she could help it !

They met Mam'zelle at the bend of the stairs, and Mam'zelle exclaimed in surprise. ' *Tiens* ! What is this ? Zerelda ! Your hair ! '

' Yes. I'm dealing with her, Mam'zelle, ' said Matron firmly. She and Mam'zelle were usually at war with one another, so Matron did not stop to talk, but swept Zerelda along to her room at top speed, leaving Mam'zelle to gape and wonder.

Fortunately for Zerelda, Matron could find no damage done to either the tablecloth or the curtain. She was quite disappointed ! She did Zerelda's hair for her herself, and Zerelda was so overcome by Matron's briskness and ability to talk without stopping that she submitted without saying a word.

Matron plaited Zerelda's hair into two fat plaits ! Zerelda had never had her hair plaited in her life. She sat there, horror-struck. This awful school ! Whatever would happen to her next ?

' There, ' said Matron, satisfied at last, tying the ends of the plaits with blue tape. She stepped back. ' Now you look a proper schoolgirl, Zerelda—and very sensible and nice too. Why you want to go about pretending you are twenty, I don't know. '

Zerelda got up weakly. She caught a glimpse of herself in the glass. How *awful* ! Could that really be herself ? Why, she looked a nobody—just like all the other English girls. She crept out of Matron's room and fled up to the dormy to try and put her hair right.

She met Miss Peters, who stared at her as if she didn't know her. Zerelda smiled a weak smile and tried to get by without a word.

' Well   *Zerelda* ! ' she heard Miss Peters say, as if she couldn't believe her eyes. Zerelda shot down the corridor, praying that she would not meet anyone else.

Gwendoline was in the dormy, and she too stared at Zerelda as if she was seeing a ghost.

' Did Matron do that to you ? ' she asked. ' Oh, Zerelda—you look like a real schoolgirl now—not a bit like yourself. Oh, I *must* tell the others that Matron plaited your hair. '

' If you dare to repeat such a thing I'll never speak to you again ! ' said Zerelda, in such a fierce voice that Gwen was quite scared. She shook her hair free of the plaits. ' This horrible school ! I'll never forgive Matron, never ! '

14   BILL IS CAUGHT !

ALICIA had not been allowed to forget the sneezing trick. All the form begged her to do it—except Sally. Sally still said she thought it was a dangerous joke to play, but Alicia laughed at her.

' You only say that because it's *my* trick ! ' she said, knowing that Sally was jealous of her friendship with Darrell. ' If it was Irene's joke or Jean's you'd be thrilled. '

Jean was torn between her desire to see the trick played and her feeling that as head-girl she ought not to be too encouraging. Still, head-girls couldn't be too strict and prim—and she did badly want to see what would happen !

' There's to be a maths test next week, ' said Alicia. ' That's the time to do it ! I bet we'll get out of the test all right. A-tish-oo ! '

Everyone laughed. Darrell hugged herself. Oh, school was such fun ! She enjoyed every single minute of it. She loved her work and her play, she loved the company of the chattering girls, she loved being third reserve—oh, everything was wonderful ! This was the nicest term she had ever had.

Then she saw Bill looking anything but happy. Poor Bill! She was worried because Thunder was still not himself. Nobody else seemed to notice it—but Bill *knew*. Thunder wasn't just homesick, as she had thought at first. He wasn't well. She was very worried about him—and the more worried she got, the less attention she paid to her work, and the crosser she made Miss Peters.

'Wilhelmina! Will you please pay attention! Wilhelmina! Will you repeat what I have just said? Wilhelmina, I will not have you in my class if you persist in looking out of the window and dreaming!' It was 'Wilhelmina! Wilhelmina!' all the time.

It was dreadful. Bill was really very miserable now, but she said very little unless anyone actually asked her about 'Thunder. She knew that Jean disapproved strongly of her continual disobedience. But she simply couldn't help it! She must, *must* see Thunder each day, especially just now.

Miss Peters was beginning to be puzzled over Bill. If the girl was so fond of her horse, why did she keep earning punishments forbidding her to see him? Miss Peters thought back a few days. Why, Bill couldn't have seen her beloved horse all the week. And yet she hadn't complained about it!

A suspicion came into Miss Peters' mind. Was Bill being disobedient? Surely not! Disobedience was not a thing that Miss Peters had to deal with very often. Girls rarely dared to disobey even her slightest word. She was noted for her good discipline.

She spoke about it to Miss Potts, who was in charge of North Tower, 'I'm puzzled about Wilhelmina, Miss Potts. I can't make her out. She is such a terrible dreamer, and yet she looks such a sensible, hard-headed little thing! Then, too, she seems so fond of that horse of hers—and yet although she knows I shall punish her by forbidding her to see him, she goes on being silly and getting punished! She can't have seen that horse of hers for a whole week now!'

Miss Potts looked startled. She frowned, trying to remember something clearly, ' Well—that's funny—I could swear I saw Wilhelmina in the stables yesterday when I went by, I looked in at the windows as I passed—and I'm almost certain it was Wilhelmina—standing beside a big black horse. '

' Yes—that would be Thunder, ' said Miss Peters, grimly. ' The untrustworthy, disobedient little monkey ! If I catch her disobeying I shall insist that the horse is sent back to her home. She can ride one of the school horses instead, I will not have her mooning all the morning over that horse, nice as he is—and being disobedient like that. '

Miss Peters was really very angry. She never could bear to be disobeyed. She went back to her room, feeling shocked and disappointed. She hadn't thought Wilhelmina would be so deceitful and untrustworthy. It just showed how little you knew about anyone !

Miss Peters felt more and more indignant about the whole thing as the day wore on. It so happened that she took the third form very little that day, as Miss Carton, the history mistress, Mam'zelle, Miss Linnie, the art mistress, and Mr. Young, the singing-master, each took the third form for a lesson. She had no chance of looking sharply at Bill to see if she looked guilty or not.

After dinner that morning there was about half an hour before afternoon school. This was a time when Bill very often slipped out to the stables. She usually went down the back stairs, out at a little side-door, and across to the stables by a path under the trees, so that, unless she was very unlucky, nobody would see her.

She slipped off to the stables as usual to see Thunder. He whinnied softly when he heard her footstep. She opened the big door and went inside. There was no one else there at all. Only the horses stamped and blew, glad of each other's company.

She went to Thunder's stall. He put his great black head into the crook of her arm and snuffled there happily. Bill stroked his velvety nose, ' Thunder, do you feel better? Let me look at your eyes. Oh, Thunder, they aren't as bright as they ought to be— and I don't like the feel of your coat. It should be much silkier. It's harsh. Thunder, what's wrong? Don't be ill, darling Thunder, I couldn't bear it. '

Thunder blew a little, and whinnied happily. He didn't feel well, certainly—but that didn't matter when Bill was with him. He could feel ill and yet be happy at the same time if she was with him.

Upstairs in North Tower, Miss Peters walked along the corridor. She meant to find Bill and have a straight talk with her. She went to the door of the third-form common-room and looked in. Wilhelmina was not there!

'I want Wilhelmina, ' said Miss Peters. 'Where is she? '

Everybody knew, of course. But nobody was going to tell. Darrell wondered if she could possibly slip out and warn Bill to come back quickly.

' Shall I go and find her for you? ' she said.

' No. I'll find her, ' said Miss Peters. ' Does anyone know where she is? '

Nobody answered. They all looked blank in a most irritating way. Miss Peters felt furious. She knew quite well that they all knew. Well, she couldn't expect them to sneak, if they thought Wilhelmina was somewhere she ought not to be—in the stables!

'I suppose she is in the stables, ' said Miss Peters, grimly.

She looked at Jean. ' You, as head-girl, Jean, ought to tell her not to be so foolish and dishonourable. You know I put everyone on their honour to obey any punishment I give. '

Jean went red and looked uncomfortable. It was all very well for Miss Peters to talk like that! Nobody could possibly make any impression on Bill if it meant that she would have to neglect Thunder!

'Stay here, all of you,' commanded Miss Peters, feeling sure that one or other might rush off to the stables to warn Bill if they got the chance. And Miss Peters meant to catch Bill herself and stop this kind of thing for good and all.

'Oh, poor Bill!' groaned Darrell, when Miss Peters had gone. 'Now she'll get into a fearful row! I say—I bet Miss Peters has gone down the front stairs. If I race down the back ones, I *might* get to the stables first and warn Bill. I'll try!'

She didn't wait to hear what anyone had to say. She shot out of the room, almost knocked down Matron outside, raced down the corridor to the back stairs, went down them two at a time, slid through the side-door and out under the trees. She shot over to the stable door and squeezed through it.

'Bill! Look out! Miss Peters is coming here!' she hissed. She saw Bill's startled face beside Thunder's black head.

Then she heard footsteps and groaned. 'It's too late—you'll be caught. Can't you hide?'

Darrell shot under a pile of straw and lay there, her heart beating wildly. Bill stood as if turned to stone, her freckled face pale with fright. The door opened wide and Miss Peters came in.

'Oh! So you *are* here, Wilhelmina!' she said, angrily. 'I suppose you have been systematically disobeying me the whole week. I am really ashamed of you. You will never settle down at school whilst you have Thunder here, I can quite see that. He will have to be sent back home in a horse-box!'

'No! Oh no, Miss Peters! Don't, don't do that!' begged Bill, even her freckles going pale with anxiety. 'It's only that Thunder's not well. He really isn't. If he was well I'd obey you. But he needs me when he's not well.'

'I'm not going to discuss the matter,' said Miss Peters, coldly. 'You have heard what I said. I am not likely to change my mind after such a show of disobedience. Please go back to your common-room, Wilhelmina. I will tell you when I have made arrangements to send Thunder home and you can say

Darrell and Bill tried to hide

good-bye to him till the holidays. It will probably be the day after tomorrow. '

Bill stood still, quite petrified. She couldn't make her legs move. Darrell couldn't see her, but she could imagine her very well indeed. Poor, poor Bill.

' Go, Wilhelmina, ' said Miss Peters. 'At once please. '

And Bill went, her feet dragging. Darrell heard a smothered sob. Oh dear—what a pity she had to hide under this straw and couldn't go and comfort Bill. Never mind—Miss Peters would soon be going, and then Darrell could fly up to the common-room and sympathize warmly and heartily with Bill.

But Miss Peters didn't go. She waited till Bill had quite gone. Then she went over to Thunder and spoke to him in such a gentle voice that Darrell could hardly believe it was Miss Peters'! 'Well, old boy, ' said Miss Peters, and Darrell heard the sound of her hand rubbing his coat. 'What's the matter with you? Don't feel well? Shall we get the vet to you? What's the matter with you, Thunder? Beautiful horse, aren't you? Best in the stables. What's up, old boy? '

Darrell could hardly believe her ears. She wriggled a little in the straw so that she could get a hole to peep through. Yes, there was Miss Peters, standing close to Thunder, and he was nuzzling her and whinnying in delight. Why, Miss Peters must love him! Of course, she was very fond of horses, Darrell knew that. But this was different somehow. She really seemed to love Thunder as if he was her own horse.

Miss Peters gave Thunder some sugar and he crunched it up. Then she went out of the stable and shut the door. Darrell got out of the straw and shook herself. She went to the door and listened. Miss Peters had gone. Good!

She opened the door and went out—and then she stood still, thunderstruck. Miss Peters *hadn't* gone! She was just outside, doing up her shoe-lace! She looked up and saw Darrell coming out of the stables.

She stood up, red with rage. 'What were you doing in

there?' she demanded. 'Were you there all the time I was talking to Wilhelmina? You were in the common-room when I left. Did you actually dare to run down the back stairs to warn Wilhelmina?'

Darrell couldn't speak. She nodded. 'I shall deal with you later,' said Miss Peters, hardly trusting herself to speak. 'What the third form is coming to I really do not know!'

15   MAVIS HAS AN IDEA

BILL would not be comforted by Darrell or anyone else. She hadn't gone to the common-room as Miss Peters had told her to. She had gone to the dormy and wept by herself. Bill boasted that she never cried, but this time she did. Her seven brothers had taught her to be tough and boyish, and, like a boy, she had scorned ever to shed a tear.

But she couldn't help it now. When she appeared for afternoon school the third-formers saw her red eyes and came round her to comfort her. But she pushed them away. Darrell was pushed away too, though Bill spoke a few words to her, very gratefully.

'Thank you for coming to warn me. It was decent of you, Darrell.'

'Bill—it's a shame,' began Darrell. But Bill turned away.

'I can't talk about it,' she said. 'Please don't.'

So the third-formers gave it up, and looked at one another helplessly. You simply couldn't do anything with Bill if she didn't want you to. Darrell took her place in class that afternoon with much trepidation. She knew she would sooner or later be called to Miss Peters' room, and she wondered what would happen to her. Oh dear—and everything had been so lovely up till then. Now she had got herself into trouble, and she had only wanted to help poor Bill.

Miss Peters was in a grim mood that afternoon. She was looking out for anyone or anything that would feed her anger. But nobody, not even Mavis, Gwendoline or Zerelda, did anything to provoke her. Miss Peters was terrifying when she was like this. Her big, heavy face was red, her eyes flashed as they looked round the class, and her short hair seemed to cling more tightly to her head than usual.

All the third-formers felt miserable that evening, with Bill sitting like a figure of stone in a corner. It was Mavis who suddenly livened them up.

'I say,' she said, in a whisper, as if somebody was listening who shouldn't be there. 'I say! Look here!'

She held up a paper. On it was printed these words:

TALENT SPOTTING!
Have you a gift? Can you play the piano well?
Can you draw? Do you sing?
Then bring your talent to the Grand Hall, Billington, on
Saturday night, and let us SPOT your TALENT.
Big prizes—and a CHANCE to make your NAME!
TALENT SPOTTING!

The girls read it. 'Well, what about it?' said Alicia. 'Surely you are not thinking of being spotted for talent, Mavis?'

'Yes, but listen,' said Mavis, still in an urgent whisper, 'what about Irene going with her music—and Belinda with her drawing—and Zerelda with her acting—and me with my Voice? Think what prizes we would win!'

Everyone stared at Mavis scornfully. 'Mavis! As if we'd ever be allowed to go!' said Belinda. 'And besides, who wants to go to a fifth-rate affair like this? Talent spotting indeed! Just a silly show put on to amuse the people of Billington! And the prizes will probably be half-crowns! Don't be so silly.'

'But, Belinda—Zerelda—it's such a chance!' said Mavis, who had imagined herself standing on the platform and filling the hall with her lovely voice, being applauded to the echo and perhaps having her name in the papers. Poor, foolish Mavis. Her conceit blinded her to what the show really was—just a village affair got up for fun.

' Mavis, you're just too silly for words, ' said Alicia, impatiently. ' Can you honestly see Miss Grayling allowing Malory Towers' girls to go to a thing like this and make themselves cheap and idiotic ? Do use your common-sense. '

' She can't. She hasn't got any, ' said Daphne. Mavis snatched the paper from Darrell, who was reading down it with a grin. ' All right, ' she said. ' If you don't want a bit of fun, you needn't have it. I've a good mind to go on my own. '

' Don't be a fathead, ' said Jean. ' Think of yourself standing up on a big platform, just a schoolgirl, singing to a crowded hall. It's ridiculous ! '

But it didn't seem a ridiculous picture to Mavis. She could see it all very clearly. She could even hear the thunderous applause. She could see herself bowing time after time. It would be a little taste of what life would be like when she was an opera-singer !

She stuffed the notice into her pocket, wishing she hadn't said anything about it. But a little thought kept slipping into her mind, exciting her, making her restless.

' Suppose I go ? Nobody would miss me if I said I was going for an extra lesson in singing. They would just think Mr. Young was making up the lesson he missed last week. '

It was a very exciting thought. Today was Thursday. Mavis decided to think about it all Friday and make up her mind on Saturday. Yes, that was what she would do—then she could make her plans in good time if she decided to go !

She thought about it all day Friday. And Bill thought about Thunder. Neither of them dared to be too dreamy in class, but fortunately Miss Peters did not take the third-formers a great deal that day, having to take duty for another teacher who was ill. Mam'zelle came to take her place, and she was in a pleasant mood, very talkative, and not very observant. So Bill and Mavis were able to do a little dreaming in peace.

Bill had not dared to go to the stables again. She was hoping against hope that Miss Peters might change her mind and relent. Perhaps she would let Thunder stay after all. So she did not go near the stables, hoping that Miss Peters would tell her she was not going to he so harsh after all.

Miss Peters still had not said anything to Darrell. The girl wished she would get it over, scold her, punish her—but not keep it hanging over her like this. Perhaps that was part of Miss Peters' plan though, to keep Darrell on tenterhooks for a few days !

Saturday came. Mavis had made up her mind. She would go ! She would tell Miss Potts she had a singing-lesson. She often had extra singing at odd times, so Miss Potts would not think it at all queer. She would tell the girls that too. She wouldn't be back early enough for nine o'clock bedtime but she trusted the girls not to give her away. She would slip in up the back stairs.

So Mavis made her plans. She looked up the buses. She meant to catch the six o'clock bus. That would get her to Billington at seven. The show began at half-past. She could easily go into the hall and find out what she had to do.

She looked up the buses back. How long would the show last ? About two hours, probably. There was a bus back at half-past nine—the last one. Goodness, it was late ! Mavis began to have a few qualms about her adventure. It was very, very late for her to come back alone in the dark all the way up the school drive from the bus-stop. Oh dear—would it be moonlight ? She did hope so !

Bill came over to Darrell on Saturday morning. 'Darrell ! Would you do something for me ? I'm not going to go to the stables again unless I'm allowed to—just in case Miss Peters might change her mind about sending Thunder away—so would you *please*, Darrell, slip down there yourself and go to Thunder and see if he's all right?'

'Yes, of course,' said Darrell. 'He wasn't out with the other horses this morning. I saw them all go off, but Thunder wasn't there.'

'No, he wouldn't be,' said Bill. 'Nobody rides him but me. Do go, Darrell.'

Darrell went. It didn't matter *her* going in the least. She kicked herself for not having thought of it before. She could have gone yesterday for Bill too.

She went into the stables. All the horses were there. One of the grooms was there too, rubbing a horse down, whistling between his teeth as he did so.

''Morning, Miss,' he said.

'Good morning,' said Darrell. 'Where's Thunder? Is he all right?'

'He's over there in his stall, Miss,' said the groom, standing up. 'He doesn't seem too well. It's my opinion he's in for a bout of colic or something.'

Colic? That was tummy-ache, wasn't it, thought Darrell. Oh well, that wasn't anything very much. She went over to Thunder, who hung his head and looked miserable.

'He really doesn't seem very well, does he?' said Darrell, anxiously. 'Do you suppose he's missing his mistress? She's not been allowed to see him.'

'Well, he may be,' said the groom. 'But it's his insides are making him miserable, I guess. Have to have the vet to him if he doesn't pick up. But I did hear something about him being sent back home.'

Darrell said no more. She ran back to North Tower to find Bill, who was anxiously waiting for her.

'Thunder doesn't seem *very* well,' she said. 'But you needn't worry. The groom said it was only that he might be going to have a bout of colic. That's nothing, is it?'

Bill stared at her in horror. 'Colic! Why, it's one of the worst

things a horse can have ! Oh, Darrell, think what a big stomach
a horse has and imagine him having an ache all over it. It's
agony ! '

'Oh—I didn't know, ' said Darrell. ' But—surely it isn't as
serious as all that, is it ? '

'It is, it is, ' said Bill, and tears came into her eyes. ' Oh, what
shall I do ? I *daren't* go to the stables in case I'm caught, and I
might spoil Thunder's chance of not being sent home after all.
Miss Peters hasn't said anything more to me about him going.
Oh, what *shall* I do ? '

'You can't do anything, ' said Darrell. ' Really you can't.
He'll be all right tomorrow. Don't you worry, Bill. Oh, blow—
it's begun to pour with rain—just as I wanted to go and practise
catching again. '

Bill turned away. Rain ! What did *rain* matter ! She sat down
in a corner and began to worry hard. Colic ! One of her
brothers' horses had had colic and had died. Suppose—
suppose Thunder got very ill in the middle of the night—and
nobody knew ? The grooms did not sleep very near the stables.
Nobody would know. And in the morning Thunder would be
dead !

Whilst Bill tortured herself with these horrible thoughts,
Mavis delighted herself with pleasant ones. She had made all
her plans. She didn't care a bit if she was discovered after it was
all over—by that time she could have been received with
wonder and applause, and Malory Towers would praise her
and admire her.

'How bold she is to do a thing like that ! ' they would say.
'Just the kind of thing an opera-singer *would* do ! All fire and
temperament and boldness ! Wonderful Mavis ! '

Nobody had any suspicion of Mavis's mad plans that night.
Miss Potts said nothing when she told her that she was to have
an extra singing—lesson, and would be having her supper early
to make time for it. The girls took no notice either. They were
used to Mavis and her odd lessons at all times.

'It's all too easy for words!' thought Mavis, exultantly. 'I shall easily be able to catch the bus. Nobody will guess a thing! Whatever will the girls say when I come back tonight! Well—they'll know I am something besides just a Voice!'

She caught the bus easily. It was pouring with rain but she had her mackintosh with her. She did not wear a hat in case somebody noticed the school-band. so her head was bare. But as the bus stopped just by the Grand Hall at Billington, she wouldn't get her hair very wet.

The bus started off with a jolt. Off to fame! Off to applause! Off to the Beginning of a Wonderful Career!

16   WHERE IS MAVIS ?

MISS POTTS noticed that Mavis was not at the supper-table. She was about to remark on it when she remembered that Mavis had told her something about an extra singing-lesson. She must have had supper early then, as she sometimes did when Mr. Young came late. So Miss Potts said nothing.

The girls thought nothing of it either. They were used to Mavis and her continual extra voice-training now. They hardly missed her. As they often said, Mavis was really nothing but a Voice and a lot of conceit.

Bill was very silent and worried, and ate hardly anything. Warm-hearted Darrell felt sorry for her. She knew she was worrying about Thunder and not being able to go to him. She whispered to Bill.

'Shall I go and have a look at him for you after supper?'

Bill shook her head. 'No. I don't want to get you into trouble. Nobody's allowed in the stables when it's dark.'

No one said anything about Mavis not being in the common-room after supper. Alicia switched on the wireless. Belinda began to do a ridiculous dance. Zerelda got up and joined her.

Everyone laughed. Zerelda could be really funny when she forgot her airs and graces.

She was pleased at the girls' applause. 'Shall I act a bit of "Romeo and Juliet" for you?' she asked, eagerly. 'I'm tired of waiting for that rehearsal with Miss Hibbert!'

'Yes, do, Zerelda!' said Gwen, at once. The others were not so keen, but they sat back, prepared to be patient for a little while.

Zerelda began. She struck a pose, lifted up her voice and began to speak and act the part of Juliet, trying to talk in the English way.

The result was so very comical that the girls roared with laughter. They honestly thought that Zerelda was being funny on purpose. Zerelda stopped and looked at them, offended.

'What are you laughing at? This part is very tragic and sad.'

Still the girls thought that Zerelda was being funny, and they laughed again. 'Go on, Zerelda! This is priceless!' said Darrell. 'I never knew you could be so comical.'

'I'm not being comical,' said Zerelda.

'Do go on,' begged Irene. 'Come on—I'll be Romeo. We'll rag the whole thing.'

'I'm *not* ragging,' said Zerelda. 'I was playing the part properly—as I thought it ought to be played.'

The girls looked at her in surprise. Did she really mean it? Did she honestly think that kind of acting was good? It was so bad that it was funny.

They didn't know what to say. They could, however, quite well imagine what Miss Hibbert would say. She had her own way of dealing with stage-struck people who thought they could act. Zerelda was appalling. She flung her hands about, made terrible faces which were supposed to be tragic, and was altogether too dramatic for words.

'She can't act for toffee!' whispered Alicia to Darrell. 'What are we to say?'

Fortunately the door was opened at that moment and a fourth-former came in to borrow a gramophone record. Zerelda, offended with everyone, sat down in a chair and took up a book. She hated everyone in the school ! Why had she ever come here ? Not one of them thought anything of her—and she was worth the whole lot put together.

When the bell rang at nine o'clock Mavis was not back. Jean noticed it at once. ' Where's Mavis ? I haven't seen her all evening. '

' She said she had a singing-lesson, ' said Darrell. ' But what a long one it must have been ! Well, she'll come along when Mr. Young's finished with her, I suppose. '

' He's never as late as this, ' said Jean, puzzled. ' I wonder if I ought to tell Miss Potts. '

' No, don't. She may be messing about somewhere, and you'll only get her into trouble, ' said Belinda. ' She'll be up in the dormy probably. '

But she wasn't. The girls undressed and got into bed. Jean did not allow talking after lights out, so there was nothing said until Jean herself spoke.

' I say ! You don't think, do you, that that idiot of a Mavis has gone off to that talent spotting affair ? You know—the thing at Billington Grand Hall. '

There was a silence. Then Alicia spoke. ' I shouldn't be a bit surprised ! She's quite silly over her voice. She might think it was a wonderful chance to air it in public. She's always wanting to. '

' Well ! ' said Jean, angrily. ' She'll just *have* to be reported then. Honestly, she's the limit. '

' We can't do much just now, ' said Darrell. ' She may be back at any minute. I forget what time the concert began. I expect she'd catch the half-past eight bus back and be here just after half-past nine. It must be nearly that now. You'll have to report her tomorrow morning. Jean—what a perfect idiot she must be, if she really *has* gone ! '

'What I'm afraid of,' said Jean, 'is that they might let her get up on the platform and sing—and, you know, she really has got such a wonderful voice that it would be bound to bring the house down—and that's just what Mavis would love—cheering and clapping and applause! She'll be worse than ever if that happens—and she won't care a bit about being reported and punished.'

'Leave it till tomorrow morning,' said Darrell, sleepily. 'She'll be along soon. Tick her off then, Jean, and report her in the morning.'

Miss Potts heard the voices in the dormy and was surprised. She came to the door—but as she heard Jean's clear voice say 'Now, no more talking, girls', at that moment, she did not open the door to scold. If she had, she would have switched on the light and noticed Mavis's empty bed. As it was, she went away at once.

The girls were tired. Jean tried to keep awake to tick off Mavis, but she couldn't. Her eyes closed and she fell fast asleep. So did everyone else—except Bill. Bill hadn't heard a word about Mavis. She was wrapped up in her own thoughts and they were very miserable ones. Thunder! How are you getting on? Have you missed me? Bill talked to Thunder in her thoughts, and heard nothing else at all.

Darrell too was asleep. She had meant to have a last comforting whisper with Bill, who slept next to her, but she fell asleep before she could say the words. Only Bill was awake.

Mavis didn't come. Ten o'clock struck, and eleven. No Mavis. All the girls were asleep except Bill, and she didn't think about Mavis. Twelve o'clock struck. Bill counted the strokes.

'l can't go to sleep! I simply can't! I shall lie awake till the morning. If only I knew how Thunder is getting on! If I knew he was all right, I'd be all right, too. But supposing he really has the colic?'

She lay and thought for a few minutes. She remembered a window that overlooked the stables. If she went to it and opened it and leaned out, she might perhaps hear if Thunder was all right. A horse with colic makes a noise. She would hear that.

Bill got out of bed, and felt for her dressing-gown and slippers. She put them on. She groped her way to the door, bumping against Darrell's bed as she did so. Darrell woke up at once.

She thought it was Mavis coming back. She sat up and whispered loudly. ' Mavis ! '

No answer. The door softly opened and shut. Somebody had gone out, not come in. Who was it ?

Darrell got her torch and switched it on. The first thing she saw was Bill's empty bed. Was Bill ill ? Or had she gone to the stables ? Surely not, in the middle of a pouring wet night.

She went to the door and opened it. She thought she saw something a good distance down the corridor. She ran after the something.

Bill had gone to the window that overlooked the stables. She opened it, and Darrell heard her and went towards the sound. Bill leaned out of the window and listened.

Her heart went cold ! From the stables came a groaning and a stamping. There was a horse in distress there, quite certainly. Bill knew it was Thunder. She felt sure it was. He had colic ! He was in agony. He would die if somebody didn't help him !

She turned away from the window and jumped violently when Darrell put a hand on her shoulder. ' Bill ! What are you doing ? ' whispered Darrell.

' Oh, Darrell—I was listening to see if any noise came from the stables over there—and there's a horse in pain. I'm sure it's Thunder. I must go to him ! Oh, Darrell, please come with me. I might want help. Do, do help me. '

' All right, ' said Darrell, unhappy to hear Bill's tearful voice.

'I'll come. Come back and get on something warmer. It's pouring with rain. We can't go out in dressing-gowns. '

Bill didn't want to stop to put anything on, but Darrell made her. The two girls put on cardigans and tunics and mackintoshes. Then they slipped down the back stairs, went through the little side-door and ran across to the stables in the pouring rain. Darrell could hear a horse groaning and stamping. Oh dear! It sounded awful. With trembling fingers Bill undid the stable door and went inside. There was a lantern standing in a corner, with a box of matches beside it. Her fingers trembled so much that she couldn't strike a match and Darrell had to light the lamp.

Both girls felt better when the light streamed out into the dark stable, that smelt of horses and hay. Bill made her way swiftly to Thunder's stall. Darrell followed with the lantern.

Thunder's eyes were big and frightened. He hung his head in misery. From his body came weird rumbling noises, like far-away thunder.

'Yes. He's got colic. He's bad. Darrell. Oh, Darrell, we mustn't let him lie down. That would be fatal. We must walk him about all the time. '

'Walk him about? Where?' asked Darrell, in astonishment. 'In the stables?'

'No. Outside. It's the only thing to do, keep him walking so that he can't lie down. Look, he's trying to lie down now. Help me to stop him!'

But it is a very difficult thing to prevent a big horse from lying down if he wants to! Neither of the girls would have been able to stop him if Thunder had really made up his mind to lie down—but fortunately he decided to stand up a little longer and nuzzle against Bill. He was so very, very glad to see her!

Bill was crying bitterly. 'Oh, Thunder! What can I do for you? Don't lie down, Thunder. Don't lie down!'

'You ought to have the vet, Bill, oughtn't you?' said Darrell, anxiously. 'How can we get him?'

'Could you possibly ride over and fetch him?' said Bill, wiping her eyes with the back of her hand. 'You know where he lives—not far off, really.'

'No, I couldn't,' said Darrell. 'I don't ride well enough to get a horse and gallop off on a dark night. You go, Bill, and I'll stay with Thunder.'

'I can't leave him even for a *minute*!' said Bill. She seemed quite unable to think what to do. Darrell thought hard.

An idea came into her head. She touched Bill on the shoulder. 'Bill! Stay here and I'll get help somehow. Don't worry. I'll be back as soon as I can!'

17   A MIDNIGHT RIDE

DARRELL raced off into the rain. She had thought of something— but she didn't want to tell Bill what it was. Bill wouldn't like it. But still, it was the only sensible thing Darrell could think of.

She was going to wake up Miss Peters and tell her about Thunder! She remembered how she had heard Miss Peters talking to the horse, sympathizing with him, and she remembered, too, how Thunder had nuzzled happily against her. Surely Miss Peters would understand and come to their help?

She went indoors. She made her way to Miss Peters' room, stumbling through the dark corridors. She wondered if she had come to the right room. Yes, this must be it. She rapped at the door.

There was no answer. She rapped again. Still no answer. Miss Peters must sleep very, very soundly! In desperation Darrell opened the door and looked in. The room was in darkness. She felt for the light switch and put it on.

Miss Peters was lying humped up in bed, fast asleep. She slept very soundly indeed, and even a thunderstorm did not usually awaken her. Darrell went to the bed and put her hand on Miss Peters' shoulder.

Miss Peters awoke at once then. She sat up and stared at Darrell in amazement. 'What is it?' she said. 'What have you come to me for?'

Darrell would have gone to Miss Potts or Matron in the usual way—but this was something so unusual that the girl felt only Miss Peters could deal with it properly. She began to tell Miss Peters all about the trouble.

'It's Thunder. He's got colic and Bill's afraid he'll die if he lies down. Can you get the vet, Miss Peters?'

'Good gracious! Have you and Bill been out to the stables at this time of night?' said Miss Peters, looking at her clock, which showed half-past twelve. She sprang out of bed. She pulled on riding-breeches and jersey and riding-coat, for she had been riding that day with the school, and her things lay ready to hand.

'Yes,' said Darrell. 'But don't be angry, Miss Peters—we simply had to go when we heard Thunder in pain.'

'I'm not angry,' said Miss Peters. 'l was worried myself about Thunder today. I rang up the vet and he said he would come tomorrow. I'll come down with you and have a look at the horse myself.'

In a few minutes she was in the stables with Darrell. Bill was amazed to see her, but very comforted when she saw how capably Miss Peters handled the distressed horse. Thunder whinnied to her and nuzzled against her shoulder. Miss Peters spoke to him gently, and Bill's heart warmed to her.

'Oh, Miss Peters—can we get the vet to come now? I'm so afraid Thunder will lie down and we won't be able to get him up again.'

Thunder's insides gave a most alarming rumble just then and he groaned in pain and fright. He seemed about to lie down, but Miss Peters took him out of his stall at once, and began to walk him up and down the stables. The other horses looked round, mildly surprised at all these unusual happenings. One or two whinnied to Miss Peters. They were very fond of her.

'Darrell! Go quickly and get sou'westers for yourself and Bill. Then take the horse into the yard and walk him round and round. I'll go and phone the vet and come back at once.'

Darrell flew off. She came back with the sou'westers. She had to put Bill's on for her, because Bill looked at the sou'wester as if she simply didn't know what it was!

'I'm going to phone now,' said Miss Peters. 'Walk him out, Bill.'

She went. She telephoned the vet's house. The sleepy voice of his housekeeper answered her. 'I'm sorry, Mam—but the vet has gone to Raglett's farm to a cow. He said he'd sleep there for the night. No, Mam—I'm afraid they're not on the telephone. You can't get the vet tonight. I'm sorry.'

Miss Peters put down the receiver. Couldn't get the vet! What was to be done? The horse needed medicine, and only the vet could bring it and make him drink it down. Miss Peters could see that Thunder's condition was serious. Something *must* be done!

She went out to the stables again. In the yard the two girls were walking Thunder round and round, the rain pouring down on them. She told them that the vet could not be reached. Bill groaned. She was in despair.

'He's at Raglett's farm,' said Miss Peters. 'That's about five miles off, on the Billington Road. I know what I'll do. I'll saddle one of the other horses and ride to the farm myself and get him. That would be the best thing.'

'What! In the dark and the rain?' said Darrell, hardly able to believe her ears.

'That's nothing,' said Miss Peters. 'Thunder is a lovely horse—I don't mind what I do for him.'

Bill's hand groped for Miss Peters' arm. She was sobbing. 'You *are* good!' she said. 'Thank you, Miss Peters. You are the kindest person I've ever known. Oh, if only you can get the vet!'

Miss Peters patted Bill's shoulder. 'I'll do my best. Don't worry, Bill!'

Darrell was struck with surprise. Miss Peters had called Bill Bill. Gracious! And she was going to ride for miles in the dark to fetch someone to help Thunder. She was a perfectly marvellous person! 'And to think I never even guessed it before!' marvelled Darrell, valiantly leading Thunder round the yard. 'People are awfully decent underneath.'

Miss Peters was soon galloping off into the night. The two girls took it in turns to lead Thunder round the yard. He seemed better when he was walking.

'Darrell—I do feel so awful now to remember all the horrid things I thought about Miss Peters,' said Bill, once. 'She's the decentest person I've ever met. Fancy riding off like that to get the vet. Darrell, I shall never be able to repay her. Shall I?'

'No. I don't suppose you will,' said Darrell. 'I think she's fine. Golly—won't the girls be thrilled to hear about all this tomorrow!'

Miss Peters was riding fast through the night. The rain beat down on her but she didn't mind. She was an all-weather person, and thought nothing of rain, wind, snow or fog! She galloped off to Raglett's farm, and at last got to the gate that led up to the farm.

There was a light in one of the sheds. Miss Peters guessed the vet was there with the farmer, and the cow he had gone to ténd. She rode up to the door, her horse's hooves making a loud noise in the night.

The farmer came to the door in surprise. Miss Peters hailed him in her loud, deep voice. 'Is the vet here? Can I speak to him?'

'He's in yonder,' said the farmer. Miss Peters dismounted

and went into the shed. The vet was there, kneeling beside a cow. By the cow's side were two pretty little calves.

'Mr. Turnbull,' said Miss Peters,' if you've finished here, could you possibly come to Malory Towers? That horse Thunder I told you about on the telephone this morning is in a bad way. Colic. He needs help.'

'Right,' said the vet, getting up. 'I've finished here, as it happens—much earlier than I thought. I'll come along now. I'll get my horse. Well, Raglett, that cow's fine now—and she's got two of the prettiest calves I ever saw!'

Presently the vet and Miss Peters were riding back over he road to Malory Towers. When they were half-way here Miss Peters' horse suddenly shied and reared.

'Hey there! Whoa! What's the matter?' cried Miss Peters— and at the same moment she saw something lying beside the road. It was a dark shape, hardly visible in the darkness of the night.

'Mr. Turnbull. Come here!' yelled Miss Peters. 'I think there's somebody here. I hope they haven't been knocked down by a car and left helpless!'

The vet had a powerful torch. He switched it on. The beam played over a huddled up bundle—a bundle with a mackintosh on!

'Good heavens! It's a young girl!' said the vet. 'Is she hurt?'

He picked the girl up. Miss Peters gave a loud and horrified exclamation. 'It's MAVIS! Good gracious me! Mavis! Whatever is she doing lying out here in the dark at this time of night? This is terrible!'

'She's fainted from exhaustion I think,' said the vet. 'Doesn't seem to have any bones broken. Look, she's opening her eyes.'

Mavis looked up and saw Miss Peters. She began to cry weakly. 'They wouldn't let me sing. And I missed the last bus, and I've been walking all night in the rain.'

'What *is* she talking about?' said the vet. 'Look, she's wet

'*It's Mavis! Good gracious me!*'

through ! She'll get pneumonia unless we're pretty quick. I'll take her on my horse. Help me to lift her up. '

Amazed, horrified and distressed, Miss Peters helped to lift Mavis on to the vet's horse. He held the girl steady in front of him. Then off they went again, this time more slowly.

They came to Malory Towers. 'If Mavis can walk I'll take her straight in to Matron, ' said Miss Peters. 'Oh dear, what a night ! You go to the stables, Mr. Turnbull. Darrell and Bill are walking Thunder in the yard. '

The vet disappeared in the direction of the stables. Miss Peters guided the exhausted Mavis into North Tower. She could hardly walk. Miss Peters half-dragged her up the stairs to Matron's room.

Matron awoke and opened her door in surprise. She exclaimed in horror when she saw Mavis. 'What's all this ? Where has she been ? She's soaked through and shivering. Miss Peters, there's an electric blanket in that cupboard. Put it into the little bed over there, will you, and get the bed hot. And put my electric kettle on. Good gracious ! What can have happened ? '

'Goodness knows, ' said Miss Peters, doing all the things she had been asked to do, whilst Matron quickly undressed Mavis, flinging her soaking clothes on the floor in her hurry to get her into a warm bed. It wasn't long before she was tucked up with two hot-water bottles, whilst Matron prepared some hot cocoa.

Mavis tried to tell her what had happened. She spoke in a poor croaking voice. 'I only went to Billington—to that talent spotting concert—but they said they couldn't let schoolgirls enter. I tried and tried to make them let me sing, but they wouldn't. And then I missed the last bus so I began to walk all the way home. But it rained and blew and I was so tired I fell down. And I couldn't get up again. So ... '

'Now, don't talk any more,' said Matron, gently. 'You drink this cocoa and go to sleep. I'll be here in this other bed so you'll be all right.'

Miss Peters had slipped out of the room, murmuring something about seeing to a horse, much to Matron's surprise. She couldn't make out why Miss Peters was in riding things nor how it was that she had found Mavis on the road. Well, the main thing was to see to Mavis. She could find out the rest of the mystery afterwards.

Miss Peters went down to the others. Bill and Darrell had welcomed the vet with joy and relief. Thunder knew him and whinnied. It wasn't long before the vet had made him drink a huge draught of medicine. 'You've done well to keep him on his feet,' he told the two tired girls. 'Probably saved his life. Now—off you go to bed. I'll stay with him till morning. Miss Peters will help me. Off you go!'

18   NEXT MORNING

BILL hadn't wanted to leave Thunder, of course. But Miss Peters spoke to her firmly and gently. 'Now, Bill—you must leave matters to us. You know that we shall do our best for the horse, and now that he has had that draught he will be all right. We'll walk him as long as necessary. But you and Darrell have done your share and you are tired out. Be sensible, Bill, and do as you are told.'

'Yes, I will,' said Bill, unexpectedly. She took Miss Peters' hand in hers and held it tightly. 'Miss Peters—I can never repay you. Never. But I'll never forget tonight and all you did.'

Miss Peters patted Bill on the back. 'That's all right. I'm not asking for any repayment! I'm fond of Thunder, too, and I knew how you felt. I'm not sending him home, Bill. You shall keep him. I don't somehow think I shall ever have to punish you again by saying you mustn't see him.'

'You won't,' said Bill, her white face gleaming in the lamplight. 'I'll be your—your very best pupil from now on, Miss Peters!'

'Well—that will be a wonderful repayment,' said Miss Peters, smiling. 'Now do go, both of you. You look so pale and tired. You must both have breakfast in bed!'

'Oh no!' protested both girls. 'We couldn't bear it.'

'All right. I can't bear it either,' said Miss Peters. 'You can go to bed early instead! Now, good night—or rather, good morning! It's nearly three o'clock!'

The two girls stumbled into North Tower, yawning. They hardly said a word to one another, they were so tired. But they were happy, and felt as if they had been friends for years! Bill slid into bed. She whispered to Darrell.

'Darrell! I know you're Sally's friend, so you can't be mine. But I'm yours for ever and ever. Just you remember that! I'll pay you back some day for all you did tonight.'

'That's all right,' said Darrell, sleepily, and was asleep almost at once.

In the morning, what a to-do! Darrell and Bill slept so soundly that not even the bell awoke them. When Jean pulled at them they shrugged away and cuddled down again, hardly waking.

'Darrell! Bill! I say, what's the matter with them both! Wake up, you two, the bell's gone ages ago. Do wake up—we want to tell you something. Mavis isn't back! Her bed is empty!'

The rest of the girls were talking excitedly about Mavis's non-appearance. Jean was very worried. She felt that she ought to have reported the night before that Mavis had not come to bed with the rest of them. She was feeling very guilty.

'I must go to Miss Potts at once,' she said and she rushed off. But Miss Potts knew all about Mavis, for Matron had already reported to her. Miss Grayling knew, too. There had been a great upset about it. Mavis was now in the san. where sick girls were kept, and Sister, who looked after the san., was in charge of her. The doctor had been to see her already.

Jean listened to all this in amazement. 'Did Mavis—did she go to Billington?' she asked.

'Oh! So you know about that too,' said Miss Potts, grimly. 'Funny sort of head-girl you are, Jean, not to have reported that Mavis was not in the dormitory last night. Very remiss of you. There are times when you have to make a distinction between telling tales and reporting. You know that. We might have saved Mavis from a serious illness if we had learnt from you that she hadn't gone to bed.'

Jean went white. 'I fell asleep,' she said, miserably, 'I was going to wait till the last bus came in—and if Mavis didn't come in then I was going to come and report. But I fell asleep.'

'A lame excuse,' said Miss Potts, who was angry with herself for not having popped her head into the third form dormy the night before, when she had heard talking. If only she had!

'Can we see Mavis?' asked Jean.

'Certainly not,' said Miss Potts. 'She is seriously ill. She got soaked through, and then lay for some time by the roadside. She has bronchitis now—and we are hoping it won't turn to anything worse. Her throat is terribly bad, too—she can hardly whisper.'

Jean went back to the third form dormy feeling guilty and alarmed. She found the third-formers gathered round Darrell, listening excitedly to her tale of the night before. Bill was not there. She had rushed off to the stables at once, of course.

'Listen ...' said Jean. But nobody listened. They were all agape at Darrell's amazing tale. Jean found herself listening, too.

'But—would you believe Miss Peters could be so utterly decent?' said Belinda, in surprise. 'She was super! How lucky that you fetched her, Darrell!'

'It *was* a night!' said Darrell. 'Bill and I must have walked miles and miles with Thunder round the yard. I wonder how he is this morning.'

Footsteps raced up the corridor to the dormy. Bill burst in, her face glowing. 'Darrell! DARRELL! He's all right. Right as rain, and eating his oats as if he couldn't have enough. The vet stayed with him till half-past seven, and Miss Peters stayed till now. She never went to bed again!'

'Golly! She's wonderful,' said Alicia, seeing Miss Peters in an entirely new light. 'Bill, why didn't you and Darrell wake us up, too!'

'We never thought of anything like that,' said Bill. 'We only thought of Thunder. Darrell was marvellous, too. Oh, I feel so happy. Thunder's all right. He's not going to be sent home. Everything's fine. And I shall never, never forget what Miss Peters did last night.'

'You will!' said Alicia. 'You'll sit and look out of the window and dream in class, just as you always do!'

'I shan't,' said Bill, earnestly. 'Don't tease me, Alicia. I feel a bit queer though I feel so happy. Now I know that Miss Peters is so fond of Thunder—and he loves her, too, fancy that!—I shall feel quite different about everything. I might even let her ride him.'

Jean at last got a word in. 'Listen to *me* now!' she said, and she told the third-formers about Mavis. They listened in horrified silence. Darrell burst out at once.

'Gracious! So Miss Peters didn't only save Thunder last night—she saved Mavis, too. But I say—fancy Mavis trying to walk home all those miles in the dark by herself. She's afraid of the dark, too.'

The girls were happy about Bill and Thunder, but upset about Mavis. They stood about in the dormy, talking, forgetting all about breakfast. Somebody came running up the corridor. It was Lucy of the fourth form.

'I *say*! What are you all thinking of? Aren't you coming to breakfast? The bell's gone long ago. Mam'zelle is absolutely furious!'

'Oh dear! Come on, everyone,' said Jean. 'I feel all in a whirl.'

The news about Thunder and about Mavis spread all through the school, and was the talk in every class from the bottom form to the top. Darrell and Bill had to tell the tale over and over again.

It was Sunday so there were no classes. In the school chapel, where the service was held, a prayer was said for Mavis. All the girls joined in it, for although few of them liked Mavis they were all sorry for her. The news went round that she was worse. Her parents had been sent for! Oh dear, thought Jean, it was all her fault!

By the next morning, however, Mavis had taken a turn for the better. Thunder, too, was perfectly all right. Bill was thrilled. It seemed impossible that a horse in such pain as Thunder had been should be quite recovered the day after. How wonderful people like doctors and vets were!

The girls settled down to their classes on Monday, glad that Mavis was better. Jean especially was thankful. Perhaps she would soon be back in school. The whole matter would have blown over. Mavis would be given a talking to by Miss Grayling, but no punishment because she had punished herself enough. Everything would be all right.

Miss Peters had had a good rest on the Sunday, and was taking the third form as usual on Monday. When she came into the classroom, she had a surprise.

'Hurrah for Miss Peters!' cried Darrell's voice, and to the amazement of the forms on each side of the third form room, three hearty cheers rang out for Miss Peters. She couldn't help being pleased. She smiled pleasantly all round.

'Thank you,' she said. 'That was nice of you. Now—open your books at page forty-one. Alicia, come up to the blackboard, please.'

Darrell looked with interest at Bill several times that morning. Bill didn't gaze out of the window once. She paid great attention to every word that Miss Peters said. She answered intelligently, and when it was her turn to come up to the blackboard, she did extremely well.

'Very good, Bill,' said Miss Peters, and a gasp went round the class. Miss Peters hadn't called her Wilhelmina as she always did. She had called her Bill. Bill grinned as she went back to her place. She looked a different person.

Darrell admired her as she watched her in class after class. Bill had made up her mind to do a thing and she meant to do it. She *would* do it, too! Darrell thought that it was quite possible for Bill to rise near the top of the class once she had made up her mind to do it.

'I suppose that's what Daddy would call strength of character,' thought Darrell. 'He's always saying that strength of character is one of the greatest things anyone can have because then they have courage and pluck and determination, no matter what difficulties come. Bill's got it. I bet she won't dream, or gaze out of the window again, or not bother with her work. She's going to repay Miss Peters for Saturday night!'

Miss Peters knew that Bill meant to repay her for that, too. She trusted Bill now. They understood one another, which really wasn't very surprising, because they were very much alike. Miss Peters was mannish, and Bill was boyish. They both loved life out-of-doors and adored horses. They had disliked one another very much indeed—but now they were going to be firm friends. That would be nice for Bill.

'Darrell! Are you day-dreaming?' said Miss Peters' voice. 'You don't seem to have written down anything at all!'

Darrell jumped and went red. Gracious! Here she was admiring Bill for being able to stop dreaming in class—and she, Darrell, had fallen into the same fault herself! She pulled herself together and began to write.

That afternoon Miss Hibbert was going to take the first rehearsal of the play in the art-room. This was often used for dramatic work because it had a small platform. Zerelda was very much looking forward to the afternoon. She sat in her place, murmuring some lines from 'Romeo and Juliet' below her breath. Miss Peters saw her lips moving and thought she was whispering to Gwen.

'Zerelda!' she said, sharply. 'What are you saying to Gwendoline?'

'Nothing, Miss Peters,' said Zerelda, surprised.

'Well, what were you saying to yourself then?' demanded Miss Peters. 'Stand up when you answer me, Zerelda.'

Zerelda stood up. She looked at Miss Peters and recited dramatically what she had been murmuring to herself.

'Wilt thou be gone? It is not yet near day;
It was the nightingale and not ...'

A volley of laughter from everyone in the class drowned her voice. Miss Peters rapped sharply on her desk. 'Zerelda! I hope you don't really *mean* to be rude. That's enough! We are doing geography, not Shakespeare. Sit down and get on!'

19   AT THE REHEARSAL

AFTER the dinner hour that day the third-formers brought up the subject of Alicia's trick again.

'You know, Alicia—I don't somehow feel as if I want it played on Miss Peters now,' said Bill.

'Nor do I,' said Darrell.

'I don't want it played at all,' said Sally, stoutly.

'Well, you're the only one that doesn't,' said Alicia. 'So keep quiet. What does everyone else say?'

'*I* don't quite like to play it on Miss Peters now,' said

Belinda. 'I feel like Bill and Darrell. You know—it seems a bit odd to give three cheers for somebody and then the very next day play a trick on them like that.'

'*I* shouldn't mind,' said Zerelda, who hadn't liked being ticked off in class that morning by Miss Peters. 'What's in a trick, anyway! Only a bit of fun. I guess it wouldn't matter at all.'

'I agree with Zerelda,' said Gwen's voice. 'Why shouldn't we? Don't you agree, Daphne?'

'I don't know,' said Daphne, who had been rather struck with Miss Peters' dramatic ride through the night. 'No—I think on the whole I'd rather play it on Mam'zelle—or Miss Carton, perhaps.'

'Well, I don't much care who we play it on,' said Alicia. 'Darrell and I will agree to what the majority say.'

'Darrell and you!' exclaimed Sally. 'What's Darrell got to do with it? It's *your* trick, not hers!'

'Oh, we've just been planning it out together that's all,' said Alicia, coolly, pleased to see Sally's jealousy flare up in public. Darrell went red. It was true she had enjoyed talking over the trick with Alicia—but she knew quite well that Alicia was only saying that to make Sally cross. Bother them both Why couldn't they all he friends together? Never mind— Betty was coming hack soon. Then perhaps Alicia would stop teasing Sally and Sally would stop being jealous and spiteful.

'Well—lets play the trick on Mam'zelle then,' said Irene. 'Mam'zelle's lovely to play tricks on. We haven't played one on her for terms and terms.'

'Right. Mam'zelle it shall be,' said Alicia. 'Do you agree, Darrell? We'll talk about the best time and so on together when we've got a minute to ourselves. It's time to go over to the art-room now.'

They all went off to the art-room, Sally looking glum. Alicia slipped her arm in Darrell's and bore her off as if she really was her best friend. Darrell glanced back at Sally and tried to take her arm away from Alicia. But Sally gave her such a sour look that Darrell was annoyed, and didn't go back to her after all.

Privately Darrell thought the hour of Shakespeare was a dreadful waste, because it was a fine sunny afternoon when a game of lacrosse could have been arranged. Still it would be fun to see Zerelda trying to impress Miss Hibbert.

Zerelda was excited. This was her great chance. If only she could bring it off—make Miss Hibbert say what a gift for acting she had. ' Zerelda, you're a born actress ! ' she would say to her. ' You have a great Gift. You must turn all your attention to building it up. You have the right appearance, too—striking, graceful, mature. It will make me very proud to teach you this year ! '

Zerelda had done a little roll of hair on top of her head again—not so big a roll as before, certainly, but still a roll, pinned up to make her look older. Her hair was not tied back so tightly either. She had made up her face a little—put red on her lips, pink on her cheeks, and had smothered herself with powder. Her hands were white. Her nails were very long and highly polished. She hoped she looked a finished actress !

Miss Hibbert did not look at all like a producer of plays. She was neat, with a well-fitting coat and skirt, and her hair, slightly wavy, was brushed well back. She wore a pair of glasses with rather thick rims. She had a lovely speaking voice, very pleasant to listen to. She was very efficient. and knew exactly how to pick the right actor for the right part.

She looked over the girls as they came in. She knew Zerelda already because she had taken her for a few lessons in the fourth form. She looked in astonishment at Zerelda's make-up. Good gracious ! What did the girl think she was up to !

Miss Hibbert had absolutely no idea at all that Zerelda fancied herself as an actress or as a film-star. Nobody had told her. Perhaps if she had known, she might have been a little more patient, even a little kinder. But she didn't know.

There was a lot to get through. For one reason or another two rehearsals had been put off, and Miss Hibbert was feeling a little rushed for time. She handed out copies of the play and looked round the form.

'Now—has anyone acted in this play before?'

Nobody had. Zerelda stepped forward and said a few words, trying to speak the English way. 'Please, Miss Hibbert, once I did Lady Macbeth in Shakespeare.'

'Oh,' said Miss Hibbert, gazing at Zerelda's hair. 'Zerelda. I don't like the way you do your hair. Don't come to my classes with that silly roll on top again.'

Zerelda went red and stepped back.

'Has anyone read the play?' Darrell and Mary-Lou put up their hands, and so did Zerelda.

'Does anyone know any of the parts? Has anyone been sufficiently interested to learn any of the speeches?' went on Miss Hibbert.

Zerelda stepped forward again. 'Please, Miss Hibbert, I know all Juliet's speeches, every one of them. I guess I could say them all, right now. It's a wunnerful part, Juliet's. I've been rehearsing it like mad.'

'Yes. She's awfully good as Juliet,' put in Gwendoline, and got a grateful smile from Zerelda.

'Very well. As you've taken the trouble to learn the part, you can take it this afternoon,' said Miss Hibbert. She looked round the class for a boyish third-former to take the part of Romeo. Her eye fell on Bill.

'You,' she said. 'What's your name—Wilhelmina—you can take the part of Romeo today. And you, Darrell, can be the nurse, and you ...'

Quickly she fitted part after part. The girls looked at their copies of the play and prepared to read and act them.

'Not very inspired,' said Miss Hibbert, after the first few

pages had been read. 'Turn to the part where Juliet comes on. Zerelda, are you ready?'

Was she *ready*? Why, she was waiting on tenterhooks to begin! She was full of it! She was Juliet to the life, poor, tragic Juliet.

Zerelda launched herself into the part. She declaimed her lines in a most dramatic manner, she flung herself about, she marched up and down, she threw her head back, imagining herself to be beautiful and most lovable.

'Stop, Zerelda,' said Miss Hibbert, amazed. But Zerelda did not stop. Heedless of the giggles of the class she ranted on. Irene gave one of her enormous snorts, and Miss Hibbert glared at her. She spoke loudly to Zerelda again.

'STOP, Zerelda!'

Zerelda stopped and stared blankly at Miss Hibbert, surprised to see that she looked so furious.

'How dare you behave like that?' stormed Miss Hibbert. 'Sending the class into fits! Do you think that's the way to behave in a Shakespeare class? They may think it comical but I don't. Those are lovely lines you have been saying—but you have completely spoilt them. And do you really think it is clever to throw yourself about like that, and toss your head? Don't you know that Juliet was young and gentle and sweet? You are trying to make her into some horrible affected film-star!'

Zerelda took in what the angry mistress was saying. She could hardly believe it. She went rather white under the pink on her cheeks.

'And why have you made yourself up like that?' demanded Miss Hibbert, roused to more anger by the giggles of the rest of the form. 'I cannot tell you how horrible you look with that stuff on your face. You would not dare to go to Miss Peters' class like that. I'm not going to put up with it. You may as well make up your mind, Zerelda, that you will never be an actress. You simply haven't got it in you. All that happens is that you make yourself really vulgar. Now go and wash your face and do your hair properly. '

Zerelda felt like a balloon that had been pricked. All her confidence and pride oozed out of her. She crept to the door and went out. Some of the girls felt sorry for her.

Rather subdued by this unusual outburst, the rest of the form went on with the reading Miss Hibbert, a little sorry that she had been so very hard on Zerelda, handed out a few words of praise. 'Alicia, you're good. Mary-Lou, you have a nice voice if you could remember to hold your head up when you speak your lines. Darrell, I can see you are trying. Next time we will all take different parts. '

'Miss Hibbert, had I better go and see what has happened to Zerelda?' asked Gwen, timidly. 'Miss Hibbert, she really did think she had a gift for acting, you know. Aren't you going to let her be in the play at all? '

'I may give her a very small part—where she can't throw herself about,' said Miss Hibbert. 'But certainly not a good part. It must be obvious even to you, Gwendoline, that Zerelda hasn't the faintest idea of acting, and never will have. Go and find her and tell her to come here to me. I want to talk to her. The class is now dismissed. '

The third-formers went out quietly. Poor Zerelda! What would she do now?

'Put a bold face on it, I expect, ' said Alicia. 'Just as she did when she was sent down to the third form. She won't care! She'll go on in just the same way, thinking the world of herself, and very little of anyone else! '

Zerelda was found by Gwen in the cloakroom. She had washed her face quite clean and tied back her hair. But she had been too scared to go back to the art-room.

'Zerelda, Miss Hibbert wants you, ' said Gwen. 'I'm sorry about that row. It's a shame. '

'*Can't* I act, Gwen?' said Zerelda, her lip quivering suddenly. Gwendoline hesitated.

'Well—you weren't very good really,' she said. 'You—you just seemed to be terribly funny. You might make a very good *comedian*, Zerelda.'

Zerelda said nothing but went off to the art-room. Even Gwen thought she couldn't act! In fact, she was so bad that she became ridiculous. Zerelda was shocked and dismayed. She dreaded hearing what Miss Hibbert had to say.

But Miss Hibbert was unexpectedly kind. 'I hear that it is your ambition to be a great actress, Zerelda,' she said. 'Well, my dear, it is given to very few of us to be that. You haven't the gift—and you haven't another thing that all really fine actresses need.'

'What?' whispered Zerelda.

'Well, Zerelda, in order to be able to put yourself properly into some other character, you have to forget yourself entirely—forget your looks, your ambitions, your pride in acting, everything! And it takes a strong and understanding character to do that, someone without conceit or weakness of any sort—the finer the character of the actor, the better he can play any part. You are thinking of yourself too much. You were not Juliet being acted by Zerelda this afternoon— you were Zerelda all the time—and not a very nice Zerelda either!'

'Shan't I ever be any good at acting?' asked Zerelda, miserably.

'I don't think so,' said Miss Hibbert, gently. 'I can always tell at once those who have any gift for it. You have let your foolish worship and admiration of the film-stars blind you, Zerelda. Why not try to be your own self for a while? Stop all this posturing and pretending. Be like the others, a schoolgirl sent here to learn lessons and play games!'

'It's the only thing left for me to be,' said Zerelda, and a tear ran down her cheek.

'It's a very, very *nice* thing to be,' said Miss Hibbert. 'You try it and see ! I wouldn't have been so hard on you if I'd known you had set your heart on being an actress. I thought you were just being ridiculous. '

Zerelda left the art-room, hardly knowing what to think. She had made herself ridiculous. She never, never wanted to act again ! All she wanted to do was to sink into being a nobody, hoping that none of the others would notice her and tease her about that afternoon.

She joined the others at tea, slipping into her place unnoticed by the girls. Miss Potts looked at her and saw that she had been crying. ' Funny thing ! ' thought Miss Potts, ' it's the first time I've noticed it, but Zerelda is getting to look much more like the others now—a proper little schoolgirl. Perhaps Malory Towers is beginning to have an effect after all ! '

20   THE TRICK !

ONE or two days slipped by. Mavis was still very ill and could not be seen, but it was known now that she was mending. Everyone was relieved. The girls sent in flowers and books, and Zerelda sent her a complicated American jigsaw.

Bill had quite recovered from her midnight adventure and so had Darrell. Miss Peters was delighted with the change in Bill's work. It was still uneven, but she knew that Bill was paying great attention and really trying hard. Zerelda, too, was working even better, and had actually asked Mam'zelle for extra coaching !

Zerelda had sorted things out in her mind. She had definitely given up the idea of becoming a film-actress. She didn't even want to *look* like one ! She wanted to look as like the others as possible, and to make them forget how ridiculous she had been. She began to copy them in every way she could.

'Isn't Zerelda queer?' said Belinda to Irene. 'When she first came here she gave herself such airs and graces, and looked down on the whole lot of us—now she tries to copy us in everything—the way we speak, the way we do this and that—and seems to think we're just "wunnerful!"'

'She's much nicer,' said Irene, trying out the rhythm of a tune on the table in front of her. 'Tum-tum-ti-tum. Yes, that's how it goes. I like Zerelda now, really I do.'

'Look—Gwendoline's scowling again!' said Belinda, in a whisper. 'I can get that scowl this time. Isn't it a beauty!'

Gwen suddenly became aware of Belinda's intent glances. She straightened her face at once. 'If you've drawn me, I'll tear up the paper!' she said.

'Oh, *Gwen*—scowl half a minute more and I'll get it!' begged Belinda. But Gwen walked out of the room, putting the scowl on outside the door because she felt so annoyed with Belinda and her impish pencil.

'About that trick,' said Alicia, suddenly to Darrell. 'Shall we play it on Friday? Mam'zelle was murmuring this morning something about a test then.'

'Oh *yes*. Let's!' said Darrell, thrilled. She saw Sally nearby, her face glum. 'Sally! Do say you agree. It really will be funny—and quite harmless.'

'I've said already I'm not going to have anything to do with the trick,' said Sally. 'I think it's a silly trick, and might be dangerous. I can't see how anyone can sneeze and sneeze without feeling exhausted. Do it if you like—but just remember that I don't agree!'

'Spoil-sport,' said Alicia, in a low voice to Darrell. Darrell sighed. She couldn't back out of the trick now just to please Sally—but she did hate it when Sally wouldn't be friends. Never mind—Betty would be coming back this week. On Friday perhaps! Then Alicia wouldn't bother about her any more. Betty had been away for more than six weeks now—it was past half-term—but she had been sent away to the

seaside, after her whooping-cough was over, because she had
had it so badly. Good gracious—there were only three or four
weeks to the end of the term! How the time had flown. It was
March now, and the early daffodils were blowing in the
courtyard.

Alicia and Darrell made their plans. 'We'll put the little
pellet, soaked in salt water, on the little ledge behind Mam'zelle, '
said Alicia. ' Let's see—who's on duty to get the room ready on
Friday? Oh, I do believe it's you, isn't it, Darrell? That will be
easy then. You can put the pellet there yourself. '

' Yes, I will, ' agreed Darrell, beginning to giggle at the
thought of Mam'zelle's surprise when she kept sneezing.

All the third-formers knew about the joke. Only Sally
disapproved. Jean didn't think there was any harm in it at all,
so she didn't draw back either. Everyone was thrilled at the
thought of Friday.

It came at last. Darrell slipped into the form room with the
little pellet and a sponge soaked in salt water. She set the pellet
on the ledge and squeezed a few drops of water from the sponge
over it. That was apparently all that was needed to make it
work.

The others came in to get ready for the class. They raised
their eye-brows at Darrell, and she nodded back, smiling. They
all took their places, ready for Mam'zelle.

She came in, beaming as usual. ' *Asseyez-vous, mes enfants.*
Today we have a great, great treat. It is a test! '

Deep groans from the class.

' Silence! ' hissed Mam'zelle. ' Do you want Miss Potts to
come and find out what is the meaning of this terrible noise?
Now, I will write some questions on the blackboard, and you
will answer them in your books. '

She turned to write on the blackboard, and got the first whiff
of the fine vapour, quite invisible, that was streaming from the
curious little pellet.

Mam'zelle felt a tickling in her nose, and felt about her

' A-tish-oo! ' sneezed poor Mam 'zelle

plump person for her handkerchief. 'Ah, where is it, now? I have a nose-tickle.'

'Your hanky's in your belt, Mam'zelle,' called Alicia, hoping that Irene wasn't going to do one of her explosions too soon. She already looked as if she was on the point of bursting.

Mam'zelle also looked as if she was bursting. She snatched at her handkerchief and pressed it to her nose. But no handkerchief could choke down that colossal sneeze. Mam'zelle always did sneeze loudly at any time—but this time it sounded like an explosive shell!

'A-WHOOSH-OOOO! Dear me,' said Mam'zelle, patting her nose with her handkerchief. 'I'm sorry, girls, I could not help it.'

Irene had already bent down to hide her giggles under the desk. Alicia glanced at her in amused annoyance. Whatever would she do when Mam'zelle's second sneeze came along. Ah—it was coming. Mam'zelle was making a frantic grab for her handkerchief again. 'Oh, *là là*! Here is another snizz. I hope I do not get a cold. A-WHOOOSH-OOOOOOO!'

Irene exploded and so did Belinda. Mam'zelle, quite shaken by her enormous sneeze, glared at them both.

'Irene! Belinda! It is not kind to laugh at another's discom... A-WHOOOSH-OO!'

But now even Alicia could not hide her laughter. Darrell leaned back weakly and tried to stop laughing because her side ached so much. Even Sally was smiling, though she tried hard not to.

'A-WHOOOSH-OOO!' sneezed Mam'zelle again. She reeled back to her chair, and mopped her forehead. 'Never have I snizzed like this before,' she said. 'It is unheard of that I snizz so much. A-WHOOOOOSH-OOOOOO!'

The last one was so terrific that it shook poor Mam'zelle right out of her chair. By now the whole class was in convulsions. Gwen was falling out of her chair. In another moment Irene would be rolling on the floor. Tears of laughter were pouring down the cheeks of half a dozen of the girls.

Mam'zelle sat staring at the blackboard wondering if the sneezing had finished. Perhaps the attack was over. She got up cautiously and went to the blackboard—but at once her nose began to tickle again and she put up her handkerchief. 'A-WHOOOOOOOOOSH-OOO!'

Mam'zelle sank down into her chair again. At this moment the door opened and Miss Potts looked in with a sheaf of papers. 'Oh, excuse me, Mam'zelle, but you left these ... ' she began, and then stopped short in surprise at seeing the whole form rolling about in helpless laughter. Whatever was happening?

She looked at Mam'zelle, and Mam'zelle looked back, trying to tell her what was happening. Another exploding sneeze nearly blew Miss Potts out of the door.

'A-WHOOOSH-OOOOOO!'

The class sobered up when they saw Miss Potts. They hoped she would go immediately—but she didn't. Rather alarmed at Mam'zelle's agonized expression, she went over to her. 'It is these snizzes—' Mam'zelle began to explain and was then overcome by another.

The vapour found its way to Miss Potts' nose. She was just about to open her mouth and speak when she too felt a sneeze coming. Her nose began to tickle and she felt for her handkerchief.

'A-TISH-OOO!' she sneezed, and Irene burst into one of her explosive laughs at once. Miss Potts glared at her.

'Irene! Do you think... A-TISH-OOOO!'

'A-WHOOOOSH-OOOO!' from Mam'zelle. 'Miss Potts what is this snizzing? I cannot stop my snizzes—A-WHOOOSH-OO!'

Miss Potts sneezed three times without being able to get a word in between the sneezes. Then a sudden suspicion flashed into her mind. She looked at the giggling girls.

'Jean,' she said, 'you are head-girl of this form. Is this a trick? A-TISH-OO!'

Jean hesitated. How could she give the whole form away?

Mam'zelle saved her from further questioning. She sneezed such a mighty sneeze that she fell off her chair. She moaned. 'I am ill! I have never snizzed like this before. I am very ill. A-WHOOOOSH-OO.'

Really alarmed, Miss Potts, hindered by two or three sudden sneezes of her own, dragged Mam'zelle to her feet. 'Open the window,' she commanded Darrell. 'Fetch Matron. Mam'zelle certainly does look ill.'

In great alarm Darrell opened the window and Mary-Lou ran for Matron. Matron came, puzzled by Mary-Lou's breathless tale of Mam'zelle's sneezes. She saw Mam'zelle's pale face and took her arm to lead her away. The pellet-vapour overtook Matron also, and she did a very sudden sneeze indeed. Miss Potts also obliged with two more, and Mam'zelle prepared for yet another. Then Matron took Mam'zelle from the room, and Miss Potts followed, to make sure poor Mam'zelle was all right.

The girls, alarmed and frightened though they were, could not stop from laughing at the sight of the three adults sneezing in chorus together. 'You were nearly caught out with Miss Potts' question, Jean,' said Alicia. 'It was a narrow shave!. Let's hope she doesn't ask it again.'

'I hope Mam'zelle isn't *really* knocked out,' said Darrell, anxiously. 'She did look rather awful. I think I'll quickly take that pellet and throw it out of the window before Miss Potts comes back and sees it!'

So she threw it out, being caught for a sneeze herself first. Then the form settled down to wait for someone to come back.

It was Miss Potts. 'Mam'zelle is not at all well,' she began, severely, handkerchief in hand in case she began to sneeze again. 'She has had to go to bed. She is quite exhausted. The strange—very strange—thing is, that as soon as we left this room not one of us had any wish to sneeze. Jean, will you please explain this to me. Or perhaps you, Alicia, would like to do so? I feel that you probably know more about it than anyone else.'

Alicia hardly knew what to say. Jean nudged her. 'Go on. You'll have to tell.'

So Alicia told. It didn't seem nearly such a funny idea when it was told stammeringly to a frowning Miss Potts.

'I see. One of your asinine tricks again. I should have thought that third-formers were above such childish things. Were you all in this, every one of you?'

'Sally wasn't,' said Darrell. 'She refused to agree. She was the only one who stood out.'

'Only one sensible person in the whole of the form!' said Miss Potts. 'Very well—with the exception of Sally, each of you will forfeit the next half-holiday, which is, I believe, on Thursday. You will also apologize to Mam'zelle and work twice as hard at your French for the rest of the term!'

21   MAVIS AND ZERELDA

IT was a sorry ending to what everyone had thought to be a very fine trick. 'I suppose that pellet had been made stronger than usual,' said Alicia, gloomily.

Sally didn't say 'I told you so', which was very good of her, Darrell thought. 'I shall give up the half-holiday just the same as you all do,' she told Darrell. 'I may have stood out against the trick, but I'm going to share the punishment, of course.'

'You're decent, Sally,' said Darrell, slipping her arm in hers. 'Let's go downstairs and see if there's anything interesting on the notice-board. I believe there's a debate tonight we might go to—sixth-formers against fifth-formers, all arguing their heads off.'

They went to find the notice-board. One of the fourth-formers was also there, looking at it. It was Ellen. 'Hallo, Darrell!' she said. 'Congratulations!'

'What on?' asked Darrell, surprised.

'Well, look—you're playing for the third match-team next Thursday!' said Ellen. 'Three people have fallen out, ill—so all three reserves are playing—and you're one of them, aren't you?'

'Oh—how perfectly wizard!' cried Darrell. She capered round the hall—and then her face suddenly sobered. 'I say—will Miss Potts let me play next Thursday? That's the half-holiday, isn't it, except for match-players? Oh, Sally—do you think I shan't be able to play because we've all got to give up our half-holiday and work instead?'

'What *are* you talking about?' said Ellen, puzzled. Darrell told her.

'Goodness!' said Ellen. 'You won't be able to play then. You can't expect Potty to let you off a punishment in order to have a great treat like playing in a match-team.'

Darrell groaned. 'Oh—what simply awful bad luck! My first chance! And I've chucked it away. Oh, Sally, why didn't I back you up and stand aside with you, instead of going in with Alicia?'

It was a terrible blow to poor Darrell. She went about looking so miserable that Sally couldn't bear it. She went to Miss Potts' room and knocked at the door.

'Please, Miss Potts—Darrell is down to play in the third match-team next Thursday,' said Sally. 'And because of the trick today she's supposed to work on that day. She's terribly disappointed. You said I needn't give up the half-holiday because I didn't agree to the trick. Can I give it up, please, and let Darrell take it instead of me? Then she could play in the match.'

'A kind thought, Sally, but quite impossible,' said Miss Potts. 'Darrell must take her punishment like the rest of the form. It's her own fault if she misses her chance of playing in the match. '

Sally went away sadly. She met Darrell and told her how she had tried to get her the half-holiday so that she might play in the team. Darrell was touched. 'Oh, Sally! You really *are* a sport! A proper friend! Thank you. '

Sally smiled at her. Her jealousy slid away suddenly. She knew she had been silly, but she wouldn't be any more. She linked her arm in Darrell's.

'I'll be glad when Betty's back and Alicia has her for company, ' she said.

'So will I, ' said Darrell, heartily. 'It's annoying the way she keeps trying to make us into a threesome. Don't let's, Sally. '

Sally was satisfied. But how she wished she could give Darrell her half-holiday! Poor Darrell—it was such a wonderful chance—one that might not come again for ages.

They met Sister and asked her for news of Mavis. 'Much better, ' said Sister. 'Her *voice* has gone though. She can only croak, poor Mavis. She seems very miserable. She can have a visitor tomorrow. She's asked for Zerelda, so you might tell her she can go to see Mavis after tea. '

Darrell and Sally looked at each other in astonishment. Zerelda! Whatever did Mavis want Zerelda for?

Mavis was very unhappy. She had been horrified when she found that her voice had gone. She had only a croak that sounded quite unlike her own voice. 'Oh, Sister—won't I ever be able to sing again? ' she had asked, anxiously.

'Not for some time, ' Sister had said. 'Oh, yes, I expect it will come back all right, Mavis—but you have been very ill with throat and chest trouble, and you won't have to try and sing for a year or two. If you do, the specialist says you will damage your voice for ever, and will never be able to become a singer. '

Mavis let the tears slide down her cheeks without wiping them away. No Voice! No singing for a year or two—and perhaps not then. Why, she might not become an opera-singer after all. Throat trouble—chest trouble—they were the two things a singer must always guard against.

' It's my own fault! Why did I creep off in the rain that night ? ' wept poor Mavis. ' I thought it was a grand thing to do. The others didn't. Perhaps Zerelda would understand though— she's going to be a grand film-actress, and she understands how a singer or an actress longs to be recognized, aches for applause. '

So, when Sister told her she could have a visitor and asked her whom she would like, she chose Zerelda! She must tell Zerelda everything. Zerelda would understand and sympathize.

Zerelda was surprised, too, to be chosen. She hadn't liked Mavis very much. But she went to see her, taking some fruit, some sweets and a book that had just come for her from America. Zerelda was always generous.

She was shocked to see how thin Mavis looked. ' Sit down, ' said Mavis, in a terrible croak.

' What's happened to your voice ? ' asked Zerelda, in alarm.

' I've lost it—perhaps for ever! ' said Mavis, in a pathetic croak. ' Oh, Zerelda, I've been an idiot. I'm sure nobody would understand but you! '

In a series of pants and croaks she told Zerelda all the happenings of that Saturday night—and how they wouldn't even *let* her sing. ' So it was all for nothing. Oh, Zerelda, what am I to do without my voice ? I shall die! The others have always told me that I'm nothing without my voice, nothing at all. '

' Don't talk any more, Mavis, ' said Sister, putting her head in at the door. ' You talk instead, Zerelda. '

So Zerelda talked. What did she find to talk about ? Ah, Zerelda suddenly found a bit of character and quite a lot of wisdom. She had learnt quite a few things already from her term at Malory Towers—she had especially learnt from her failure at acting. And she told Mavis all she had learnt.

It wasn't easy to tell what had happened in the Shakespeare class—but when Zerelda saw how Mavis was drinking it all in, paying her the very closest attention, she spared herself nothing.

'So you see, Mavis,' she finished at last, 'I was much, much worse than you. You really *had* a gift. I never had! You were proud of a real thing. I was vain of something false, that didn't exist. I'm happier now I know, though. After all, it is more sensible to be what we really are, isn't it—schoolgirls—not future film-actresses or opera-singers. You'll feel the same, too, when you've thought about it. You can be *you* now you've lost your voice for a bit.'

'Oh, Zerelda,' croaked Mavis, slipping her hand into the American girl's, 'you don't know how you've helped me. I was so terribly miserable. I didn't think anything like this had ever happened to anyone before. And it's happened to *you* as well as to me!'

Zerelda said nothing. It had cost her a lot to make such a confession to Mavis, of all people. But with all her faults, Zerelda was generous-hearted, and she had quickly seen how she, and she alone, could help Mavis.

Sister put her head in again. She was glad to see Mavis looking so much happier. She came right in. 'Well, you have done her good, Zerelda!' she said. 'She looks quite different. You're friends, I suppose?'

Mavis looked eagerly at Zerelda. 'Yes,' said Zerelda, firmly. 'We're friends.'

'Well, two minutes more and you must go,' said Sister and went out again.

'I'm going to make the others see that I wasn't only a Voice,' croaked Mavis. 'Zerelda, will you go on helping me? Will you be friends with me? I'm not much, I know—but you haven't got a friend, have you?'

'No,' said Zerelda, ashamed to say it. 'Well—I suppose I'm not much of a person either, Mavis. I'm just a no-account person—both of us are! We'll help each other. Now I must go. Good-bye! I'll come again tomorrow!'

22   THINGS GET STRAIGHTENED OUT

MAM'ZELLE soon recovered from her fit of 'snizzes', and returned to her teaching the next day. At first she had felt very angry when Miss Potts had explained to her that it was all because of some trick the girls had played.

But gradually her sense of humour came back to her and she found herself chuckling when she thought of Miss Potts and Matron also being caught by the trick and sneezing violently too.

'But I, I snizzed the greatest snizzes,' said Mam'zelle to herself. 'Aha!—here is Mam'zelle Rougier. I will tell her of this trick.'

She told the prim, rather sour-faced Mam'zelle Rougier who did not approve of tricks in any shape or form. She was horrified.

'These English girls! Have you told Miss Grayling? They should all be punished, every one.'

'Oh *no*—I haven't reported them to the Head,' said Mam'zelle Dupont. 'I only do that for serious matters.'

'And you do not call this a serious matter!' cried Mam'zelle Rougier. 'You will overlook it, and not have the girls punished at all! That Alicia—and the mad Irene and the bad Belinda— it would do them good to have a hard punishment.'

'Oh, they are all being punished,' said Mam'zelle, hastily. 'They are to give up their half-holiday and work instead.'

'That is no real punishment!' said Mam'zelle Rougier. 'You are poor at discipline, Mam'zelle Dupont. I have always said so.'

'Indeed, I am not!' cried Mam'zelle Dupont, annoyed. 'Have you no sense of humour? Do you not see the funny side?'

'No, I do not,' said Mam'zelle Rougier, firmly. 'What is this "funny side" that the English speak of so much? It is not funny. You too know that it is not, Mam'zelle.'

The more that Mam'zelle Rougier talked like this the more certain Mam'zelle Dupont was that the joke had been funny. In the end she quite persuaded herself that she had really entered into it and laughed with the girls.

She almost felt that she would like to remove the punishment Miss Potts had imposed. But Miss Potts would not hear of it. 'Certainly not! Don't be weak, Mam'zelle. We can't possibly let things like that pass.'

'Perhaps not,' said Mam'zelle, a sudden idea coming into her head. 'The bad girls! They shall come to me for the whole of Thursday afternoon, Miss Potts, and I will make them WORK.'

'That's better,' said Miss Potts, approvingly. She found Mam'zelle very difficult at times. 'Keep them at it all the afternoon!'

'I shall take them for a walk,' thought Mam'zelle. She hated walks herself, but she knew how much the girls loved them. But when Thursday afternoon came, it was such a pouring wet day that not only was no lacrosse match possible but no walk either.

Darrell saw a notice up on the board beside the list of players. 'MATCH CANCELLED. ANOTHER DATE WILL BE FIXED LATER.'

'Look at that!' she said to Sally. 'No match after all. How frightfully disappointed I'd have been if I'd been playing—and it was cancelled. I wonder if there's any hope of my playing on the next date it's arranged. I suppose the girls who are ill will be better by then, though.'

The girls went to their classroom that afternoon, to work, while all the other forms went down to the big hall to play mad games together, and to see a film afterwards on a big screen put up at the end of the hall.

Mam'zelle was waiting for them, a broad smile on her face.

'Poor children! You have to work this afternoon because of my snizzes. You must learn some French dances. I have brought my gramophone and some records. I will teach you a fine country dance that all French children know.'

In surprise and glee the third-formers put back all the desks and chairs. They hoped Miss Potts would come by, or Miss Peters, and see what kind of work they were doing on their forfeited half-holiday! What sport to see their faces if they looked into the room!

But Mam'zelle had made sure that both these mistresses would not come that way. Miss Peters had gone off for the afternoon. Miss Potts would be in the big hall with her first form. Mam'zelle was safe!

'The coast is bright!' said Mam'zelle, gleefully. The girls giggled. 'You mean, "the coast is *clear*",' said Jean.

'It is the same thing,' said Mam'zelle. 'Now—begin! Form a ring, please, and I will tell you what to sing as you go round to the music.'

It was a hilarious afternoon, and the third-formers enjoyed it very much. 'You're a sport, Mam'zelle,' said Darrell, warmly at the end. 'A real sport.'

Mam'zelle beamed. She had never yet been able to understand exactly what a 'sport' was—she only knew it was very high praise, and she was pleased.

'You made me snizz—and I have made you pant!' she said, to the breathless girls. 'We are evens, are we not?'

'Quits, you mean,' said Jean, but Mam'zelle took no notice.

'I shall tell Miss Potts you have quite exhausted yourselves in your hard work this afternoon,' said Mam'zelle. 'Poor children—you will be so hungry for tea!'

Zerelda had enjoyed herself as much as anyone. In fact, she was very surprised to find how much she had enjoyed the whole afternoon. Why—a week ago she would have turned up her nose at such rowdiness, and would only have joined in languidly, pretending it was all beneath her.

'But I loved every minute!' thought Zerelda, tying her hair back firmly. It had come loose with the dancing. 'I must have been a frightful idiot before. No wonder the girls laughed at me.'

She saw her old self suddenly—posing, trying to be so grown-up, piling up her hair in Lossie Laxton's terrible style, looking down on all these jolly schoolgirls. She wouldn't bear to think of it.

'It's *fun* to be a proper schoolgirl,' she thought. 'Lovely to be just myself, instead of trying to be like Lossie. What an idiot I was—far worse than Mavis, who did at least have a *real* gift!'

Mavis was getting on well. She looked forward immensely to Zerelda's visits. Many of the third-formers had been to see her now, but she looked forward to Zerelda's visits more than to anyone else's. She thought Zerelda was wonderful—wonderful to have learnt a lesson that she, Mavis, meant to try to learn, too. It was a little comfort to Zerelda to feel that someone did think she was wonderful, even though she knew now that she wasn't. Now that Mavis had stopped talking about her voice and her marvellous future, she seemed a different kind of person—simpler, more natural, with a greater interest in other people.

'I'm never going to mention my voice again,' Mavis told Zerelda. 'I'm never going to say "when I'm an opera-singer" again. Perhaps if I'm sensible and don't boast and don't think about my voice, it'll come back.'

'Oh, it'll come back, I expect,' said Zerelda, comfortingly. 'You did your best to get rid of it though! Oh, Mavis—you're just like me—reduced to being a schoolgirl and nothing else. But, gee, you wouldn't believe how nice it is to belong to the others, to be just as they are, and not try to make out you're too wunnerful for words!'

'Tell me about Mam'zelle and the sneezing again,' begged Mavis. 'You do make me laugh so. You're terribly funny when you tell things like that, Zerelda.'

Zerelda was. She could not act any part, but she could tell a story in a very humorous way, and keep everyone in fits of laughter. Privately Alicia thought that that was Zerelda's real gift, the ability to be really funny—but she wasn't going to say so! She wasn't going to give Zerelda any chance of thinking herself 'wunnerful' again!

The girls admired the way Zerelda gave her time so generously to Mavis. They thought a good deal more of her for taking Miss Hibbert's rather harsh ticking-off so well, and for taking to heart all she had said.

'I didn't think she had it in her,' said Darrell to Sally. 'I really didn't. I thought she was just an inflated balloon—and when Miss Hibbert pricked her, I thought she'd just deflate and there'd be nothing. But there *is* something after all. I like her now, don't you?'

'Well—I always did think she was very generous, and I liked her good nature,' said Sally. 'But then I didn't have such a dose of her silliness as you did—I didn't come back to school till so late.'

'I'm glad Betty's back, aren't you?' said Darrell. 'Thank goodness! Now Alicia has got someone to go round with, and she doesn't always want you and me to make a threesome. I wish Bill had a friend. She's rather one on her own.'

'Well—I don't mind making up a threesome with Bill sometimes,' said Sally. 'Though Bill doesn't *really* need a friend, you know, Darrell—honestly I think Thunder takes the place of a friend with her.'

'Yes. He does,' said Darrell, remembering that dark rainy night when she and Bill had walked Thunder round and round the yard. 'But it would be nice for Bill if we let her go with us sometimes. She's a sport.'

So Bill, to her delight, was often taken in tow by Darrell and Sally. She thought the world of Darrell. 'One day I'll repay her for that night,' thought Bill, a hundred times a week. 'I'll never forget.'

She was very happy now. Thunder was quite well. Darrell and Sally welcomed her. She was doing well in class. And Miss Peters was Simply Grand!

Bill was a simple person, straightforward, natural and very loyal. These things made a great appeal to Miss Peters, who was much the same. So there grew up a real understanding between the form-mistress and Bill, delightful to them both.

'I'm so happy here,' said Bill to Darrell. 'I didn't want to come—but oh, I'm so *glad* I came!'

23 A LOVELY END TO THE TERM!

THE term was coming to an end. Darrell as usual was torn in two over her feelings about this. 'I do so love going home—but I do so love being at Malory Towers!' she said to Sally.

'Well, you're lucky to have both worlds,' said Sally. 'So am I. I love being at home—but I love school, too. It's been a good term, hasn't it, Darrell?'

'Yes,' said Darrell. 'I've only had one bitter disappointment—and that was, that after all the practising I've done, and all the extra coaching I got, and the help that Molly gave me—I never played in the third match-team after all.'

'Did they play the match that was cancelled?' asked Sally.

'No. The other school hadn't a free date,' said Darrell. 'We break up next week—so there's no chance now. That's the only thing that has really spoilt the term a bit for me—and you being so late back, of course.'

'Isn't it a gorgeous afternoon?' said Sally, as they strolled out into the courtyard, and looked at the daffodils growing everywhere there, dancing in the March breeze. 'T'here's half an hour before dinner. What shall we do?'

'Let's go out to the lacrosse field,' said Darrell. 'It will be lovely there. I feel restless after sitting still so long. A bit of running and catching will do us good.'

Sally didn't really want to. She was not as good at games that term as usual, because she had come back so late. But she saw Darrell's eager face and put aside her own wishes.

'All right. I'll get the sticks. You go and ask for a ball,' she said. They met again on the field, and were soon running and catching and passing.

They were the only ones there. Molly Ronaldson, passing by, smiled to see Darrell out there again. What a sticker she was! She really did stick to whatever she made up her mind to do. Molly liked that kind of thing.

She called to Darrell. 'My goodness, you deserve to play well, Darrell! Have you heard that we are playing Barchester after all, next week—you know the match that was cancelled the half-holiday Thursday? We thought we wouldn't be able to fix it up again—but Barchester have just let us know that they can play us next Thursday—the day before we break up.'

'Oh, really?' said Darrell. 'Molly—any chance of my being in the reserve three again? Do say yes!'

'Well, last time, apparently, you would have actually *played* in the match, as all the reserves were to play,' said Molly, 'but I heard that you played the fool, you and the third form, and got the half-holiday forfeited. So you wouldn't have been able to play after all.'

'Yes, that's true,' said Darrell. 'But I haven't played the fool since. Put me in the reserve next Thursday, Molly, please do. Not that I've much hope of playing in the match this time, because everyone who was ill is all right again!'

'True,' said Molly. 'Well, I shall be making a new list of match-team players, and you may be in the reserve or you may not. I'm making no promises! I'll come and watch the third and fourth forms playing lacrosse on Monday afternoon. I shall only want a few players from them for the Barchester match, so it's up to you to do your best!'

'Isn't Molly marvellous!' said Darrell to Sally, her face in a glow as Molly walked off.

'Well—I think she's very good as a games captain,' said Sally, who didn't get quite such wild enthusiasms as Darrell got. 'Anyway—you play well on Monday, when Molly's watching, and see if you can get in the reserve again, Darrell.'

So Darrell did. She was nimble and swift, she was deft at catching, unselfish in her passing, and very sure in her attack on goal. Molly was on the field, watching the various games being played there. She walked from one to another, sturdy, deliberate, her sharp eyes noting every good pass and swift rush.

That night the names of the girls in the third match-team were to be put up. The names of the reserve girls would be put below the team-list. Darrell hardly dared to go up to the notice-board and look to see if her name was in the reserve.

Surely it would be! Surely she had been better than most of the fourth-formers, and certainly far better than any other third-former! She glanced hopefully but fearfully at the names of the three reserves.

Hers wasn't there! In real dismay Darrell read down the three reserve names again. No—her name was not there—not even as third reserve, which she had been before! Molly hadn't thought her good enough to put her in the reserve this time. What a terrible disappointment.

Sally came running up. 'Darrell! Is your name down? Are you in the reserve?'

Darrell shook her head. 'No,' she said. 'Not this time. Oh, Sally—I'm awfully disappointed.'

Sally was too. She slipped her arm through Darrell's. 'Bad luck, old thing. I *am* sorry.'

'Oh well—I'm as bad as Zerelda used to be—imagining I'm good enough at lacrosse to be in the reserve for the Barchester match,' said Darrell, her voice a little shaky. 'Serves me right!'

'It doesn't, it doesn't!' said Sally. 'You *ought* to be at least *first* reserve—yes, you ought, Darrell. You are *awfully* good—super—at lacrosse. And you've practised so hard, too.'

'Don't rub it in,' said Darrell, Sally's eager championship making her feel much worse. They went to the common-room together. Mavis was there with Zerelda, for the first time.

'Hallo, Mavis!' cried Sally, in surprise. 'I thought you weren't coming to join us again till tomorrow. I'm so glad you're back.'

'Welcome home again!' said Darrell, trying to forget her disappointment. 'I'm glad you're all right, Mavis. How do you feel?'

'Grand,' said Mavis, in her changed voice. She no longer had the deep, delightful voice she used to have. It was hoarse and had lost its lovely tone. The girls were used to it by now, but poor Mavis wasn't. She couldn't bear this horrid, creaky voice! But she had made up her mind not to grumble or complain. 'I'm glad to be back, too. Sister was awfully nice to me, and it's cosy over in the san.—but I did miss all the fun and noise of school.'

She coughed. 'Don't talk too much all at once,' said Zerelda. 'You know Sister put me in charge of you—and I've got to deliver you well and healthy up to Matron tonight, before you are allowed to sleep in our dormy again!'

'I'll be all right,' said Mavis. 'Darrell—are you in the reserve? Zerelda said you were sure to be. I'm looking forward to seeing a match again.'

'No. I'm not,' said Darrell, and turned away. Zerelda looked up, surprised and sorry.

'Gee, that's too bad,' she said, and then stopped as Sally frowned at her to stop her saying too much about it. Darrell was feeling it very much. She couldn't understand why Molly had left her out of the reserve this time. It didn't seem fair, after all she had said!

Darrell went out of the room. Sally didn't follow her,

knowing that she wanted to be alone and get over her disappointment before she faced the rest of the form.

There came a clatter of feet down the corridor. The door burst open and the rest of the third form poured in. 'I say! Where's Darrell! My goodness, has she seen the notice-board?'

'Yes. She's frightfully disappointed,' said Sally. The beaming third-formers looked immensely surprised.

'Disappointed!' echoed Alicia. 'Why? She ought to be so bucked that she's doing a war-dance round the room!'

Now it was Sally's turn to be surprised. 'But why, you idiot? She's not even been put into the reserve this time!'

'No—she hasn't—because, idiot, she's in the team itself!' cried Alicia.

'Yes. Actually in the *team*!' said Bill, joyfully. 'Isn't it an honour?'

Sally gasped. 'Gracious! Darrell must just have looked at the names of the reserves—and not looked at the names in the *team* at all! How like her!'

'Where *is* she?' demanded Alicia, impatiently.

'Here she is!' yelled Belinda from the door. 'Darrell! Come here!'

Darrell came in, looking rather subdued. She gazed round in surprise at the excited third-formers. 'What's up?' she said.

'*You* are!' cried Irene, slapping her on the back, 'Up on the notice-board, silly! In the TEAM!'

Darrell didn't take it in. The others all crowded round her impatiently, talking at the tops of their voices.

'You're in the TEAM! Don't you understand?'

'Not in the reserve. You're PLAYING on Thursday against Barchester.'

'Look at her—quite dumb. *Darrell*! Do you mean to say you only looked at the names in the reserve and not at the names in the match-team itself? Well, of all the donkeys!'

Light suddenly dawned upon Darrell. She seized Alicia's

wrists joyfully. ' Alicia ! Do you mean it ? I'm in the TEAM !
Golly—I never thought of looking there. '

Then there was so much shouting and congratulating and
rejoicing that Matron came in to see whatever the noise was
about, and to find out how Mavis was standing it.

Mavis was standing it very well. She was smacking Darrell on
the back and calling out ' Jolly good ! Jolly good ! ' in a cracked
but most determined voice. Her face shone with pleasure, just
like the faces of the rest.

Matron went out again without being noticed. She smiled to
herself. ' All because someone's put into the team ! ' she
thought. ' Well, well—what a thing it is to be a schoolgirl ! '

It was a lovely thing to Darrell at that moment. She thought
she had never been so happy in her life before—just when she
had felt so disappointed and miserable, too ! She was almost in
tears when she saw the pleasure and pride of the others. ' Why,
they must like me an awful lot ! ' she thought, happily. ' Oh, I
do hope I play well on Thursday. If only we can beat Barchester !
We haven't for a whole year. '

She could hardly wait till Thursday came—but it dawned at
last, sunny and clear—the ideal day for a match. It was a home
match, and as it was the day before breaking up, all girls who
wished to could watch it. Most of them turned up to cheer the
Barchester girls when they arrived in their coach. Then they all
streamed to the field to find seats on the wooden forms.

Darrell was nervous. She was cross with herself for this, but
she couldn't help it. Molly came by, and grinned at her. ' Got
stage-fright ? Wait till you're on the field—you'll soon forget
it ! '

Molly was right. Once on the field, with her lacrosse stick in
her hands, dancing about joyfully, all Darrell's nervousness
went, and she was eager for the match to begin. She was on the
wing. She glanced at her opponent. She was a big, sturdy girl.
Oh dear—probably she could run even faster than Darrell !

She certainly could run very fast and she was powerful too,

getting the ball from Darrell nearly every time by tackling strongly and swiftly.

'Play up, Darrell! Play up!' yelled the watching third-formers, every time Darrell got the ball and sped off with it. 'Oh, well passed! Oh, well caught! Play UP, Malory Towers!'

Goal to Barchester. Goal to Malory Towers. Half-time. One all. Slices of sour lemon being brought out on plates. And here was Molly beside Darrell, talking to her earnestly.

'Darrell! You're tiring the other girl out nicely. She's good, but she gets winded more quickly than you do. Watch your chance, tackle her next time she comes up, get the ball, pass to Catherine, run level, let her pass back to you and then SHOOT! Do you hear?'

'Yes. Yes, Molly,' said Darrell, almost swallowing her slice of lemon in her eagerness to take it all in. 'Yes—I think my opponent's tiring. I can out-run her. I'll do what you say if I can. Tell Catherine.'

'I have,' said Molly. 'Now—there's the whistle. You're all doing well. But I think it will have to be you who does a bit of shooting this half, Darrell. The others allow themselves to be tackled too easily. Good luck.'

Molly went off the field. A chorus went up from the watchers. 'PLAY—UP—Malory TOWERS! PLAY—UP—Malory TOWERS!'

And Malory Towers played up. Darrell and Catherine passed beautifully to one another, and Catherine shot. Two goals to Malory Towers! Then the Barchester team got going again. Second goal to them. Two all. Fifteen minutes to play. 'PLAY—UP—Malory TOWERS!'

Darrell felt the time slipping by. Two goals all—Malory Towers must shoot again before time was up. She took a fine pass, and ran with the ball in her lacrosse net. Her opponent tackled her. Darrell dodged her very neatly and sped down the field.

'Go it, DARRELL! SHOOT! SHOOT!' yelled everyone,

but Darrell was too far from goal to do that. Instead, she sent the ball to Catherine, who, alas ! muffed the catch, fell over, and let the enemy snatch it up from where it rolled on the ground. Then down the field rushed the Barchester wing, back towards the Malory Towers' goal.

But there the goal-keeper stopped it valiantly. Hurrah ! Saved again ! Up the field came the ball again, and Darrell made a remarkable catch, leaping high in the air.

'Go it, DARRELL!' yelled the onlookers. Darrell ran towards the Barchester goal. Catherine kept level with her, watching carefully for a pass. When she was tackled Darrell passed the ball deftly to Catherine, making a lovely throw. Catherine caught it, but was tackled immediately. Out of the corner of her eye she saw Darrell, watching.

She threw. It was a clumsy throw, but Darrell ran to catch the ball. Once in her net she kept the ball there, dodging cleverly when she was tackled. A great cry came up from the onlookers.

'SHOOT! SHOOT! SHOOT!'

And Darrell shot. She threw the ball with all her might at the goal. The Barchester goal-keeper came out to stop it. The ball struck her pad, then struck the goal-post—and rolled to the back of the net.

'GOAL!' What a cry went up. 'Jolly good, Darrell! Fine shot! Hurrah! Three goals to two!'

Almost immediately the whistle blew for time. The two teams lined up and cheered one another. Darrell was trembling with excitement and joy. She had played in a match—she had shot the winning goal!

'Well played, young Darrell!' said Molly's voice. 'You did well. That was a very fine goal.'

Darrell went off to the big tea provided for the two match-teams, her heart singing. This was a great moment for her. The third-formers all crowded round her, clapping her on the shoulder, praising her, delighted that one of their own form should have shot the winning goal.

Darrell was very tired and very happy that evening. What would her father and mother and her sister Felicity say when she told them all this? Thank goodness she was seeing them tomorrow, and they would know. She could hardly wait to tell them!

All the third-formers shared in Darrell's delight. They cheered her when she came into the common-room, and she stood there blushing and embarrassed.

'Good old Darrell! So modest she didn't even think of looking in the team-list for her own name—and so marvellous that she shoots the winning goal!' cried Irene, and thumped Darrell on the back so hard that she coughed.

The last day came. All the packing was done, except for a few things that the car-girls were bundling into their cars at the last minute. Good-byes were said. Addresses were exchanged and immediately lost. Matron tried to find Belinda who had completely disappeared. Miss Potts tried to find Irene, who also seemed to have disappeared. There was a tremendous noise and confusion, in the middle of which seven boys appeared on seven horses in the drive among the cars!

'Bill! Good heavens! Here are all your brothers again!' yelled Darrell. But Bill was getting Thunder from the stables and was not there. She appeared a moment later on her horse, and yelled with delight to see all her brothers and their horses in the drive.

'You've come to fetch me! Look at Thunder! Isn't he in good condition? Get up, Thunder! Oh, he's so pleased to see you all.'

The train-girls went, and there was a little more peace. Irene wandered round lamenting that someone had taken her suit-case. Gwen went round scowling because nobody had yet come to fetch her, and she didn't want to be the last. Belinda stalked her with an open sketch-book and pencil.

'Gwen! It's my last chance! Let me sketch that scowl!'

Darrell laughed. How like Belinda to do that when her

mother and father were waiting patiently in the car for her outside!

Zerelda popped up to say good-bye. How different she looked now from when she came. She wore her school hat for one thing—a thing she had said she would never do! 'Good-bye,' she said. 'See you again next term. It's been wunnerful here. I'm glad I came—and gee, I'm glad I'm coming back!'

'Good-bye!' croaked Mavis, waving to everyone as she climbed into her car. 'See you next term.'

Bill galloped off with her brothers, calling a mad good-bye. Mam'zelle Dupont watched her go in amazement. 'In France such a thing could not happen!' she declared. 'That Bill! I think at home she must let her horse sleep with her in a corner of her bedroom!'

Darrell giggled. Belinda came by with a wooden box of bath salts she had suddenly remembered leaving in the bathroom. She collided with Mam'zelle and the box fell to the floor.

A green powder covered the hall, and a green cloud rose up into the air, with a very strong smell.

'Now, Belinda, I ...' began Mam'zelle, and then paused with her mouth wide open. She felt frantically about her plump person for her handkerchief. Just as Miss Potts came up with Miss Peters, Mam'zelle sneezed. It was one of her best efforts.

'A-WHOOOOOSH-OOOOOOO!'

'Good gracious!' said Miss Potts, startled. 'I never knew anyone sn...'

'A-Whooooooo——' began Mam'zelle again and Miss Potts ran for shelter.

Darrell and Sally giggled helplessly. They remembered the afternoon of the Trick. Darrell suddenly picked up somebody's umbrella and opened it.

'Now sneeze, Mam'zelle!' she cried, holding the umbrella over Miss Potts and Miss Peters. 'I'll protect everyone!'

Darrell's mother, coming up the steps in search of her, was amazed to see this sight. Darrell flung away the umbrella joyfully and sprang at her mother. ' Oh, here you are. I thought you were never coming! Sally, are you ready? Good-bye, Mam'zelle, good-bye, Potty, good-bye, Miss P., good-bye, Matron. See you all next term! This has been a SUPER term!'

' Good-bye!' said Matron. ' Be good.'

' Good-bye,' said Miss Potts and Miss Peters together. ' Remember your holiday reading!'

' A-Whoooosh-ooooo!' said Mam'zelle, and ran forward to wave. Gwen just saved her from falling over the open umbrella.

The car drove off. Darrell waved frantically till they were out of the front gates. Then she leaned back contentedly and began.

' Mother! Daddy! What DO you think? I played in the third match-team yesterday against Barchester School—and I shot the winning goal. Mother, I—'

Sally listened contentedly. Good old Darrell! She had had a lovely term and enjoyed it. She was sorry it was over. But there would be the summer term—and the autumn term—and the winter term—oh, terms and terms and terms!

' Here's the last glimpse of Malory Towers, Darrell,' said Sally, suddenly. Darrell opened the window and leaned out.

' I'll soon be back, Malory Towers!' she called ' Good-bye for a little while. I'll soon be back!'